During This, Our Nadir

Joshua Amses

Fomite
Burlington, VT

ISBN-13: 978-1-942515-51-7
Library of Congress Control Number:

Fomite
58 Peru Street
Burlington, VT 05401
www.fomitepress.com

For Sam

"Who invented the human heart, I wonder? Tell me, and then show me the place where he was hanged."

—Lawrence Durrell, *Justine*

I.

"So. I have inspected my conscience and found it non-existent."
—Robert Ruark, *Uhuru*

I PULL THE LETTER TO CORDELIA from beneath my seat somewhere outside Hartford, Connecticut, looking over what I've written on the back of a semi-official notice informing me that the loans I took out for a degree I didn't complete have gone into default. This is page one, sadly. Meanwhile, Officer Laurel navigates a police van packed with our things up route 91-North. We're not talking much.

It's 5PM on a Friday in August. I can't be sure of the exact date, but I've traveled this road many times, and have never seen it so empty during rush hour. Empty of cars, that is. As we enter the city limits, divisions of professionally comported men and women begin appearing on the road, most lurching in concert along the shoulder, but some bumbling their common way down the centerline. No one has any reason to expect traffic.

I touch Officer Laurel's knee, but she's already seen them, and slows down. Or perhaps they see us first. The faces of the office workers heading from the insurance firms girding the rim of the interstate turn in dull unison at the sound of an isolated engine, and watch the police van pass as if it is a sort of mobile buffet, and they a contingent of starving zeks drawn fresh from the gulag. A woman points; a folder drops from beneath a man's arm, littering the passing lane with licensing agreements, addendums, and reams of usurious, impenetrable policy. Several people extend their thumbs in what may be a joke.

"You'd think they'd find an alternate route..." I say, watching mild disappointment etch itself across the made-up features of a windblown secretary as the van passes. Her left shoe is missing a heel, likely surrendered to the barren face of the entrance ramp leading from Aetna or the Lincoln National Company headquarters. "...Rather than just walking the way they would drive. That woman has broken her shoe. How sad."

"They probably don't know how to get home any other way," murmurs Laurel, as we proceed through the foremost clutch of Hartford's peripatetic business community. "After I moved to Forest Hills, the transmission went in my Camry, so I had to get myself to work on the train from out there. It was scary. I'd never done it before, so I didn't know how to get from my own house to the precinct where I was supposed to show up. It's hard to redraw the map."

"Schrodinger says that's the only way to assure consciousness."

"What is?"

"Redrawing the map, Laurel. Taking the road less traveled."

"Usually, if no one's traveling on it, that's because there's construction or something and traffic will be worse."

I don't respond but return to reading. The letter from the loan company is postmarked July 10th, a date for which I have no significant association, other than it happening before many other more recent things, events that have placed me not so much at the epicenter, but the corona of various circumstances culminating in my current position: the passenger seat of a NYPD vehicle beside the lovely Officer Laurel, who does not know I will abandon her when we reach Springfield, Massachusetts, some forty-five minutes away. I'm not proud of it. She's done more than her part for me, and I'm sorry I can't return it in the way she expects.

Of course, I wish I could choose a better place than Springfield for the scene of our parting. It may be a very nice town, but I only know it based on two experiences. The first was during a bathroom break at a Greyhound station that looked like a Serbian railway platform, and the second a detour taken with Cordelia, during a trip similar to this, only heading toward New York City rather than away from it on a return from Vermont. We exited the freeway looking for something to eat amid the Styrofoam brick arcades, driving in endless, unrewarding circles through the baked lots of one commercial ghetto after another while the dog cried in the back seat, and our mutual blood sugar plummeted. We exited an hour later with sandwiches made by a machine, and a dent the size and depth of a nectarine delivered to the side panel of our rental car by an Iraq war veteran's wheelchair. It escaped from beneath him as he was leveraging himself into his vehicle and rolled several spaces down into our car, and since he was about our age, but missing a leg, we didn't say anything. He said he lost the leg in Ramallah, and seemed to be awaiting congratulations of some kind. I considered a high-five, but Cordelia just scowled at the damage, got in the car, and ate her factory-pressed sandwich in unbroken silence until we reached Connecticut.

But I chose Springfield for Officer Laurel for practical reasons. It's exactly halfway between New York City and Acheron, Vermont, and is the point on the journey between the two where the landscape begins looking less human, which is to say: hideous, and more natural, lush, and verdant. The road narrows from four lanes to two after passing Holyoke, the first of many Lesbian college towns en route, and the concrete embankment dividing the road from the single-use zoning of diabetic shopping plazas fades to a pleasantly sinister shoulder of dark, Teutonic forest or open farmland, interrupted only here and there by a stray thresher or bevy of cattle. God's country, postcard-friendly, upon whose emerald meridian I will disjoin from my companion and escape through the unlatched gate of New England. I've already begun drafting an apology, which I plan to leave in the space Officer Laurel expects to find the van.

"Thanks for doing this," I say, perhaps to obviate some of the guilt I feel as we pass a sign indicating the mileage to Springfield.

"I chose you," she replies just as the sour weather disperses, allowing a narrow fan of sun to fall in the empty parking lot of a Cracker Barrel a quarter mile ahead. "I think I did before I found you, Walter. I loved you before we met."

She's said this before, and to be honest, I had to bite the inside of my cheek the first time she told me, in the backyard of a rowhouse she owned in Queens, where we sat having breakfast on the patio the morning after she found me wandering around the burned-out husk of Breezy Point, shivering and talking to myself. What she said reminded me of the sort of aphorism found on the back of a matchbox or interior of a fortune cookie, devoid of currency, unsound. But she was dressed for work, her Glock 9 strapped to her broad, gorgeous hips, her blond hair stuffed beneath a peaked cap, and her badge reflecting sunlight reflected from the windows of a housing coop backing up against the yard directly into my eyes. I blindly chewed a stale muffin, drank weak coffee, and said then what I say now.

"That makes sense."

This response has satisfied her up so far, and if need be, I'll alter it. But for the moment, her plump lips smile with a vague contentment as the weather re-sours beyond the front window. How did I end up with a woman who talks the way a motivational calendar looks? If Cordelia met her, and the full succession of events were discussed and understood, it would embarrass all of us. In short, if everyone were honest, we would all be disappointed, which is both very fair, and very sad. This is why I have to maroon Officer Laurel in Springfield, and return to Acheron, and Cordelia, alone. There is little less attractive than not knowing where someone has been, though knowing where they've been can sometimes be worse. If not for the smallest of fuckups on my part, Cordelia wouldn't have to ask because I would have been with her, in the passenger seat as I am now with Officer Laurel, heading toward Acheron. Same direction, wrong driver, and several days late. But I'm hoping Cordelia will understand. We often spoke about how a downward spiral isn't actually a spiral at all, but a more or less straight line from apogee to perigee. Cordelia used the image of falling from the top of a tree to the forest floor, and compared each bad decision or importune circumstance to a branch you, or I in this case, hit on the way to the ground.

So the past several days have been a continuous plummet on my part, with each branch delaying my return to her, and the final impact with solid earth being my relationship with Officer Laurel. Though I credit myself with managing to parlay this into a ride to Acheron, Cordelia and I haven't spoken since the day she left, the day of the storm, and even though the town is my home as much as hers, I can't help feeling I'm showing up unannounced, dropping by, being a pest.

Thus: the page in my hand, part of the incomplete letter I've written to her on loose stationary over the past few days; junk mail, bills, receipts, a menu from a Polish deli in Queens, an application for loan consolidation, anything I could grab and scribble on while Officer Laurel's back was turned, all of it clipped together and jammed under the passenger seat until now. The Koran was originally written this way, I tell myself as I shuffle the irregular pages. On bones, leaves, rocks, whatever was around, and stuffed in a trunk. Surely it too was unfinished and unsatisfying, at some point. I try not to be intimidated by the mess I've made of my recap of the past few days without Cordelia, something I intend to slip under her front door or inside her mailbox when it's complete. Explaining everything this way is cowardly, but safer. I've lied so much recently I no longer trust myself to speak on my behalf. And even if I did, what would I say? Aiming high only makes sense when you're shooting at a blimp, I think as I reshuffle what is already beginning to feel like a deck of marked cards, and stow it back beneath my seat.

*　　*　　*

Dear Cordelia,

I suppose this is meant to be a work of literature, but I should warn you: I have no formal training in this area. As you know, during the three terms I spent with you at St. Margaret's, I took mostly art and philosophy classes, and one term of elementary Latin. That was a mistake. To be: Sum, es, estis, sumus estis sunt. To love: Amo, amas, amat, amamus, amatis, amant. To corrupt: infici, inficis, inficit, inficimus, inficitis, nficiunt. I'm ashamed that's all I remember. But like most people who didn't finish college and read a lot to compensate, I have enormous regard for formal education. Still, when you finished your degree and got a job in New York, I didn't want to be alone in Ohio. Thank you for inviting me along. It made thematic sense. I followed you to Julian Falls from Acheron. I'd follow you to Brooklyn too. This seems to be my role. Dogging and basking in your shadow, a toehold I've come to love.

So then: Acheron, Vermont. Julian Falls, Ohio. New York City, New York State. If you connect them on a map you get a squashed triangle. An axis of failure, or trajectory of several errors, if you like, all mine. I'll get to them later. But for now, I should explain why I failed to meet you on Friday before the storm. I'm sorry you had to load my things in the moving van yourself, my books and clothes, and but thank you for leaving the bed in the apartment. How deeply thoughtful of you. Not that I've slept there since you vacated it, but it was nice to know you didn't expect me to snooze on the floor like a migrant worker. Anyway, I'm glad you made it out of the city before the weather turned.

The Monday after you left began well. I was arraigned at 6AM and out of jail by 8AM, but the subway was shut down for the storm, and the bridges were closed to traffic. I already knew you were gone, because I called you from a holding cell in Chinatown to say I was in a holding cell in Chinatown. But when you asked where I was, I said "someplace bad," instead of something more accurate, because I was embarrassed. And we didn't talk about it again. I hung up when I realized you were talking to a tollbooth operator who said "$6.50," in the background of the call, meaning you were over the Whitestone Bridge, entering Connecticut, moving back to Acheron alone. So that was it. I hung up, and handed the duty cop my phone through the bars. Earlier in the night, while being fingerprinted, he looked me up and down and said: "What are you doing in here? Someone break your Dave Matthews CD?" and we both laughed. But when I handed him the phone, he said, "You're going downtown in a minute," meaning the city jail, and neither of us laughed. I wondered if I would be raped there, and tried to *mentally prepare myself for this. You told me a man's prostate is somewhere in his anus. Maybe I would enjoy it. I listened to the cops tease an underage Chinese kid sitting across from me in the holding cell. They told him to get his Vaseline, and he puked in his mouth, but swallowed it. His parents showed up an hour later and took him away, just as I was removed, handcuffed, and driven three unremarkable blocks to the Tombs.*

Bartleby died here, I thought, as they led me beneath what looked like a freight entrance, down some stairs, into a cellblock with walls the color of an empty, sunbleached pool, a milky diluted blue green. I stared at the floor until told to raise my head for the man taking my mugshot. He asked me to remove my glasses, and I had to remind him I was handcuffed. The officer who brought me to have my picture taken folded my spectacles, and tucked them in my pocket. After the photographer was satisfied, I had to ask the same officer to return them to my face so I could see.

Trusties gave me a bag lunch. Cheese on bread. Not quite a sandwich. Milk in a carton, like kindergarten, Acheron Elementary, 1990, if you recall. Mrs. Downing trying to control her tremor as she divided skim from whole, blue and red, like diametric shades of donated blood. Parents selected the strain for their kids, checked a box on a form sent home at the beginning of the school year, and mine chose skim for some reason, but I always wanted red, because I thought it was sweeter. When I was finally caught, I said I didn't know there was a difference, and the school nurse tested me for color blindness. When I passed, Mrs. Downing wanted to call me a liar, but decided to distribute the milk herself therein, her trembling hands frothing it as she passed me. Anyway, I reached into the bag and removed an inedible orange. That was it. I sat with my prison fruit and watched prospective rapists use the rotary phone across the cell. A sign nearby ex-

plained the phone was a courtesy. Trusties mopped the floor. The room seemed too hot and bright for violent sex, and I was comfortable enough to fall asleep. I didn't dream so much as recite, remembering the vacation we took to Croatia the year earlier, and how someone at the tourist office in Rab found us a suite of rooms in the house of an old woman who put coins in our shoes when we left them in the foyer, and how the shutters opened onto the Adriatic, which was black with urchins that season, so we had to swim without touching bottom. I wasn't a strong swimmer, and I nearly drowned trying to pursue you from one end of the parapet to the other. I floundered in the shade of the bell towers casting oblong shadows across the water as the afternoon grew hot and still. Later, we drank coffee in the shade of a single Holm oak in Freedom Square, the presence of which had something to do with Mussolini using the island as a concentration camp, a favor to Hitler, I presume. We ate fruit and cheese with the coffee, and I watched you become limitlessly beautiful in the shade of a belfry.

I woke from this at 5AM to the sound of a stranger calling my name. An ombudsman with a rolling rostrum approached the cell and asked what I did for a living. Even though I'd handed in my notice a week earlier, as a preparation for leaving the city behind, I gave her my card through the bars.

Walter Ratliff

Research Coordinator
Brooklyn Association for Community Organization Now!

"What does this mean?" she asked, returning the card, though I meant for her to keep it.

"It's a non-profit," I said, and she shrugged and sent me back

to the rapists, who were just beginning to stir. I sat down and immediately stood up, because a huge black corrections officer opened the door, and told us to line up in the hallway.

"No cameras here," he said, waving at the absence of them. To be in state custody means you're no longer on the map, I thought, as the CO stalked the line from end to end. "So, if any of you half-homos want to step out of line, talk to your buddy, maybe take a poke at me, you do that. I want to be part of your education. So, here it is: put your doo rag in your pocket, or step out of line. Please. Come on, you underwear models. In this particular instantiation, I got the long dick."

No one moved until they were told. The CO led us upstairs and into a holding cell behind the courtroom, where I met my court-appointed lawyer in a Plexiglas booth. He advised me to enter a guilty plea and disappeared, only to reappear twenty minutes later to make a desist gesture when I tried to hand the judge my card. No sale. Fine. I'd been passing them out to get rid of them anyway, not wanting to remind myself of the bleak four years of my life spent in a cubicle on the second floor of a decommissioned movie theater in Downtown Brooklyn. The offices of the Brooklyn Association, for short, were equidistant from a methadone clinic, a halfway house, and the New York State Parole Board in a neighborhood so bad the wait-staff at Applebee's across the street carried box cutters with their scratchpads. Black Nationalists dressed like Erykah Badu blocked the entrance to my bank between two and three times a week, howling about 'white devils' as though transported from some orphaned wing of history, and distributing literature. I often had to cross Atlantic Avenue to withdraw money for lunch or deposit my paycheck. Despite the proximity of the Atlantic Mall, the Barclay's Center, the area resisted gentrification with the stoic resolve of

Simeon Stylites, chained high-atop his pillar in the Syrian desert.

This was the area in which I made my half of our living, making spreadsheets, collecting news articles, and writing memos to oblivion. It was never clear which of us was more embarrassed by my job. You had a grown-up position managing an art school library in a neighborhood with regular trash pickup and a student sensibility. I worked for a non-profit that cajoled minorities into giving monthly donations in exchange for a voice, as they said. We both agreed: a non-profit is not a real job. It was a relief to quit, even though Gordon seemed surprised I was still on the payroll when I knocked on his office door and gave my notice.

"You working on anything I need to pass off or be aware of?" asked my supervisor, the orotund, charismatic deputy director of the Brooklyn Association. He seemed nervous at the thought of anything new, and likely useless if it came from me, entering his orbit. It was a perfunctory question, and I gave a perfunctory answer that left us both happy.

"Nope."

He shook my hand, and walked me the three steps out of his office before closing the door. No commemorative watch or good luck card. Just mutual relief. I stuck to the campsite rule, leaving no great mess for Gordon to clean up. But even if I wanted to, I wouldn't know how. I read an article published in some completely unreliable location saying office workers accomplish three hours of actual work per eight-hour workday. When I shared this with you, we agreed the number sounded generous, if not Pollyannaish. We agreed again: nothing important ever happens in an office or between the walls of a cubicle. I proved it whenever I arrived home, and you asked me about my day, and then watched me struggle to remember something to make it not so much interesting as referential, some small point of identity to confirm I had

*actually gone to work, and hadn't just imagined it while sitting in
the apartment all day. After a while, you stopped asking, because
it was obviously causing me pain.*

*The judge set a court date for some time in the future and turned
me loose, judging my risk of flight low with the bridges, tunnels,
and airports closed for the storm. The lawyer said he would call
me, and disappeared again. I exited out the rear of the building,
and walked along the edge of Columbus Park without my shoelaces. I'd forgotten to claim them, and worried this might mark
me as a recidivist, but no one passing noticed; the solipsism of
the entire city was overcome with the sense of assured unwell
presaging the hurricane brewing at sea.*

*Twenty minutes later, I was crossing the Brooklyn Bridge
toward an empty apartment in a bad neighborhood, returning
on foot to the West Indian ghetto near Prospect Park we called
home. Animal blood on the sidewalk. Chicken feathers in trash-
bags or aerated by the rush of a passing truck. The invocative
panting of an exorcism performed at 2AM across the airshaft.
Voodoo is a syncretic religion, so we never knew exactly what
to expect. But I was pretty sure the guys who drove the dollar
vans were ex-Tonton Macoute. Straw hats, sunglasses, a machete
under the passenger seat. Bag men. The name means Uncle Gun-
nysack. These characters scared the shit out of me on a daily
basis.*

*The sky over the East River was a uniform blue gray as I crossed
the bridge. The wind blew cyclists into the pedestrian lane, and
pedestrians into the bicycle lane as both rushed home with bags
of provisions: candles, jugs of water, bottles of whiskey, loaves
of bread, canned peaches, condoms. The storm was scheduled
to make landfall sometime in the evening. Parts of Long Island*

were already seeing rain and high wind. It looked generally bad. I gathered impressions of the impending hurricane from car stereos, loose talk from passerby, and televisions wedged like icons in the upper corner of hookah salons and pizza parlors along Bedford Avenue. They were calling it Hurricane Eula. I knew no one by that name, except the irresistible Mrs. Varner nee Snopes, given by marriage to an impotent, venal man whose only joy was macerating the air of Frenchman's Bend between teeth I always imagined blunted by chewing tobacco. You always reminded me of Eula, the earth of her simple perfection run through with the clumsy harrow of young male desire. I've watched men watch you since I began watching you in ninth grade, Acheron District School, unaware of yourself, or them, or me, in Mrs. Bates' physical education class, fifth period, falling unfortunately after lunch. Mrs. Bates had a yogic conceit that year, and perhaps drawing a cue from the classes she took on her own time in Burlington, asked you to demonstrate a pose that required you to lie on your back, and draw one knee against your chest. And as you did this, I watched a tangle of strawberry gold pubic hair emerge from beneath the cuff of your athletic shorts, like the feathered head of a small bird netted in your underthings. I don't know whether anyone else saw it, but I kept this emergence with me for the rest of the school year, only allowing it to withdraw after I got to know you as something more than the girl whose pubic hair I saw once in gym class.

When I reached Grand Army Plaza, I noticed a police cruiser blocking the entrance to Prospect Park, and was told it was closed because of high wind.

"Someone might get hit with a branch from a tree," said the officer from the window of his patrol car. "Or a tree branch. You better get home. It's coming."

I said thanks while standing unnaturally close to the vehicle to prevent him from seeing my laceless shoes, and walked along a barren Prospect Park West, until I reached the parade grounds, crossing them between the tennis pavilion and baseball diamond, both deserted beneath the infringement brewing overhead as I turned onto Caton Avenue. Home at last, on the bad side of the park, I thought, trying to feel good about reaching a place I didn't want to be. I felt alone because I was alone. I assumed you took the dog, but was amazed and relieved to find I was wrong. She greeted me at the apartment door, expecting a walk I was too tired to deliver after ambulating from 100 Center Street. A note left in the place where the coffee table would have been read: "She likes you better." This may be true of Ruby, the foolish, one-eyed Pekingese with hip dysplasia we adopted three years earlier from a mobile shelter on 23rd Street. Still here, I thought. And in far better shape than myself, even after a lifetime of bumping into walls and chair legs.

No matter. I hoisted her into bed with me after checking to see what you left behind. My clothes, and books were gone. Too much trouble to unload them, I imagined. A useless, oscillating fan that neither cooled the apartment nor oscillated. One mug, one glass, one dish. A bag of jasmine rice. Two cans of beans. A quarter roll of toilet paper. The bedside lamp. The sheets on the mattress, of course, and one pillow, with case. I should thank you for your generosity. This was really all I needed.

I thought I might explain to someone later how I put on "Have You Forgotten?" by the Red House Painters and forced myself to cry while staring at an empty wall, a wall that formerly displayed a rather awkward portrait of us drawn by you for a visual arts class at FIT, and based on a photograph a friend took during our only summer together at St. Margaret's University, Julian Falls,

Ohio. We were in bed pretending to read whilst preening for the camera. The photographer was a girl from San Francisco who bit her on-campus boyfriend so hard during coition that his bruises looked like keloid lesions. That was a good summer. You had missed me, I think, during our time apart, the years between you leaving Acheron, and my arrival in Julian Falls, a period of time I wasted working for my brother in his grocery store, taking a class in Wildlife Management at the local college, and fatalistically believing I wouldn't ever see you again, though now, I realize how unlikely this was. Even if I had remained in our hometown, we would always have Christmas, and the odd Thanksgiving. And I thought I might make a decent game warden because I hated working in a grocery store. But you realized I was in a rut before I did, which I think is why you told me to apply to St. Margaret's before I started furnishing it, my rut. You said it would be easy, and you were right. By time, I'd already failed the Wildlife Management class, so I didn't even have to worry about transferring credits.

The song unspooled, somber, humorless, apposite. I wanted to feel like Mark Kozelek when he wrote it, or how I imagined he must have felt. Solitary, and gifted, conveying grief for an audience. But I had only the dog to watch me, and though her single eye remained fixed on my ersatz sorrow, it occurred to me she might have been hungry, even starving. I had a habit of forgetting to feed her. But as I entered the kitchen to serve her dinner, I saw the empty sack of kibble stuffed in the trash, and the bag's contents spilling over the rim of a mixing bowl in which you normally prepared pancake or muffin batter. You couldn't cook, but you could certainly bake, and I'm honestly shocked you didn't take the bowl with you. I should apologize in advance for it not being part of the luggage in Officer Laurel's van, but you'll see why later.

*"Have you forgotten / how to love yourself?" asked Mark Ko-
zelek as I returned to the empty living room.*

*"No," I answered through a curtain of false tears, answering
him because I wanted to resemble him, I think. Instead, I felt
more like Hitler in Vienna as the first current of Hurricane Eula
launched a sheet of rain against a window set in an empty wall:
an isolated, transient failure in a secondhand overcoat. Shirer
said the raiment resembled a caftan. An active, cluttered mind in
an old cloak. That was more like it. Wouldn't you agree?*

*Yes, the rain began then, and something of the wind promised
by the broadcast impression I'd gathered from loose talk and
stray newspapers during my shamble between the city jail and
our apartment. I also heard the phrase 'evacuation zone,' but
had no idea if I was in one or not. The nearest water was the
lake in Prospect Park. Could that flood? I suppose it could, but
everyone seemed more concerned about the sewers being inundated, and belching the water they were meant to filter from the
city back upon it. I took Ruby beneath my arm and walked with
her to the bedroom window overlooking Caton Avenue. A livery
cab fishtailed down the street. Several dolts walked past trying to
remain dry under dollar umbrellas. A Mexican delivery boy rode
a bicycle into the rain, smelling his hand.*

*"Seems peculiar," I said to Ruby, her tail beating against my
ribs. "But not dangerous."*

*In fact, it likely was dangerous, and I would have been better
off sitting alone with my books, and waiting it out. I read later
that even by 6PM, the wind was taking down trees, and tossing trashcans around the street. But to be honest, I was less
concerned with the storm, and more worried about the inevitable solitude entailed in being stranded in our rattrap apartment
with just two cans of beans, no candles, and only myself. Could*

I survive that? You were gone, and normally, I found peace in this, because I knew you would return at some point, and interrupt the strange, cultivated weirdness I'd come to regard as my special time alone. I needed to be around people, if only to prove I actually existed without you.

Catalina answered Arvin's phone, and had obviously been expecting a call from someone else. But she listened patiently to me explain why I was still in New York, excising the jail time and the reasons you left without me, since I didn't fully understand them myself.

"We had a fight," I said, which wasn't exactly a lie. I often retreated to Arvin and Catalina's when you and I weren't getting along, because I knew she would listen to me while at least one of the two attractive young women who shared the first floor of the house on Rugby Road pretended not to listen from the kitchen.

"How bad?" asked Catalina, sounding not quite bored with the topic, but prepared for it. This made sense. In the past few weeks, these visits had become clocklike in their routine parts. Fight with Cordelia. Leave apartment. Turn left out of door. Walk until neighborhood becomes not shitty. Turn left again. Stop at liquor store by train tracks. Buy pint of bourbon. Left on Rugby Road. Ring first bell. Greet Catalina with an overlong hug if Arvin isn't watching. Pretend to listen to her when Danielle enters the kitchen in a sports bra and yoga shorts. Make oblique eye contact. Stumble home.

"Well, I'm here," I said. "And she isn't."

"Maybe she'll come back for you."

"I don't think it's like that, Catalina. I'm going to come over now if you don't mind."

"Of course. Be careful," she said, which made me feel heroic, even though what I was about to do was essentially foolish, *and meant to make only me feel better. I packed the rice, beans, kibble, a chew toy shaped like a buzzard, and a library copy of* The Alexandria Quartet *I'd been meaning to read in a daypack, secured Ruby in her harness, and left the house.*

The weather had gotten significantly worse by the time I reached the head of Rugby Road and passed through the quiet, empty, and inchoately flooded suburban district below the park. Several people were out in the rain, securing shrubs, or tying down lawn furniture, but most were shuttered indoors, I imagined, or inferred from the dull interior light of televisions igniting windows up and down the block. Ruby was struggling to keep pace with me on her leash, and didn't like being wet in any case, so I tucked her beneath my arm as I had earlier at the window, and continued walking. She didn't like being picked up either, but the wind and rain pummeling the street and houses lining it left us with few choices.

"We all have to make sacrifices," I assured her, though I didn't know what I meant as I pulled my coat around her to keep the dog's backside dry. "Let's hope the liquor store is open,"

I wasn't a drinker, but perhaps retracing the route I had so often wandered after fighting with you awakened some revenant dipsomaniac in me. Part of my brain was thirsty, or had been thirsty since the night before. Jail deliberately, I think, provided me with the opportunity to inventory my shortcomings, so it was inevitable that while listening to the rapists bedevil the rotary telephone, I would think of you, and Lionel. I never disapproved exactly, but I found it hard to exist in any universe where the sun didn't circle me, Planet Walter, of the Ratliff System. So when I met you for yoga several months before the storm, and asked how you spent your day off, because you looked so cheerful, I

20

found the reality of your orbit no longer encompassing me in the way I'd imagined hard to stomach.

"Making out with Lionel Little," you said, because we had long ago agreed not to punish each other in this regard. We both admitted early on, while still students in Ohio that the idea of fucking only each other for the rest of our lives seemed ludicrous. Part of me being fine with this arrangement had much to do with both of us assuming I'd screw up first. Thus, a pre-absolution seemed important, if not necessary.

Still, I proceeded through a sequence of dull poses with a lump in my throat, not from sadness, but frustration. Why didn't I have a Lionel Little of my own to balance the scale tipping extremely in your favor? I didn't look at you throughout the class, even when a crone who looked like she fed poison apples to children farted like a Howitzer during constructive rest, and spoke minimally throughout the evening, except to answer "nothing" whenever you asked what was wrong. After class, we shopped for groceries in silence, which is both difficult and nerve-wracking when your items are confined to the same basket. But I watched it fill slowly with the same food as the previous week, understanding the boredom of this errand as I understood the necessity of it, but drawing nothing that could be called an even conclusion. Of course, buying the same Greek yogurt at the same time each week isn't aphrodisiacal. But must it slay desire entirely?

I wasn't getting it, but, to your credit, neither were you. You seemed genuinely surprised I was upset, and it's possible the depth of my despair shocked me as well. Even that evening, when we arrived home and had the sort of feverish sex only possible as a result of an upheaval, an after-funeral or post apocalypse sort of sex, the kind we might have had if you stayed with me during the storm, I had what might have been an out of body experience. Your thighs were clamped around my head so tight that I couldn't hear anything you said, but I watched your mouth move, and thought I saw your lips form and expel his name. And from my own position, I remember thinking, "Someday, I will be Lionel," meaning soon he will be where I was at that moment. Male desire being a stateless self-servant, this thought didn't take me out of myself enough to dissolve or ruin the act, even though I knew you were fucking him through me. But as we came together, I saw myself in the mirror by the bedroom closet, and thought: You have no pride, while wilting inside you.

Please note: I'm saving the apology for the end of this letter, because I know that repeating myself, even if I'm saying what you want to hear, is not the way to your heart.

The liquor store was closing when I arrived, and all my normal choices were cleaned out, so I bought something that looked like it wouldn't embarrass me in front Arvin and Catalina. He brewed beer, and they both drank it, which put them way ahead of me in terms of understanding why alcohol is more than a palliative. The clerk noticed Ruby nosing out my coat when I handed him the money, and smiled.

"You and your friend got a place to go?" he asked, concerned, but not overmuch.

"Uhyut," I replied, lapsing unconsciously into the affirmative of Acheron's lower, woodcutting class. Where did that come from? "I mean, yes, sir. Sure do. Just down the street. Pretty girls there."

"Well, take care then," he said, flicking a light switch behind him and darkening the store. "I'm closing up here myself."

He thinks I'm homeless, I thought as I wandered down Cortelyou Road toward the junction with Rugby. This was mostly true.

22

There was little chance of me tackling the rent for our ghetto palace on my own. The only real money I had was my half of the security deposit, sitting in a soggy fold in my pocket. The clerk at the liquor store either hadn't noticed or didn't care that I was walking around with several hundred dollars in cash. In New York, a critter in your coat spells homeless.

I reached the dooryard of Arvin and Catalina's house before discovering I still wasn't wearing shoelaces, and only then because a passing police cruiser drove through a puddle moating the sidewalk, soaking both Ruby and myself. I glanced down at my body, saw the empty grommets, and looked up in time to see the white and blue Impala returning in reverse. I tried to look as small and inconspicuous as possible, and considered diving into the hedge beside me, but as you know, I can't make a choice when cornered, even if it might save my life. So I stood paralyzed in the rain as the officer rolled down his window.

"I splash you?" he said, shouting to make himself heard over the wind.

"No, sir. I was already wet."

"Sorry," he shouted, his eyes apparently taking all of me in for the first time. "You going someplace?"

"I think so," I shouted back, knowing it was the wrong answer, but not wanting to contradict him if the question was rhetorical. At the same moment, the whiskey bottle slipped through the bottom of the sodden paper bag in my right hand, and would have shattered on the sidewalk separating me from the police officer, if I hadn't caught it with my left. I was so pleasantly shocked with myself that I grinned like a lunatic at the cop, who seemed to be in the middle stages of sizing me up.

"You're not drinking that here, right?" he said, with a certain preparedness.

"Uhyut. I mean, no sir. In there," I said, waving my hand at the broadside of the house behind me as Ruby emerged from beneath my coat. "With other people."

"What's that in your jacket?" he asked, squinting at the dog.

"A dog. My dog."

"Why's it got one eye?"

"I'm not sure. She came that way. But she doesn't get along so well with other dogs, so what we think happened was she got in a fight, because the person at the shelter told us…"

"Great," he said, closing the window, and continuing down the block, far too fast, in my opinion, considering the street was alive with a directionless flow of water. I climbed the steps to the door, and set Ruby at my feet before ringing the bell. My finger hovered above it before retracting, and uncapping the bottle. A nip seemed in order now that the officer had disappeared. I'd earned it with the walk over.

Arvin opened the door as I was tilting the bottle back, which made me feel like an overweight child caught with his mouth around a can of Reddi-wip. Ruby wandered between his legs, and inside; the world is her house. I lowered the bottle, and wiped the mouth on my sleeve before handing it to him.

"We heard shouting," he said. "And saw a cop drive off. Everything okay?"

"Sure. Why wouldn't it be?" I replied, a little too loud, and off kilter to convince Arvin, who stepped out of the doorway and hugged me. We'd hugged before, but it was always a man hug, a kind of way to show each other and anyone watching that we were secure enough in our sexualities and relationships not to worry whether embracing another man made us look gay. But I no longer had a relationship, so the hug meant something else. It reminded me of the way my brother and I hugged after we

24

tossed the commingled ashes of our parents into the wind atop Mt. Abandon. You were in Ohio at the time, but I remember you calling, and saying you would come on the first flight out of Columbus or Dayton, and how I somehow knew what kind of sacrifice that would entail for you academically. When my parents died from smoke inhalation in the middle of your sophomore term, I told you to stay in Ohio, because I wanted to believe I wasn't the sort of selfish person I became after you started visiting Lionel on your day off. This postponement may have bought us a decade, but it's impossible to tell now.

"I'm sorry," said Arvin, perhaps to escape me, because I was clutching his tall, thin, endlessly sympathetic frame as though it belonged to Grover. Maybe I've made it a little gay, I thought, letting him go and wondering if I looked as needy as I felt. Arvin held the door for me, and I followed him inside, even as the apology returned me to the doorstep of my parent's house the morning after the lining in their woodstove caught fire in the cabin up by Kranion Pond, and basically smothered them in their sleep. Sheriff Blivet delivered the news, and the same apology with tears thawing on his roseate cheeks as he stood in the mudroom, and explained it to me and Grover. A kettle whistled from the kitchen until the water evaporated. And a few days later, he and I watched skeins of ash disperse on the mountaintop above Acheron, which were really just cinders from the remains of the deer camp where our mom and dad spent winter weekends, snowshoeing and shooting things after retirement. It didn't make sense, and we had to climb a mountain in the middle of winter to do it, and I'm not sure either of us felt any better afterward. But I felt well enough to tell you to stay in Ohio. I think we can both agree this is the closest I've come to a sweeping gesture, so far.

An hour later, I sheltered beneath the back porch of the house on Rugby Road, beside Danielle, because she wore the yoga shorts/ sports bra combination mentioned earlier, and had cigarettes. I'm not sure why. Perhaps because of the outfit, I judged her lifestyle healthier than my own. But as I inspected her more closely, I noticed the finer points of her body faded from irregular use. I knew Danielle meditated, but that was all, and judging by the pout of her butt beside my own on the top step of the back porch, she seemed accustomed to resting on it. I thought of Eula again, the woman, not the storm, her indecent body forever at ease in a chair or the seat of a buggy, and tried to apply this luscious template to Danielle without success. She just looked like she sat on pillows a lot.

"...Yeah, so, at the Institute for Boddhisattva Studies, that's where I go to meditate because it's a good community, a lot of people who all want the same thing, and that can be nice, you know?" she asked, but saved me from having to answer by continuing to speak. "But the lectures have covered pain mostly, and how pain is derived from fear, you know, because we're afraid, we lash out, and cause pain because we're in pain, and I totally get it because I can be a total bitch sometimes and I think maybe it has to do with being lonely because I haven't been in New York that long, and I'm unemployed, and it can be kind of isolating, looking for a job, by yourself, you know? But the point is that we can free ourselves from pain, yeah, it's totally possible, by eliminating unhealthy desires, by just, you know, being, in ourselves, without anything else, so I've really been trying to do that lately, just exist without desire and training myself to recognize temptations..."

I nodded as though I understood this, sipping from a bottle of chocolate stout brewed by Arvin, and wondering if Danielle was delivering some sort of cue. Did she recognize me as temptation, or did she want me to nominate myself as a potential bridge from pain? Her company was honest murder, but it was becoming apparent that without a woman in my life, I lacked an immediate compass. Everything since the evening of my arrest seemed ambiguous, and warlike. So even as I watched rain bead in the oil on her forehead, and tried to ignore the smell of bongwater emanating from her wet hair, I stayed rooted in place, secretly afraid of allowing an opportunity for stability to elude me. Dotty as she was, I had somehow reached the unsound working conclusion that Danielle might be the only woman ever interested in me again.

And my running criticism of an essentially nice person made me morose. Danielle wasn't as attractive as you, but she was far prettier than some of the women I'd failed with, and I wasn't entirely sure I could do any better. I realized it had been many years since I was on the market, and when this occurred to me as the storm shook the house behind Danielle and I, and churned the backyard into a mire at the foot of the stairs, I didn't feel gleeful, and nearly had to leave the porch. Not to escape her, but to lock myself in the downstairs bathroom, and evaluate what I saw in the mirror. I needed the sort of objectivity only you could provide, so I remained, terrified of what I might see if I excused myself.

"How's the job hunt going?" I asked, somewhat muddied from the sweet and heavy beer. I try not to drink unless I'm around people who make me want to drink, and Danielle was certainly one of them.

"Not wonderful. I'm working for this musician I guess for like twenty an hour as like his assistant, but he's having trouble finding work too, so he hasn't actually paid me yet because there isn't anything for me to do."

"If you want, I could…" I began, thinking I might be able to find her a place at the Brooklyn Association before remembering I didn't work there any longer. She either didn't care what I had to say, or hadn't recognized the thought as incomplete, because she continued talking.

"There's this yeshiva that almost hired me on Avenue H and Ocean, but I haven't done the birthright thing yet so they seemed kind of skeptical. I've just been riding the train a lot. I get off at stops with names I like, and walk around handing out resumes."

"You should ride a bike," I said, actually meaning it. *"It's far better than the peasant shuttle."*

"Are you kidding?" she asked. *"I love the subway! How could you not? So many different people, all forced to stand together and mingle. I think it's great. I love to start conversations with them. I talked to this homeless guy, poor man, yesterday who invented Christmas lights. No, really, he said he came up with that shit, and it was stolen from him, and then he got bitten by a lion while working as a cage cleaner, and now he can't work at all, so he has no place to live. Isn't that sad and amazing?"*

This was everything I hated about public transit, plus a few items more. But I chuckled like an ass, and tried to sip from the empty bottle of stout. She lit a cigarette, and passed it to me, our wet hands touching, but the gesture was more kind than erotic, even though I suspected she did it to keep me from leaving the porch.

"Sorry she left," said Danielle, meaning you, and speaking with a measured caution so unfamiliar it was spooky. I shrugged. *"I know you probably wanted to go with her. I didn't think she would leave without you."*

I couldn't tell if she was trying to malign you in some way, or just saying what she thought I wanted to hear. Her manners

28

weren't excellent, but they were irreproachable enough to make me feel like a beast. Oddly enough, Lionel possessed the same quality and ability, a kind of daft earnestness that left me feeling physically disfigured when speaking derisively to you about him, because what did I really know? We'd only met once. I'd come to see you after work in Fort Greene, and you and he were sitting in the sculpture garden outside the campus library where the two of you worked, smoking marijuana, a drug that gave me panic attacks. He was pretty, polite, and smaller than me, all of which made him seem non-threatening. And he was a desk clerk, your desk clerk. You were his boss, so I figured there was probably some ethical problem in philandering among your minions, but again, what did I know? I'd never been in charge of anyone.

But I might have guessed Lionel believed in something beyond himself even before you told me. His manner suggested it the day we met in the sculpture garden, so genial and apparently pleased to meet me that I instantly felt like a savage beside him, a block-headed, lumbering heathen dragging his dull thumbs in the dirt beside this cheerful, bright little person. Of course, he was high as a crow's nest, and when you told me he was quietly religious afterward, I may have snorted with a kind of superior pity at his nescience, but I wasn't surprised by it. However: after your first afternoon together when I sat silently beside you in a yoga studio smelling of old lady farts, I grew slowly grateful you'd chosen a man of the church with whom to test my own dubious faith. Of course, he turned out to be the sort of Catholic who was kind to animals and old people rather than dogmatic and miserable, more like an Anglican shaped like a papist. But we both realized this was the only obstacle standing between you and sex with him, and so I apologized to Lionel's god privately, thanking it for leaving your relationship unconsummated, and our own somewhat intact, and apologized for all the shitty, unfounded things I said about him after you began seeing each other. I don't want to repeat them. I know you remember.

I'll admit I've come to regard the relief I felt after leaving the Brooklyn Association early to meet you on Nevins Street as a religious experience, having no other point of comparison. You were crying athwart a Marathon Bank where you had deposited our rent money, and, not ironically, a church. I did my best to offer comfort, though we both knew I was celebrating internally. A month of strangely tame grope sessions in his studio on Parkside Avenue passed before Lionel dumped you after you made him watch Harold and Maude, *a film you loved, and he found grotesque. You told me he said, "I would have sex with you," the week before, but wanted to take things slow for some reason, making this rupture all the more curious. You weren't sad. You were disappointed. The two are different though we often treat them the same.*

Though we all knew the live-in actuality of me was simply too much for him, he had enough tact not to mention it, saying he was seeing someone else instead, someone "who also happened to be single," as he put it. In short, he explained it kindly. You hadn't been rejected since middle school, but managed to absorb it with enough grace to make it to Nevins Street with the rent money and call me before breaking down. And I came to think of the Bible as occasionally useful, so we all learned something. Lionel began dating a Korean exchange student who worked with retarded children, and we returned to our grocery shopping and yoga classes, the same comfortable monotony that had bored you into seeing him to begin with. But when you clung to me on Nevins Street crying in the rain, and said, "I never wanted to replace you," I thought perhaps we'd turned the corner on

*Lionel, and whatever he represented. Though when you blew
your nose in your hand and added, "I shouldn't have shown him
that movie," I was less certain.*

*I followed Danielle inside when the weather made smoking or
talking impossible, and the complete darkness at the foot of the
porch stairs made it seem like they led to an abyss rather than the
yard. Where the grass had been, a small, muddy lake reflected
the glow of the porch lamp, but not the funereal candlelight from
the windows of the apartment building beyond the back fence.*

*"They've lost power," I said, gesturing toward the building as
she rose from the stairs. "That's probably an indication of something bad, right?"*

*"Maybe. Come inside," she said, tugging my shirt. I might as
well, I thought. We hadn't said much beyond what I've already
described, but I felt better about you after sitting with someone
else. So I stood to follow Danielle, and immediately slipped on
the stairs, falling into her, and toppling us both from porch, to
yard. We were unhurt because the yard was entirely mud, and
the water was up to our calves. It was too dark to seem much
of anything, but I heard Danielle thrashing around in the murk
somewhere nearby, and tried to help her up, reaching blindly in
the darkness, wind, and rain, and grasping what I thought was
her forearm, but turned out to be her inner thigh. She squeaked
when I mistook her vagina for her armpit, confusing one pulse
with another, and cupping it like a hard-boiled egg as I tried to
haul her to her feet this way before realizing I'd made a mistake.
But it was too late. Her chin clonked my teeth in a sort of kiss,
shattering whatever tension remained. Both of us said, "wait," at
the same moment, and there was an awkward, blind pause before
one of her hands began to climb my body until it found my face.*

"Okay," she said. I heard her feet stir the water as she walked forward and pressed her lips gently against mine. Though we haven't spoken about it, I think we were broken up at this point, so pardon me if I skip the apology.

"Tree shaker," I said, as she broke from me, and something shook the tree above my head.

"I know, right?" she replied with a kind of frightening gusto. I allowed her to tug my shirt again, drawing me from the water to the porch like a lifeguard. What have I done? I wondered, truthfully not understanding any of it.

Inside, I exchanged my empty bottle for a full one, placing it in a rack beside the beer fridge in the living room. Arvin saved them for the next batch, although with the sense of doom in the air, a next batch seemed unlikely. Danielle twittered in the kitchen to Billy, a confederate of hers from college who was even newer to New York, but had lived in the house on Rugby Road long enough to develop a shitty opinion of me. We were introduced during a July 4th barbeque in the backyard, if you recall, and when you asked her why she moved to the city, Billy answered with something absurd and polite, but not untypical, about it being the greatest city in the world or loving the energy or something. Of course, we were planning our mutual escape at this point, feeling we had done our time in the septic metropolis, and perhaps because of this immanency, you were able to smile, and let the remark pass. I, however, had been drinking gin and tonics since noon, and the bell above one of the churches on Dorchester Road tolled six times as I launched into an antithetical, incoherent, and too loud sermon about how Brooklyn was an unlivable abomination, and she, Billy, should do herself a favor and move back to wherever she came from. This turned out to be southern California.

Since then, she had caught me several times at the dining room table beside Catalina, leering through a curtain of bourbon at Danielle in the kitchen. Billy was prettier than her friend, but seemed entirely unaware of it, and almost asexual. She'd gotten into the habit of deliberately blocking my view of Danielle's sports bra/yoga shorts combo with her own, less-exposed, but finer body, a maneuver that suited me fine, though I found it puzzling. How could a woman so pretty not understand that rather than shielding her friend, she was simply upgrading the view? Billy's sexual life intrigued me only because there was no evidence she had one. I never saw her with a suitor of any kind, and when I asked Danielle about this, she just said, "Billy likes soccer players," which made me scoff, until she added, "At least she knows what she likes." I couldn't argue with that.

Catalina saw me come in with Danielle from the back yard, the both of us covered in mud and soaking wet, and was alternating her somber, witchy gaze between the two girls in the kitchen, and me in the living room as I struggled to open another chocolate stout with Danielle's cigarette lighter. She furiously stroked the coat of a large, ginger cat spread across her knees like a carriage blanket, while Ruby snored beneath her chair. She looked matri-archal, handsome, and extraordinarily pissed off about whatever had gone on in the back yard between Danielle and myself. When sexual tension fades, all that remains is contempt.

I don't know how attractive Catalina and I found each other the evening Arvin introduced us at a Japanese restaurant on 5th Avenue, but it had been two years since the meal, with nothing untoward taking place between us, aside from a small transgression at her birthday party. I had drank far too much, and went to her and Arvin's room to lie down, and at some point during my caesura, she appeared in the doorway, and when I closed my eyes for a moment, she had moved to the bedside in strange bit of illusory motion, like part of a thaumatrope. I opened my mouth to say hello, and her nipple entered it, though at what point she raised her shirt, I couldn't recall. Neither can I remember how long this went on, her nursing me in the back bedroom of the house, while the sounds of her birthday party rose and fell from the living room. But at some point it ended, and I was left with only my uncertain memory, and raw lips. I think Arvin knew, and didn't care, and I know you laughed when I told you. But I had no idea what Catalina thought, because we never discussed it.

"Are you jealous?" I tried to joke, sitting beside her at the dining room table. I caught Billy's eye from the kitchen, and smirked as Danielle chattered in the middle-distance.

"It's none of my business," said Catalina, tasting a goblet of wine at her elbow, and returning it to the table without looking at me. "But this is my house."

Before I could ask what that meant, Arvin appeared from the basement.

"So, we're in an evacuation zone," he said to all of us, kissing the top of Catalina's head as he joined her and me at the table. "Anyone feel like evacuating?"

Before we could answer, the lights went out.

How can I explain paranoia? It's worrying that the building superintendent who caught me dropping a bag of dog shit in his bag of recycling which I didn't know was recycling will assault you as revenge. It wasn't my fault. He hung the sack of bottles and cans from the fence dividing the grass median between the building and the sidewalk, which was something building managers did to supplement the dearth of municipal trash cans in the neighborhood. My mistake. I agonized, worrying he might punish you for my sin, or swat the dog to death with a broom. Nothing happened, but paranoia remains shark-like, continually moving with or without a fixed target. By the time I realized I was being absurd, I was worried about something else.

But as the homes up and down Rugby Road fell into darkness, I realized paranoia does have purpose, although in this case, I'd failed to grasp its import until Arvin's landlord, who lived in the house next door, appeared on the porch dressed like a lobsterman to say he wasn't leaving, but if it got bad, he for some reason had a canoe. Arvin thanked him, and closed the door as Billy and Danielle began lighting candles. Catalina hadn't moved from her chair, but continued to sip her wine and stare vaguely in my direction. I knew I was trapped as I watched water climb the base of the flagpole in the front yard out the dining room window, but by then it was too late to escape. So I sat with Ruby between my feet, and allowed Catalina to glare at me in the candlelight. My paranoia had already navigated to something else; I began worrying whether I would be able to perform with Danielle, if the evening came to that. It seemed likely, but part of me hoped we would all be washed away in the flood before she put the unspoken question to me, because for many years, it had been only you, Cordelia. I was frankly terrified at the possibility of having to prove myself to another woman. I choose not to believe in karma because it precludes me from having to behave like a gentleman. But most often, this only shortens the number of steps I take before I'm in above my head. I hadn't meant to hoist Danielle out of the floodwater by her vagina, but there was nothing I could say to convince her it was a mistake. Still, as I noticed her drawing nearer through the dark of the dining room, her orbit around me elliptical as she lit one candle, and then another, conjuring a trail of light toward where I sat beside a fuming Catali-

na, I knew that in some abstract part of my loneliness, I wanted her, or at the very least, whatever she represented. It's easy to forget desire when you're consumed with fulfilling it.

Of course, you don't remember the last person I slept with before joining you in Ohio, because I never told you. Not that we didn't discuss that sort of thing. I almost shared the story of my season with Martha, because she reminded me of you, and I thought saying so might be cute. But before I could, you told me an ex-boyfriend used an identical excuse to justify crushing the piñata, so to speak, with a chubby Unitarian in the back an Econoline van while you were away on an internship in San Francisco. Ole! So I bit my tongue, grateful that someone had saved me from stepping on my dick, even though recalling this remained raw for you. I took it as an omen; I probably shouldn't say anything about Martha at all, and thus she remained a lacuna in the romantic history I shared with you. But there's no reason to keep it to myself any longer, and I don't want to make the same mistake again, which is why I'm writing this. And since you're reading it, I'm going to assume you're considering allowing me back into your life, so you might as well know that during the fall of my last year in Acheron before I rejoined you in Julian Falls, I slept with a woman in my Wildlife Management class named Martha.

She wasn't actually in the class, but a graduate student of forestry working as a teaching assistant with a professor who moonlighted as the game warden for the Mt. Abandon Trust. Martha had the bad luck to receive her fellowship during Vermont's deer season, so she ended up with most of his course load. I had informally dropped out by the time she stepped in, and only attended one of her classes because rumor had it the new professor was sexy in a hillbilly sort of way. This turned out to be true, but wasn't enough to cement me on the college track. So I slunk back to my brother's grocery store, and assumed with a kind of fatalistic stupidity that Martha and I would never see each other again, though Acheron is neither vast, nor a particularly easy place to hide.

Still, I was surprised several weeks after recusing myself from her class to find us chest to chest on the doorstep of the house she rented on Town Hill Road, she freshly showered and wearing a red flannel bathrobe decorated with small game, and I in an apron and nametag with a crate of her groceries at my feet. The collar of the robe furled a bit as she leaned in the doorway, exposing the point of her clavicle and the parabolic contour of a breast as she said, "So you're a grocery boy." I tried to explain my brother owned the store, and I was only doing deliveries as a favor because some hungover undergraduate didn't show up. But this didn't impress her at all, and made me sound ashamed of myself, which I was, and to a certain extant, remain. She told me to bring the groceries into the kitchen, and explained how I could still pass her class as I put them away. If I helped her with a project over the weekend, she promised to return my grade to its former low average, provided I continued attending the class therein. While she explained the nature of the work, I watched the uncertain shape of her body beneath the robe, wondering if the raiment belonged to a boyfriend, or worse, a husband. No matter, I thought, scouring the fingers on both her hands for some dent, shade or impression of a ring recently removed. She asked if I thought I could do whatever she asked me to do, stooping past me to remove a box of cereal I'd stationed in the refrigerator. I drew back to watch the flannel tighten against her behind as she bent over, and said, "Uhyut."

The following Saturday, we were in a deer stand in the woods *at the base of Maybrick Peak, drinking coffee from a thermos and watching a doe-shaped mannequin through a spotting scope. It was an interesting arrangement, but I still had no idea what was expected of me, though I realized Martha may have just wanted company when her knee dropped against mine beneath the space blanket we shared. And frankly, Cordelia, I was touched. I couldn't remember the last time I'd spent an afternoon half as intimate with anyone except Grover, and even then, we were usually working at the store. I was so overcome by the aspect of our shared heat on the narrow platform high above the forest floor, and the raw scent of her wafting from some vent in her camouflage coveralls, that I nearly mistook her asking me what exactly I wanted to do with my life for some sort of invitation, until I noticed her staring at the nameplate affixed to the apron beneath my jacket. Martha wanted to know if I had any plans for myself other than delivering things for my brother. This was the correct moment to mention you. I know that, Cordelia. All my plans seem to involve hitching myself to your wagon, and I'm not ashamed of this. Still, as Martha's knee dropped against mine, it felt like the wrong moment to mention anyone else, and I hope you won't blame me for telling her I wanted to be philosopher, which is the grown-up equivalent of a six-year old saying he or she wants to be an astronaut. But it seemed like the only career path that would allow me to remain otiose and intellectually committed to you without closing myself to whatever Martha might represent. She asked first why I was in her class if that's what I wanted, and added that, depending on how you looked at it, being a philosopher was a very achievable goal. These were the words she used, and I buried myself in them for only an instant before the report of a high-powered rifle sounded from the direction of the access road, and the celluloid deer's head exploded.*

"Nice shot," said Martha. An engine revved and a tire spit loose earth and road salt into the wheel well as a vehicle fled. She checked the time, made a note in a logbook between us. "Shame about the dummy. But I guess we're about done for the day. Unless you think there's anyone in this town dumb enough to try and take down a headless decoy out of season."

I said it seemed unlikely, and followed Martha down the ladder to the ground, wondering if the rifle report had interrupted the perfect moment for a kiss and perhaps a grope.

"Too late now," I said aloud, idly and accidentally, and asked why Martha allowed the deerjackers to escape to cover myself.

"They didn't," she said, as we walked out into the clearing to collect the headless doe. "I got six trap cams set up all the way down to the hill to the main road in places where anyone would take a shot from, whether they know what they're doing or not. So we got their picture and plate number at worst. I'm guessing they fired out of the cab, around camera four, and if we go down there, we'll probably find a couple empty cans of Lowry's and the shell casing. But unless you want a souvenir, no need."

We drove back to her house with the dummy wedged morbidly in the back seat, and after I'd helped her bring it and the rest of the equipment inside, she asked me to stay for a glass of wine, which became a bottle, which became an invitation to dinner. I accepted and offered to help, and so we banged giddily around the kitchen for half and hour, dropping pans, burning vegetables, and allowing pots of oil and water to boil onto the stovetop. It felt like a kind of warfare, but we managed to combine enough of the groceries I'd delivered earlier that week into meal to pad the two bottles of wine we drank during it, and the one afterward. I can't say what became of us after 8PM. But I woke at 4AM with my face resting in Martha's armpit as she snored like a brush hog, *not entirely certain the day had been a success. We were both naked, which was good, but at some point during the night, the headless decoy was relocated to the foot of Martha's bed, where it sat in a rhombus of light falling through the window from a streetlamp like a sort of heathen offering. The room smelled of sex, so hopefully no one was left disappointed, though my eyes were swollen as if I'd been crying, and when I felt the mattress beneath my head, it was damp. Is it possible to cry in your sleep? I don't know if Martha noticed, and almost would have preferred wetting the bed, which seemed more normal. Even more peculiar: I couldn't recall the source of my grief, only the feeling of it, which is not unlike the way people remember dreams. It was the sense of having been not so much abandoned as surpassed; like when someone says they've changed rather than saying you haven't.*

Paranoia is the inability to flush the urinal at the offices of the Brooklyn Association with my hand, and using my wrist instead. And when caught by a coworker, knocking the back of my forearm against the apparatus like a victim of some atavistic palsy, augmenting the motion rather than trying to conceal it, as if to say, "I am not a lunatic, and I have nothing to hide! This is how I respond to your germs!"

After Gordon caught me performing what must have looked like a kind of toilet ritual, he stopped acknowledging me in the street, and began conveying all his instructions for me either through other people or email, even though he worked within conversational range of my desk. It didn't help that the canvass manager had forgotten to open a window before his 10AM sharp evacuation, leaving the men's room smelling like the rhino enclosure at the Bronx Zoo. And I knew even if I wasn't the scent's author, Gordon would forever associate it with me. I saw it in the expression of mingled pity and disgust he directed away from me at the urinal and toward himself in the mirror before leaving the bathroom without doing anything in particular.

I directed my own expression to the floor, and the effluent, alkaline lake of urine lying springless between my feet, and considered the concept of backsplash. One man misses his target, dribbling on the floor, and so the next must either step in the puddle, or aim from further away and risk contributing to it. And so the mess grows, snowballing from one initial mishap or act of wanton negligence, until you might as well just piss on the floor, because what difference would it really make? In a way, this described my life in New York City perfectly, but still, I made sure to open the bathroom window on my way out. Exiting the bathroom without any hope at all felt dangerously easy.

Still, after that day, Gordon began turning his head away from me when we saw each other outside the office, or even in the office, when he had no direct business with me. I tried not to take it personally, but did anyway. I'm not weird, Gordon, I thought, as he passed me outside the Flatbush Grill, absorbed by whatever was unfolding on his Blackberry. You're not so awesome either, I continued, as we passed within slapping distance of each other. What exactly makes you so goddamn unique? The only outstanding anecdote I could recall about Gordon was that he was the only person I knew who had gotten into a fistfight in the departures lounge at LaGuardia. He and a cohort of organizers en route to a convention in Fort Lauderdale ran across a bevy of orthodox Baptists on their way to picket a stranger's funeral in Orlando, and the situation got predictably ugly. I only know the story because Gordon shared it during a mandatory staff retreat at the Marriott by the courthouse on Adams Street as sort of mo-

tivational parable. The punchline: he and the other staff members still made the flight to Florida. I didn't get it then, and I don't get it now, but as you've told me many times, I'm in the wrong line of work. We haven't been able to agree on what I should be doing, though I think it was thoughtful of you to point out that I would have made an excellent saint if I wasn't so selfish and nervous.

So other than being the only person I know who's been in an airport brawl, I don't know anything about Gordon that makes him so much better than me. I only bring him up because when I stood on the porch with Danielle, watching a bold neighbor paddle a small kayak down the center of Rugby Road, I realized I probably wasn't leaving the city any time soon, and might need my job back in order to remain comfortable until I could make you love me again.

*   *   *

Poor Officer Laurel. By the time she asks what I'm thinking, I've already checked my expression in the sideview mirror to make certain I look honest when I tell her how happy I'll be when we get to what I've been euphemistically referring to as 'New Hampshire' since realizing she could help me escape the city after the storm. What I'm actually thinking is something along the lines of how relieved I'll be in a little under twenty minutes, when she and her love for me are firmly in the rearview. Until then, I babble away about New England's merits like I'm en route to a harvest festival, a little spooked by how easily this satisfies our different needs in the moment, but plowing along anyway. I'm hoping to round out this last pack of lies on a high note.

"I thought it might be something like that," she says, ignoring either her intuition or law enforcement training or both as she

42

steers the van past a derelict automobile on the shoulder of 1-91. "You look a little like a dog when it needs to go out."

"I probably do," I admit, wondering if this might just be my resting expression after spending so long in New York. I don't know what else to say, so I place my hand on her uniformed thigh resting against the gearshift. I do like her, and the time we've spent together hasn't meant nothing to me. She appeared when I needed her most, and for that, I will always be grateful. But is it love? No, I'm sure of that. Love is what I felt when Cordelia told me she was finally ready to leave Brooklyn. It had gotten too crowded, she said, and in many ways, too small. She missed the green hills of Acheron, the slate gray dome of Holmes Hall sitting like a third nipple between the bosomed contours of Maybrick Peak and Mt. Abandon, the calm, leafy, and slightly homogenous streets populated by people with advanced degrees in the humanities. In short, she missed home. But for so long, it had been only me, suffering New York privately. The city seemed to grow stranger and more alienating the longer I remained, and this seemed as good a reason as any to leave it behind, feeling as though I had done my time. I had paid $1725 for a second floor firetrap in a dangerous neighborhood. I'd smelled the exhaust of long haul trucks as I lay in bed and they passed beneath my window. I'd spent the Fourth of July in Prospect Park, when the ground was so littered with picnic refuse and smoking charcoal that there was no place to lay a blanket and watch the fireworks. I'd been hit by cars, and attacked by motorists while riding my bicycle. I'd watched people wait in line for Cronuts. I'd waited in line myself for dumber things, and paid more for them. In short, I felt I'd had an authentic New York experience, and was ready to return to the campestral backwater I called home.

But I never thought Cordelia would agree to leave. She loved

working around art students, even if she wasn't an artist herself, and seemed to feed upon the raw tension of undergraduate
creativity. We both enjoyed not having to own a car, but she
more than I, since driving seemed a fine compromise for what
it allowed me to flee from. She liked the energy of millions of
people crammed into an acreage that might suit a hundred in
Vermont, and often talked about the collective unconscious. She
enjoyed the energy of the city, an energy Waugh dismissed as
kind of neurosis in *Brideshead Revisited,* a book she never read,
but one I always thought she'd enjoy. New York for Cordelia
was a place where progress happened, and people did interesting things, so I knew coming home to me each night couldn't
be easy; sitting in the dark with a plate of wilted peirogi in my
lap, screening the same twelve stale episodes of *Fawlty Towers,*
fresh from a desk job that humiliated me, and so generally depressed I could barely remove the food from my body to greet
her at the door, and when I did, it was the same hug, the same
kiss, the same questions about her day as Ruby climbed her leg,
each night, for a minimum of four years, perhaps more. I know
whatever that was, it didn't look like progress, and wasn't interesting. She said she knew I was struggling, but thought I had
decided not to enjoy myself anymore, and all I could say was: it
wasn't a decision I made deliberately. This made me sound like
I was clinically disassociating, or feeble-minded. I then said I
hadn't had a bowel movement since getting doored by a motorist on Ocean Avenue, and asked if she thought this was unusual.
It was the wrong question to bookend what may have been an
overture.

Too late now, of course, but regret is part of what I'm calling
my experiments in hope, a term I coined when Cordelia finally
began talking about leaving New York, settling us in a place with

good schools and decent hospitals, because she wanted to have children with me. Even though it wasn't mentioned, I think we both knew I would make a better father elsewhere. This is the last moment I remember feeling love, when I realized that despite how maladjusted I had become, she still wanted a family with me. I didn't particularly want children, but was willing to have them if she was willing to leave with me; at the time, this seemed like the correct arrangement. But I remember the love specifically, the swollen throated sense of complete and utter admiration crippling me as I set my plate of wilted peirogi aside, silenced Basil Fawlty, and hugged her long and deep against my body.

And apparently her wish to leave was greater than I thought, because here I am with Officer Laurel, and there she is, somewhere beyond the soft cut of the Berkshires in the distance, perhaps blowing tufts of cigarette smoke into the cool night from the front porch of her father's house on Summer Street. Even this memory is pregnant with love for me, which is how I know I don't love Officer Laurel, who seems to have returned to whatever occupied her before she noticed me proofreading. It's unfortunate my not loving her doesn't make her ugly, or repulsive in some way. That would make this transition much easier. Instead, she looks handsome in her work clothes, armed and sturdy, tough and sexy, more woman than most men, including me in all honesty, could competently handle. Our first night of lovemaking in the second floor bedroom of her house in Queens left me feeling like zoo animals attacked me. I still don't understand why she agreed to abandon her job, her life, and her home to come live with me in what she now knows as New Hampshire. But then, I suppose that's love as well, irrational, dog-like, and entirely beyond the control of those over whom it has thrown a saddle.

After Danielle and I got tired of watching the storm, we left Ruby asleep with the cats upstairs, and she lit candles around her bedroom in the basement, as water washed against a window set in the foundation. Even though the candles were necessary, they reminded me of a girl we went to high school with, Lily, if you remember her. She did the same thing; invited me to her room, lit candles, and put on possibly the same song as Danielle (something arty and atrocious by Jeff Buckley), just before she asked me to take her virginity. I didn't balk, but I felt as if a trap had snapped shut on my leg as soon as the request tipped from her lips onto my to-do list. She took so much time to arrange the ideal scene to surrender her maidenhead. Even if I wanted to say no, it would have been hard. A therapist might refer to this sort of arrangement as a 'guided choice.'

I was about eighty-five percent sure Danielle wasn't a virgin, and she looked lovely in the candlelight. But still, the anxiety of expectation mingled with the sense of myself nosing toward a precipice of some kind kept me pawing at the bookshelves for something to comment upon, and pecking the keys of an electric keyboard as if I knew anything about music. But the room was too small to avoid the obvious.

"Take your shoes off," she said. I mistook it for an invitation to relax, missing the room's far Eastern motif; paper lanterns, fans tacked to the wall above the bed, a tatami mat in place of a rug, a kimono suggesting itself from the closet, a wilted orchid in an austere vessel from the bodega at the head of the street. I obliged, not wanting to disrespect anyone's adopted customs, and sat beside her on the bed since it was the only place to sit.

The room's solitary chair now held what had been on the bed when we came in.

"Take your coat off," she said, leaning over me in the formerly alluring sports bra/yoga short combo that had tempted me for so long, now within reach. As a sort of reflex from life with you, I reached out, and cupped her hips as she leaned over me, tugging on the jacket, and though nothing yielded as tension might suggest, she put her face against mine and whispered something I couldn't hear. Instead of asking her to repeat, I just nodded, as though I knew exactly what she said and agreed with it.

"You're sure?" she said, drawing back from the bed and looking me in the eyes.

"Absolutely!" I replied, wondering what I missed, but only for the time it took her to kiss me, wetly and with a measure of abandon, since whatever I didn't hear had obviously been the only palisade between us. I had the sense of a trap closing around my leg once again, but managed to return the kiss and finish removing my jacket, an old, blaze red Woolrich my father wore to stack wood. It was really the only thing in life I was afraid of losing now that he and my mother were dead, and you had disappeared. Even though the Tombs were like a recidivist sauna, I'd been allowed to keep this garment while interred there, and used it to cloak my head in an earnest attempt at sleep, inhaling the fine odor of autumn labor and smoke burnt into the woolen lining, and remembering my father standing between two cords with his chin pinched between his thumb and knuckle as he decided where to start. It stood out like something from Thomas Kincaid, the sort of purely rural image you considered insipid, but allowed me to express because it involved a tragedy. I know you gently suggested other jackets, gifting me things that were fashionable, and slightly more urban, clothing to help me blend

in and perhaps have more fun. It must have been embarrassing to walk beside me on Atlantic Avenue while I was dressed like a deer hunter, and answering any affirmative question with an 'uhyut.' I suppose this was my way of saying I would remain essentially woodsy, even if there were no woods to be had. I know I said I would save my apology for the end, but please believe I'm sorry for how little fun I had become.

Danielle snuffed the candles except one, and left the room. A toilet flushed down the hall, and when she returned, she wore the kimono, her hair was pulled into a bun, and she appeared to have put on makeup. A geisha joke made it halfway out of my mouth before I managed to silence myself, and Danielle snuffed the remaining candle without hearing it. She padded over to the bedside, and kissed me again. Despite the trap manacled to my leg, the kisses were good, alien and entirely new. It suddenly seemed so strange to have spent the past several years only kissing you, Cordelia, and at the same time, the sense of having not kissed you enough during that time remained. While Danielle stood above, I slid my hands beneath the robe, and was somewhat dismayed to find the yoga shorts absent, but understood this was done for our mutual benefit. Her butt felt good in my hands, and I was so amazed by my own enthusiasm that tried to press my face between her legs, but she tapped the top of my head.

"Let me do you instead," she said, kneeling in her robe, and fiddling with the clasp on the front of my pants. I hadn't rethreaded the belt taken and returned to me during my time in state custody, which was beginning to seem like a remote fever dream. I liked this new, laconic Danielle, who wore costumes to bed, and was primarily generous; she seemed to know exactly how to approach me. I realize, Cordelia, this last statement makes me sound like a wildebeest someone is trying to photograph, but

wasn't it you who said our sexual chemistry was a problem when Lionel Little was briefly in the picture? The two of you had the chemistry we lacked; I remember this distinctly because it made me feel so awful. Part of me thought with a kind of infant diplomacy that everything would be fine if we were just nice to each other, and calmed down a bit. But later I began to think we knew each other too well to hide our selfishness; I might be willing to suffer a Lionel Little every year or so, provided I could continue my experiments in hope, as mentioned.

"I like you," I said stupidly as Danielle crawled atop me, and cast away her robe, ecstatic at how little guilt I felt, and hoping whatever happened next wouldn't come back to haunt me later. But I was willing to take the risk, even if it meant the absence of a condom. Off to an irresponsible start, I thought, as she rode me like a broomstick, smacking her pelvis against mine with a kind of witchy vigor, and a sound like a welcome mat beaten clean against the side of a house. What fun we had, Cordelia, the risky kind that turns out poorly more often than not, but fun even so, the sort you and I might have managed if it hadn't been for the incompatibility issue. I know comparisons are hurtful in this context, my love, but the point I'm making is that I found myself agreeing with you as the warm flush of Danielle's climax began percolating within her, while I, no closer to coming, but enjoying myself even so, lay beneath, just as the window above the bed began to leak, and drain onto the two of us below. Paranoia is expecting the sky to fall, but allowing yourself to be shocked, even outraged, when it does.

I saw the water coming, and was prepared for something bathetic. But Danielle had not, and when the torrent from the side-yard breeched the window, spilling mud, grass, and rain over the rocking, ghost-white contour of her shoulders, she was too shocked to scream, her mouth contracting into a bead of qui-escent agony as she slipped from my body onto the floor, and scrambled out of the room with the kimono tangled around one foot, trailing her like the tail of a kite. I stood, trying to follow the moist slap of her feet through the humid darkness of the base-ment room, and managed to stagger to the door with my pants coiled around my ankles before collapsing somewhere short of the upstairs landing. This is where Arvin and the rest of the house found me, my legs snared in the suddenly literal trap of my own clothing, which I had to remove entirely in order to stand. I ex-pected Billy to turn away, but instead her horrified gaze fell on my lower half, illuminated by a flashlight extended indecently from Catalina's arm. Even before I had glanced down at myself, I heard them say in unison, "You're bleeding," and yes, there was some blood, not much, but enough to cause concern, particularly in that region.

"No, it's not that," said Danielle from somewhere to the right of Billy, the white of her skin reshrouded in the kimono, and her eyes invisible beyond the beam of the flashlight, though I had the sense they were staring at me as if I was meant to explain whatev-er she had whispered earlier, so low I couldn't understand it but agreed anyway, because I'm accommodating, Cordelia. I'll agree to anything as long as I don't have to deal with the consequences.

"It's okay," I said, nodding in the direction of everyone. "No need to stigmatize anyone. I'll just go…wash myself off."

"Ew," said someone, probably Billy.

"Shower's out," said Arvin, taking the flashlight away from Catalina in order to give everyone a break. "You might have to just go stand in the rain a while."

"I'll do that," I said, trying to sound cheerful, as people began going back upstairs. I pretended to follow, but returned instead *to Danielle's room, wrapped myself in a wet blanket and curled up beneath the party dresses and seemingly endless stock of decorative, oriental robes in her closet. I assumed she would probably sleep in Billy's room, since her bed was soaked, and all I wanted was a moment to myself in order to remember who I was without you, Cordelia. It had been a big day, and I just wanted five minutes alone to reinvent myself. But I realized this would take longer than I probably wanted to spend on it, so I slept half naked in the wardrobe, trying to call you, and never connecting as the storm shook the house, and rainwater seeped into the foundation.*

*　　*　　*

Paranoia is the morning I awoke in complete darkness in a shelterbelt fringing the abandoned golf course on the edge the St. Margaret's campus without any idea how I'd arrived there. I'd been drinking, that was clear, and slept standing at attention like a draft horse in a frock of trees bearding the cornfield on the Greene/Miami county line. Dawn seemed remote, as did the exact direction of Julian Falls, or the bonfire I'd departed from for no reason, possibly to return to my dormitory and call you in Baltimore, even though I had the sense you wouldn't be available. I was lost in Ohio, and bleary with drink, but had the presence of mind to check my phone, and yes, there were several calls placed earlier in the evening in an effort to reach you, Cordelia, each spaced five to ten minutes apart, as though I'd called you, taken between ten and twenty steps in the opposite direction from where I meant to go, forgotten, and called you again. Your phone had become harder to answer when your internship began, even though it was a part time gig throwing paintings around an art museum. I wasn't sure what you did with the rest of your time in the city, but I knew it had something to do with a painter named Nathan Moore, who dumped you and dropped out of St. Margaret's long before I arrived, and moved to Baltimore to live in an unheated cellar and read Ezra Pound on the toilet. When I learned this later, I wondered whether your breakup with him had something to do with encouraging me to join you in Ohio, but decided as long as you wanted me there, the reasons didn't matter.

Still, as I staggered out of what passes for wilderness in Southern Ohio, and began walking toward what I hoped were the lights of campus far in the distance, I wondered what I was doing there exactly. It couldn't be described as academic or personal progress, and since the internship in Baltimore constituted your final term, I assumed I wouldn't be staying in Ohio without you. And yet, there I was without you anyway, feeling Schafer and Stroh's cans collapse beneath my shoes in the cool early morning grass as I passed the bonfire from whence I departed at some vague point earlier in the evening, and where Marlowe, a fellow Vermonter and elderly freshmen still sat with several sturdy looking women, drinking off the remainder. We exchanged a wave, which helped me remember I was still corporeal, and could feel pain, and I recognized this sensation somewhere between my stomach and head, but waited until I was beyond the purview of the bonfire to raise my shirt and examine myself. No injury. But I was hurt even so, as if I knew then that while I lost myself in the trees trying to reach you, Nathan was sharing his Klonopin with you in Federal Hill Park, and talking about the various and combined minor tragedies preventing him from getting a job or dating you seriously. I imagine, Cordelia, he stared intensely at the inner harbor, while feeding you his medication like breadcrumbs to a shore-

bird. I only found out you slept with him when you wrote a poem about it two years later, and asked me to read it and give you my thoughts. By then we were already in New York, and becoming angry felt unproductive. You described the sex as "unsuccessful" and we both left it there.

Still, I always wondered why you stopped taking my calls altogether. Granted many were placed rather late, and it wouldn't have taken a third eye to guess I was incoherent on my end, and I never had much to say anyway, since it was obvious by the hour of my call and timbre of my voice what I was up to. I only called to hear yours, Cordelia. And the point of all this is that whether or not you ignored my calls during the night I spent in the bottom of Danielle's wardrobe, or whether you simply were not available, or whether the storm had made it impossible for the call to go through, all I wanted, then as now, was to know you would answer if you saw it was me. To just answer the phone, and say, "I won't speak to you if you're just going to be drunk the whole time," and hang up. That seemed moderately reciprocal to me, and was really all I wanted.

But when I woke encoffined in the wardrobe with the phone's keypad pressed into the side of my face from where I'd slept on it, and staggered upstairs to check on Ruby, I couldn't relieve the immediate and familiar pain roiling from somewhere between my stomach and head, which I only recognized then as a derivative form of loss when Danielle passed me on her way to the toilet.

"You can totally stay here again tonight if you want," she said impatiently before mincing into the bathroom. Is that what I want? I asked myself. No, not at all. But do I have a choice? Probably not, I thought, as Ruby climbed my leg for a walk. I got her into her harness and put on my shoes and even poured myself a mug of coffee before realizing there was absolutely no place to

take her when we stepped outside. The street was still awash with inches of rainwater, and blocked by the shaggy trunks of several uprooted shade trees. It looked like the aftermath of thunderstorms I'd seen in Ohio, but more importantly, it made the possibility of returning to the rattrap on Caton Avenue to sit in the darkness with only my thoughts and the dog no longer a choice. For the time being, Danielle's wardrobe was my home.

I pitched a tenuous sort of camp between the front gate and the porch, allowing Ruby to nose deposits of flotsam and relieve herself on a hummock girding the birdbath, and dialed Gordon's number, unsure of what else to do. The soggy bankroll in my pocket would only sustain my limited needs for so long, that much was clear. True, I'd survived on far less in Ohio's medieval economy. But as I watched several dour-looking people pass on the street, wheeling shopping carts and hand trucks presumably encumbered with their belongings through the water, I realized that depending on the exact scope of the storm damage, it was possible money wouldn't do much good.

I considered Camus: "…and to state quite simply what we learn in a time of pestilence: that there are more things to admire in men than to despise," *and wanted to believe order would remain in the city, and I wouldn't have to use my half of the security deposit as tinder to cook my shoes. But paranoia in one form is just a heightened breed of pragmatism, which is why I'd inspected the larder inside Arvin and Catalina's home the night before, and while it wasn't exactly bare, there certainly wasn't enough food to sustain five adults, two cats, and one dog for much longer than a few days. As I shifted cans of pumpkin pie filling remaining from Thanksgiving in the candle light, and listened to a disconsolate broadcast from a portable radio in the living room announcing that Breezy Point was on fire, I tried to calculate my chance of surviving whatever happened next. I'm not stupid, I thought, blowing the dust from a tin of Kipper Snacks, and wondering whether anyone in the house would notice it missing. But by nature, I am not useful, either to others or myself. And it is obvious to everyone. The odds seem high that I will be within the first division of social parasites shucked from the lifeboat. On an impulse, I slipped the Kippered Snacks down my pants, only to have them clatter out of the cuff onto the tiles as Billy entered the kitchen to get a glass of water, eying me with not so much suspicion, as confirmation. In that moment, it was unclear whose trust issues were more pronounced.*

So I had to think with the sort of practicality you embody, Cordelia, and from which I had always benefited without absorbing. Thus, I sat on the saturated steps of Arvin and Catalina's porch, hoping Gordon would take my call. The Brooklyn Association was likely mobilizing a relief effort of some kind, meaning the conference room at the downtown office would be a vault of non-perishable food and warm clothing, perhaps even kibble for Ruby. If they wouldn't give me my old job back, or a new job with pay, I'd volunteer. Non-profits will refuse to do many things, but in my experience, accepting free labor isn't one of them. It only occurred to me that volunteering for relief work with the non-categorical intention to steal food might constitute a sort of amoral terminal velocity after Gordon had already answered the phone and listened to me explain why I wanted to help.

"We need people out at the point," he said. "It's still burning in places, but most of the fires are out. The problem now is residents are basically cold, and hungry. Rumor is that FEMA has a barge parked off shore somewhere, but it's like the Flying fucking Dutchmen, and we can't wait for them to finish jerking off the mayor's office while folks are dying of exposure. Do you have transportation?"

"Yes," I said, eying an unattended bakfiets across the street. I was willing to steal a bicycle if it meant securing a food source. "I can be there in an hour."

"That'll work. Call me when you arrive. We're setting up a distribution center on Oceanside Avenue if the fire department will allow it. As far as I know, the Wedge is closed off, but if you have any trouble getting in, show them your work I.D., or have them call me. And thanks for this."

I said it was no trouble while I was already mounting the cargo bike, and steering it into the center of the street. It was heavy enough to cut gracefully through the water, and traffic would likely not be an issue. I scooped Ruby out of the yard, and placed her in the luggage bucket, before pedaling the bicycle to the intersection of Dorchester Road, and concealing it behind a hedge, just as the owner emerged from the building, and began a fruitless hunt for the machine he'd orphaned at the curb. Normally, this would make me feel something other than a sense of victory, I thought as I watched him from the interior of the hedge, with Ruby tucked beneath my arm. And yet, I feel only as much empathy as triumph will allow, which is to say, very little; the pity of a king receiving an oath of fealty from a deposed rival. Perhaps I am not yet a bad person, but I recognize this as a future possibility.

When I returned to the house, Danielle was just exiting the bathroom, and appeared both disappointed and proud when I explained the spurious nature of my sojourn to the Irish Riviera, and then asked her if she would mind watching Ruby while I was in Queens.

"No of course not," she murmured, smiling "I'm sorry we can't spend the day together, after last night. But I think it's wonderful that you're willing to go down there to help."

"May I borrow this?" I asked, holding up a canvas bag I'd discovered in what Acheron residents might refer to as 'the mud-room', but New Yorkers would likely call a 'shoe enclave' or 'coat transept' or something. The bag was large enough to hold a load of canned goods, but small enough to conceal inside my father's jacket. My plan was to loop my arms through the straps, allowing the bag to billow beneath my coat, and form sort of a grocery brassiere. As long as I was careful, I could slip food and whatever else I needed down my collar, and into the bag without anyone noticing.

"Absolutely," said Danielle, her opalescent eyes shining with an admiration I hadn't earned, but was unwilling to smother. "Do you want breakfast before you go? I think we have a few eggs from a rooftop farm in Red Hook. They're great! Nothing like farm fresh, am I right?"

"Absolutely," I echoed, suddenly recalling the chickens my parents kept in the backyard of our house on Loomis Street, and the crisp, buff center of an egg with two yolks broken in a cast iron skillet, while tears of grease popped and stained my mother's robe as she stood before the range, a garment not dissimilar from the one Martha wore when she answered the door. Red flannel, decorated with adolescent white tails, and plump pheasants, a robe I associated with illness, because I only saw it when she stayed home with me while I was sick. And yes, I know, Cordelia: My inability to move beyond memories like this may have been what poisoned our relationship, or my character, or simply pre-vented me from having a good time, as you indicated. And yet, as I stood in the kitchen on Rugby Road, trying not to associate a woman who had menstruated upon me the previous evening with my mother, even as she puttered and fussed around the kitchen, but most particularly, yipped with a kind of delighted surprise *as an egg broken against the edge of the frying pan offered up two yolks, I wondered if your disregard for my particular history had more to do with the shelter it provided me, and excluded you from, rather than some instantiation of my inability to grow up. But isn't that New York's single, undeniable gift to its residents? Eternal, decrepit youth for every denizen? Manhattan being a near analogue for the Land of Toys, and Brooklyn itself one large, liberal arts campus on which you can forever be exactly who you were sophomore year. Welcome home! Are these not simple truths, my love? I wanted to make you happy so badly, though I suspected post-Lionel Little that you didn't want happiness from me, but a sort of emotional scaffolding until you could find something better. You'll recall, or perhaps you won't, that my experiments in hope reached a kind of recondite apotheosis at this time. The day before I went to jail, and you left the city without me, I remember experiencing a twenty-minute period of euphoria while listening to you explain how a mortgage worked, and thinking I would love you forever, if allowed.*

"Someone's going to be married soon," said Danielle, placing a helping of charred scrambled eggs before me. "I suppose that will be Arvin and Catalina…"

"I suppose so," I agreed, shoveling the food into my mouth as though it were my last meal on planet earth, and ignoring the ellipsis. She absorbed my silence as though swallowing a cannonball. I wanted to inform her that she had mistaken me for someone with something to offer, but thanked her for the meal instead, grabbed the canvas bag I planned to use to plunder food from the needy, and walked down the street to the stolen bike with which I would transport it.

I'll admit it was impossible to rid myself of the thought, or, more

*accurately: the memory of you as I shuttled south down the aban-
doned center of Flatbush Avenue, toward what the black-headed
Gull in* Watership Down *referred to as "big water." New York
City suggests an ocean the way certain solitary men at the truck
stops and rest areas between the Pennsylvania/New Jersey border and Julian Falls, Ohio suggest a history of domestic violence.
My first informal introduction to one of these took place after
visiting you in Baltimore over Columbus Day weekend. We had
fun, didn't we? You lived on the top floor of a row house outside
a liquor store whose automated bell never stopped ringing, and
thus accompanied the corybantic love we made in your room,
deep in the afternoon. We drove between museums, and went
to a book festival near Mt. Vernon, where I met Nathan, theoretically reading a free weekly on the stoop of his building like a
social media portrait of relaxed, groovy urbanism. While using
the bathroom in the oubliette in which you would eventually
fuck him, I noticed that while there wasn't toilet paper, there was
a copy of Kierkegaard's* Diary of a Seducer, *which would have
suited my needs just fine. This only seemed ironic, or perhaps
congruent, years later in New York, when I noticed you reading
this particular book and tried to convince myself that some co-
incidence rather than regular communication with Nathan had
guided your choice, while trying to imagine how he might feel if
I gave the girlfriend he didn't have a copy of* Lady Chatterley's
Lover, *or* Sexus, *or fucking* Justine, *for god's sake. I decided Nathan would likely feign libertine indifference with such skill that
his authentic feelings would be impossible to withdraw from the
histrionic warren of his personality, and that, as far as you were
concerned, he had won this round. Vae victo, I suppose.*

*The point of all this, my darling, is that on the way back, after
reconnoitering somewhere between Maryland and Washington*

D.C. with the St. Margaret's classmate who had driven me down, we stopped for a piss and pommes frites *around 1 AM on the border between Kentucky and Ohio, and while standing at the urinal, I felt the iron eye of the giant beside me, the sort of universal man beast as likely to be found in the woodlots of the northeast as the natural gas fields of the far west, fall upon my part. I worried that struggling to conceal myself might offend or possibly encourage him, and yes, as mentioned, a vague ferocity seemed to detach itself from the rogue eye of this seasonal laborer and settle like a turkey vulture upon my exposed root, as though the two of us had reached a silent agreement herein; indeed, sir, I will allow you to watch me pee, as long as you don't hurt me with your hands. Some people might call this rape. I preferred to think of it as motivated bargaining, or another guided choice.*

Thus, the dubious sea leers at the New York horizon the way this man leered above the partition between urinals. It's always beyond the corner of the next building, implying itself without ever presenting until you've crossed Avenue U, and bypassed the King's Plaza Shopping Center, which seems to be the unnatural boundary between lesser Brooklyn and Marine Park. And of course, even before I passed the shuttered plaza, and the barren lot beside it, down the normally congested lanes of Flatbush Avenue, I thought of the few times you had cajoled me into riding to Fort Tilden with you, and how those afternoons had always turned out well. We'd wandered among the razor clams, and seen men teaching their daughters how to use a surf-casting rod, passed beneath the shadow of several shuttered seaside clubs with their patio furniture bolted to paint-flaked terraces, and inspected the abandoned bunkers remaining from when the beach was used as a military base during WWII. There are moments, as I'm sure you know, when it is possible to tumble briefly into love, and as

the surf climbed our ankles, and the sunset guided our peregri-
nation toward a piling we'd used to lock up our bikes, I felt this,
and I know you did as well, though it naturally faded by the time
we'd returned to the apartment.

The cargo bicycle cut through the four to five inches of rain-
water as well as any boat, and I only needed to tow the thing
out of deep water twice before reaching the Marine Park Bridge.
South Brooklyn didn't look abandoned so much as in hiding.
Even though the storm had passed, the stores along Flatbush
were closed, and many were boarded up. The air smelled like
smoke, and standing water. I only saw three people, all look-
ing lost and bellicose, and one police van, between the house
on Rugby Road, and the emergency barricade at the head of the
bridge. The officer on duty waved my bicycle to the side, and as
I fished my soggy work I.D. out of my coat, I wondered irratio-
nally whether they might have already received a report about a
stolen bakfietz ridden by an idiot heading south down a vacant
Flatbush Avenue. Most of New York City is either underwater or
on fire, I thought, as the officer inspected my identification with-
out any real care, and gestured me beyond the cordon and onto
the bridge. And I'm worried about being arrested for stealing a
bike. Despite everything, my self-esteem is obviously healthy, and
functioning well. I am the light of the world, etc.

I called Gordon after crossing the bridge, and he directed me
to the fire station off Rockaway Point Boulevard, where I posted
up in the bathroom, removed my jacket, and slipped my arms
through the straps of the grocery bag I'd borrowed from Dan-
ielle. I looked at myself in the mirror before zipping my coat
over the theft hammock hanging empty against my chest, and
tried desperately to like what I saw in the glass. A twenty-nine
year old, possibly single, white male, superficially handsome,

blind without his glasses, and smartish, but: no money, no job or career, one handicapped dog, semi-criminal record, not a problem so much as a fascination with alcohol, and the peculiar inability to exist without the guidance and support of a strong, high-achieving woman. Also: steals.

Through the bathroom window, sheets of black smoke gathered and hung over the sections of the neighborhood continuing to burn. I cracked the door, and watched a shuffling queue of residents terminating at a brace of folding tables manned by Gordon, and several other former coworkers, an evident heap of goods behind them spilling from the open hatch of a minivan with New Jersey plates. The line of people seemed as polite as could be expected, evincing only fatigue and a mild impatience as they accepted a share of whatever the Brooklyn Association had managed to haul out here on the spur of the moment.

"There will be more," I heard Gordon assure one middle-aged black woman in her pajamas. Two children flanked her, also in sleepwear. "We have a panel truck en route now, so please, tell your neighbors."

"I don't have a place to prepare this," she said, removing a can of minestrone soup from the box Gordon had given her. "I don't even have an opener. And my house is gone, sir. Do you understand that?"

Gordon told her to use the firehouse kitchen if the kids were hungry, and then said something to Chanel, the PR coordinator, about getting some cots and cooking gear set up in the basement of a church off West Market Street. She nodded, and stepped away from the table to make a phone call. Can I realistically steal from these people? I asked myself, as I exited the bathroom to join them. Yes, I answered. But I won't enjoy it.

"Your call surprised the shit out of me," said Gordon, as I

stood woodenly beside him at the table, trying not to invest the nearby mound of food and supplies with too much attention. "I get you, in a way. This is a job, and I seeing you come to work everyday, I got it. You did your work, and went home. I was never going to rattle your cage or anything when you disappeared for an hour to read under those trees outside Long Island University. It seemed like you needed it, and as long as the work was done, it wasn't my problem."

"What trees?" I asked, plainly embarrassed by the fact that in addition to my bathroom difficulties, he knew about my midmorning ritual. You're familiar with it of course, because it was all I had to talk about when you asked me about my day. I would escape the office, wander down the street, and sit beneath a tree in a public plaza outside LIU with a book open in my lap for an hour. This seemed like the sort of civil disobedience the Brooklyn Association would welcome, in theory, and turned out to be the only assured method of nurturing a sense of quotidian progress in what I began to call 'my stupid life' in conversation with you, and whoever else would listen. Don't think I didn't notice it: the commingling of concern and regret in your face when I responded to any question about my workday by delineating the plot of After Dark, My Sweet *or* The Plague Dogs, *not just to fill the silence between us, but because this was the only way I knew how to live. Would you have preferred to hear about the spreadsheets I made of foreclosed properties in each county in New York State, or the memoranda on public pool closures in and around Hempstead which I wrote, circulated, and ultimately knew was unread? I always tried to share what I believed was worth sharing, my love, even if that meant neither of us had any clear idea what I did from the hours of 10AM to 6PM.*

"Doesn't matter," said Gordon, as though I had confirmed something for him. "The point is: you surprised me today, and I appreciate that. And you rode here on a bike? Good man. It was hard enough getting the van out here. Speaking of which, what I need from you is to go out back. There's a Mazda crammed to the fucking ridgepole with food, clothes, diapers, that kind of thing. Leave the food except formula, and pull out the kid stuff, bring it back here. We're running low, and I have no idea when the next load will cross the bridge. NY1 is making this out to be some alleged valley of desolation, when families live here, and they need help. FEMA's fucking ghost ship may show up today, tomorrow, or never, so someone has to fill the gap, and you saw the smoke above the Wedge; it's a huge fucking gap. So, thanks."

"Don't mention it," I pleaded, accepting the keys and stalking toward the parking lot in the rear of the fire station. I wasn't sure I could take much more of this. Though the bag around my neck was empty, it seemed full of cinderblocks as I unlocked the door of the car, and began sifting the supplies jammed in the back seat. I tried to prevent myself from either screaming obscenities at my reflection in the rear view mirror, or slamming my own head in the door by focusing on the actual task Gordon had given me, while silently mulling over the evasive nature of pure evil. It seemed that without you nearby, Cordelia, I had become a rudimentary person, or collection of base needs cloaked by enough personality to pass as human. While I would hate to presume that your love made me whole, it certainly shaded the patchier, lacunae-like areas of my character.

And yet, after handling the diapers, baby formula, and other non-perishable detritus from the Brooklyn Association cupboard, the idea of slipping any of it beneath my collar was abhorrent. This seemed so simple several hours earlier. Human, I thought, or *quoted. All too human. Even so, I should at least try to steal from the homeless, if only to make the trip a success.*

I removed a canister of peaches from between the passenger seat and console, and dropped it into the bag beneath my coat. It didn't feel exactly right, but it didn't feel wrong either. I could do this. And I had to do this, because, and I think we both can agree, it was what you would have done. I tried several more cans; green beans, corn, tuna fish. Each clonked neutrally against the other within my jacket. The bag grew heavy, the straps biting into my shoulders as I added pears, several packages of instant noodles, and another can of peaches, suddenly remembering their taste from fifth grade, Acheron Elementary, 1995-ish, on a day I'd forgotten the bag lunch packed by my mother, and was forced to either starve or eat whatever the school provided. This turned out to be a glutinous shepherd's pie, with a crust like the carapace of a snapping turtle, and the interior filled with creamed potatoes that could have caulked a sewer pipe, but suspended peas like expended .22 caliber bullets instead. I made it halfway through this mess before trading it to a young Henry Hoffmann, who had a reputation for dourly mowing through whatever was placed before him with the stoic fortitude of a dispossessed Roman consul, and appeared to derive some veiled benefit from trading his dessert of peaches in treacle for the half-eaten wedge of pie abandoned in my tray. Over his shoulder, I watched a young you deposit your own tray and silverware in a plastic tub of blue solution before rejoining your table, which, even then, I noticed was fuller than my own.

All evil has a place in the world, I resolved, standing and smacking the back of my head against the Mazda's chassis hard enough to drop the box of children's items I'd been removing from the car onto the ground. I wondered if this might be god's way of telling me I was wrong, or some demon's way of saying I was on the right track, but resolved to proceed as normal, or what suddenly passed for it, though this became noticeably more difficult as I stood with the box, attempting to adjust to the weight beneath my coat in a way that wouldn't make me appear suspicious, and made eye contact with Gordon who had emerged from the rear of the building to smoke a cigarette. Act casual, I thought. You have no idea how long he's been watching you. It's unlikely, but possible, that he saw nothing unusual.

"So, I'm in there wondering what's taking you so long," he said, holding an unlit cigarette as if it was lit, and gesturing toward the door with it. My hope receded. "And I come out back, and see you staring at a can of pears for nearly ten minutes, like you're maybe waiting for it to open itself. Then it disappears under your coat. Do you understand why this behavior might concern me?"

"They were peaches," I said, setting the box of diapers and things at his feet.

"I have the feeling you will make a career out of partially fulfilling extremely low expectations," said Gordon, offering me a cigarette. "Exactly how much food is concealed beneath your coat?"

"Enough for my dog and me, I hope," I said, accepting the cigarette without wanting it, but feeling as though denying the overture might further indict me in some way. "My partner left two days ago. I am alone here. I am sleeping in a woman's closet, and she may be beginning to love me ferociously. I can't imagine why."

"Me neither."

"I want to help others, but I'm worried that I may starve to death if I don't help myself."

"You could have just gotten in line."

"I hate lines."

"This is not a productive conversation. Return what you took to the car, get on your bike, and go back to your closet. Obviously, I'd fire you if you hadn't already quit."

"A reference is probably too much to hope for in the future."

"Absolutely not!" said Gordon, grinding his heel into the spent end of his cigarette with a kind of unnatural glee. "I would be more than happy to explain why you suck to whoever will listen."

"Whomever, I think you mean."

"Build an ivory tower. Spit out the window," said Gordon, as I handed him the car keys. "If you're still lurking around back here in five minutes, I'm calling the cops on the bridge. We went to high school together. They'll take good care of you."

"In solidarity," I said, as the door slammed in my face, and I rounded the side of the building to get my bicycle. Failure feels like failure, I thought obliquely, but with the sort of clarity that ordinarily arrives after having been caught in an act both casually amoral, and objectively stupid, like blowing your nose in a tablecloth, or resting your beer on a headstone.

But as I pedaled back toward the bridge, I recognized the suddenly familiar weight of the overfull grocery bag beneath my coat, and felt less like a failure, and more like a criminal. Perhaps this was what Gordon meant by partially fulfilling low expectations. I left when asked, but returned nothing, and was fleeing back to Brooklyn with my non-perishable plunder toward my temporary home in the lady's closet. Had I meant to do this? Steal, that is? Judging by the tide of anxiety lapping at the fraying cuff of my equilibrium as I turned the bicycle onto the bridge, I would say not. I've tried to describe this sensation to you before, and each time I have failed to convey the exact feeling of a panic attack. But I remember you listening to me try, while rooted in the sort of stolid, internal stasis that inhibits the entrance of empathy. Baghdad or Brooklyn, it made no difference. You were at home in the world, and I was not, hence: my trouble. I now recognize that it probably took great discipline to feel so little. But at the time, as I sat with you in the living room, gasping and barking an incoherent summary of the issues I'd been having since we returned from spending Christmas in Holland, I wasn't angry or hurt by you so much as ashamed of myself when you said you couldn't deal with head shit, and left the apartment to go shopping in Manhattan.

Head shit, I thought as the door closed behind you, and freezing rain pattered the apartment window. I considered rolling myself up in the living room rug, and spending the rest of winter that way. As long as you slipped food twice a day into the end where my head was, there wouldn't be a problem. How had I tried to explain the feeling of anxiety, brewing at such a feverish and frenetic pitch that it expelled the breath from my body, and left me gasping and choking in my cubicle at work, or in the center of a crowded B train, or even while receiving an echocardiogram a week later, to make sure my head shit wasn't a result or symptom of heart trouble? I prayed for mitral valve prolapse, and was told my heart beat fast, but there was nothing wrong with it, or anything else. All the medical professionals said so, even the young, beautiful Pakistani resident who seemed shocked when I used my limited breath to explain why I would accept no medication other than aspirin, while sitting so rigidly on the examination table in her office that I looked like the human equivalent of a Gordian knot, hugging my shallow chest with one leg locked over the other, and my chin resting in the cup of my manu-

brium, all while watching the reflection of this anxious display in a window with a sign on it that read: PLEASE DONUT OPEN THIS WINDOW. And from deep in my throat, a low-toned hum emerged, like the sound of a lawnmower heard many yards distant during an especially hot and still summer day, a kind of sustained murmur, which unsettled the other patients in the waiting room. Even the Pakistani resident found it off-putting enough to ask why I was growling, forcing me to explain through my constricted breath that it wasn't a growl, but a sort of sidecar to the generalized anxiety disorder she had just diagnosed me with, and while I didn't enjoy making the noise, I was afraid of what might happen if I stopped. She asked if it helped me breath, and I said I wasn't sure, but it definitely helped pass the time until I could breath again, at which point she sent me to get blood drawn and have my thyroid checked.

Or later, when I told the baleful, Aryan scarecrow of a doctor in the ER at Park Slope Methodist how badly the thin muscles of my torso ached from trying to breath through the feeling of catastrophic, irredeemable, and baseless harm shuttling toward me from what seemed like every corner of New York City, he looked at me with the sort of surrender the hopeful reserve for the hopeless and said he'd looked through my labs, everything was fine, and this should be good news. In theory, I agreed, but knowing it was all head shit, as you suspected from the beginning, and not something that could be repaired by looking under the hood, so to speak, made me feel more alone than I had when you'd left me alone in the apartment after I'd compared the sensation of a panic attack with the adrenal, semi-lucid feeling of falling in a dream. I think you understood that, and perhaps even appreciated the accidental poetry of it, but left me alone anyway, maybe hoping by the time you returned, I would have a plan to fix myself outlined, and taped to the refrigerator. But later in the ER, as I sat on the examination table purring like a small engine, I looked over the instruments in a jar beside the sink with envy, the scalpels and surgical scissors, and then looked at the face of the doctor who had just given me a diagnosis of incurably batshit, and wondered if begging him to cut me open and have a look anyway would produce a kind of mutual progress, or further strengthen his verdict.

It didn't help that Christmas in Holland had been what we both needed, and, as a result of the suffocation and anxious growling on my part, we discovered it was possible to ruin a joyful, rich experience weeks, even months afterward. Going forward, I will do my best to keep this in mind. But by the time I began to control myself later that year, no longer venturing out into the city with the sort of neophyte excitement I once had, but able to shop for groceries at Key Food without growling toward the exit when the check-out line was too long, or ride the train without tying myself in a quivering bundle as I had during my appointment with the Pakistani resident, it was too late. The memory was already polluted, wasn't it? Landing at Schilpol at 5AM on Christmas morning, and debarking the train at Utrecht only to wander the cold and deserted streets beneath the obelisk shadow of the Dom tower as the sun rose slowly along the Oudegracht, and the city came to partial life. It was all, in fact, for nothing.

But I recall it anyway with only as much regret as the ineluctable vault of the past will allow: Most stores and restaurants were gesloten, *so after we checked in at our hotel, we returned to Amsterdam, bought bread, fruit, and marijuana, and napped on the train as the uniform winter plain of the land unspooled past the window, and smoke rose from the chimneys of farmhouses bulwarking the fields and saddles of scrubby forest. For some*

70

reason, my foremost recollection of that tired afternoon with my face against the train's window: a lone man in an gray overcoat and red driving cap pedaling a bicycle beside the tracks. It remained with me later, as Ruby towed me down Caton Avenue while I hummed to myself like a Cessna, and counted my steps; one, two, three, and if I made it to ten without losing my breath amid the internal Tartarus of grief and shame I'd developed following the afternoon you left me alone in the apartment, I considered it a good day. I read somewhere that counting your steps was supposed to be calming, and could even be considered a form of meditation. But each footstep during the grim midwinter after our return from Holland seemed as if it fell in some dreary no man's land separating irretrievable loss from the possibility of further loss, even with the New Year's fireworks we watched from the hotel balcony as we emptied the minibar still echoing in their formerly poignant casket, or the bicycles we rented and rode through the forests of the Hogue Veluwe, or the lunch at the art museum deep within it, where I recall with a certain jealousy the extreme pleasure you evinced while eating Brie and honey on a halved baguette at the café therein, only because I can't remember you ever being as happy with me as you were with that Dutch fucking sandwich. But then, this may have been the last time we were truly in love, Cordelia, and, if I may, I will cling to it like a cat on a screen door, with both the desperation and skill that come with practice.

Either Faulkner or Aristotle may have said something about a man needing to do what he must to do what he must. I suppose the problem is that I've never known what I needed to do. But after I began panicking my nights away in bed beside you, I wondered if perhaps my little job in life was to needlessly suffer. Someone has to do it, right? I can already hear you laughing, as I'm sure you will when I slip this beneath the door of your father's house when I reach Acheron. If we ever talk about it, I know you'll say my inability to do anything practical with these kinds of memories except idealize and regret them, not necessarily in that order, is probably the exact reason you left New York without me. But I was never much of a learner, which is why you finished college and I didn't, and likely the reason I was willing to follow you to the city, all things considered, and also partially to blame for my collapse on the Marine Park Bridge in front of Officer Laurel and two of her coworkers.

To be fair, ignorance wasn't entirely responsible for the fall. There was also the canvas grocery bag stuffed with stolen canned goods hanging from my shoulders redistributing my weight in such a way that as I stepped off the bicycle and bent to catch my breath, which was off to a running start and fleeing like a triumphant hyena over the horizon. I took three steps and collided with the railing, and two more, before toppling onto my face.

Cop shoes moved toward me, and a woman's voice speaking in a central Queens dialect ask if I was all right. This was Officer Laurel, who I should have recognized from our interaction an hour earlier when she checked my work I.D. and waved me through the barricade. As two of her cohort raised me to my feet, and leaned me against the railing of the pedestrian walkway, I considered the water beneath the bridge. Jumping into it could save me and most of the people I knew an immense amount of bother. The ballast supplied by the canned goods would likely draw me to the bottom of the slough like a conquistador in his armor, a bag of Aztec gold strapped to his sword belt, and a faith receding with each bypassed fathom. I truly had no faith to lose, and was certain if I didn't return, Danielle would see to Ruby, if only from sentimental attachment to me. But that would be *enough to tide the dog over. It bought you and me at least three years.*

"Why are you growling?" asked Officer Laurel. I recognized her as beautiful for the first time that day. "Or, what's that noise you're making?"

"I'm sorry," I said, as waves of adrenal fear galloped across my chest, cinching it like a corset across my ribs, and squeezing the breath from my body. I wanted to add something about the nature of panic, or try to contextualize my strange behavior for the three police officers who had probably seen weirder. But the desire to say more was less than the desire to flee toward some neutral hinterland far beyond the range of my legs, but propelling myself toward uncertainty seemed better than remaining with what felt like assured disaster, and so I was off, running at full speed for perhaps five steps before one of the officers who was not Officer Laurel seized my collar, jerking me like a dog at the end of its lead, and knocking me back onto the pavement hard enough to eject several cans of food from beneath my collar and send them rolling across the asphalt plane of the bridge.

"Why's he got food under his jacket?" asked one of the cops as I purred, flopped, and gasped fish-like on the ground at his feet, wondering whether it was even worth trying to sit up.

"I think he's having trouble breathing," said Officer Laurel, kneeling beside me and unzipping my jacket, thus exposing the flank of my already partially revealed shame. I realized everything was either going to be fine, or I was going to pass out. My vision was beginning to grow indistinct at the edges, and no matter how deeply I tried to inhale, it was impossible to draw a full, salubrious breath into my lungs.

While I know a panic attack has never killed anyone, I thought, it acquaints the victim with the endless working reality of incursive, irretrievable doom, like a torturer who each morning takes his torturee to the edge of a sheer cliff, and dangles him or her over it without ever actually letting them fall, thereby familiarizing his client with the impending finality of death without the big finish, until both of them grow equally ambivalent regarding it. Anxiety kills you enough times in rehearsal to make actually killing you a sort of technicality. One can only confront the abyss so often before it's just a hole in the ground. So, given my history, I thought further, I'm already dead. Wonderful. If I could breathe long enough to speak, I might share this with my new friends, the bridge police. Couldn't be any weirder for them than the growling.

"What the hell is that?" asked one of the cops who wasn't Officer Laurel, gesturing at the partially empty bag hanging against my chest. "Looks like maybe he was trying to hide it."

"Should we call the ambulance?" asked the other, removing his radio from the circlet of utilities around his waste, and holding it the way Hamlet is often seen holding Yorick's skull, a sort of defeatist contemplation, as if the officer had a copy of my medical record in his squad car.

"It won't get here fast enough even if it can get here," said Officer Laurel, threading her arms beneath mine and hoisting me to my feet. "I'll take him. Can you walk?"

"He could run a second ago," said the cop with the radio.

"Uhyut," I managed, taking one step before collapsing in a heap like a magician's sheet used in a vanishing trick. This is my life now, I thought, as Officer Laurel heaved me over her shoulder like a sack of unwanted kittens destined for the river, and rolled me into the rear of her patrol car at the base of the bridge.

"There's a bag from Luigi's on the floor by your feet. I think you should breath into it. I'm going to drive very fast," she said, calmly gunning the engine. "Is that going to bother you?"

I tried to say it would, and when this didn't work, I tried to say thank you, but couldn't form the words, wheezing and humming through them instead as I placed the bag over my face and tried to regulate my breathing. I know rebreathing is supposed to work by recycling exhaled carbon dioxide, but it always seemed like bullshit to me, and far too obvious to be of any use except in private. Am I supposed to just whip out a paper sack on the subway and hang it over my face like a feedbag whenever I'm suffocating? Yes, New York has seen weirder things, but not from me, and as you know, Cordelia, I try not to be overgenerous when contributing to the world's already vast collection of sadness. Still, I did as Officer Laurel suggested, purring my thanks into the bag, before passing out somewhere between King's Highway and Nostrand Avenue. What I remember most, and last: her blonde hair blowing in a breath of storm wind from the open driver's window as she removed her peaked cap, and the orthodox womanly scent of it reaching me through the portcullis dividing the center of the police cruiser as I tipped to the side like a wall-mounted ironing board and fell asleep.

*   *   *

Paranoia is wondering whether Officer Laurel will emerge from the Starbuck's on the outskirt of Springfield before I've finished composing what I hope will be a lovely, assuaging note thanking her for everything she has done to get me this far. I couldn't have done it without her, and I am truly grateful. But how best to convey this? I remain stuck on the proper salutation. "Dear Officer Laurel" sounds both formal and jejune, and belies the undeniable, platonic regard I have for her. "Laurel" manages to be both intimate and terse, as though we know each other too well to bother disguising our mutual boredom. "Darling" is sweet, cute, and closer to the truth about us, as she might see it. But when I imagine her passing from the hermetic interior of the roadside coffee shop into the parking lot, with a steaming paper cup jailed in either hand while her head oscillates to the left, and then the right, wondering whether she forgot where she parked the van, I can't imagine the love which travelled like kudzu across the retaining wall separating Officer Laurel's mating instinct from her fathomless heart will feel any less betrayed at my choice to begin an I-dump-thee! letter with Darling. I'm also abandoning her in a Springfield, Massachusetts strip mall during a gas shortage, Not mollifying, I think, as I transfer Ruby from my lap to the passenger seat and start the van. I care for you very much. Thus: goodbye. Talk about mixed signals. Best to remain economic, and unemotional. I dispense with the salutation, and write: THANK YOU! I'M SO SORRY!, meaning every word of it, and fold the paper once so it resembles a card.

In some sense, I wonder if I'm not inflicting on poor Officer Laurel the same treatment and circumstance Cordelia inflicted on me. Far from home, with a tailored beverage I will never drink steaming in the gray, impersonal air of northeastern American, wearing her work clothes on which the revenant imprint of my hand remains where it moved in a sort of ghost migration down her thigh only ten minutes ago. As she stares at the impregnability of the parking lot, now void of anything save the note I've weighted with my unread library copy of *The Alexandria Quartet* atop the two totes, and one handbag comprising her share of the luggage I've left occupying the parking space formerly held by the police van, she will wonder what changed between my hand combing her thigh, and this moment.

I wish it could be less similar to Cordelia discarding me a few days earlier, and if I wasn't acting as both an enemy and accomplice of love, it's likely I would be unable to circle the van out of the parking lot, and guide it to the mouth of the interstate, my course charted three hours north for Acheron and the woman I love enough to abuse the trust and manipulate the goodwill of those around me. It's possible romance will make a chimera of anyone, though some surrender to it easier than others; being suddenly without love makes me feel handicapped.

I would be ashamed of this experience, my experience, if I weren't manacled to it, though I'm speaking mostly of the days following my awakening in the guest bedroom of Officer Laurel's row house, a hospital-like space, made only the more clinical by the sterile evening light illumining the slats of a vertical blind to my left, the guttural drone of an A/C unit partially concealed behind it, and a small, muted flat-screen television sutured to the wall opposite the bed. As I tapped the remote, raising the volume on the evening news enough to learn it was still the same day, and I had only slept for three hours, I searched each horizontal plane in the vicinity for a segmented tray, but found nothing, and felt relieved. I am not in an asylum, a jail, or home for wayward idiots, I thought. This is obviously someone's house.

But whose house? I wondered, as my gaze swept the room, absorbing the inoffensive shades applied to the wall, and chosen for the furnishings, the carefully balanced lighting, and mundane selection of reading material adjoining a baby monitor I mistook for a clock radio on the night table. Time is immaterial, I thought, wondering why the appliance failed to display the hour of the day as I sat up in bed, and allowed the sheet to descend my naked torso, and then raising the remainder bunched at my waist to find the rest of my body stripped of not only the theft brassiere, but clothing as well.

How curious. I didn't remember undressing myself, but I suppose that doesn't mean it didn't happen. That early fall morning
in 2001 shortly after Halloween when I awoke in my parent's
hunting camp to snow drifting beyond the frosted glass, and Cordelia, age 17, breathing beside me with the quilt drawn just below
her breasts. And as I stood to feed the sections of tinder she'd
split the evening before into the woodstove ticking at the foot of
the bed, I realized I was naked, and didn't know what we'd done,
but wasn't seriously worried about it. A bottle of peppermint
schnapps her father received as a sort of gag gift when he was
tenured at the college sat on the bedside table, partially purged.
We hadn't drank much of that, just enough to sand the sharp
edges of our mutual nerves to a finer, more agreeable contour.
We were not each other's firsts; we'd discussed it: Cordelia lost
her virginity to a Portuguese exchange student named Raul, since
departed back to somewhere in the Algarve, and my own was
jettisoned with the help of Millicent Oliver, whose foster family
gave her a room in an unfinished attic where the only furnishings
were a bed and a radio, playing constantly. Even as we bounced
against each other during a grey autumnal Wednesday several
years earlier, Vermont Public Radio tooted the kind of martial,
Wagnerian selection my father always characterized as music that
made him feel like Tartars were riding over the hills of Acheron
to kill him and loot his household.

So Cordelia and I weren't new to this. But the liquor helped
us proceed calmly where we might have otherwise fumbled, or
grown frantic at key points, and perhaps even helped me remain
phlegmatic when Grover appeared in the doorway of the camp
with a shopping bag in his arms, setting it down beside the
place in the hall where he might have removed his boots if he
hadn't spotted me naked, feeding the stove in the center of the

room, and turned on his heel like a Byzantine sentry pacing the walls of Theodosius II, and walked back outside. Cordelia remained asleep as the door slammed behind him, I fumbled into my clothes, which seemed to have been flung about the room with the categorical aim of making them impossible to collect, and ran outside barefoot in the snow to catch my older brother where he stood smoking in the yard beside his car. He was in his sophomore year in college then, studying sustainable business management or something similarly practical, and the smoking was a habit he did either in private, or in front of me, but never in front of our parents, who we both knew would flatly disapprove. I apologized for what he had seen, not really meaning a word of it, proud in a way to have him witness evidence of my ability to sleep with a woman.

It didn't matter. He laughed and said he knew my car didn't have snow tires, and when he saw the weather report this morning, he came up to the camp to make sure we got back to town okay, since our parents, and Cordelia's father, thought the two of us were places we were not, and he didn't want to see us stranded, and having to admit to both lying, and fornication, by default. I asked what was in the bag he'd left inside, and he said some coffee, and stuff for breakfast, eggs, vegetables, bacon, that sort of thing. He thought we might be hungry. And before I knew it, I was hugging him, and he was lurching away from me, smiling, embarrassed, but happy to participate in this minor conspiracy. He said he would wait out in the car for us, and I told to him to come in and eat some of the food he'd brought. Cordelia appeared in the doorway wrapped in the quilt, bidding us both good morning, and as I looked from her to Grover, I remember thinking these were two people I would always love, beyond condition, geography, or anything else that impedes this kind of reckless sentiment. The feeling persisted as we sat at the kitchen table later on, eating scrambled eggs with red potatoes, and green onions, while Grover discussed college programs with Cordelia, and I listened, feeling no need to participate, but knowing I would go wherever she did.

"Does loving you this way make me stupid?" I asked the empty room in Officer Laurel's house as this memory receded, and then: "Please excuse me. My life without you is a dungeon of choices. Free will has a cost for people like me. You always knew that. And yet, you allowed me to cling to the tail of your coat…I, lamprey. Why? I never wanted to compromise your life. I only wanted to watch it pass with you, benignly, if possible…Also: I have enormous respect for all the things you know that I do not. And I adore the way you managed to keep the world at bay. Meanwhile: this room is a sort of purgatory, I suppose. No surprise there. For years I've sensed a kind of limbo erecting itself around me…On that note, please forgive my insistence on memory to get by. It's all I have to generate the sort of feeling that could easily be misfiled as an experiment in hope, but is closer to what I imagine a mother must feel the first time she nurses a child. Or perhaps it's what the child feels. Anyway, I've just realized that I'm speaking aloud into a baby monitor. I'll possibly submit this in letterform, or I may just eject it wholesale on your doorstep whenever I have the opportunity to return to you, though I can't say when that will be. This news program reports all roads, tunnels, and bridges into or out of this toilet of a city are closed until further notice, and that gasoline will be unavailable to private citizens. A state of emergency has been declared. I couldn't agree more."

The baby monitor emitted a salient pop as I inadvertently combed it from the nightstand while reaching for an outlying copy of *Mysteries* there. The cheap interior speaker shattering as it hit the floor, and I immediately felt guilty, and then afraid as I heard footsteps approaching from the hall. I turned off the television, and drew the blanket to my chin, hoping feigning sleep might help me avoid blame. The steps paused beyond the door, as if unsure whether or not to enter, and in a plane of light falling between the vertical blinds, I quickly refreshed myself on the plot of the book in my hand: "…an eternal foe of the establishment." Sounds about right, though I recall it making no sense whatsoever when I read it last, except as a sort of deliberately absurd joke Hamsun concocted to puzzle and disappoint anyone who enjoyed *Hunger*. Still, based on the décor, and the sort of modern cheerlessness of the room, it's about the last book I'd expect to find on the nightstand. Or perhaps it fits perfectly. I suppose it depends on whoever is turning the doorknob at this very moment.

Afraid to be caught doing anything unusual, I stuffed the book beneath the sheets, and closed my eyes, projecting an almost comically false snore in the direction of the door as it swung wide, admitting, though just barely, Officer Laurel's uniformed shape into the room like the figurehead of a galleon emerging from a wall of pale sea fog. So it's you, I thought, unsure of what I meant, but watching through the crack of one eye, and feeling a sudden sense of delicious shame as she crossed the room to adjust the blinds, or perhaps the air conditioner. I couldn't be sure which, because the honeyed cascade of hair spilling down the back of her navy uniform fixed my attention, filling me with the sort of greed a career glutton must feel as he passes the window of a confectionary. Six foot two at least, one hundred and seventy-five pounds at most, all of it some combination of brawn and what the woodcutters of Acheron might refer to as 'log-sense.' Watching her fuss with the room as she tried to decide whether or not to wake me, I imagined her standing beside Odin upon the gelid floor of Valhalla, and tried to shoehorn myself into this tableau without success. She is clearly some kind of goddess, I thought. And I am a bespectacled twerp who steals canned peaches to survive. Nothing about her equipoise suggests she's in the market for a scavenger.

Yet there I was anyway, naked in her guest bed, shuffling between shame, desire, and a kind of latent fear of not so much what she might want, but whether I would be able to provide it. Despite my fumbling with a post-menstrual Danielle, I still felt unprepared for intimacy after Cordelia, whose outline I'll admit to transposing upon Officer Laurel's silhouette as she stood in the window, just to see how many of her might fit inside it. I judged two and half Cordelias to one Officer Laurel, a figure that only augmented the inadequacy that had made my heart a sort of purlieu, or three-season home, since Lionel Little, or perhaps as far back as Nathan Moore. Of course, any man who reads Gertrude Stein while taking a dump isn't husband material, which would make me feel better if Cordelia wanted a husband. But apparently, the worst thing I could have done for our sex life was not being the kind of partner who consumes three beers and six Clonazepam before falling asleep in a plate of Tofurkey during Thanksgiving dinner with her father. Who knew? I have trouble learning from this sort of mistake.

I tried the same trick with Martha. She seemed like the only woman I'd known intimately who came close to measuring up to Officer Laurel. In terms of what, I can't say exactly. The ratio was somewhat better, as I judged it: one and a half to one, though I wasn't sure if Martha and I had managed to make any whoopee the night I spent with her and the decoy, so rather than resurrecting my confidence from the abyss into which it had withdrawn, the figure reminded me instead of a good opportunity I'd ruined through some combination of strong drink and poor planning.

And while I knew this process of stacking one woman's imprint against another's wasn't scientific, or even particularly quantitative, it was definitive enough to galvanize the fear I felt watching Officer Laurel pace the room like Cerberus in search of honeyed bread. It was also fitting: early evening has always been the time when I try to tally and index the day's botched opportunities, not so much to learn from them as cannibalize their tragic possibilities for anything that will make me feel like a victim of God rather than myself.

"I'm tired of pretending you're not awake," said Officer Laurel, settling heavily on the bed, her weight on the mattress edge causing my leg to roll log-like against the swell of her uniformed bottom. "I came to see if you're hungry. I can make the food you brought, or something else."

"The food I brought," I echoed, realizing I'd given myself away only after hearing my own voice aloud, and thinking: Wherever I am, I packed food before arriving here. This is an example of good planning. Perhaps I am an adult after all.

"The cans you had hidden under your coat," continued Officer Laurel. "There were peaches, I think. Maybe tuna. Do you want peaches and tuna?"

"No thank you," I said. Her face was angled away from the light, so I couldn't tell whether or not this menu suggestion was a joke. "Why am I here? And where is this?"

"My house. We're in Ridgewood. I can take you to a hospital," she said slowly, calmly, with only the suggestion of an edge; a law enforcement voice, accustomed to predicting trouble. "But you'll be lucky to find floor space with what's going on in the street right now. You also don't seem like the sort of person who enjoys waiting for things, and if you're just having a fit, you'll be waiting a while."

"It's not 'a fit'. They're panic attacks. There's no cure, and most people think I'm lying, or that I was molested as a child when I try to explain why I sometimes find the world overwhelming and terrifying for no obvious reason."

"You don't seem molested."

"Well…I'm not entirely sure what you mean by that. But good, I guess. Thank you, in fact, I…"

"And the world is only as scary as you allow it to be."

"Okay, that's maybe half true. But I suppose in your line of work you…"

"What are you hiding under there?"

For a moment, I thought she meant something other than the book resting like a morgue attendant's clipboard against my sternum. Why am I afraid of this woman? I thought as I withdrew the Hamsun from under the covers, ashamed at my relief when this seemed to answer her question. The worst that can happen, I thought further, as she took the book and returned it to the nightstand. Is that my penis refuses to rise when called, like Bartleby from his prison bunk, simply preferring not to.

"I hate that book," she said.

"Me too," I replied, suddenly ecstatic to find we had something in common. "Though in terms of sympathizers, or collaborators, if we're being honest, I prefer Celine, and not just the approachable, by comparison, work: *Journey to the End of the Night*, or *Death on the Installment Plan*, you know, the ones you find on the shelf at warehouse booksellers in the Midwest. I mean *North, Castle to Castle*, and even *Normance*. An author writing his way through brief personal trauma is compelling, but Louis F.'s nervous breakdown lasted from the First World War until his death, in my opinion, in an apartment full of cats and anti-Semitic pamphlets. Ginsberg, the gnome prince of North

84

American middle-achievement, and Burroughs, his jester, visited him around then, and were disappointed, I'm guessing. So sad, in a way. He loved his wife and animals dearly. But I suppose the good artist is his own iconoclast. The Teutonics never learned that: Grass the tank commander, and his moment with the Waffen S.S., or Fallada on his farm, and his sheltered, uncritical silence in the face of it all while Goebbels championed *Wolf Among Wolves*. And poor Boll: refusing to join the Hilter Jugend only to end up in the Wehrmacht anyway, finishing the war as a mangled POW. He is what might happen if Faulkner were born a good German, I think. Something about all this equals a Nobel Prize. Have you noticed?"

"You sound like Johan Nagel," said Officer Laurel, raising her soft chin toward the nightstand where the book had come to rest. "And I don't understand a word of it, which is why I didn't enjoy the book. The library down the street had a sale, and this sounded interesting. It wasn't. That's all I have to say about it. I still don't know if you're hungry. And why did you break this?"

"It was an accident," I said, as she plucked the carcass of the baby monitor from the floor, examining it as if its destruction, however sad, remained congruent with her expectations for the day. "Why do you have that anyway? Is there a child in this house?"

"No," she said. "At one point, I thought I was pregnant, and got excited. So I picked up some things. But it turned out to be a mistake."

"I'm sorry, I think."

"I didn't want a baby overmuch. I just thought it might be interesting to care for something that makes me feel ignorant. My dad said he never knew how little he knew until I was born."

"My father said the most terrifying moment of his life was

the afternoon he and my mother returned from the hospital with me, and realized they had no idea what they were doing. My girlfriend…pardon me, my ex-girlfriend wanted children very much, though I don't think she wanted them with me…But I wasn't sure I wanted them with her either, mostly because I didn't think we could survive being trapped together in a position of mutual terror…and ignorance, as you mentioned. I always had the feeling she might poison me if it proved advantageous in some way. I think I was a placeholder."

"My last boyfriend told me he wanted to have a family shortly before we broke up. It wasn't clear if these two things were related. He didn't ask what I wanted."

"What did you want?"

"A family," said Officer Laurel. "But not with him. We were both placeholders. So it worked out. What do you want?"

"I just want to go home," I said, suddenly wondering if Officer Laurel tossing me in a squad car and depositing me naked in her guest bed qualified as kidnapping. Would she allow me to leave whenever I wanted, or would I have to plot an escape? And did I even want to leave? The bed was far more comfortable than Danielle's closet, or the bare mattress in the nearly empty apartment on Caton Avenue, which, when compared with the anodyne modernity of Officer Laurel's guest room, had all the composite ambiance of a Balkan caravansary after Cordelia made off with everything worth showing people. So, even if I was being held prisoner, I was comfortable, and if Ruby were with me, I would consider my life temporarily complete.

"Where are you from?"

"New…Hampshire," I said, meaning to say New England, but lying for some reason, as if I already sensed that Officer Laurel, in all her stolid loneliness, might be my express ticket home, even if I was unsure of how exactly she would fulfill this capacity, or if it would behoove me to deceive her. Depending on how lonely you are, life in New York can make you either overgenerous with your personal information, or so guarded that you eventually come to believe most of the lies you share with people. New Hampshire is beside Vermont, I thought, watching a matrix of light fall from the vertical blinds upon the soft, earnest features Officer Laurel, decamped on my beside like a Viking nurse practitioner, and showing no sign of retreat. So, considering the geography, it's less of a lie, and more of a generalization, I thought further. I was never precisely lonely until quite recently. Still, old habits persevere.

"I've heard it's beautiful there," she said. "I've always wanted to visit."

"Oh, it is," I replied, actually believing myself as I continued. "The foliage is incredible in the fall. The maple syrup is like auburn gold, and makes an excellent treat on fresh snow. There are green mountains, glacial lakes, abig, dark woods. It continues to be the only place I've ever lived that didn't feel like a spiritual prison."

"That sounds more like Vermont."

"Well, we are neighbors," I said, feeling as if the conversation had come full circle, and was thus a success. Did I feel guilty for abusing her hospitality in this way? No, not really. Surely, if she cared to find out the formal details of my life, her profession would make them available. Maybe she already had, and her question of origin was a test. Perhaps, she removed my wallet while undressing me for bed, and ran it through the computer at the precinct house or something, and was simply probing to see if I was as suspicious as I probably appeared when she scraped me off the Marine Park Bridge. I have no idea how police manage the information available to them, but I always assume it's safe to lie when someone asks a question they could easily answer on their own. When shared, paranoia is sometimes just a form of sympathetic lying employed to discover an ideal truth, or unearth a common motive. What I've gathered so far from Officer Laurel: she is lonely, passively heartbroken, and while not desperate, more than willing to reveal the autobiographic timbers buttressing her disappointments to me; winning her sympathy was like bass fishing with hand grenade.

"I still don't know if you're hungry," she said.

"Why are you so eager to feed me?"

"Because I don't want you to be hungry."

"That...makes perfect sense," I said, watching her features tangle in an expression of genuine confusion, perhaps mirroring my own. After my years with Cordelia, the appearance of empathy in strangers perplexed me to the point where I often mistook it for love. "Well, no thank you. I'm not hungry. If I am, you don't need to wait on me, Laurel. Do you-"

"Officer Laurel."

"Of course, my mistake, please pardon me. I wasn't aware that you prefer to be called by your professional, and I'm certain well-earned, title. But I have to ask: Do you have any pierogi?"

"There's a Polish place down the street. I can pick some up."

"No trouble, Laurel...Officer Laurel. I can go as soon as you tell me where my clothes are hidden."

"They're not hidden. They're in the dryer."

"I see...Did I...make a mess?"

"You smelled like rainwater, burning tires, and menstrual blood. It seemed like you were having some trouble, outside of the obvious."

"I see. So I can go to the Polish place on my own when my

clothes are dry?" I asked, hoping the question would help me determine whether or not I was being held prisoner without revealing my suspicion.

"You could," said Officer Laurel, slowly, as if I'd asked whether I had two legs and a brain. "But if they're open, they close in ten minutes, and I wouldn't have thought you were so particular about what you eat considering what was under your jacket. If you want to go yourself, Donald left some clothes here. They won't fit."

"Is Donald someone I should know?"

"My ex. He was bigger than you."

"Many men are bigger than me," I said, my attention entirely captured by a filament of blond hair detaching itself from behind the Venusian contour of Officer Laurel's ear. In the breeze from the air conditioner, it appeared to nod in my direction. I felt encouraged by this.

"I don't understand what that means," said Officer Laurel. "Donald knows the job, but didn't know shit otherwise. It only hurt when he left because it felt like a career move. For me, it was a lateral trade. I've noticed disappointment is always shaped like a person who makes too much sense. I guess he taught me what I want isn't what I think I want, most of the time."

"Yes, Cordelia leaving showed me how useless I am to strangers," I said, wondering idly if it were possible to balance a tea cup on Officer Laurel's bottom lip, which had begun to protrude like a kind of shelf at the first mention of Donald.

"Why did she leave?" she asked.

"I'm not sure. I think I would have been able to answer that question accurately if you asked it before she left. Now I don't know. But I could have generated a few theories if the question were theoretical, or presented as a kind of thought experiment. In retrospect, I can't decide if I always thought she'd leave, and was just experimenting with hope in the meanwhile, or if I honestly thought she would stay with me forever, and that we would be very happy."

"Which sounds more likely?"

"I don't know, Laurel. Officer! Officer Laurel! Crediting myself with foresight seems compensatory. What I want, and what I know are often antipodal. Have you ever had that experience?"

"When I saw you on the bridge," she began, as one of her hands traveled the comforter with an aspect of abandon toward the suggestion of my fingers beneath it, but halting, as though recalling itself from the rim of a crevasse, the uncertain gravity of risk suddenly falling upon her like a predator inevitably colliding with prey. A tensile silence engulfed the room. I wasn't sure she had finished speaking, but I knew she no longer frightened me. How had this happened? Accidentally, I imagine. I waited in silence, watching her hand withdraw from the bedspread as she stood, and left the room.

That went well, I thought, tugging the comforter to my chin, and glancing at the television sputtering mutely from its emplacement. A program called "Fat People Tell Stories About Falling Down" was just beginning, and I adjusted the volume to a susurrus, no longer afraid of my host, but wondering if she had just revealed a vestige of something significant. What had it been? I told myself I would have chased her down to find out if I hadn't been naked, a superficially valid, yet practically flimsy excuse, but an excuse nonetheless. I employed worse with Cordelia, citing work as an excuse to opt out of her invitation to go sweater shopping somewhere in Red Hook one Saturday afternoon over the summer. In this case, sweater shopping was a euphemism. She was too proud to say that she wanted to spend time with me, doing nothing in particular somewhere other than the apartment. I never took anything home from the Brooklyn Association, so the idea of work on a Saturday was clearly hogwash, and we both knew it. But the word itself was part of the same duplicitous grammar as sweater shopping, with work standing in for the time I thought I needed to sift the tired bone matter of the acute depression I'd come to accept as an urban reality. Aside from answering the dreaded necessities of life, laundry, groceries, walking Ruby, why would I leave the apartment on a day off? To have fun, and enjoy life, according to Cordelia. But our definitions of fun were different; when left alone in the apartment, I bumbled between rooms, read a few pages in a book, watered plants, walked Ruby, and eventually ended up in front of the laptop, watching John Cleese physically abuse Andrew Sachs, pacified, relieved to have passed the time without some calamity befalling me. Another day down, I would think, always. How many more to go?

But this particular Saturday, Cordelia offered to buy me lunch if I came along, and I still refused, hating myself as I watched her try to conceal her disappointment beneath an overpainting of ambivalence. It reminded me of my mother trying to spend quality time with me when I was an inward, unpleasant thirteen-year-old. Acheron, VT, 1998. She'd offered me food in exchange for company as well, hadn't she? And then, as now, I'd refused. I knew this hurt her, but didn't see another way it could be; I wanted what I wanted even if I didn't know why I wanted it. In the case of my mother, this meant brooding in front of an ice cream parlor in downtown Acheron with a detail of concomitant dipshits, and a skateboard beneath my arm. Years later, the peer group would dissolve, and a book would take the place of the skateboard. Otherwise, little had changed; I remained essentially selfish. But when I saw the expression of my departed mother break the surface of Cordelia's sadness, I was suddenly thirteen again, rediscovering the first moment I realized it was possible to hurt people by just being myself. So I'm a bad person, I thought then, as the door clicked shut behind Cordelia, and the tick of bicycle receded down the hall. That settles that.

I dozed off during the closing act of "Fat People Tell Stories About Falling Down," and when I awoke several hours later, the television was mute once again, and a tray with a plate of tepid pierogi occupied the nightstand.

I stayed with Officer Laurel for a few days without going farther than her backyard. I only discovered what the front of her house looked like the morning she drove me to back to Brooklyn to pick up Ruby and the few things I'd left with Arvin and Catalina. This was the day we left, of course, and even then, traveling north on a nearly abandoned Van Wyck Expressway, with the Whitestone bridge looking bereft against a rain-choked horizon and Ruby panting on my lap as Officer Laurel guided the police van through the backmatter of the hurricane, I tried to storyboard the events since Cordelia left in a way that would make sense, in letterform or otherwise. The bushel of notes beneath my seat seemed like evidence of something important to say; it hadn't always. When I began the letter to Cordelia one morning shortly after breakfast with Officer Laurel, I had already told enough lies to make the truth feel like an accessory to them. Shouldn't it have been the other way around? I hoped writing about where I'd been and where I expected to go might remind me what I actually wanted in case I started believing myself.

She says she loves me, I thought then, and kept thinking, or it kept recurring because she kept reminding me of it whenever our conversation lulled during the drive, which was often. When she first said it, we were breakfasting beneath a picnic shelter on a terrace in her backyard. She was dressed for work, eating far less than I would expect of a person her size and strength, a strength I'd felt the intimate end of the night before. She calmly consumed half a poppy seed bagel with a rime of vegetable cream cheese and nugatory helping of lox, while I sat across the patio table swaddled in Donald's bathrobe, erratically disheveling a grapefruit. I thought she was going to ask if I wanted help eating it, but said she loved me instead, and then continued her breakfast like a duchess who had just ordered someone out of the dining room.

"That makes sense," I offered, setting the mangled fruit on my plate with a clatter, and hoping to be ignored. I was naked under my robe, and as a stiff, tertiary storm wind blew beneath it from somewhere in the direction of Long Island, I winced, feeling every raw knot. I assumed what she had done to me the night before had everything to do with what she was revealing now, though the sudden embarkation of Cordelia left me feeling I knew far less than I thought I did about what actually constituted love. Before the storm broke, I assumed it was something unevenly shared between two similar people over a lengthy period of time, the proportion shifting based on context and compromise, but always with one half of this arrangement shouldered by the weaker of the two. Me, in this case. Though we'd known each other since we were children, my adult relationship with Cordelia felt like an apprenticeship, and I was fine with that. It seemed like a natural outcome.

During a particularly lyric moment, I might tell her how I'd fallen in love after watching her break her arm on the jungle gym during third grade recess at Acheron Elementary. I was the one who ran for help, across the soccer field, through the double doors into the fifth/sixth grade hallway, and down the corridor terminating at Mrs. Bones' office in order to disrupt her lunch, and drag the school nurse out to the playground. June Bones knelt beside Cordelia with flakes of lettuce from the extraordinarily dismal salad she consumed each day still clinging to her blouse, and examined the girl's warped forearm, which, even as a child, I knew was broken. Cordelia stood bravely, crying less as the crowd around her grew, and watched her and Mrs. Bones depart toward the fixed shape of the school hugging the tree line. Our eyes didn't meet or anything, and Cordelia never thanked me for going to get the nurse. But this was where I marked the beginning of my side of our love, though Cordelia often dismissed this anecdote as a textbook hero complex, and asked me why it was I needed to see a women helpless and in pain order to fall in love with her? It was a technically smart, emotionally lazy question, and I never had an equally smart response prepared, though, in a rare moment of private honesty with myself, I might admit whatever layer we occupied within the stratigraphy separating romantic failure from success, it took a while to reach it. Not so with Officer Laurel; love for her was a checked box.

" What does that mean?" she asked. "How does what I said make sense to you?"

"I don't know," I said, slowly, trying to measure my words in a way that would exonerate me from her affection without entirely slaying it. I had options to preserve. "But I think the word 'love' would mean something different if I said it."

"What does it mean when you say it?"

"It means," I began, as if I was edging my way to the terminus of a plank set above a roiling, unfriendly sea. "Well. I think you're a wonderful person who deserves the very best from the people around them. Unfortunately, I can't offer you that."

"You have the emotional responsibility of someone who was

94

homeschooled," she said, clattering away from the table, and lumbering toward the terrace door. Her plate, coffee cup, and I sat abandoned beneath the picnic shelter. I watched her cross the lawn with the moist wind blowing up Donald's bathrobe, wondering if I should just go ahead and collect the crockery, and hoping the even peace I'd reached with my breakfast fruit might somehow transfer to the post-coital dynamic with my host. I didn't want to go back to Danielle's closet, or the empty apartment on Caton Avenue. I wanted to go home, and when I'd expressed this to Officer Laurel the afternoon she installed me in her house, or last night, when we'd lain in bed together after the maiden voyage of our intimacy, she said she would like to see New Hampshire.

And so, I repainted the picture of Acheron, Vermont masquerading beneath this sobriquet, the one I'd provided earlier in the week; shading the sketch and brightening its corners, until it became a masterpiece of well-intentioned deceit, because wasn't I doing this for love? The summer forest girding the municipality of Acheron came alive in the darkened bedroom, the smell of sun-warmed, embowered earth, the widowed call of a loon plying the surface of Kranion Pond in the static estate of an autumn evening, the cuff of fresh snow encircling my ankle as I staggered toward the firetower crowning Maybrick Peak on snowshoes several winters ago. I neglected to mention Cordelia staggering along with me, and thus felt I'd reclaimed the memory. I told her about the stand of woods behind Acheron College the students decorated for Halloween, distributing pumpkins, scarecrows, and other seasonal grotesqueries around the forest, and touring their work in costume on All Hallow's Eve. And I told her about the view from Mt. Abandon, which led to the time Grover and I spent together there, casting the ashes of our parent's deer camp into wind. This generated the sort of obtuse sympathy people reserve for the death of strangers. Still, she said she would like to go there with me, and when I began to express how nice that would be if it were not impossible with the bridges and tunnels flooded and closed, and gas already being rationed, and only then to emergency personnel, she looked at me as if I'd forgotten who she was without her uniform.

And yes, without her blues, she was simply a brawny naked woman who had joined me in bed around 11:30PM, according to the clock radio that had replaced the baby monitor on the nightstand. I didn't hear her coming, and was nearly asleep when I realized she was naked at the foot of my bed, towering above me and everything else in the room. We'd had wine with dinner, and her breath suggested chardonnay as her limbs depressed the mattress in a kind of crab walk toward me, until her mouth was beside my ear, asking if I minded her there, and saying she would leave if I were uncomfortable. Of course, I'm uncomfortable, I thought. But then, this is nothing new; everything makes me uncomfortable.

I've always had an easier time with women who know what they want, and it was evident Officer Laurel had a design. Had I known falling in love was part of it, I probably would have done nothing different. I was pinned to the mattress by her thighs and pelvis, in any case, and felt a bit like a Shetland pony mounted by a berserker. Escape was impossible, and seemed ludicrous at that point, though less ludicrous than the sidelong image I caught of us in the vanity across the room. The piston-like movement of Officer Laurel's body against mine was impactful enough to simultaneously raise my feet and head six inches off the mattress with each collision. Together, our lovemaking formed the inverted shape of a butterfly corkscrew, doing its good work. I hate myself, I thought, watching it happen, and praying I would exit this congress without rupturing anything, or getting thrown out of the house. It didn't feel bad, but it didn't feel good either, and I surprised myself by politely ejaculating in unison with Officer Laurel's supernumerary orgasm. Thank god, I thought further, but too soon. She collapsed against my chest like a Corinthian pillar rocked from its plinth, knocking the wind out of me, and upsetting the television remote. The screen across the room winked to life, displaying the bereaved aspect of Gordon. Behind him, the mouth of the Breezy Point fire station expelled a dolorous queue of people, not unlike those I'd stolen from earlier in the week.

"Whatever you're doing right now," he said into a NY1 microphone brandished before him. "Just remember: people down here are hungry, cold, and homeless. I don't want to throw the responsibility for this on anyone, but a thing to think about is that the food you're not eating right now, or the shirt you're not wearing could go to someone who needed it yesterday. I'm sorry if you don't have gas to get work, or if your basement is flooded, or your power is still off. But when things like this happen, we have to remember that being a New Yorker means you're a part of making this the greatest city on earth. And we don't let people go hungry."

Simple-minded urbanite chauvinist, I thought as I struggled for breath beneath Officer Laurel, who appeared to be dozing. A stiff wave of panic broke against the levy of my dubious sangfroid as I wondered if this would be how I die. Suffocated beneath the queen of Valhalla while listening to the Brooklyn Association's deputy director extoll the virtue of a city I had come to regard as something between a purgatorial clearing house for unimaginative failures and an open sewer. I slapped at the remote to silence the television and succeeded only in raising the volume.

"Some people," continued Gordon stentorially, "might treat this situation as an opportunity to act on their own worst impulses, and I'm not talking about looting or riots or anything like that. This is New York. We don't have that here. I mean: treating the grave misfortune of others as a meal ticket. I've seen it, even among my own people on the ground. But as a city, I know that's not who we are, and that we hold ourselves to a higher moral standard. So, please: whatever you can spare, spare it. And, as I said, if you see this as a chance to be on your worst behavior, I encourage you to leave for good as soon as the bridges open. We don't need you."

I don't need you either, nescient fuckstick metropolite, I thought, as I watched Gordon speak over Officer Laurel's bedewed shoulder. He appeared to glare at me from the television. I took this as a cue. If I managed to survive this *peine forte et dure*, I'd flee the city as fast as whatever mode of conveyance I chose would allow me. Because hadn't that been the plan originally? To return to the places and people who had succeeded, against all odds it seemed now, in making me more or less human? I'd watched the city age Cordelia, and erode the person she had been not long ago, when we were kids in Vermont or students in Ohio. She was always the sturdier half of our pair, so I wondered: beyond the categorical depression, agoraphobia, and routine panic attacks, how else had New York impacted me? I wanted to believe I was better than the place I lived, but most evidence suggested otherwise. I remember watching a man weep several benches down from me in a public park beside the Wyckoff Gardens housing project, howling like a werewolf, and cradling his face in his hands while children danced in a tepid fountain, and the plangent bell on an Italian ice cart sung in the empty summer afternoon, and all I felt then was irritation; I was racing through an overdue library copy of *Little Man, What Now?*, trying to finish and return it, and here was this belligerant, inspecific mourner wailing as if he was giving birth, shattering my concentration.

Or the woman sitting on a campstool beside the front door of the Brooklyn Association, in the obvious first stage of a drug overdose, toothlessly chewing the foul air of Flatbush Avenue to herself as her head swung like the directionless prow of a boat set adrift, vacantly watching traffic in the sun. I went upstairs and alerted the office manager, transferring the problem rather than solving it, and only doing anything at all because having to walk past an indigent to get into the building made me nervous and would likely attract more, I suspected.

Or the American Staffordshire Terrier I'd seen passively walking on a leash held by a young sadist, who intermittently yanked the dog's chain hard enough to contort the animal's body into a sort of angled bracket, or airborn greater-than sign. It happened five times in the space of one minute, and when I looked away from the half-wit torturing the animal, my eyes fell on a chunk of concrete detached from the sidewalk, and I wondered: should this be where I make my final, or only, ethical stand? I didn't necessarily want to kill the young man, but knocking him on the head with a paving stone and absconding with the dog seemed like the only way of forestalling an inevitably miserable life for the latter, and complicating if not concluding the unexamined existence of the former. If he doesn't understand the casual torment he's inflicting on this animal enough to even bother concealing it, thereby sharing what evil he has to offer the world with not only the dog at his side, but strangers consigned to share the neighborhood with him and his cruelty, what is this man's life worth to me, or anyone else for that matter? I wondered, but then, as he and the dog passed me by: And if I do nothing, what is mine worth?

During what became regular moments of uniform regret, I would sit with these two people and one dog, the man from the park crying steadily, the inebriate woman nodding to herself, the pit bull hissing breath through a pinched trachea, and apologize to them, codifying my apology by explaining how I obviously wasn't the person they needed, but I knew this didn't excuse me from doing nothing except bearing witness.

Is it possible to be haunted by people or animals who may still be alive? I asked Cordelia when she arrived home from work one evening, and we shared an expression a profound concern. Mine was endemic; her own appeared hamstrung between sympathy for me, and frustration with my inability to shake the deportment of a horrified bumpkin lost in the big city where he had oddly enough lived for seven years. She broke from me wordlessly to shelter in the bathroom for nearly forty minutes, while I sat with the remains of my pierogi, trying to guess the nature of the answer she hadn't shared with me. This was three weeks before we planned to leave.

It's possible I was always a useless, ethically muddled coward, but I didn't want to exist any longer in a place where being this way helped me blend in. In a normal human living arrangement, I thought, once from beneath Officer Laurel, and again the following morning as I pursued her inside from the patio, being a selfish or sadistic piece of shit would leave you ostracized and clanless. But if the people of Brooklyn can't fuck it, they'll eat it. And if neither are possible, it gets ignored. I had to get back to Acheron, if only to remember what it felt like to be a semi-realized human being.

So when Officer Laurel stormed inside, I followed her with dishes clattering between my hands, and wisps of grapefruit dangling from my chin, and found her crying at the sink in her uniform and running warm water over her hands. I knew whatever happened next could decide whether I would return to Acheron and Cordelia in enough time to repair whatever had become of our love. If I convinced Officer Laurel to leave with me, there might be hope, or something like it. I didn't know I would abandon her then, or even what I would do if she actually agreed to drive me in some pseudo-official capacity to the place she had come to know as New Hampshire. For now, I needed to provide her with a reason to leave. Thus, I consigned myself to the *auto de fe* of her apparent love. This was the first time I can remember ever wanting anything bad enough to be my own martyr.

"You remind me of someone I went to college with," she said, as I dumped the plates in the sink, turned off the hot water, and took her pink, soggy hands in mine. "He wanted to be a woman."

"You're trying to hurt me," I said, managing to both sidestep her weird remark, and throw a saddle over it. "I understand it. I hurt you, just now, when you said you loved me, and I said…"

"I don't understand it," she said, turning toward me and blocking the muted sunlight from the kitchen window; I occupied her shadow as she spoke. "If I did, it wouldn't be hard to not tell you. I knew you might not care, but you're the only person who could possibly care, if you did. With Donald, love was mutually unexpected. I wanted to love someone. And I wanted to be loved, I did. Just not by him. I sound dumb. But I want you to know how I feel, so it isn't entirely my problem from now until whatever happens next. Even if you don't love me, you can stay here until you find a way back to New Hampshire. I like having you here, even if you can't say it, or can say it, but don't mean it. I like having you here because I haven't gotten this close with anyone before, and if you go…"

"I don't have anywhere to go," I said. It wasn't entirely true, but I was hoping to buy a modicum of time, if only to remind myself to proceed carefully. Officer Laurel was intent on cudgeling me with her feelings, regardless of how I responded to them, but I was relieved to discover I wasn't a prisoner in her home, and that whatever bizarre attachment to me she had formed in the past few days likely had enough gravity to evict me from the city. I felt cruel, but I knew from experience it would pass.

Your feelings are not my fault, I thought as I looked into the viciously earnest face of my host, her blue eyes appearing almost deliquescent as filaments of tears coursed either cheek. Soundless crying has a deeply unsettling quality, because it seems like a preface of some kind; a thundercloud blotting the horizon, the sudden caesura of birdsong, a shadow falling over your shoulder. But in this case, I stood within her silhouette, knowing I had nothing to fear, and thus felt bold enough to comb the moisture away from her cheek with my thumb while cupping her face in my suddenly very small-seeming hand, as my mouth recited an apposite grammar of intimacy, or many of the things I would have said to Cordelia if she were there, or I was in Acheron.

This became my trick. When I needed to remind Officer Laurel of my love, or when she needed to be reminded of it, I imagined the masterless Fourth of July evening during summer term as St. Margaret's when we'd sat in a cushion of grass at the Julian Falls rec field beneath a ceiling of fireworks shortly after dusk fell. It was a poor display, especially by middle-American standards, and as cinders drifted onto us from the rockets exploding above, we rolled ourselves into our blanket for protection, which dovetailed into a nearly silent course of public intimacy as Cordelia lifted her skirt and drew me inside her while using her hips to pinch the blanket tighter and tighter around us until we became what several fellow students who witnessed this later described as a sex burrito. While things continued to explode overhead, we existed in the wordless darkness of our cowl, trying to keep our movements inconspicuous for the benefit of the families scattered around the baseball diamond, and across the face of the acclivity bulwarking it to the north, even as we came mutually with the breathless relief of bank robbers crossing a national border. My back rolled against something hard, and I assumed it was a tree trunk until we unfurled the blanket, and I realized I'd come to rest against the khaki leg of a Julian Fall's deputy, whose face was obscured beneath the brim of the Stanton he wore like an occluded halo in the moonlight. It was clear time had passed from the sudden stillness of the night outside the blanket. The sky was empty of smoke, and sown with stars; only a lingering expression of cordite remained in the air above the sport's field. Below the hill, the thin beacon of headlights spotlit ovate men in muscle t-shirts carrying coolers in their fists and lawn chairs beneath their arms, while sunburnt women in halter tops guided children toward the parking area. I remember thinking: America on the move, after the tent has fallen. It was clear the fireworks were over, though it was impossible to tell when they had ended. The sheriff didn't say anything, and seemed only mildly interested in us. He'd likely seen similar, or worse.

Even so, I stood, and helped Cordelia out of the tangled blanket, saying something oddly proleptic in his direction about us being engaged. I liked the way this sounded spoken aloud, and as Cordelia and I joined hands and fled toward the parking lot, I said something about how the only thing to do with a person who can swallow the sound of a fireworks show with a simple movement of their pelvis is propose to them. She said the stillness we'd experienced was a gift; and I wanted to say I would remain still forever, with her, if allowed. But it felt disjunctive, so I asked if she could ever imagine marrying me when it made sense. She said it never made sense, but if it did, then yes, she could see it. That was enough for me. I hoped it would be enough for Officer Laurel.

"I don't understand what you mean," she said, my hand still cupping her face. "How is stillness a gift?"

"It has to do with achieving consciousness," I said, hoping the pirated line would have the impact on her that it did on me. No luck. I tried expanding on it. "When I'm with you, like we were last night, I am still. Time appears to halt. I lose the sense of process that guides every stupid thing I do each day. I am only with you. And that is a gift."

"I want that to be true, I think."

She seemed to absorb this reluctantly, but with a sense of resolution, like a person trapped beneath a broken umbrella. We could both agree I was certainly better than nothing. This could be progress. I didn't want to cannibalize my past too greatly, and propose marriage, even in the same cowardly vein as the night of the fireworks in Julian Falls, but was willing to do it if I ran short of other options. Fortunately, Officer Laurel appeared satisfied with the remark I'd borrowed from Cordelia. She kissed the palm of my hand, and began tidying the kitchen.

"I'll do that," I offered. It seemed like a natural follow-up. I suddenly felt like I needed something to hide behind.

"Thanks. I have to go to work," she said, adding, not cruelly: "If you're afraid to be alone, you can come."

The headline: 'Bring Stupid to Work Day!' marched before my eyes as I politely declined, wondering how she should would explain my presence to her coworkers, or any criminals they might wrangle during the course of the day. I am the natural offspring of a gigolo mated to a tramp, I thought, watching her straighten her uniform in the hallway mirror. The bizarre elements theoretically explaining what I was doing in her house didn't seem to accurately explain them. Love at first sight felt too easy. Desperation in the face of impending doom seemed like cant. An alchemy between boredom and loneliness was the obvious answer, the smart answer, and I've always been willing to accept the obvious when trenching deeper might tire me or cause pain. The latter certainly explained why I remained, lonely then, roosting on a kitchen stool in Donald's voluminous bathrobe staring at the door through which Officer Laurel left the house. The inevitability of her return, and what it might promise, was enough to keep me there.

Also, I was actually afraid to be alone, but only realized this after I'd allowed Officer Laurel to kiss my face and leave the house, wherein the terrible stillness, either completely unlike or identical to the stasis I'd described earlier to her in the kitchen, crept forward and settled somewhere between my head and my stomach. I feel a sense of desolation when a woman leaves a room. I'm not sure why. Some peevish annex of my heart assumed I would never see Cordelia again whenever she exited the apartment. I would sit terrified, anxiously raking at Ruby's coat, as the tick of her bicycle faded in the stairwell, and listening again for the impact of her handlebar against the door of the building as she dragged her apparatus to the sidewalk. I was always afraid she would die in traffic, but this was unrelated to sense of loss I experienced watching her leave for work. The world might swallow her, as it had swallowed the part of me that was once well enough to walk freely in it at her side. I was afraid she would blame this sort of thinking on what happened to my parents if I ever shared it, so I didn't.

I withdrew my phone from the pocket of the robe, and dialed

Cordelia's number. Service was unavailable in my area. Likely a disruption related to the storm. I hadn't tried to call her since the night in Danielle's closet because I sensed remaining mysterious might benefit me if Officer Laurel ever got us out of the city. Better to present myself on Cordelia's doorstep without warning than give her time to draft a rebuttal.

I transferred my sense of unwell to the terrace where I'd ruined breakfast, terrified at the prospect of having the day to myself. The residue of the hurricane remained above the house graying the sky, and showed no sign of departure. Though it was now clear I wasn't a prisoner in Officer Laurel's house, I felt like a specimen jailed in a commodious yet limited enclosure as I sat beneath the picnic tent, wondering whether killing myself would be simpler than waiting for the day to end. The house seemed to snarl at me from edge of the patio. Nothing to do, I thought, trying to avoid the leer of the dormers. Except rifle the medicine cabinets, and toss a few drawers. Learn a little more about the lovely young woman I'm hoodwinking. I owe her that much.

It was a cruel, idle thought, and I only realized I had allowed it to consume me after catching a reflection of myself in the wardrobe mirror in Officer Laurel's bedroom, elbow deep in her hope chest as I reclined like a sultan in the belly of her closet. There was nothing explicitly private about what I found there. Old photographs of her as a child on the beach at Montauk, the lighthouse rigid as an orthostat in the background. Awards for various sporting achievements; soccer, volleyball, and equestrianism, somehow. A degree in psychology from Stony Brook, and a MA in criminal justice from John Jay. The material of her history was so inevitable that sifting it in secret felt redundant. No wonder Donald left, I thought meanly, tugging his bathrobe around me. He was probably bored out of his mind.

Once again, my galloping criticism of someone who was basically a decent, normal human being began depressing me, as it had with Danielle. When Cordelia was here to share my derision, it was fun. But without her, pillorying someone for the ability to lead a life not at all resembling my own felt recklessly indulgent, and quite sad. I was a man painting a bridge to nowhere.

I resettled the raw material of Officer Laurel's life back where I thought it had come from, replacing the photo albums, trophies, and framed degrees amid the shelves, and wondering whether there was anything to drink in the house, and if it was too early to begin drinking it, before remembering I had nothing to do, and nowhere to go. This somewhat tapered the desire. Drinking to forget is only useful when you have something to forget. Since Cordelia left New York, I couldn't shake the sense of having forgotten something important, yet nearby, and close enough to reclaim. Millicent Oliver shared a similar feeling with me as we lay half naked in the garret her foster family allotted her, listening to what sounded like Wagner, as the curtain fell on a gray autumn afternoon beyond the attic window. She said she wanted to remember what it felt like to look forward to something, but nothing suggested itself; each day was subducted beneath the next, entirely free of anything notable, and devoid of prospects in either the near or immediate future. So for Millicent, time had flattened.

This may have been the place to suggest myself to her as something to anticipate with a measure of joy, but at the time, her discontent rang tritely, even coming from a fifteen-year-old foster child with a green Mohawk, tactically shredded black stockings, and an Aus-Rotten t-shirt. How sad for you, I remember thinking as I tucked myself into the uniform corresponding to my own, mostly anchorless discontent; pegged black jeans, combat boots, and a denim vest with the words POLICE BASTARD framed by an assemblage of conical studs across its shoulders. Unlike Millicent, I had no real reason to be angry at the world, which may be why it took me fifteen years to both experience what she meant, and what it represented. When enough clichés converge, sometimes they produce an ugly, prognostic truth. Millicent's future was inevitable. She became pregnant a few years later by a localized pool shark and deer-jacker, fled Acheron with him, and now lives between an amateur racetrack and a granite quarry in Barre with a different drifter, who may be a cousin of the former. But here in the story, rumor trickles into unprofitable speculation, and I'm left only with what Millicent and I had in common: the inability to move forward without something ferocious chasing us.

Still, I went downstairs to prowl the kitchen cupboards, and interior of the refrigerator until I found a bottle of chardonnay bedded in the vegetable drawer, and after removing the cork, returned to Officer Laurel's bedroom. The closet felt less threatening than the rest of the house, and I wasn't entirely finished boring myself with its contents. I drank the chardonnay from a plastic cup since the wineglasses seemed far to small for whatever I needed to accomplish. Surely, there must be something interesting or unexpected in here, I thought as I shifted shoeboxes containing shoes, and slid hangers with things hung on them aside. Everything insufferably in its place, I thought further, brooding now and growing furious at the irreducible, solitary order of people who live alone. Where are your secrets, Officer Laurel? Don't you have anything you wouldn't want a person like me to see? You must! But where is it? Where is your shameful treasure? I'll find it if I have to tear this closet apart!

And I might have done so, if a black rubber dildo the size and girth of rolling pin hadn't tipped from some nether sanctum in an upper cubby and fallen like a warhead, tip down, into the tumbler containing my wine. The cup rocked a little before upsetting itself across my bare feet. Not entirely unexpected, but also not what I was expecting. Fair enough. I righted the cup and was so eager to refill it that I didn't bother removing the dildo until after I'd taken my first sip. How interesting, by comparison, I thought, withdrawing the cock, and trying to guess how much larger it was than what nature or god had provisioned me. Twice seemed like an economic estimate. But you are rubber, I thought, suddenly angry at the polymer dong in my fist. And I am all man. Or mostly. Therefore: you lose. I will drown you.

I dunked the dildo back in my wine, stirring viciously, as though it were a toothpick spearing an olive or a quartered pickle, and trying desperately to feel superior to it. She loves me, according to her. This proves my shortcomings are forgivable, or easy enough to ignore, and I am not interchangeable with a dildo, even if I do not quite measure up. Besides, it looks brand new. When was the last time Officer Laurel employed it?

I raised the implement to my nostrils, smelling only wine and rubber, and finding no residue of sex beneath. But in an uncharacteristic effort to be thorough, I placed the bulbous head in my mouth to see if taste could detect what smell could not. Nothing but white wine and black rubber once again. I will not allow this to make me feel inadequate, I resolved with my mouth full, just as Officer Laurel stepped into the frame of the closet door. The dildo made a soft pop as I jerked it from between my lips, and repatriated it in the tumbler as if this was where it belonged.

"I was saving that," said Officer Laurel, unmoved. It was unclear whether she meant the dildo or the wine.

*　　*　　*

Greenfield, Massachusetts passes in a flurry of wooded rest areas without facilities. I stop at the last of these to allow Ruby to comb the compound of human and animal waste amid the grass for something particular to her. With Officer Laurel occupying my rear view, I am suddenly my own responsibility. I'd worry about this if the amplitude of my choices were not plotted before me; a sign shortly past the final rest area indicates the distance between Brattleboro, Vermont, some fifteen miles, and myself. Below this, I imagine Cordelia's name printed with the mileage to Acheron beside it.

The letter to her remains widowed on the seat beneath Ruby. I'll have to recuse myself for several days after I arrive in order to finish it. Since Cordelia isn't waiting for me, she won't mind, and Grover will likely have no reason to let her know. It's probably best to omit the parts about Officer Laurel, which will make completing the epistle a bit easier. Likewise sleeping with Danielle, which would make her laugh for the wrong reasons. And I don't want my missive to be comedic. No, after several revisions, it will hopefully be as dry, devoted, and deceptive as it needs to be for her to cancel my manumission, and welcome me back. She knows I lack the courage to experience the world alone, and the commitment to kill myself, so my choices are essentially limited.

On that note: Paranoia is the experiment in hope concealed within a marriage proposal both predating and allowing the van to slip now across the Vermont state border, and into the small part of New England I understand. Home at last. I never expected trumpets. But home at what cost? Answer: Excluding the tariff levied on Officer Laurel's emotional credulity, nearly free. She procured fuel through some intestine channel of the New York City Police Department, and I used the remainder of the security deposit wadded within an overlarge raincoat abandoned by

Donald and appropriated by me during the final stage of packing up the house in Ridgewood to purchase road food. We didn't eat well; the region directly North of New York City is where fast food comes to die. But it was all I had to practically contribute. And she seemed happy enough watching me toddle around the parking lot of a Long John Silver outside New Haven in her ex's rain slicker with 'N.Y.P.D.' stenciled across the sagging shoulders. A paper bag occluded by clouds of grease steamed in the humidity where it hung from my hand like an extinguished lantern. A rictus split between easement and beatitude surfaced past a windshield pebbled with moisture as I returned to the van. I wanted to warn her then; to say that trusting me was a terrible idea, and accepting the offer of marriage I'd proposed immediately after she caught me in the closet chewing her dildo was a mistake, but not for any obvious reason. Also: That I liked, but did not love Officer Laurel. That her loving me earnestly and with devotion meant I could no longer expect to be an anodyne problem; I would have to learn how to participate, and actually make her happy in some way. And that I didn't really want anything from life except to hitch myself to the wagon of someone who actually did want things (other than me), and hope we had something in common. So how would I live? I couldn't imagine it. I should have spoken then. But no: my silence, and several bags of fast food were my price, making the move from New York somewhat expensive for her, but rather cheap for me.

To her credit, she didn't accept immediately. I ran short of options, as I knew I would, since there weren't many to begin with. She stood in the bedroom, more saddened than horrified it seemed to me, but whichever it was, or in whatever measure, I saw my escape to Acheron growing more distant in the barrel of her closet as she retreated from the doorway, away from me. I had to act. The proposal seemed to roll from not so much my mouth or throat but the general direction of my body, out of the closet toward where she had taken refuge in the en suite, the door delicately cracked like the spine of a book, as though she intuitively knew shutting it would be dishonest to us both. It would open shortly; we understood this as the moment for a grand gesture, because sweeping motions always appear when it is too late to excuse yourself otherwise. I had more to obviate than the simple weirdness I presented; the privacy invaded, the wine impeached, the sex toy gobbled. It was apparent I had to do something with the feelings she had left in my care regarding each of these, certainly, but I needed to show her I was more than the sum of them. Even if it isn't true, I thought. Life at any cost. I set the scuttled dildo aside, and directed my nuptial request to the empty bedroom, once, twice, and somewhere between the second and third recitation, the bathroom door opened, and she emerged, naked, obvious, and compliant.

"No one has ever asked," she said, tipping me onto the bedspread. I felt like a coatrack being laid to rest.

"There was nothing else to say," I said. It was true.

"I don't understand why I've never wanted someone to ask more."

"I need to leave."

"I know."

"I need to be in a place where I can be the husband you deserve."

"I know."

"Will you take me there?"

"Yes."

"When?"

"I'll put in my notice," she said, her mouth opening and closing against my neck. "Even if you didn't ask me to be your wife, I would have left with you."

112

I tried and failed to console myself. There's no such thing as a safe bet, I thought. It never hurts to hedge. And I didn't ask her to quit her job. But I would have eventually. So, in addition to being jilted at the altar, Officer Laurel will also be unemployed, with shabby references, since she abandoned her post during the middle of a state of emergency. Well done. Perhaps I should also ask her to burn the house down before we leave, just to make a clean sweep of things. If I'm going to have her ruin on my conscience, it may as well be complete.

Of course, seeing my father didn't help. He stood in a corner of the bedroom beside the closet, dressed in beaten Carhartt dungarees and the red Woolrich jacket Cordelia always hated, waiting to meet my eyes above the horizon of Officer Laurel's shoulder before imparting the sort of advice I'd come to expect from him, the sort I'd never taken.

"You're constantly surprised," he said, lighting a Cohiba in the crisp air of an autumn afternoon as he leaned on the foremost row of firewood stacked against the house. The sun hugged the shoulder of Maybrick Peak through a girdle of grey cloud above the valley; a fire smoldered in a pit at our feet, the smoke billowing toward a bank of spade-like evergreens at the foot of the lawn. "You both underestimate the people around you, and the world you live in, to the point where when something happens, you notice it too late, and have to compromise. I don't think you do it out of meanness. I think you assume people aren't paying attention because you aren't, and since you don't seem to have very high expectations for yourself, you assume they don't either. I've never been much for strong motion myself, so you probably got it from me. But remember: people will take the shortest route to get what they want, or to escape from what they don't; you'll understand this better not so much when you find something you want, but when you have something to risk for it. For me, that was your mother. You have to figure out what it is for you. Whatever that might be, it will hopefully leave you farther than to the immediate right or left of neutral."

What were we really talking about? I can't remember. I know I'd helped him stack wood for the better part of the late morning and afternoon, after returning from Millicent Oliver's house. He perhaps sensed I was up to no good, regarding her, and wanted to remind me that even if I assumed everyone was as passionless and complacent as myself, I shouldn't be shocked when my actions had an impact on the people around me. The import of this elementary lesson in interpersonal physics didn't escape me; even fifteen years later, as Officer Laurel and I roiled the bedspread, and she murmured 'yes' against my ear over and over again while I tried to imagine how ashamed my father would be of me at this very moment, even then, I knew simply being aware of my impact didn't obviate the responsibility for it.

And afterward, as I lay in bed pretending to doze, and she went downstairs to prepare dinner for us, I wondered whether I had turned the corner on the dispassion characterizing my young adulthood, and was now in the rudimentary stages of an evil life. Since my ambition, or what passed for it, had never involved the living of a categorically good life, leading one of incidental evil didn't feel like a failure, or deviation. Even so, it was too late to save Officer Laurel. The situation was beyond a simple mercy killing. And who knew what form her wrath might adopt after the initial disappointment. I didn't want to go back to jail, but saw myself back on the stainless steel bunk anyway, waiting to be arraigned as storm water drained from the courtroom. No, I'd crossed the Rubicon; evil was necessary to preserve my comfort, and liberty.

Explaining any of this to Danielle wouldn't have done me much good, though based on how surprised and worried she looked when I appeared at the door of the house on Rugby Road a few days later, she seemed to crave an explanation of some kind. What could I say? Whatever we shared earlier in the week when the floodwaters inundated our lovemaking meant something different to both of us, and for once, I didn't consider myself entirely culpable for her disappointment. I truly had nothing to explain. But the police van purring at the curb, obviously waiting to receive me, didn't dispel the unspoken yet apparent notion that I'd found my way into trouble of some kind since we last saw each other.

"I don't have much time," I said, trying to preserve this impression. It felt like the only way to assure a quick entrance and exit from Danielle's home without having to tell some lie, and I was tired of lying; not morally, but actually mentally fatigued from the zephyr of bullshit I needed to keep afloat in order to leave New York City. This was the final leg. It was all arranged. I was engaged to Officer Laurel, and would wed her duly upon arrival in New Hampshire, where she would get a job with the local constabulary, and I would continue to survive on the periphery of employment and thus: adulthood, a spectator, as always, when it came to the important things in life. She wanted a small wedding. Since it made no difference to me, I assented, but would have done so even if she had insisted on the sort of nuptial holocaust many good Americans mistake for a civil right. It was all fantasy anyway. Why not give it spurs?

Billy absorbed the police van at the curb and my tenure in the egress as though she had expected to see it for some time, and acted as if transferring Ruby to my care constituted an ethical problem. She's my dog, you harridan, I thought, trying not to draw any conclusions from the outline of a merlot bra beneath the white t-shirt she wore as she handed me the canine like a loaf of bread, upstaging Danielle, as usual. That's obviously new, I thought further, as they stood side by side in the foyer, Billy mute as a tongue-less bell, and Danielle ejecting little beyond the beginning of whatever sentence she thought might prompt me to explain myself.

The dog beneath my arm surveyed all with her single eye in a spirit of indiscriminate amity, her tail beating against my shoulder as I realized how little space the material evidence of my life occupied. At some point, one of the women handed me a bag I had brought with me. It still contained rice, beans, kibble, a chew toy shaped like a buzzard, and the omnibus edition of *The Alexandria Quartet*. The luggage of an ambitious immigrant, I thought, and most of it pertinent only to the dog, whom I consider a ward, rather than a possession. So: I have examined the physical content of my life, and found that I inadvertently live like a homeless person. Too late now. It didn't occur to me how little space I took up until Cordelia emptied the apartment, and drove away with the contents. If it weren't for my driver's license, the question of whether or not I actually existed would be undecided.

"Where are you going?" asked not Danielle or Billy, but Catalina. She stepped from the kitchen door into the hall the way a spider lowers itself on a strand of filament, with a rogue steadiness, like she was wheeled into position on a dolly. "Are you in trouble?"

"I can't tell," I said, which was true enough. "I just came to take Ruby."

"She can stay," said Billy, taking a step forward as if she meant to take her away from me. "It might be better. For her."

"You don't even know what I'm doing," I said, rotating toward the door with the dog beneath my arm.

"Neither do you," said Danielle, completing what was beginning to feel like an interrogative chorus. "You can stay here. With me, if you want that."

"What does that even mean?" I asked over my shoulder as I practically ran down the walk toward the van. Billy looked appalled beside her friend, and Catalina looked disgusted from within the shadow cowling her in the foyer. It was so dark in the entrance that her head seemed to be in orbit beyond Danielle and Billy, both of whom stood on the porch like they were seeing me and the dog off to war. Arvin appeared from the backyard, and seemed to hesitate, unsure of whether he might be joining the wrong camp by approaching me.

"Are you finally leaving?" he asked. I nodded, and so did he. "You always wanted to. We'll miss you."

I had troubled believing that, but it effected me enough to spur me across the yard, and, even though Ruby was still beneath my arm, into a ponderous hug. At some point, Catalina descended from her roost in the doorway and joined us. Danielle seemed to hold back for Billy's sake, but appeared even so, the smell of bongwater still clinging to her hair as her lips met my cheek. Billy transitioned from porch to yard, feeling left out, but not willing to actually touch me in order to feel otherwise. As we broke, she offered a handshake as a sort of compromise. Good enough, I thought, even as her eyes caught my own reappraising the roseate undergarment surfacing beneath her t-shirt. Obviously, it was time to go.

"Are you going to miss your friends?" asked Officer Laurel after we had joined with the oddly vacant artery of Bedford Avenue.

"No," I said. "But I'll think of them well."

"Is there anything you want from your apartment?"

I thought of the mattress, on which I'd disappointed Cordelia numberless times, and the useless, oscillating fan. One mug, one glass, one dish. A bag of jasmine rice. Two cans of beans. A quarter roll of toilet paper. The bedside lamp. The sheets on the mattress, of course, and one pillow, with case. Most of the clothes that embarrassed her, and a few books remained. All of it could stay. I imagined arriving in Acheron with everything she decided to leave behind, the detritus of our time together, in tow. It would be the opposite of refreshing, and a precluding argument against the kind of progress I needed to mimic in order to remind her why she had almost agreed to marry me when we were just students in Julian Falls, watching fireworks.

"Let's just get there," I said, which seemed to impel Officer Laurel. She depressed the accelerator, transferring the weary verdure of Prospect Park to our rear view as the van cornered the triumphal arch at Grand Army Plaza, and tore down Vanderbilt Avenue, barren of traffic, and dark with storm water. Trash billowed in our wake, and pedestrians looked on with a kind of localized oblivion as we crossed Atlantic Avenue, inches from the intransigent waste of Queens. By the time she'd merged onto the Jackie Robinson Parkway, with Cypress Hill cemetery announcing itself to either side of the van, I was beginning to experience the enormity of what I had created, and perhaps to compensate for this, I asked Officer Laurel if there was anything she would miss about the city.

"The sameness, maybe," she said. "It's always one way. That's New York. It doesn't change. No seasons. No revolutions. No progress. That's comforting, I think. You can get absorbed in how little happens here. It's also what I won't miss, because who can seriously live that way and be happy?"

"No one here is happy."

"Is there anything you'll miss?"

"No. New York is a dumping ground for people who lack imagination."

118

"I think some part of you thrives on being at odds with your environment."

"Do you know me well enough to know that?"

"You're not that hard to figure out."

That's what you think, I thought. For some reason, her statement regarding the uniformity of the city reminded me of Millicent Oliver wondering what it was like to anticipate something, and my wondering whether I was an answer to this question. I was horrified by the possibility of Officer Laurel echoing this in some way, but smothered my horror with a question about Ruby, who was resting her jowls on Officer Laurel's uniformed thigh as she piloted us onto the Van Wyck Expressway.

"Oh, she'll do just fine," she said, stroking the dog's head with a kind of militarism. Do just fine? What did that mean? It seemed Officer Laurel had penciled in the finer points of the blueprint for life in greater New Hampshire I'd presented to her in bed. Was this my fault? No, I didn't think so. I was willing to absorb the blame for most of what would happen in the next six hours, but I'd only deployed a template for our life together. However Officer Laurel imagined it was her own responsibility.

When the van runs out of gas, I briefly assume some mechanical failure is responsible for the vehicle stuttering to a halt in a wooded rest area without facilities just past the Waterbury exit on 1-89. I'm so unused to driving that I paid absolutely no attention to the fuel gauge, which has been steadily dropping micrometer by micrometer since the service station outside Danbury, Connecticut where Officer Laurel flashed a sheaf of credentials at the clerk, and filled up the tank. So what now? I think, watching a convoy of thunderheads approach from the lip of the horizon.

Outside the cockpit, the day, or evening by now, is humid,

gray, and pregnant with the possibility of a storm. A curtain of gloom fifteen miles north and six or seven miles east, descends between my torpid vehicle and the hamlet of Acheron, sitting only eight miles away, as the crow flies. Ruby noses around the remnant of what was once a picnic shelter as it occurs to me how lonely I would be without her.

The interstate in either direction is devoid of traffic, the gas crunch on the eastern seaboard having extended a finger even this far north, an hour from the Canadian border. The barren land, the funereal sky, the silence of everything except the wind and the anxious, atonal polka playing in my head. An apocalypse may have already occurred here, where the pavement ends, and been eclipsed, from a media perspective, by greater problems back in New York: the destruction of ports up and down the Hudson River, the inundation of the subway system in all of lower Manhattan, and FEMA sitting like a decoy mallard in Jamaica Bay while Breezy Point burnt to the ground. I'm sure all of this is newsworthy, and most people in New York City probably don't even realize Vermont is a state. So who has time or motivation to report on the wellbeing of a New England college town with a population lower than the average Brooklyn housing project? I never followed the news during the best of times, and Officer Laurel and I didn't switch on the radio once during the four hours it took us to reach Springfield, though we hadn't spoken much. Where did the silence go? And afterward, I was too occupied with my escape to wonder whether I might be waltzing toward calamity. Knowing my father's position on solipsism, I'm sure I haven't made him proud.

So it's possible I'm walking into desolation, an Acheron unfixed from civil order. I imagine my brother's grocery store looted and destroyed, unpopular or weak residents enslaved by the strongest to fortify Acheron College campus, and the women,

120

including Cordelia, treated like chattel and bartered for ammunition, liquor, or safe passage. I don't know why I imagine the warlords of Northern Vermont as inherently venal and despotic patriarchs. In truth, I never knew anyone like this growing up, and always assumed I would be safe in Acheron if everything went to hell. And even if she were manacled to the throne of some post-reckoning bandit king, I could still imagine Cordelia laughing at this, as she did whenever I shared it aloud. But the possibility of being ignored is part of why I enjoy Vermont; I imagine the world could end without ever seeming to reach it.

Of course, that's wrong, which is most of the reason I'm able to load the bulk of my idiot possessions and the dog in the cargo bucket of the bakfiets I stole from outside Arvin and Catalina's house, and peddle it down the attenuated centerline between the two northbound lanes of I-89. I don't know why I insisted on bringing it along. Officer Laurel assumed it belonged to me when she scraped me off the Marine Park Bridge, and after we'd emptied the house in Ridgewood of her things, and packed them in the back of the van, I felt left out in not having my own luggage. Since I didn't have anything else, the bicycle fit well enough, and having it now, as I pass a sign indicating my destination is only eight miles away, I feel lucky for the first time in perhaps five to seven years.

Until the wind picks up, the trees begin to nod, and the sky emits an eructation of thunder from what sounds like the space directly behind my left shoulder. The storm is nearly on top of me by the time I reach the exit, and at the bottom of the ramp, I remove Donald's raincoat, and secure it around the cargo bucket in order to keep Ruby dry.

"It's only three more miles. We can make it," I tell her as a rift of lightening fractures the sky ahead, and a nodule of hail bounces off the geometric center of my head. Another clicks the lens of my glasses as I glare stupidly upward at the roiling sky, as if expecting to find an imp with a bucket of ice straddling a tree branch above me. The dog doesn't appear worried. She sits content in a bed of my belongings, swaddled in my father's coat beneath the ersatz parasol I've constructed as I pedal through a downpour interspersed by sheets of hail with the size and seeming velocity of rubber bullets. Oddly enough, the frigid rain offsets the impact, numbing my body until I don't feel much of anything beyond a slight sputter of joy as I clatter past a sign welcoming me to Acheron.

"We've arrived," I announce to no one as I see the lights of town, and the college occupying the hill above it, glowing in the bed of the valley like the beacons of a rescue fleet. "It's all down hill from here!"

I mean this literally, of course. I've already begun coasting limply through the descent that becomes Clamence Street when it reaches downtown. Mt. Abandon and Maybrick peak sit to either side of view into which I half ride, half topple, as rain complicates the calipers cinching my tire; squeezing the handbrake actually seems to accelerate the bicycle, leaving me no choice but to ride it out, and wait for the hill to end. The downtown streets are devoid of traffic as I coast through two of three reddened traffic lights before bearing left on Loomis Street, toward my family's house. Though it mostly belongs to Grover. After the funeral, he took over what was left of the mortgage without asking me to help. I was already working part time for him at the grocery store, and living in the house to save what little I earned for no real purpose, so he knew I had nothing to offer. That much hasn't changed. When we stood together in the hallway of the house, straightening our funeral clothes in a mirror by the stairs, he watched me attempt to knot my tie as if it were a noose before reaching over my shoulders and organizing the thing correctly around my neck. Since he is my older brother, and my inability to properly dress myself for our parent's burial offered Grover the chance to edify me, I expected a lesson of some kind. But he said nothing. The tie was knotted, miserable and perfect as a chastity belt beneath my chin, even as his hands shook from the hangover beneath which we both passed the better part of the morning. I wondered whether he had given up, and later, when he allowed me live in the house as if I was still in middle school, and gave me a job I didn't want, without asking me to contribute anything, I felt certain he nursed no hope of me ever becoming something he wouldn't have to correct and support in equal measure. The most irresponsible I had ever seen him be was the night before the funeral, which was passed listening to Boccherini on our mother's turntable, and disheveling our father's liquor cabinet in the front room until we couldn't stand it any longer, and drove to the blackened foundation in the snow in which our parent's cabin had once nested. We never figured out who drove. Grover thought I did, and I thought he did, and it was a miracle we didn't end up wrapping the front end of his sensible little foreign made sedan around a tree on our way to or from the scene of the fire. We didn't ask much from the evening. Merely to reveal the absence of what had once existed in a wash of the car's headlights, and be disappointed in what people in these situations mistake for unfairness, but is actually just the muted shock of finding exactly what you expect exactly where you expect to find it. The same thing happens when people visit a tombstone; they're disappointed to find it still there.

But some part of us wanted the cabin to be there; the windows lit, a vein of smoke slithering from the chimney, and the calm faces of our parents passing like slides within the scenery. I suppose in revisiting the physical evidence of loss, we were confirming the fact that each of us was now our own problem; or, more accurately: that Grover would see to things from now on, including me. Unlike many of the adults I knew, including Cordelia, I'd never learned to hate my adolescence, and always thought of it as a time when things were easiest and comfortable. And even before the fire, I was aware some part of me would never be fully capable of living comfortably as an adult, and the best I could do was find people who would tolerate this. Cordelia was an unlikely choice, I knew that; from the age of fifteen until the evening before she abandoned me in Brooklyn, I'd watched her nebulous ambition grow between us like a malignant hedge, the root of which I'd somehow managed to stand upon while loving her clumsily throughout my young adulthood, and only discovered after Nathan, and Lionel Little. And by then, it was too late; paranoia was essentially piloting my life, needing nothing to legitimize it, and what moments weren't spent wondering who Cordelia might be fucking while I munched away on my pierogi, elapsed in periods of suffocation, broken only by a quiet growl in anticipation of the day, hour, or minute when I would once again be able to catch my breath.

And yet, she reminded me always of how little progress I needed to make in order to remain not happy, but stable. How could I not stay with her? Whenever my father or mother mentioned how abrasive she was, or how they'd never been comfortable with us together, especially in as shitty a place as New York, I always wanted to tell them it would be fine; she would get over the need to succeed, we would move back to Acheron, and move in with our families, get unimpressive jobs, until we'd saved enough money for our own place, and take it from there.

124

Repeat our adolescence as adults. That was my plan for us.

But even then, I think I knew my parents were right about how it would all shake out. So I just said I had no idea what they were talking about and changed the subject.

II.

"I considered the wonder of the things that befell me, convinced that my life was the best omelet you could make with a chainsaw."
—Thomas McGuane, *Panama*

I HOPED MY UNEXPECTED RETURN TO Acheron would be a pleasant surprise for Grover, and did my best when I arrived to sneak quietly inside the house, and up to my room. I only emerged after I'd realized I was too hungry and adrenal to fall asleep, and clattered around in the kitchen until I found a bottle of wine, and some leftover pasta and withdrew with these and a copy of *The Riddle of the Sands* to my room, waiting until morning to reveal myself.

But now, as he stands in my bedroom doorway with Ruby tucked pacifically beneath his arm, watching me awake in litter of sunlight from the window like a newly minted boy king, it's clear my brother was aware of my presence in the house the moment he arrived from work.

"I found this wandering in the garden," he says, nodding toward the dog beneath his arm. "And I slipped on the footprints you left in the front hall, and nearly broke my pelvis. So I assumed you were here."

"Did I leave a door open?"

"Doors."

"Sorry, Grover."

"Uhyut," he says ambivalently, setting Ruby down on the bedspread. She wanders toward my face, but veers at the very last moment to nose the plate of gnocchi and pesto I left on the unoccupied side of the mattress. On the nightstand, the copy of Childer's only novel is nearly afloat in a pool of Syrah. I'm dimly aware of attempting to use the wine bottle as a bookmark the night before. My brother absorbs all this with a sainted resignation before occupying a chair between the window and myself, leaving him silhouetted and me with the compulsion to apologize to his shadow.

"I'm sorry, Grover."

"You said that. You don't need to."

"I want you to be happy to see me."

"I am happy to see you. You are my brother, therefore: I love you."

"Therefore?"

"And I'm glad you managed to get out of New York. I couldn't reach you. I was worried."

"You still sound worried."

"You're smart enough to know that you suddenly being here means I'm now in an interesting position."

"I want interesting to be good."

"It isn't bad," he says, half his face now revealed in the light from the window. The part I can see appears to be in pain. "Cordelia wouldn't tell me anything about why she was here, and you weren't with her, and frankly, I think she's avoiding me, which I would normally prefer, if it didn't involve a question mark regarding you."

"You saw her?" I ask, as if Cordelia is a comet, or the Loch Ness monster. The wonder in my voice appears to disturb Grover.

"Briefly," he says. "She was leaving the library. She works

there now, it seems. Rodney mentioned how glad he was to have her back when I brought my books to the counter, thought I can't imagine why he choose to share this with me."

"He was probably in ecstasy. Was the front of his trousers damp?" I say, remembering the attention paid to Cordelia by the director of the Acheron Free Library, even, or perhaps especially, when I arrived to meet her after work. Rodney Downing would be inescapably at her side athwart the shelves, or hovering above her at the desk, sweat pearling along his brow, and one plump hand resting upon her shoulder, cranium, and in one instance during summer vacation, the honeyed skin of her thigh, as he held forth on some minor point of catalogue doctrine. But the thigh: she hadn't been at the check-out counter, so I'd come around the desk to seek her out, and found them sharing a desk in the administrative wing, her attention captured by a computer screen, and his fixed on me as I entered the office. We made eye contact, but Cordelia didn't see me. I nodded to him, turned around, and walked outside to wait in my car. Some part of me wondered whether this sort of heteronormative protestant lechery was normal, even healthy. I understood the harmless attention of an overweight man who always smelled like his last meal fed something deep inside Cordelia, and refused to mention it, even when Rodney began assessing late fees on books I hadn't taken out, and misplacing books I'd returned. I just started using the library on the Acheron College campus, and asked her to meet me outside whenever we made plans after work. This felt like a draw to me, but I'm certain Rodney viewed it as a victory. Considering the current state of things, I'm inclined to agree with him.

"I didn't examine him that way," says Grover, standing up. "I've made breakfast. It may be a bit cold, but if you're hungry, I'll fix you a plate."

I follow him downstairs, with Ruby leading the way down the sloping staircase to the kitchen as though she was raised in the house as well. Grover has already plated a bowl of the soggy kibble I hauled from Brooklyn, and the sound of her enjoying her meal seems to assess the absence of conversation between my brother and me. Is it possible we've already discussed everything there is to discuss? We've always been close, and any sort of rivalry never troubled our relationship; neither of us ever wanted to compete with anyone, certainly not each other. And I always assumed he would win if we did. Grover was never so much interested in being perfect as competent, and even at an early age, competence eluded me. An example: the plate of scrambled eggs he places before me are technically flawless; fluffy, buff, lightly seasoned, with a suggestion of cheese and perhaps paprika, or something spicy at any rate. I know he can produce this meal at will, and each time it will be the same: adequate, and delicious, passionless, and forgettable. My scrambled eggs are passionately awful; they refuse to be forgotten. Somewhere here is a balance neither of us can strike, and the mutual awareness of it is perhaps why I love him almost maniacally and worry he might ask me to leave before I can explain myself. But would an explanation do any good?

"You're having that with your eggs?" he asks, nodding toward my hand. Apparently, somewhere between the kitchen door and table, I poured myself a glass of wine.

"Yes. I mean, no. I'll get rid of it," I say, walking toward the sink like a marionette.

"And now you're just going to dump it. You opened a seventy dollar bottle of wine."

"I opened it as well?"

"How do think it got out of the bottle and into your glass?"

"I just assumed..." I begin, unsure what I'm trying to say, and feeling unwelcome. Grover sighs deeply as he takes the bottle from the counter, gets himself a glass from the cupboard, and draws me outside into the backyard. Ruby pads along, gulping the shreds of scrambled egg tipping from my plate as we follow him outside. The wooded slope of Mt. Abandon a mile or so distant sits calmly against a sky blank as a fresh canvass. When I was young, I imagined the mountain creeping closer to the house each night in an effort to devour it. A suggestion of the storm the night before remains in the air, chilling the grass beneath our feet, even as the sun begins drying the trees dripping on us as we sit beneath them in a brace of Adirondack chairs.

"Don't you have to go to work?" I ask, watching him fill his glass.

"Do you not know it's Sunday?" Grover asks back, sipping the wine with a delicacy I can't even mimic.

"I just forgot you weren't open on Sundays," I lie, guzzling mine, and staring into it. "This is nice."

"I am open on Sundays. But I give the store over to Oliver Himmel, the produce manager."

"Grover: You can't seriously expect me to remember your work schedule? Do you know mine?"

"Do you have a job?"

"Not anymore, but that's not the point. Assuming I did, would you be able to say when I would be there?"

"No, I suppose not," he says, after a famished-seeming pause. "I'm sorry. Glad you like the wine. An adjunct to living alone is easily forgetting the world doesn't follow your schedule."

"I'm sorry my being here interrupts whatever you had planned for the day."

"It doesn't. I can't even remember what I was going to do. And I'm glad you're here, as always. This is your home as well."

The silence following this comment is not unwelcome. We watch Ruby patrol the tomato cages in the garden, and listen to the brook beyond the back fence slosh into a culvert. A family of deer occupy a corner of pasture in the middle distance. I'm about to comment upon them when Grover asks the one question I'm not prepared to answer.

"I've been wondering how you got here. From what I understand, the city is locked down until they can drain it, so to speak. You couldn't possible have ridden that ridiculous bicycle all the way here."

"No," I say, after trying to silently calculate whether or not this is actually possible, and if Grover would believe me. "No, nothing like that. A friend drove me. She worked for the city, and knew the right people to get us out. I dropped her in Springfield, and drove from there myself. But I ran out of gas around Waterbury...and just rode the rest of the way."

"She gave you her car? How generous."

"Yes, well, no. I'm borrowing it, for the time being."

"Where is it now?"

"At a rest stop. Awaiting fuel."

"Will she be arriving to claim it?"

"I hope not," I say without thinking. "I mean: I'm planning on bringing it to Massachusetts and taking the bus back or something. You know, when things become a bit more regular."

"Does this friend of yours have anything to do with why Cordelia arrived here without you?"

"Yes," I say, seizing this inchoate narrative for what it will save me in man-hours spent explaining why exactly Cordelia abandoned me to my fate on the cusp of Hurricane Eula. Retrieving the soggy bindle of documents from the bicycle's cargo bucket in the front yard and dumping them in Grover's lap would do no good; the letter remains incomplete, and I'm not confident it would illuminate anything for him even if it were finished. Or perhaps it would confirm what he had suspected when I refused his invitation to come home shortly after spending Christmas in Holland. He'd listened to me gibber and purr into my phone, while trying to assure him of how great, no, not great, terrific I was feeling, a word he had never heard me use to describe myself, and set about arranging several calls with a behavioral therapist, who suggested I imagine my anxiety as a cloud floating past my window, and drink plenty of hot water with lemon.

But when Grover asked why I wouldn't leave New York, even for a few weeks, just to give myself a break, I said something about how I couldn't leave Cordelia alone in the city, because if I left, especially under an aegis of vulnerability, it would be too easy for her to see how little I contributed to her life aside from rent money and dog stewardship. I imagined her finding someone new within the week, a hulking, financially solvent man-beast with a real job, the sort of renaissance asshole who knows how to properly anchor bookshelves, and speak intelligently about Saul Kripke while fixing dinner and a toilet. In many ways, this reiver had already made his way into the apartment, and watched me coolly from across the room as I explained the theoretical side of all this to my brother over the phone. Grover had said he hoped this wasn't true, but allowed me to stay, calling each day to check on my lack of progress, and even speaking several times with Cordelia about it, though I gathered these conversations were not reassuring from remarks he made later.

"That's actually a relief," says Grover, dribbling a bit more wine into our glasses. From somewhere, he produces a tin tray with several cheeses, a wedge of smoked salmon, sliced apples, and a jar of mustard. "When I realized you were here, I was afraid you came back for her. Cordelia, I mean."

"Oh, no. Absolutely not," I say, deciding to allow Grover's version of events to flourish in place of the actual. In all honesty, I want Cordelia more than anything, and this desire has only grown more acute since arriving in town. And as soon as my brother grows bored with me, I'm going to find her. "I couldn't want anything less."

"You don't need to hear my feelings on any of this. I know you understand them. But I think mom and dad would have been glad to know you finally got out from under her."

This strikes me as an extraordinarily morbid remark, but I don't say anything about it. I don't know the exact measure of how little my family enjoyed being around Cordelia, but over the years, I watched it grow, fathom by fathom. The tension between her and my mother was enough to sink a passenger ferry; the years my mom spent working for Hunger Mountain Mental Health Resources had left her with a tendency to pathologize the people around her, assigning them a diagnosis the way I imagine field biologists tag large, wayward animals with radio collars. This seemed harmless enough, until Cordelia, returned for the summer from her first term at St. Margaret's, asserted her disbelief in mental illness during a family dinner after my mother suggested Henry Hoffmann, a classmate of Grover's, was a sociopath. Her evidence had something to do with Henry stealing a dog from a Hunger Mountain client, or blackmailing her into giving the animal away. It was unclear, and Grover, who worked with Henry at the time, couldn't offer any sort of confirmation or denial. Still, the collar was in place: Henry Hoffmann, sociopath.

My mother didn't know Cordelia had nursed a public longing for Henry when we were all in high school, a longing that remained unfulfilled for reasons particular to him. I never understood any of it, but I remember occupying the sideline of her desire, seeing nothing wrong with being benched, because it meant I still had a chance of setting foot in the game, while she paraded before Henry after fifth period Spanish in a halter top she'd concealed beneath a Gin Blossoms t-shirt, her back flawless, of course, her breasts obvious, her midriff tanned from the previous weekend she and I spent on a sandbar in the Wendigo river. Only I know where those tan lines end, I remember thinking. But for how long? I wondered, as Henry scanned Cordelia with the jaded, appraising eye of a middle-aged pawnbroker. Now, I easily see the template for our time together exhibited in this interaction, but at the time, I was satisfied when Henry abandoned her to me. It was the uncommon circumstance in which second prize is exactly the same as first.

I couldn't tell if Cordelia was defending him during dinner with my family, or just wanted to test drive whatever she'd learned interning at a farm for lunatics in Amish country during her inaugural term at St. Margaret's. But she said the experience caused her to disbelieve in mental illness, and change her major from psychology to women's studies. Grover made the point that every female undergraduate between Boston and Chicago majors in psychology at some point, wherein Cordelia called him sexist, and my brother responded by saying it seemed like the change was working well. My father had combed the remaining food from his plate to the kitchen trash early in the conversation, and returned to watch it develop, but seemed to be searching the dining room for something to clear away, a means of escape. He had recently retired from a position as a special education coordinator in the Acheron public school system, working with children who grew up to be adults exactly like Cordelia, and was probably surprised to find his work had not only followed him home, but was eating dinner at his table.

I wanted to say something palliative, but could only point out a picture my mother had painted and recently framed, hanging on the wall beyond the table, and ask Cordelia what she thought of it. Art, in comparison to whatever the conversation had become, seemed neutral. She barely took in the painting, an aqueous, impressionistic landscape of Kranion Pond painted from the porch of a friend's camp earlier that summer, before dismissing it as 'pretty,' and 'too colorful.' I couldn't bear to look at my mother during this critique. I realized later I'd shown Cordelia the painting some weeks before in my mother's studio, but couldn't tell if she remembered this or not. What I knew for certain was my mother's radio collar was already bridling Cordelia by the time I excused us from dinner, and each evening with my family going forward landed somewhere between mutual toleration and a Mexican standoff. As Grover and my father did their best to remain impartial, and my mother fecklessly probed Cordelia for something innocuous to pass the time, I would stare bleakly into the bottom of my wineglass, privately rationalizing the Damoclean blade hovering above the dinner table as fair remuneration for the promise of a life with Cordelia. What is love without collateral damage? I wondered, quietly appalled at my own lack of insight, but willing to live with it.

"Mom always thought she was fucking crazy," says my brother. "She never said anything to you, which meant the responsibility for hearing it all devolved on me."

"Thank you and I'm sorry."

"You should have heard it; bi-polar hypomania, oppositional defiant disorder, borderline personality. Nights when you weren't here, she sat with a glass of Pinot Grigio and the DSM open in her lap. I just listened."

"This feels like picnicking on mom's grave, Grover."

"Mom placed particular emphasis on the last one. And I don't understand what you mean by picnicking. I'm telling you what I know, which is what mom wanted you to know, but was too kind to tell you."

"I wish you shared that kindness."

"I wonder how you've gotten so far in life hearing only what you want from the people around you."

"Practice?" I suggest. Grover stands, appearing disgusted, and handing me the half empty bottle of wine, and gathering the remnants of our meal on the tray.

"I love you," he says, seceding from the conversation as if this remark can only lead him to ruin. "You're always welcome here. If you need money, you can work at the store, and I'll float you until the first paycheck. Meanwhile, I don't have any advice."

"I didn't ask for advice," I call to his average back as it retreats across the lawn toward the house. "And I don't need money! Or a job!"

As soon as I finish speaking, I realize I need all three of these things, and consider shouting an apology, or a clarification of some sort, but my brother is already inside. Shocked as I am to find a remnant of foolish, self-immolating pride remaining after the years spent with Cordelia in New York, part of me wishes I'd stapled my tongue to the roof of my mouth before going to bed last night. Even Ruby knows not to bite the hand that feeds before dinner. And Grover is my older brother; even if I wasn't an itinerant problem and diminishing return in his life, even if I resembled the domestic carpenter, sous chef, and graduate student in formal logic who I always assumed would take my place if I ever left Cordelia alone, even then, he would still offer me advice, and help, because this is what people who care for other people are supposed to do. Share information, and try to solve problems together. Why do I always feel as if I'm rediscovering this? Perhaps because the only recent advice I can remember receiving from Cordelia was something about how if I didn't start getting my life together, I couldn't expect it to remain easy. Was this a warning? She had just been admitted to a second or third graduate program, this one in philosophy, and seemed to be reassessing my pedigree apropos of this. The decision for me to drop out of St. Margaret's and move to New York with her had been mutual; how could it suddenly be wrong? Instead of asking this, I asked her why wanting an easy life was a problem, but by then she'd already left the room to prepare for class.

But all this is in the past, and if I want to make Cordelia love me again, I need to begin thinking about the future. Simply revealing myself with a soggy, incomplete letter and no prospects on the doorstep of her father's house has an unwise, Ghost of Christmas Past theatricality. I need to appear as if I've returned to Acheron with the specific intention of doing something worthwhile, like going back to school, and studying something that will not only impress Cordelia, but the people whose opinions matter to her. Since I don't even have an undergraduate degree, the possibilities suddenly appear limitless. Going forward, I should try to remember this moment, and treat my ignorance as an asset. The world is blank page to the man who knows nothing.

But in the shorter term, I need to find a job obviously not given to me by my brother out of pity. Since Cordelia is likely living with her father, I don't need to get my own place before revealing myself to her, which is good, because I don't want to live alone just to prove a point. But I should have an income from something not idiotic and partially respectable before planting myself on her doorstep with my unfinished letter and imprecise plans for the future. I suppose I'm seeking to display evidence of change without actually changing anything; if I'm lucky, this will be enough. Though I always doubted my impact on our relationship, I'd like to think Cordelia's time with me accustomed her to the middle class ritual of settling for less.

*　　*　　*

Paranoia is the following morning, when I see Cordelia for the first time in a business week as she enters Fatale: Women's Clothing & Accessories, where I've come to apply for the job of "saleswoman," according to a notice in the display window. A bell over the entrance chimes merrily as her leonine head appears in the doorway. Before the rest of her body follows, I conceal myself in a circular rack of dress slacks, abandoning my resume with the young woman at the register, who watches the place where I withdrew into the hanging clothing like a seam between the closed curtains of a puppet show. I feel stupid, yes, even before I see my curriculum vitae whisked from the counter into a wastepaper basket through the screen of women's clothing.

I should have realized I might come across Cordelia before I was ready; Acheron isn't large. But applying this knowledge to my job search might have saved me some embarrassment. What exactly am I doing applying to be a saleswoman in what used to be her favorite place to shop before the pestilence of choices beneath Houston Street supplanted it? I'll have to watch myself closely going forward, and try to avoid being drawn into places like this by the gravity of our combined history. Old habits have a way of steering you into a bridge abutment when you let them drive. If I could learn from anything I know but don't act upon, I would choose this.

The saleswoman's eyes drift once again toward my hiding place as Cordelia approaches the counter, clearly trying to decide whether it's more trouble to remove me or let me remain. Her attention returns to Cordelia for the time being, leaving me free to examine the woman who more or less explains my presence in the shop. A honeyed, muscular little blonde, with owlish blue eyes, dressed in spare cutoffs, and a halter-top that crash-lands somewhere between lingerie and swimwear. My inability to tell the difference would make me a terrible saleswoman if my resume didn't speak for itself. It's probably, undoubtedly, for the best; Cordelia appears familiar with the staff behind the counter, so she's probably here often. I could imagine no worse introduction than reappearing in one of her purlieus. Greetings, Cordelia! Remember when you thought you left me in Brooklyn? Surprise! How can I help you today? Oh, and by the way: I love you. Remember?

Just as I'm beginning to get comfortable amid the women's pants, a low, predicative purr stirs in my chest, and exits my mouth, returning the eyes of the saleswoman to my emplacement. I haven't given away my position so much as reminded her of it, but Cordelia's attention remains fixed on a catalogue spread between them on the counter, even as I nearly throttle myself trying to stifle anything further. They speak for a few minutes before Cordelia affirmatively taps the catalogue on the counter, thanks the clerk, and exits the store. I drop my hands from my mouth and emit what can only be called a bark, as if the compound shape of whatever I've been trying to stifle has grown rather than receded during the interim. I feel briefly victorious until I recognize what I'm celebrating. The saleswoman has had enough of it, and coaxes me from the interior of the rack to the counter, where she fishes my resume from the wastebasket and returns it with a sort of mute acknowledgement of the obvious.

"I'm sorry," I say, returning the document to the trash, and examining a circled item in the catalogue on which my elbow rests; a men's blazer, the sort of semi-formal urbanite horse blanket in which Cordelia always attempted to enshroud me. I tap the illustration as she did a moment before. "Are you special ordering this for that woman who came in just now?"

"The one you hid from?" asks the clerk, smirking, unafraid. Apparently, my harmlessness couldn't be more pronounced.

"I wasn't hiding."

"Okay. Why were you growling at her?"

"I wasn't growling at her."

"Okay. Can I help you with anything else?"

"Does this place have a back entrance?"

"If I tell you where it is, will you use it?"

I assure her I will, and only realize she didn't answer my question after I'm in the alley behind the building, walking back toward the place where I left the bakfiets. I consider returning to the shop and speaking with the clerk again until I feel satisfied, but can't imagine what either of us would gain from another interaction. On my end, the saleswoman job is out of the question. Cordelia, in her managerial capacity, once said she would never hire me. You project a lassitude so embedded, she said, it easily overwhelms whatever you do to hide it. Everything about your face says you don't give two shits. Or one fuck, if you'd prefer.

I've never interviewed myself for a job, so I have no idea whether this is true. But when I surrender my resume to a potential employer, I always assume they see an employee they don't want, just as I see a job I don't want. If we somehow still manage to meet in the middle, we usually both expect to be disappointed, so I've learned to thrive in an environment of unshifting low expectations, as Gordon pointed out. I start from the bottom and work my way sideways.

I tried to explain this to Cordelia shortly after she and I attended a funeral with my coworkers at the Brooklyn Association. I referred to it as a 'work funeral,' a cavalier phrase I'm certain I used to offset the grief I felt when Paul, the office manager, died of a heart attack on a Wednesday night a week before Christmas. He was forty-two, sleeping with a female body-builder named Linda from Bergen County and would occasionally leave fruit on my desk, kumquats or tangelos from the bodega beside the subway station in East Harlem where he caught the train into Brooklyn each day.

We worked together for two years, and somewhere toward the middle of the second year, I realized he was probably the closest I'd ever come to forming an adult male friendship of my own in New York City. We took breaks together on the roof of the building to drink instant coffee, and watch traffic whip down Flatbush Avenue toward the hopeless mouth of the Brooklyn Bridge as he calmly explained how tired he was from fucking Linda all weekend in a hotel room somewhere geographically proximate to Red Bank, New Jersey. It was a grim, pervert's poetry, and at some point, I stopped listening. When I tuned back in, he was talking about a day he'd spent in Copenhagen with his ex-wife. They both worked in finance at the time, and she was attending a conference. But Paul had nothing to do, so he rented a bike, rode around the city, and lay in the sun along the waterfront. I expected a punch line, and when one didn't arrive, I realized he had become agreeably mired in the recollection of what, for him, had been a nice day. I didn't have anything to add, so it was easy to leave him alone with it, the memory he had tried and failed to share with me, as the crepuscular barbarism of Brooklyn unspooled beneath us.

At the time of his death, I still had several Christmas presents for Cordelia hidden beneath his desk, and for some reason, this is where my mind went when Gordon texted me on Thursday morning to ask if I was all right; I wondered if the gifts I'd left at the office would survive the week without Paul to guard them. Things had been disappearing; cell phones, several purses, and a laptop, and he'd been working on some sort of initiative to curb the thefts. I don't know what he had in mind, but I couldn't face the office to save the Christmas gifts. I took the day off to reacquaint myself with the sort of pain I hadn't experienced since burying my parents. Cordelia did the best she could with what she'd been given, which wasn't much; she took me out to dinner at a bleak Cuban restaurant in or around the part of Park Slope where strollers outnumber bicycles, and watched me cry silently into my paella while staring like a lunatic at the clock on the wall behind her trying to estimate how much more time I could realistically put in before going to sleep.

I missed Paul less after seeing him in a coffin at a storefront funeral home in Sunset Park. He no longer seemed real, and at the time, I was fine with believing the person I apparently knew more about than anyone present, including the family, was actually a figment of my imagination. He was laid out in an Oxford shirt and khakis, much the same as he had been at the office, and when I said something about how even in life, Paul was dressed for burial, trying to lighten the mood as much for myself as the people who were beginning to speak on his behalf, no one laughed.

Paul was adopted, and reconnected late with his legitimate family, a warped, affluent clan of Connecticut tennis brats who were content to remain on the sideline while their prodigal son's coworkers lamented his death with paeans to his skill at ordering coffee for the office, making sure the canvass staff always had Metrocards, and how he always had a kind word for everyone, which was an absolute lie. If Paul had been allowed, he would have fired three quarters of you, I thought to myself, leaving with Cordelia shortly after the canvass manager pointed me out during her speech as Paul's 'road dog.' I wondered how much this would embarrass Linda if she had been there.

It was more than either of us could take, but helped me answer Cordelia later in the evening when she said my basic problem was that my coworkers at the Brooklyn Association were stupid, and she didn't understand how I could work there. I told her no one expected me to be better than anyone else, which usually meant no matter how bad I was at my job, there always someone worse. When I used the term 'job security' to describe this, she seemed to disagree, but by then, I was crying in silence again, so she left it alone.

When I reach my bicycle, the stack of resumes left in the bottom of the cargo bucket have been leafleted up and down the street by the combined wind descending from Mt. Abandon and Maybrick Peak. So much for being covert. If Cordelia missed me yowling in the sales rack at her favorite boutique, there's always the chance my resume will end up stuck to the bottom of her shoe.

I collect what I'm able to find of the formerly important seeming documents, and deposit their tattered remainder in a curbside trashcan, feeling oddly accomplished in having gotten through them all in a single morning. Still, the incorporeal sense of having martyred myself to the afternoon is already present as I stoop to retrieve a final rogue resume in what turns out to be the forecourt of St. Simeon's. As I straighten up, a phalanx of residents along the flowerbed look past me into the street; those not already smoking a cigarette roll one between trembling, yellowed fingers, while a stray contingent manacle bicycles to the fence before joining a queue outside the front door. Most people are sunburnt. One man is missing a hand; another a leg. Several residents tap around the patio on canes or crutches. Crude tattoos with some relationship to either faith or family speckle the intact limbs among the crowd arrayed beside the entrance. A symphony of neglect hangs in the air, or more acutely, between the two oak trees bracing courtyard and filtering sunlight onto the shoulders of the men and women passing the time below. Standing with them now with my resume crumpled in my fist, I might as well be Mungo Park, blundering among the Moors as I trace my way toward the source of the Niger River. I seem to have wandered off the map of things I can comfortably ignore; it becomes rapidly apparent that none of those sharing the courtyard are remotely interested in me. They appear to be waiting for something, which turns out to be Martha, of all people. The entrance clanks, admitting her with a circlet of keys hanging from her wrist, and a lanyard with a laminated photo slung around her tan neck. She looks much the same; woodsy, and capable, and I'm embarrassed by a twinge of wistful, idiot desire at the memory of us drunkenly banging into each other in her kitchen as we dog-paddled our way through preparing an evening meal. Though I don't recall our congress, the preamble was quite good, and for a moment, the possibility of rekindling whatever we almost had the day in the deer stand feels like an excellent next step in the new life I appear to be trapped by since Cordelia left. Martha is too smart and motivated to take me seriously in the long term, but an evening or two before things get back on track seems plausible.

I'm reminded this really isn't the place for unfixed carnality when a man who smells vaguely necrotic and looks like a kind of hard-luck St. Nicholas passes by on his way inside, returning me sadly to earth, and the reality of Martha in the doorway. Despite the circumstance, I notice she wears no wedding ring on the hand waving clients inside, and wonder how far away I have to stand from her before she begins detecting my desperation.

"Check in!" she shouts, surveying the courtyard like a mustering officer, her eyes drifting past me as the residents begin shuffling past her into the building.

"If you're not checking in, you need to leave the property," she adds to the dwindling queue; several people squeeze past where I've positioned myself in the gate, my arm waving in a crescent as I try to capture her attention. I must look like I'm trying to signal a boat, but it's been years since we've seen each other. I assumed she would have left town by now to patrol rangeland or fight forest fires or something. But no, here she is, framed in the doorway of the local homeless shelter, her stern gaze softening with neither recognition nor pity when she notices me waving from the sidewalk like I've been shipwrecked.

"Checking in?" she hollers across the courtyard. I stop waving and rotate in place, examining the barren street for someone else she might be talking to.

"No, I-" I begin, after finding myself alone.

"Do you need a sack lunch?"

"No, thank you, I'm not hungry. It's just-"

But the building has already swallowed her. The door clanks shut, and I find myself staring vacantly at a sign partially covering a shattered web of security glass in the sidelite:

CHECK-IN IS AT 7:30PM EVERY NIGHT. IF YOU ARE NOT CHECKING IN, YOU MUST BE OFF PROPERTY UNTIL 4AM. BETWEEN THE HOURS OF 1AM AND 4AM, WE WILL NOT ANSWER THIS DOOR. IF YOU ARE ON A VIOLATION OR PERMANENT OUT, PLEASE RING BELL FOR ASSISTANCE. UNDER

NO CIRCUMSTANCES ARE YOU TO ENTER THE BUILDING WITHOUT STAFF APPROVAL. FAILING TO COMPLY WITH THESE POLICIES WILL RESULT IN TIME ADDED TO AN EXISTING VIOLATION, OR POLICE INTERVENTION.

I suppose the years have been unkind to me. Or kinder to Martha, at any rate. No one would ever mistake her for homeless. As I wheel my bicycle away from the shelter, I try to derive some comfort from the possibility, or theory perhaps, that Martha was only pretending not to recognize me. Maybe she'll call later this evening, offering to buy me an apologetic drink, still chuckling over the ripeness of the opportunity I presented, standing in the gate of St. Simeon's with my dirty resumes, dumb clothes, and stolen bicycle. How could she not resist? Of course, if Martha knew anything about my current mishandling of my own affairs, she'd also know pretending to confuse me with one of the trembling smokers perched along the flowerbed is a little too congruent to be a good joke. Most of them are probably looking for work too.

I pause at the end of the block before turning onto Loomis Street, trying not to be discouraged by the possibility that nothing about my life is funny anymore as I glance back at the looming, mid-century house containing Martha, and wonder whether it will someday be my home. Something here feels inevitable. Hopefully it isn't that.

Grover is sitting on the porch with Ruby asleep in his lap when I arrive home, a glass of red wine at his elbow, and a copy of *Earthly Powers* open between his knees, the spine resting across the dog's back. Ruby is natural lectern. Unless there's food around, she'll stay wherever she's put.

"A venerean strabismus," he says without looking at me as I sit beside him. "What might that be?"

"I think Burgess meant 'cross-eyed', " I say, stuffing the stack of disheveled curriculum vitae beneath the cushion on a porch chair in order to conceal it from my brother. He spent the better part of the morning helping me transform it from a summary of under-achievement to a index of professionally plausible lies, and went into work early to print them on the stationary used for deli menus at the grocery store. I didn't know how to be properly grateful; I thought if I didn't find a job, the time spent looking for one this af-ternoon might provide me with some idea of how to demonstrate this, but I've I arrived at the house bereft, my goals diffused.

"How do you know that?" asks Grover, as Ruby snores in his lap.

"I don't know. It's the sort of stupid thing I remember and can't forget. You're probably the first and last person who will ever ask me what it means."

"When I listen to you speak, I have the sense that you've cast yourself as the primo uomo in a highly personal tragic opera of some kind. I'm concerned that you believe other people see exact-ly what you think is wrong with you."

"If we could discuss our separate relationships with paranoia in order to identify commonalities, I'd be grateful."

"You're hemorrhaging self-pity," says Grover, turning a page. "If I didn't love you so much, it would be nauseating. Any luck finding work?"

"I applied for the position of saleswoman at Fatale."

"So, no, it sounds like."

"It occurred to me after I'd already given them a resume that in order to sell clothes, you need to look like you enjoy wearing them. My wardrobe could probably use a spruce."

"You arrived here with that red jacket dad used to stack wood, and a NYPD rain slicker. I don't want to know how you came by that. Take whatever you need from my closet until I can drive you up to Burlington, and use the eight dollars I left in the pants you're wearing to buy yourself a haircut."

"I didn't know it was so bad."

"Your hair looks like a hat."

"That explains it," I say, recalling Martha.

"Explains what now?"

I try summarizing my earlier experience outside St. Simeon's without including the detail about chasing my resumes, which makes the story sound as if I wandered over to the homeless shelter just to see how it felt to be there. Grover looks appalled.

"I'll take tomorrow off," he says, closing his book. "We'll go up to Burlington to find you something to wear that doesn't project flaneurism."

"Cordelia was in Fatale ordering a men's blazer. I've decided to believe it is a present for me."

"Did the two of you speak?"

"No. I hid."

"If that doesn't embarrass you, I won't allow it to embarrass me."

"If a women I've theoretically slept with mistaking me for a bum doesn't, why should that?"

"We worked in the kitchen there on Thanksgiving once. Do you remember that?"

I suddenly do, but wish I hadn't. Our father corralling an eight-year-old me, and a twelve-year-old Grover into the frosted interior of his Isuzu, and presenting the three of us to the staff at St. Simeon's in the half-light of an early November morning. One man, one woman, both young with identical sets of keys chiming against their hips, both having worked the entire night rolling drunks out of the dryer vent on the side of the building, or counseling residents for whom the holiday was a sort of recurrent milestone along the artery which had eventually led them to St.

Simeon's. My father's question: What can we do to help? definitively stumped them, though it was obvious help was needed, even to me. A number chalked on a blackboard behind the desk in the staff office denoted the tally of occupants still in bed upstairs: 110, and more to come when they served the midday meal.

My father asked the same question again, patiently, calmly, expecting nothing; and again, they merely looked at us, and then each other, as though seeking not so much a resolution, as solace from having to find one. It occurs to me now they may have been in love, because this is often how I looked at Cordelia when life became a threatening riddle.

We were eventually given over to the kitchen staff, my father prepping turkey in an apron with Freedom from Want emblazoned on the corpus, Grover running the industrial dishwasher, and I helping a scarecrow-like sex offender dry the crockery ejected from it. My father knew the man through some internality of the school district, and watched closely. All I remember is a tall, toothless man in his middle fifties talking to me about baseball, something I had no interest in and knew nothing about, but it was an important enough topic for him to require almost nothing from me except a perennial indication I was still listening. The other residents referred to him as 'Sticks', and this is the name he gave the reporter from the Acheron Monitor who strode into the kitchen with a photographer an hour before lunch, and took our picture together for some holiday piece he was composing for the paper. The caption reads something like: 'Eight year old Walter Ratliff helps Sticks, a resident at St. Simeon's Shelter, dry dishes on Thanksgiving morning.'

My mother clipped the photograph and accompanying text, and preserved it in a frame above the worktable in her studio. When I learned years later about Sticks being convicted of sexually abusing several of his children (he had five), I chuckled and referred to my appearance with him in the town paper incorrectly as ironic in front of my father. He said something about how stigma is never funny, even when it's earned, and expecting the worst from people is always easy, and exactly why people like Sticks have the choice between living in a shelter or under a bridge. He said a good, firm belief in intractable evil makes us all great citizens and god fucking awful people, a remark I think I've only begun to understand after my meeting with Martha this afternoon.

"No," I lie to Grover. "I don't remember that."

"We washed dishes with a localized pederast for charity."

"I sometimes think it was the last nice thing I did for anybody."

"Going forward, I'm not going to ask you if you remember anything," he says, slipping a hand beneath Ruby as he stands up, and depositing her in my lap. "I'm hoping this will be the last time your histrionics evict me from my own porch."

"You're evicting yourself!" I say, but my brother ignores me. The screen door clatters in the jam as he withdraws inside the house, not at all disturbing the somnolent shape of the dog in my lap, but reminding me for some reason of the door of St. Simeon's slamming in the twilight an hour earlier, after I told Martha I needed nothing; another lie.

An hour later, in what remains of the sunlight helmeting the crest of Maybrick Peak, I watch the main entrance of the Acheron Free Library from a municipal bench on the shoulder of the Castle Memorial Recreation Trail running along the rim of an escarpment across the street. At my side sits a brown-bagged container of Loup Garou malt liquor, the finest beverage I could afford with the change I pulled out of Grover's davenport, and a long-handled wicker basket my mother used to gather wildflowers, repurposed by me as a sort of litter to transport a sonorous Ruby to the peak of the acclivity where we sit, having what seems to me like a picnic. Passerby, evening joggers, mountain bikers, strollers, appear to enjoy the cornucopial aspect of a small, crippled dog snoring in an antique basket until it becomes clear I have something to do with it.

Lights begin dimming in the windows of library's upper story. Employees depart, in cars, on bicycles and foot; I have a dim recollection of what it was like to have a job. At the very least, my tenure with the Brooklyn Association left me convinced nothing I did had any real value. This was a sort of succor. I was never burdened by the possibility of missing out on anything, and often imagined myself fading like a photograph left in the sun, pleased by the retiring entropy of this image; it seemed to explain New York and what I was doing there, though I think I may have mistaken the city for Cordelia, or perhaps they were the same. It's hard to tell now.

I know when I shared this during an intermission at the Metropolitan Opera, I disturbed her by treating it as an epiphany. We were seeing something by Giordano based on the life of Andre Chenier, an emotive poet guillotined during the Reign of Terror. She seemed to suspect me of drawing a crooked parallel between the lead tenor and myself. This was shortly after Paul died, so she had no idea what to expect from me, but was doing her best to be sympathetic without being indulgent. When she asked if I was enjoying the opera, I said yes, because it gave me the opportunity to cry in public. That didn't help anything. She spent the rest of the evening hunting for a neutral topic as I fed bits of a pretzel she bought me to some birds by the Revson Fountain.

Rodney Downing appears beneath the library's portico, meaning Cordelia, if she worked today, won't be far behind. And yes, I see her, tapping past the director in a pair of sensible flats down the stairs, toward the rack where her bicycle is lodged with him loping along in her wake like an engorged remora. He appears determined to waylay her, and for once I'm happy he's decided to act on his lower impulses, because they give me enough time to scramble down the ridge to the street with my libation and dog basket. I haven't stood up since opening the bottle of Loup Garou, but the full measure of its effect becomes apparent when I reach the bottom of the declivity, and walk with a kind of deliberateness into a lamppost as Cordelia departs on her bicycle, a heavy, antediluvian Schwinn. She clanks off the sidewalk into the street, passing within ten feet of my bivouac before disappearing into the night.

Catching up to her is impossible; I missed my window, or perhaps it closed on my shirttail. Either way, I know where she lives, and, if I remember correctly, her father's yard contains a scalable maple with an orchestra seat on her bedroom window. That would do; if I'm going to hide in the dark, drinking and not making any big decisions, I may as well do it from a tree branch with a view of what I'm missing.

I don't realize Ruby is awake until she's already debarked from the basket, and waddled into the street. She sniffs the pavement once, directing her monocular glance in the direction of Cordelia's commute, inhales the road once more, and looks at me, as if weighing the chance of life in my care becoming better or worse against the familiar stability encoded in Cordelia's scent. I feel like a civil defendant awaiting the obvious verdict of a custody dispute.

"Ruby…Please, don't go!" I say, realizing I sound like I'm begging. The dog realizes it too; she sniffs the ground once again, glances at me, and takes off down the street. Turncoat bitch, I think, laughing bitterly to myself as I plod off into the darkness to retrieve my pet. She reaches the head of block, and momentarily resumes her inspection of the pavement, before turning right and disappearing at the corner. I'm running now, with the empty basket swaying from wrist, and the swill remaining in the bottle of Loup Garou splashing on my clothes as I belt mangled apologies in the direction Ruby went.

"I'm sorry! It won't always be like this! Please! Come Back!" I shout, my voice redounding in the vacant night as I try to believe what I'm saying. "Things can only get better from here! I promise you! Please, Come back!"

I'm generally disturbed by the possibility of the dog and I needing each other equally as I reach the corner, and find no trace of her among the row of placid Victorian homes lining the street. From a window left open in one of these, the voice of Maria Callas singing the opening bars of Ave Maria casts an aspect of ridicule over my steadily mounting panic as I frantically search driveways and front yards for a sign of Ruby. I expect more of myself than this, I think. At least, in an abstract way.

Something moves beside a mailbox up the street, and I run toward it, bellowing the dog's name, only to find I've chased down a plastic bag from Grover's Market caught in a fence. If my brother were here, I'm confident nothing he saw would be surprising enough to disappoint him. The thought briefly comforts me, but the relief is rapidly swallowed by anxiety; my breathing grows short and peculiar, and I'm purring in between gasps before I can stop myself, humming like beehive in a stranger's dooryard and reeling a bit as I try to imagine whether Cordelia could ever be more disappointed with me than I am with myself in this moment. Maybe she doesn't realize how bad I am at taking care of myself without her around, I think, swaying a bit, dumping what remains of the beer across my shoes. If ninety-nine percent of cruelty is a result of ignorance, than leaving a pet in my care is basically animal cruelty. But hers, or mine? Maybe both.

I'm too dizzy to walk straight, and try to steady myself on a gate I mistake for a section of fence. It swings open as if agreeing with some subterranean part of my intentionality, and rolls me into someone's backyard. It's too dark to tell where exactly I've landed, but I smell basil beside my face, and a tendril of pumpkin vine is coiled around my ankle. I've come to rest in a stranger's garden. The basket has somehow remained on my wrist, and when I'm caught in a flashlight beam as I stand, I'm momentarily at a loss to contradict the voice speaking from behind it.

"Last time I caught someone robbing my garden, he got a lot more than a county bracelet."

A twelve-gauge shell drops into a chamber from the direction of the house.

"Of course, he was a gopher, and as far as I know, they don't make an ankle lock in his size, so it had to be."

The knowledge of a gun and its relationship to the voice speaking from beyond the purview of the flashlight augments the tremulous purring in my chest to an uvular wail. I'm too scared to be embarrassed.

"You growling at me, boy?"

Whoever this person might be, they have the sort of campestral gravity of speech that more or less answers itself, so I don't say anything. I suppose every question is rhetorical when a gun is pointed at you.

"So why don't you quit growling in my pumpkin patch and come on inside now. If anything about this arrangement troubles you, we can roundtable it while we wait for the sheriff."

This seems reasonable enough. Explaining how I ended up in his garden will take some time, and understanding it requires compassion on his part. I'd be startled by how patient I've become if I wasn't so glad to be in complete agreement with someone, even if they're holding me at gunpoint.

The path is clear: I cross a patio illuminated by the flashlight, and enter the house through a sliding glass door, smelling something stuffy and barn-like in the opaque interior. My jailer declines switching on a light as he follows me inside, and latches the door. Behind me, I hear the suck and pull of a refrigerator, and the half note of glass ringing against glass. A beer. Well, why not? The flashlight rests on a kitchen counter, briefly illuminating a patch of wall with some sheet music framed on it: The Kranion Pond Overture. I suddenly know whose garden I invaded, but don't say anything about it, even as I'm led deeper into the farm-smelling house by my host, toward the living room, according to him. Though, for all I can see, he could be leading me into a vat of micro-brewed quicksand or a homespun *trou de loup*. Still, I have no choice but to trust my guide, who seems to know the location of every impediment in his home, navigating it mole-like, and taking it personally when I blunder into what feels like a drop-leaf table in the hallway.

"Boy, can't you even make it between rooms in a house with destroying something? Don't make me throw a leash on you. Walk softly."

I don't answer, but nearly scream instead as something floppy and large waddles across my shoes. What in the fuck was that? A dog would have barked by now. A cat would probably be put off by the diffuse odor of Ruby. The same thing, or something very similar to it, bumbles curiously against my calf as I enter the ostensible living room.

"Take three man-size steps forward and then go ahead and sit yourself down."

"Where?" I ask. I'm so tense I can't even hum to myself. I don't know how to explain to my warden I'll collapse on the floor if I don't find a chair soon.

"Where what?"

"Where am I supposed to sit?"

"On the sofa there."

"Yes, I believe you when you say there is a sofa here. But it would be far easier to sit down while you call the sheriff if I could see where you want me to wait for him."

"Oh. Right. I see what you mean. Here you go. *Fiat lux.*"

Something clicks, revealing eight to twelve rabbits nesting, or whatever rabbits do, in a mezzeluna of light cast from a standing lamp, and Mr. Orville Gould, as I suspected from the music framed in the hallway, enthroned in an armchair with the light's dangling bead pinched between his thumb and index finger. His eyes appear to simmer as he watches me, or something very close to where I stand. The animals retreat beneath furniture, and reappear around corners, making an accurate count impossible. Their droppings, black and brown pellets the size of a chocolate covered raisin, litter the floor, the seat of couch, Mr. Gould's knees. He offers no explanation for this domestic warren, but once again encourages me to take a seat on the sofa. My elbow knocks against the gun stowed barrel up in an umbrella stand by the door as I lift my arm to avoid a rime of rabbit shit on the armrest. Retirement for an elementary school music teacher is apparently one self-imposed pitfall after another.

"You really fucked up my Christmas concert," says Mr. Gould. "You know that?"

No point in asking what he means, or trying to deny it. I absolutely did fuck up his Christmas concert, or, as he likely saw it, the public debut of his overture to Kranion Pond in the auditorium of Acheron Union School, December, 1997. I was a member of what Mr. Gould called an orchestra, but was really more of a prison band. Two days a week, the combined fifth and sixth grade members met in the FEMA-styled trailer our teacher was allotted for a classroom while the school solicited funding for a more permanent wing. It was a grim winter; trees swayed in the alpine wind from Mt. Abandon, raking the tundra that was once a playground as the orchestra marched across it with their instrument cases toward Mr. Gould's oubliette. We would sometimes hear the sound of a piano above the wind, rising in a tonality of grief from somewhere inside the trailer as we approached, or worse: a quavering tenor enjoining the notes of the piano as though trying to siphon something of their vitality. It was the score to a house fire in which all is lost.

Mr. Gould was obviously a decent and talented man, literally marginalized by the primacy of more foundational subjects, but our rehearsals in the classroom trailer never transcended our maestro's aspect of banishment. The torpid horns and dormant woodwinds seemed to toot and squeal from an outpost at the end of the world as the wind shook the flimsy walls of our conservatory, and Mr. Gould conducted us through what would become the opening movements of his overture to Kranion Pond with an energy that would have been sadistic if his spirit were not so clearly broken. When the tempo lagged, he pounded it correctly with his baton against the offending music stands, while chanting the count in his breathless tenor, his eyes wild and red-veined as flecks of foam blew from his lips upon the polished bells of the brass section. He was mostly out of control, but remained impossible to fear. Even though he taught me to read music and play the trumpet (not well, but *fortissimo*), I never got past thinking of him as a kind of humorless birthday magician, though less so after what happened at the Christmas concert.

In a way, the entire fiasco was Mr. Gould's fault for demoting me to the penultimate chair in my section at the final rehearsal before the performance. I had no reason to take it personally; I didn't care much whether or not I was any good, and he had been shuffling things around in the orchestra for weeks preceding the concert, so it wasn't surprising for him to put me where I could do the least damage. Even my parents expressed a kind of delicate regret in forcing me to join the school band after listening to me practice; my father once rushed inside after arriving home from work because he thought he heard my mother screaming, only to find her sitting with her head cupped in her hands at the kitchen table as I bleated hopelessly from my room.

So it was a salutary choice for everyone involved, even me, because on the night of the concert, I found myself seated behind a young Cordelia, then first chair of the flute section. The slight tilt of her head as she rested her lips against the embouchure transfixed me, and as the music rose, I missed several cues, which didn't matter, since I was so low on the orchestra's totem pole. Occasionally, I lifted my instrument to my lips and pretended to play for the benefit of my parents, marooned somewhere in the audience. But I made no actual music that night because I couldn't stop pretending Cordelia was offering me the side of her neck from the seat below, and knew I had to say something. I didn't know what. Anything would do. It felt like the perfect moment.

During a mutual rest, as several other sections churned away, I leaned down, placing my mouth beside her ear, realizing only after I had begun reciting some lines from a poem my mother often read to me,

"Let us go then, you and I"

that Mr. Gould's eyes were locked on us from his rostrum. I met his glance with a kind of ambiguous ownership of what I was doing; during no moment between us had it ever been clearer what I thought of him: one part minstrel to two parts rodeo clown. I continued reciting,

"When the evening is spread out against the sky"

knowing I would be sunk after the first stanza, having retained nothing beyond it, and almost relieved when Cordelia turned around and spoke.

"Desist, shitdick! I'm going to miss my cue!"

"In the room the women come and go," I said, rushing it. "Talking of Michelangelo."

And because I was hissing these disjointed lines into her ear, Cordelia did miss her cue, as did the others in her section waiting to take theirs from her. The evening became calmly doomed. I watched Mr. Gould, ramrod straight in the slightly undersized tuxedo he wore to concerts, listening to his overture tweet, lumber, and lurch to a halt, and watching me amid the unnatural conclusion of what for all I knew then or know now could be his life's work, his eyes twin pools of deep failure reflecting me as I tooted my horn amid the collision I had caused, like Nero capering and strumming his lute as the capital city of his empire burnt to the ground. This was the only moment I remember seeing Mr. Gould neither angry nor excited, but still: his baton rose as it so often did during practice to corral the orchestra into some sort of order, and walloped the nearest music stand, which happened to belong to

Purvis Blivet, the sheriff's son. And here, the head of Mr. Gould's truncheon snapped free from the handle and landed across the bridge of Purvis' nose. It immediately began to bleed. He cast his bassoon to the floor with a clatter and began to wail, making no attempt to staunch the flow of blood from his nostrils. Mr. Gould approached, offering his sleeve since a box of tissues was nowhere to be found, and apologizing, but Purvis slapped his hand aside.

"Leave me alone, you big homo!" he shouted, into the imperfect silence of the school auditorium, definitively closing the evening. The same school nurse who saw to Cordelia on the playground, left her seat to bandage Purvis, and the rest of the audience stood as if on cue.

Though none of us knew it then, this was the point at which Mr. Gould's tenuous dominion over his musicians faded to shadow of what it had never been. He understood he would never get any music from us again, and we would always remember him as the big homo who bloodied Purvis Blivet during the coda of The Kranion Pond Overture. In the days that followed, his classes became more frenzied and authoritarian, but, like some Olympian punishment, with each fascist measure he employed to retain control of the classroom, it slipped further from his grasp. He could scream, stamp, and cautiously pound his baton all he liked. It only took one student whispering 'big homo' to another to resurrect the memorial. He bore all this with as much dignity as possible, continuing to wear his tuxedo during school concerts, while parents and administrators looked on. None of them really knew what to do with him except applaud. Meanwhile, my father saw the entire thing, and knew it was my fault. Before the post-concert bake sale had even run out of lemonade, he was dragging me by the collar of my jacket toward the parking lot, and helping me draft a syllabus for the apology I would make the following Monday.

"I'm sorry," I say, not really meaning a word of it. I'm frankly sort of disturbed by the concert being what Mr. Gould remembers first after recognizing me, but relieved not to be once again mistaken for a vagrant or criminal. I would never have recognized him. Teaching children to play Sweet Georgia Brown on the French horn, and sing My Favorite Things through the glottal minefield of early adolescence would put years on anyone; Mr. Gould has come out of it looking like Saul of Tarsus in a woodcutting costume.

Rather than replying to my apology, he leaves the room, returning shortly with two beers, handing one to me, along with a folded piece of construction paper. I know what it is before opening it: A picture drawn in marker the Sunday after the concert; a maniac resembling Mr. Gould playing a massive set of drums beneath an even more massive bank of spotlights. Below this, a crowd appears to cheer. Written in my developing scrawl is the phrase: 'SORRY YOU'RE A GREAT TEACHER,' which sounds as if I'm apologizing for his ability. I only saw Mr. Gould play the drums once or twice during class, but I noticed how much he appeared to enjoy it.

"I'm surprised you still have this," I say, looking for an area not spattered with feces to place the missive. My handwriting has barely changed in twenty years. Should that worry me?

"It helps me remember," begins Mr. Gould, hoisting one of the rabbits into his lap, "my music isn't the only thing that makes me happy. When you gave me the card, I realized how little I would ever achieve."

"You're welcome?" I venture.

"No one got to hear what I spent years composing in that freezing fucking trailer between classes, and second prize is an apology that looks like a developmentally delayed person made it. I didn't hear god's voice when you gave that to me, but I heard his laughter. It was more than enough to keep me from abducting you at the bus stop, and letting your parents work it out. And now, I'm happy. Are you?"

"No. I lost my dog," I say, wondering how close I was to being a set of incomplete remains in a culvert off the Mt. Abandon access rode. Based on the amount of things I plan to do without ever doing them, I'm guessing: not very.

"Want a rabbit?"

"No thanks."

"Another beer?"

"That's kind of you, but I haven't finished-"

"Well, if you want," says Mr. Gould, leaning forward with a sort of conspiracy in his chair, and nearly dumping the rabbit in his lap onto the floor, "we could toss the beer and that gun in the back of my pickup and drive up to the quarry near the old boy scout camp. You ever shoot bats? I know that weirdo Henry Hoffmann has some kind of resort up there now, but I checked the deed at the library, and a good half of that fucking quarry is on public land, so he can go piss hard up a wash line for all I care about it. We'll take the pickup, as I said. I popped a spotlight on that bitch just the other day so we won't be shooting in the dark."

"Can you drive? I certainly can't. Or can, but shouldn't."

"Then I'm out of ideas," he says, deflating. "No pleasing you I guess. I know how absurd all this must seem. But I'm very happy."

"Miserable people always tell everyone how happy they are."

"People who question other people's happiness are pretty sad too."

"Uhyut, I'm not disagreeing with you at all on that one," I say, a bit too loud for the size of the room. Several rabbits scatter, and one shits freshly in the geometric center of the carpet. "Am I still being held against my will?"

"I imagine whatever's wrong with you would probably thrive in a jail cell, and I want no part in nurturing it. I like to sleep with a clean conscience."

"Then I'm going to leave, if it's all the same to you," I say, standing. "And there's nothing wrong with me that you know of; or nothing I'm willing to share."

"Uhyut. We're surely all very normal hereabouts. Nice to see you all grown up and doing things."

I make it through the Stygian rooms of the house and out into the street without finding a decent rejoinder to this remark, or even understanding what exactly Mr. Gould meant. Maybe that was the point. It would be easier to leave if I felt he took me seriously in some way, but I suppose the fundament of our reunion precludes this. He caught me snarling to myself and laughing at my own jokes in his pumpkin patch, as he said, and there's nothing I can do about that. Seeing the way he lives should make me feel better. But I envy the stability of his weirdness too much to feel smug about it. At least he has an income and owns his own home. I suppose it takes a village to raise an idiot, but being acutely jealous of someone who is obviously deranged for how well they've managed to conceal it has the dangerous feeling of a proto-ambition, or something I might look forward to when I'm also old and warped.

The question of whether or not I should be learning something from all this appears to have no good answer, even as I catch myself fiddling with the latch on Cordelia's mailbox on my way home. I don't expect to find much, and assumed I would be able to pass the house without attracting attention to myself. You guessed wrong! a voice seems to shout from inside the mailbox as I draw down the door, and reach inside, allowing my knuckles to knock against vacuity within as I search for some minor plunder to make the evening feel less internecine. The house, a haunt-ed-looking Victorian planted on a sort of hummock above street level, seems to judge me from its perch as I withdraw my forearm from the postbox. What next? An anticlimax feels imminent. Even if I wanted to climb the tree in the backyard, and spy on Cordelia, all the windows are dark, the house appears sullen, and whatever activities of hers might interest me are over for the day.

There's always tomorrow, I think, with a sudden and reckless species of hope. The possibility of resuming my invasion of Cordelia's privacy puts enough of a skip in my step that I'm barely surprised to find Ruby in bed, snoring on my pillow when I arrive home. If anything, her ability to successfully navigate the dark streets of Acheron half-blind proves the superfluity of my presence in her life. How could she even have gotten inside the house at this hour? I grasp the leash still attached to her collar, soiled from a long drag homeward, wondering if I wouldn't be better off with the thing around my neck as I remove it for the night.

*　　*　　*

While fixing a sort of idiot's breakfast the following morning, toast left undone on one side, eggs solemnly burnt, and rubber-ized vegetarian protein strips meant to summarize bacon in some way, a cloud passes the window behind me, darkening the kitch-en to an eclipse-like halftone, and instantly tipping my sangfroid into a kind of free-fall. The locusts have finally come, I think, leaving a trail of raw soy flesh for Ruby to follow outside as I clatter onto the front porch with my breakfast tray, hoping to greet the day with something other than fear.

I'm somewhat relieved when the cloud blocking sunlight from the window turns out to be Boris Huld's back. I haven't seen the town lawyer for years, but I remember him being a large, gregarious man with a vinous smell who didn't seem to do much other than remain on retainer for Acheron Property Management, and lunch loudly at the Herrenhof Inn. But I'd forgotten how large, and also how gregarious; the boards of the house seem to howl as he raises himself from the porch swing to greet me, slapping aside the hand I extend to swallow me in an embrace like the collapse of a circus tent, and sending Ruby after my tray of carelessly prepared food as it tips from my hand onto the lawn.

"Your brother said you were asleep," he says, gesturing toward wherever Grover might be. I'll have to take Huld's word for it. My vision is entirely occupied with a meadow-like expanse of Brook's Brother's charcoal gray. "I didn't think I'd get to welcome you home!"

"Yes, well, I'm here now!" I say, irritating myself by inadvertently mimicking the lawyer's inflection. The hug is unfamiliar and bizarre. I wasn't aware he was a friend of the family. But the wine odor is still there, though with a prandial undercurrent that's either new or I'd forgotten. The man smells like a generally good meal. Good for him.

"Nice to see you!" he says, cupping the back of my head like a chicken egg for a moment before cruising like a forklift toward the porch swing. The chains suspending it from the roof creak a sort of orison as he resettles himself; the lawyer may very well bring the entire house down on our heads. I finally notice my brother, sitting beside Huld in one of the seemingly endless detail of Adirondack chairs he arranges and rearranges around the property, looking a little like a ventriloquist dummy at rest beside the much larger man.

Whatever conversation Huld interrupted to envelope me in his suit jacket and food smell resumes slowly, and I wonder if perhaps he was so glad to see me because I'm being prosecuted. For what, I don't know. I'm certain stealing Officer Laurel's van is probably enough, though questions of jurisdiction abound. But the world is a punitive place, and borrowing a police vehicle is likely an act of terrorism nowadays, even when done for love. I've never heard of Boris Huld doing anything except drafting real estate paperwork for the Castle family, but I suppose he could put me away for a while if he wanted to. I'm oddly okay with the idea of spending a few years in jail, as long as it's somewhere nearby. Northern State Correctional in Newport is like a country club according to my mother's former clients. If I got a cell overlooking the south bay of Lake Memphremagog and a job in the prison library, I could live with that. Mentally preparing for jail time feels important. I don't expect Officer Laurel to let me get away, but haven't completely given up on the possibility. Choosing someplace a little farther off than New Hampshire to send her on a wild-goose chase would have been a good idea. The state border is less than an hour east. She could get lost and find me by accident. Perhaps Huld will represent my side of things if she shows up in town. I should think of way to ask him for help without explaining why I might need it.

"The offer is generous," begins Grover, recapturing the thread of whatever was going on before I appeared. Huld nods with a kind of glee. "Still, I have the store to consider, and there is only so much I'm willing to delegate. Buying in bulk is becoming a sort of thing people do, and I need to oversee the installation, the bins, the ordering. Really, I should have done it years ago when the coop in Montpelier was being built. I allowed my produce manager, Oliver, Oliver Himmel, you know him, of course, to draft the prospectus, and frankly, I'm unsatisfied with the result. This is not the sort of town that can function without its tamari almonds and genocide-free coffee beans. I'm going to decline. But

166

I'm sure you knew I would."

"I did, and I'll only ask you to sell the store to Acheron Property Management once more before leaving," says Huld, actually kicking his feet in the air to build momentum on the porch swing. "Cash in hand, plus a continuing interest, shall we say, since we'll keep the name. People like it, and so do we. Meanwhile, you work seasonally for Releaf Tours. Pick an office. We have many. River view? Not a problem. Pick a title. Executive director, something you like. When the leaves turn, this town becomes the foliage gateway, as we all know, and are tired of hearing, but all gateways need a gatekeeper. Be our St. Peter."

"I need a job," I say. They both ignore me.

"Mr. Castle would never have pressured me like this when he was alive," says my brother. "I can only think Henry has some sort of design worth the time it takes to ask the same question over and over again."

"If he does, I'm not party to it," says Huld, reaching down to scoop Ruby off the porch with one hand and array her on his knee. He plucks a remnant of dry toast from her jowls, places it in his own mouth and begins chewing and scratching her coat with the same cadence. He appears to hear a song. "But then, Henry saw at least ten years ahead by establishing a foliage tourism company, especially in a town where the leaves are no more or less vibrant than anywhere else in central Vermont. In any case, he likes you, and the way you work, and everything you've done for Releaf Tours and believes not that he knows your value, as each man's value is particular to himself ergo: unknowable, but that he can approximate it in some way by offering a position you deserve doing work you do well. He admires you. He doesn't admire just anybody."

"Admiring someone for how they or their property can be

used is the same as not admiring them, Huld. The three of us, you, myself, Henry, are beyond flattery by now; we are an old enough marriage, so to speak. Ergo, to borrow from you, I would ask you to ask Henry to forgo pissing in my ear so he can hand me a towel. I can remain as a consultant with Releaf Tours, and operate my store, or I can help him find someone to fill my position, if necessary. You've given me one option; I'm providing two. I think that's generous."

"I need a job," I say again, watching Huld ignore me, and nod almost cataleptically at Grover, as if whatever is going on is all the same to him. People who nod at things they disagree with are always up to no good in one way or another, but an opportunity seems to be sliding by, something I could dangle in front of Cordelia when the time is right as evidence of upward mobility. I'd work for Satan if it would leave an impression on her.

"I'll certainly pass a portion of that along," continues Huld, his vigor unreduced. "Though I'm sure you can expect, as we all can in one way or another, further knocks on your door, if not from me, than someone with more to gain from the acquisition, one the buffoons from the APM office, for example. I ask you to be kind to them, they know not what they do. You may have guessed this, but I personally see no need for it, Grover; we own most of the buildings on Clamence Street, the Herrenhof, of course, the tour company, the land trust, and now this fitness club out by the quarry. All of this generates what you might call regular wealth for the Castle estate and those of us who manage it on the family's behalf. So please, consider me an emissary rather than advocate of this proposition. I, for one, admire your unspoken but, to me, quite apparent commitment to remain independent of our mutual friend, Henry Hoffmann, while being indispensable to him. Though I love him like the son I never had and didn't want, the man is a kind of human salt mine. And I think he appreciates the irony of being referred to as a small business owner when he in fact owns all the small businesses; or collects their rent, in most cases. It amounts to the same thing, Grover: you resist, therefore you are. One could say I don't, therefore I am not, though by virtue of my position, I think we can both agree resistance would be needlessly contrary. In any case, this is what I believe Henry acknowledges rather than admires, in you, or your position. Perhaps it's a test, the way we tug the handle of a door we've just locked with a key we know to work. I will standby for a list of names, though he won't want them. This is between you and him, I think, I trust."

"I'll do my best to make it attractive," says Grover. I understand maybe half of what he and Huld are discussing, and am astounded neither has noticed me scooting my chair within spitting range of their colloquy, politely suggesting myself. I suddenly wish I had a bell to ring as Grover launches into another explication of what he and Huld both already know. "Though there is lack of talent in this town for anything concrete and realistic. I know you and Henry have to scrape the MBA barrel up at the college in order to find brokers without a degree in the humanities. When I want a nice, artless individual with a bachelor's of science and a CPA license, I end up with Oliver, who studies military history."

"A sad, over-inspired state of things," nods Huld. "Then again, whenever anyone tells me their child is going to law school, I want to say: Oh. They'll grow out of it."

"While on the other hand," continues Grover, "if you want someone to fix you up a multicultural mural for the side of a civic outbuilding, you could be taking bids from the lumpenproletariat for months."

"I would like the job, a job, any job, please," I say, almost or actually begging as Huld rises from the porch swing like a freighter leaving port; the house seems to convulse with joy at his departure. I tug the voluminous hem of his jacket, which does no good, although Grover notices.

"Ah, that's something else," he says, halting Huld who rotates with a peculiar grace at the sound of my brother's voice, as if his feet are affixed to a Lazy Susan, until we both fall within his antumbra. "Walter here needs a thing to do; for money, of course. I don't suppose anything occurs to you?"

"Well now, Wally!" bellows Huld, as if Grover has announced my marriage. "Why didn't you say something?"

"I did, I think," I say, though this is swallowed beneath a petitioning creak from the porch swing as the lawyer reclaims it. I repeat myself, just to be sure we're all on the same page: "I would like a job. Now, or soon."

"Obviously," he begins, speaking to Grover, but looking at me; I feel like a specimen. "We can't just stick Walter here where we want you. It isn't the sort of position one can treat as a sinecure, no offense meant. Unless of course, your brother has commensurate experience of some kind? Logistics, copywriting, customer service?"

"Let's assume he has none," says Grover.

"Well, that solves that. We do always need brokers at Acheron Property Management, though as I look upon your brother here, I find myself wondering whether he knows how to properly knot a necktie."

"He doesn't," says Grover.

"Tell me, Wally, and don't be ashamed: have you ever had a job that required you to appear each work day not as you are, but as your employer wished you to be?"

"I was never entirely sure what anyone who hired me actually wanted," I say.

170

"I see," says Huld, his eyes traveling longitudinally from my head and settling on my feet. "Let me put it to you a different way: are those the only shoes you own?"

"They weren't," I say, examining the foam-rubber sandal with my footprint branded on the sole in a silhouette of dirt; it dangles with a kind of insouciance from my big toe as I raise my foot from the porch for a better look. I'm hoping this answer might be mysterious enough to fool him into giving me a desk job anyway; of course, there's room for improvement here, acres of it, and work to be done. No chance of hiding that. But surely Huld sees my incompetence is only skin deep; a haircut, and a trip to Eddie Bauer would make all the difference.

"I'm not seeing as many possibilities here as I would like," says Huld to Grover while staring into my face as if he expects it to contradict him in some way. "We sort of learned our lesson while Mr. Castle was alive. I mean about putting people where they absolutely do not belong in order to be kind to them and keep them off the streets."

"Off the streets?" I echo.

"You remember Coach Dennis, of course?" continues Huld. "Nice enough man, absolutely incompetent in terms of real estate, but no one much minded since he kept the girls soccer team in the state championships or something like that; I don't follow sports, local or otherwise. But when it came out about the pictures he was taking, all his star players if you remember, and I know you do, lying in their flower beds or hanging from the eaves like an alley cat with his camera aimed at some poor girl's bedroom window. Well, I'm sure you see my point; charity has a place, I suppose, around the holidays and whatnot. We just need to make sure we're not humping the leg that kicks, so to speak."

"I don't want to take pictures of anybody doing anything,"

I say, wondering if Huld somehow caught me eyeing the oak in Cordelia's side yard the other night.

"I know you don't, Wally, but suppose you did? How would we look? I want to believe you, but there is always human nature to drop a flowerpot on your head when you least expect it."

"I promise I am not a deviant," I say.

"I don't know that there is any correlation between Dennis' vocational dissatisfaction and his deviance," mutters Grover.

"Actually, most serial killers are found working beneath their potential in positions that afford them little credibility or power, and thus they act out," I say, startled to find I'm defending the wrong side of the argument; if Ruby were not lying across my feet, I would try to kick myself in the face. Grover looks shocked, Huld nods like an oil derrick.

"Glad you see my point, Willy," he says, his mind apparently wandering far afield enough to preclude the lawyer from addressing me even semi-correctly. "It simply won't do, and I apologize for giving you the impression that it would. However, if something which doesn't require licensure, or basic clothes, skills, know-how, that sort of thing comes up, you'll be the first person I call."

As though to provide an exclamation, Huld's phone rings. He takes the call on the front lawn beside the birdbath, speaking loud enough for Grover and me to follow the conversation from the porch. My brother says nothing, but watches me as if I'm drifting far from shore on a wedge of pack ice as Huld roars from yard:

"He said what I said he would said, say rather, and several things more…You see, it isn't up to me. My role here is clear, Henry. I'm not a magician…I knew that joke was coming; it's been in the pipeline for weeks, but if you really thought I belonged at a children's birthday party, we wouldn't be having this repartee, would we now? I'm not worth the time it takes to bully because I am by the nature of my work, contract, and interests on your side...He isn't interested, as I said...Yes, correct, which leaves us exactly as we were before: solvent. Be proud...Before the what? Ah! I thought you said 'ball.' Before the fall...Right, sounds like a have-not proclaiming himself, I wouldn't write it into your charter just yet, still...Well, no, here we are again, with the same sort of question. When a thing doesn't work, you're on to the next, without waiting for us, your thralls, to catch up. To answer you: I'm still here because Wally, Walter, you know him, Grover's younger...Yes, that Walter. He's in town, seeking employment, and I was...Well, we sort roundtabled the idea of him brokering at the real estate office, but that went the way of the buffalo, quickly but quietly, I mean, after Dennis we must... Interesting, he made the same claim. However, we're talking not only paying for the courses, the exam, the license, the board fees, et alia, but an entire new wardrobe...Yes, it is really as bad as that...Have you ever known me to exaggerate in matters of deportment, Henry? He looks...I understand, but he looks like something out of National Geographic, a wartime issue...Even so, as your attorney I advise...Now, wait...Ah...Yes...Well, it hadn't occurred to me, frankly, it's a new project or venture, as you said, and I've had the feeling you want me to stay out of it, so I have, but...Right, I see...For once I would like us to forsake assigning blame whenever a good idea emerges that you thought of first. It undermines the nature of solving a prob-lem...How?...By pointing out the people who didn't solve it, Henry...Right...Fine...I'll check...Wally! Do you enjoy work-ing with people?"

"Say yes," says Grover. I make an affirmative gesture at Huld, who continues his call.

"He says he does…Any issue wearing a uniform?" he shouts across the lawn.

"I'd prefer not to," I shout back; Grover winces in the foreground.

"No problem with the uniform," says Huld into the phone, giving me the thumbs up. "When would you like…Now? Of course, I'm sure Grover will help him get up there…Why must I bring him? Henry, I'm driving a price point BMW, your compound is on a two-track logging road without cell phone reception…Sorry, yes, I'm sorry, I won't call it a compound again…I understand, but if you want to talk to me, that can be done as we're doing it now, can't it? So, why…Good…Fine…Yes…I'll tell him."

Huld seems to be fighting the impulse to toss his phone into the underbrush as he returns to the porch.

"You have an interview," he says to me, recovering himself. "And I am giving you a lift to it. Shall we?"

"That was Henry," says Grover.

"It was," says Huld, to me. "I believe you know him. You went to school together, yes?"

"We did," I say, trying to separate what I know of Henry Hoffmann from Cordelia's fascination with him throughout the years of our mutual schooling. Tall, dark, and handsome Henry, yes, I know you: your appearance was enough to disarrange an entire month's worth of planning. I still see it: Cordelia's seventeenth birthday, a picnic basket on my arm, sloughing line from the drift boat I'd rented from Morton Downing for three packs of Parliaments and watching the lee of a small island in the remotest bay of Kranion Pond, for this was our destination. The day suggested rain in a ribbon of murk above the mountains, true north. No problem, as in addition to the wine, baguette, and soft European cheese I'd stowed in the boat, I also brought camping gear, having even purchased a tent, which promised to be waterproof, for the occasion. I had something sheltered and gently erotic in mind, followed by stillness; I saw myself reading her John Bellairs by the light of a Coleman lantern, naked in a bed of sleeping bags zipped together. This is what I imagined until Henry appeared, riding his bicycle down the access road to the pond like the lead horseman of my private apocalypse.

I knew Cordelia would hale him, and I knew he would stop, if only to see what could be gained from it all. This is what I saw in him and she never did; the interest of a python in something small and willing to scurry. It didn't matter, because before I could distract her, she asked Henry if he wanted to go for a boat ride, and there they were drinking the wine I'd stolen from my parents' kitchen in the forecastle of the drift boat as I paddled them like a Gondolier toward the summer home on the far shore where Henry was house sitting. I still don't know who owned it, but there was a Jacuzzi and sauna; so an excuse for Cordelia to strip naked and caper around the place in only a towel for most of the afternoon, while Henry fixed whiskeys for himself and me, and ignored her. I don't know whether he did this out of sympathy for me, or just assumed I would probably want one after noticing the camping gear stowed in the boat, and realizing his part in botching a perfectly reasonable, perfectly private birthday celebration. I've come to think it was neither; he was fixing himself a drink, so he might as well fix two, and since he had no interest whatsoever in Cordelia, there was no reason to confuse her with small favors. Other people from our school showed up; she may have called them. Henry didn't seem to care or mind, but withdrew with me when the Jacuzzi became a sort of cauldron full of naked people we both knew. He and I sat on the dock with the bottle of whiskey between us, watching an evening storm approach the property. This is the closest he will ever come to an apology, I remember thinking just before I puked into what I thought was the water, but turned out to be part of Morton Downing's boat holding my camping gear. It started to rain, and I started to cry as Henry hoisted me to my feet, and said something about how I could stay in the house if I wanted, but the rest of those fucking kids had to go. I had no choice, and neither did Cordelia for that matter; we awoke around 7AM the next morning, somehow in the same guest room, twined together on the floor, with our heads roaring, and she thanked me for a wonderful birthday as I rowed us back to where we'd left the car. I felt accidentally successful, which is to say, not successful at all.

"Fantastic!" says Huld, spinning a ring of modern-looking keys around a finger the size of a zucchini. "I'm sure you two have lots of catching up to do! Let's shove off then. Big day for you, big day for me as well, lots to do. Come along! I'm parked some fucking where nearby. Let's go see where exactly."

As Huld leads me out of the yard, I look down at myself, my flip-flops, the abused looking athletic shorts remaining from my brief middle-school career in intramural sports, the sleeveless t-shirt, advertising the Shade A Somali Foundation, freshly stained from breakfast; what kind of job could I possibly be applying for today? I check my reflection unwisely in the window of a parked car, and find that my hair resembles a hat, as Grover said, and after running into the lightpole the evening before, my glasses sit crookedly on my face. I glance back at my brother; Ruby is cradled in his lap, chewing a filament of scrambled eggs with a calm relish. He makes an encouraging gesture, which seems to say: nothing can go wrong that hasn't already.

Paranoia is Huld driving the Mt. Abandon access road as if he expects it to attack at any moment, and leave us stranded in the foothills outside Acheron. Two men and a defunct BMW lost to the palette of old growth forest bulwarking the road to either side, and laid cloak-like across the shoulder of the mountain before us. A sketchy but complete grid of the town is visible through the back window. Whenever a stone clinks in the wheel well, Huld winces and checks the rear view, as if wondering whether, in the event of some disaster, we will be able to walk the five miles back to the retreating town before nightfall.

I'm uncomfortable as a passenger; his nervousness makes me nervous, and something about being isolated in the lawyer's company makes me feel like a pet. Here I sit, I think, being taxied to a reunion with a man against whom I have always finished second. Henry Hoffmann's perennial dismissal of Cordelia was matched in fervor only by my devotion to her, which made me feel like the sort of person who goes around a bar finishing drinks people leave behind. Walter Ratliff: He'll take what you can get! Henry seems to have done rather well for himself in the intervening years, and today, he may even give me a job. How lucky am I? It would be easier to hate him for this if current circumstances didn't cast him as the objectively better choice. For once, I'm glad Cordelia isn't here.

Huld has been steadily decelerating since leaving my brother's house around 10AM, transforming what should be a twenty-minute drive into a what feels like a New England safari; he taps the brakes when a brace of warring blue jays flutter across our path, and nearly guides the BMW into a drainage ditch as a whitetail deer flits from a stand of birch onto the road so far ahead of the car that I initially mistake the doe for a pony. I have some idea of where we're going; at this rate, we'll be there by sunset, and though the land is comforting and familiar, I find myself wishing I'd brought something to read. A strange thought when I consider the afternoons spent beneath the single tree outside the gates of Long Island University, muddling through *The Rise and Fall of the Third Reich*, and wishing for the narcotic calm of these woods as Flatbush Avenue ululated behind me. Perennial dissatisfaction marks me as man, I think, wondering how this would sound spoken aloud, or sung. Huld himself ultimately limits the chance of getting any serious reading done. His loquacity seems engorged by the baleful possibility of his car making it up the mountainside never to come down again, stranding us within musket shot of town. Two idiots driving a luxury automobile up a logging road within city limits isn't really the stuff of Gary Paulsen, but then: it's possible the lawyer has never missed a meal in his life. For a man of his size, this could be crucial. For some, the razor's edge is only the distance from hand to mouth.

Just as I feel myself careening toward pity for my chauffeur, he takes a right-hand turn, and surrenders the car with a clunk like the hitching of a freight elevator to a washed-out two-track slithering deeper into the forest. The tires spit gravel, seeking purchase, as Huld attempts to advance us up the mountainside toward the former Boy Scout camp, the history of which he has been delineating for the past half hour.

"After they closed it back in...1962? 63? Doesn't matter, you weren't born then and don't know, but after they closed it, the place got bought by some silly, frivolous charlatans with big ideas from out of state. Now where were they from? Yellow Springs? Missoula? I can't remember, but possibly somewhere as far off the fucking reservation as Portland. Oregon, not Maine...or possibly Maine. Somewhere with a surplus of solidly middle-class, homogeneous college dropouts and a job market bad enough to make them believe forming a self-sustaining community of unemployed people is a superior idea; a revolution whistling away in a teakettle. Anyway, one of them had family money, I believe, and wanted to make the camp into a sort of ashram or commune or analogous nonsense. Bake bread, fly kites, swim naked, live tax free; sort of like a liberal arts campus without a college attached. When Henry bought it, their sign, or talisman, or juju mural was still in place. He's replaced it with his own now. That may have been the first thing he did after receiving the keys; hubris for Henry is the sort of no man's land in which he feels perfectly at home...What was I saying? Ah, yes, the former sign. When I was initially forced to drive up here and give my opinion of the property, an opinion Henry ignored entirely except in terms of organizing the papers, the gate still had 'Frith' painted above it."

"I've heard that before," I reply. "I think it means-"

"Yes, Henry seemed to know what it meant too, but didn't get attached to it, as I said. I, on the other hand, don't know what it means, and don't care right now, Wally. We're approaching a nasty bit. Hold tight."

To what? I wonder, glancing around car's interior for steadiment, and finding only the lawyer's arm sitting stiffly between us like a falconet awaiting a cannoneer. Does he expect me to clutch him? I wonder further, as the front tires drop with a kind of animus into a cleaved section of road; my jaw clicks, and something partially detaches from the chassis and begins dragging beneath it. This could spell the kind of trouble Huld has imagined since leaving pavement; an exciting possibility. I examine him for signs of distress, but his eyes remain fixed on the road ahead rather than the town in his rearview. Something has changed. Or everything is the same, and I just assumed I knew what Huld thought, but was wrong about it. The second of these seems likelier.

"If you stop," I begin, wanting to appear helpful in case some tension I'm unaware of is mounting; I seem to be mostly wrong about things today. "I'll get out and see what that is."

"What what is?"

"Whatever is underneath your car. Making that noise."

"Doesn't matter. If it falls off, I'll collect it on the way down. Nothing I can't bill the estate for. Damages, damages, damages," he clucks, doing a wonderful job of cheering himself up. He's actually singing Warren Smith by the time we clatter to a halt outside an imposing metal gate set in a grid of humming electrified wire; the fence extends off into the woods to either side, and is around nine feet high. All of this suggests the word 'compound.'

"*Somebody saw you at the break of day*," warbles Huld, well enough:

"Dining and a-dancing in the cabaret,
He was long and tall,
He had plenty of cash,
He had a red Cadillac
and a black moustache,
He held your hand and he sang you a song,
Who you been lovin' since I been gone?
Who you been lovin' since I been gone?"

"Henry opening some sort of preserve?" I say to Huld's empty seat. I'm so occupied by both the fence and trying distance myself from identifying with Smith's rhetoric that I didn't notice the lawyer leave the car to fiddle with a keypad planted in the gate's left-hand abutment. Above this hangs the answer to my question, more or less. A neutral sign quietly lit by three small gooseneck fixtures proclaims:

"He changes the fucking combination each week for security reasons, of course, because that's not in the least neurotic," blusters a returning Huld from somewhere outside the vehicle. The lawyer drops into the driver's seat with an elemental defeat, tipping the car just enough for me to roll into the crook of the arm he's using to dial Henry's number, presumably. I'm not exactly trapped, but neither am I at liberty to move around as I would like. Huld doesn't seem to notice my body clamped to his chest as he completes his call. It's an odd position; my ear is close enough to Huld's stomach to hear him digesting whatever he ate last, and I myself feel partially swallowed, Jonah-like perhaps.

"Yes, we're here," says Huld, waving through the windshield at what must be a camera somewhere in the trees. "I don't know because you didn't tell me, so if you could just…"

The gate opens in complete silence, and Huld pockets his phone, releasing me.

"Think of it this way," he begins, as if we were having a conversation. "Our monuments do not make history, but alter history in order to show those who come after us not who we were, but who we wish them to believe we were. If you look at what's been done here as Henry's cenotaph, it makes far more sense, though not from a legal perspective. However, we are speaking grandly, or globally; he inherited the works of Joshua Castle, and now he must build his baths of Caracalla, his Theodosian walls, his Hagia Sophia, or his…whatever this is, really. He hasn't allowed me past the parking area since after he began renovating the property, and he'll probably make you promise not to share anything you see inside with me, and frankly, I'd also prefer you didn't. I'd rather sign the paychecks in hell than share its joys with those consigned to a life of eternal damnation. So at this point, it's between him, Mr. Todes, and Mr. Steige."

"Are they friends of his?" I ask.

"Investors. Some mongrel breed of European. I only met them once and only then because I told Henry I wouldn't help him move this forward until I was introduced to all parties involved in financing it. There was a lot of money needed, and yet, it kept appearing. Henry makes it impossible to trust him. I began feeling like a secretary to a bank robber or something. Anyway, no idea where they flew in from. One said Belgrade, the other said Zagreb, both of which sounded like lies. Frankly, the more time I spent around them, the harder it became to tell them apart. I have no idea where Henry finds these people, but he's apparently able to produce them at will. Ah, here we are. Welcome to Camp Crystal Lake. Abandon all hope ye who enter, etc."

Through a break in the trees, the BMW enters a dirt parking area filled with other performance automobiles; Audi, Mercedes, Porche, Volvo, Alfa Romeo, Rolls Royce, Aston Martin, Maserati, a vintage Ferrari Testarossa, a Lamborghini Diablo, and a Bugatti with its tailpipe missing. All of them appear similarly bemerded from the journey up the mountain. Huld parks beside a Bentley with a missing side mirror.

"The cars of the clientele, or so I'm told," he says, shuttering the engine. "No reason to lie about that, I suppose. Is that a Maybach over there? Fuck the world, Willy. Let's get this over with."

As we're leaving the car, Henry Hoffmann emerges from one of two gates sunk in a tall wooden fence hemming the parking area, and, I assume, the rest of the camp. Yes, it's him; even at the distance of a parking lot and many years, I instantly recognize the tall, broad-shouldered, handsome young man who not only

siphoned the lion's share of Cordelia's mercurial interest, but also
made something of himself in the meanwhile. I spent most of
high school panning the horizon like a periscope operator for any
sign of him, and now, here we are: master and man. Henry wants
to offer you a job, I think, trying to talk myself into viewing
whatever happens next neutrally as he crosses the parking area
toward Huld and me. He would like to give you some money.
Don't take his success personally. I mean: successes.

As Henry approaches, I'm allowed to gloat for only a moment
at the circlet of fat girding his torso, until I realize I've mistak-
en the child he's carrying in a chest harness for the genesis of a
paunch. A family man. What a surprise. No one bothered men-
tioning this. Nice to see him off the market, albeit a decade or so
too late. No matter. Wishes granted in the rear-view still count,
I suppose.

As we shake hands, the child glares at me through Henry's
eyes without blinking from beneath a swarthy, Hitlerish crest of
hair. I have the disturbing sense of Henry wearing a t-shirt of
himself, and also that the child can speak, but chooses not to,
scowling at me with the steadiness of a gargoyle instead.

"Thanks for coming up on short notice," he says, neither unfriendly nor welcoming, but reptilian, and calculable. As before,
as always, it seems. "The last time I saw you was the funeral, I
believe."

"You were there?" I ask, surprised.

"I drove by," he says, turning to Huld, but speaking to me.
"We're going to talk for a moment. Then Huld will leave, and I'll
meet you inside. He doesn't come in."

"I told him that," says Huld, already walking back toward his
car. "You didn't need to tell him again."

Henry says nothing, but purveys a business card with the door code somewhere on it, presumably, and stalks off toward the lawyer with the mute, demoniac infant rocking against his torso like an egg sac. As they pass me, the child opens and closes its toothless little mouth in a silent snarl, eliciting a reflexive, anxious bark from somewhere in my throat. I haven't seen Henry for over a decade, I think. And here I am, already on the defense and yipping at his newborn. This will not help me make friends or get a job.

Huld firing up his BMW thankfully covers the noise I've made, but the silent snarl may as well have been a punch in the throat. I wasn't over-prepared for the interview, but I'd managed to cultivate a reasonable calm during the drive up the mountain, a sort of collectedness someone dumber than Henry might mistake for genuine, and which he might be willing to settle for, depending on how badly he needs my kind of help. But it's all out the window now thanks to junior; something about the child demands a human sacrifice, or a slow march toward the temple, at the very least.

To distract myself from the acute menace of Henry's firstborn I try to count the cameras nesting amid wreathes of concertina wire atop the fence, wondering briefly if my brother has conspired with him and Huld to jail me for the time being, until they decide what to do with me. There is a very good, and very real possibility I won't make the decision myself, and I'm sure Grover knows that; I'd lock me up until a solution could be found. I'm mostly unmoved by the chance of all of this being an elaborate trap. I peck at the keypad affixed to the door, knowing I'll go quietly and gently with whomever or whatever awaits me on the other side.

This turns out to be Isidore Castle wearing a khaki uniform, peaked cap, and hobnailed jackboots like some costumed and revenant instantiation of my past shuttled forward in time to teach me a very specific lesson. Are you to be my warden? I wonder, trying not to gape like a sport fish as he reaches around me to close the gate. I haven't seen or thought about the late Joshua Castle's son since the time we attended Acheron Union School together, and even then, he was a few years ahead of me, and didn't appear to do much other than wedge his ungainly form in a corner of the lunchroom to play Magic: The Gathering and eat rufescent Jell-O with others who couldn't afford not to have anything in common. Even when he and his retinue left school early in period costumes to attend the renaissance faire in olde Waterbury with someone's parent's minivan standing in for noble steeds or a palanquin or whatever, I quietly envied their self-containment. I never made Isidore's radar then, so he has no reason to recognize me now; he only made mine because my father was somehow involved in preventing him from being held back a grade towards the twilight of his junior year, and it came up during a family dinner. This is the only time I'm aware of that Joshua Castle and my father had any direct communication; dad said he was an ass, but a nice man, without expanding on either thought.

Something about Isidore's current deportment screams middle management; he's taller than Henry or myself, but the uniform fits poorly. The cuffs of the shirt and pants creep toward mid wrist and ankle. The coat breaks no father than the bottom of his ribcage, and seems to creak across his shoulders as he takes the card Henry gave me, and burns it after closing the door.

"He insists," says Isidore, meaning probably Henry, as he combs the ashes against the wall of the stockade in which we're standing with the toe of his boot, and gestures for me to follow him.

I visited the summer camp during middle school, long before

Henry's renovations or security measures, and remember a small pond with several abandoned cabins arranged in a crescent along the shore, and a dining hall and staff buildings planted among the shade trees on the petticoat. From what I can see at my end of stockade, Henry seems to have kept everything mostly the same. The weirdness of whatever happens up here has yet to emerge. I follow Isidore through another coded door, in a kind of gatehouse built beside the fence, and into a modernist reception area with Barcelona chairs, sculptural house plants, and windows high enough to prohibit a view of anything going on outside. "Looks like a waiting room in the Weimar republic," I say to Isidore's back as he retreats through another door and down a corridor. I pause, expecting him to chuckle, but hear nothing, wondering if there is anything poetical in awaiting laughter that never arrives. The non-echo of misplaced pithiness seems to mock me as I bumble after him down the hallway, passing another clerestory of high, viewless windows on the left, and a series of rooms on the right. The first contains only a stainless steel table and two chairs bolted to the floor on either side of it; the second is some kind of medical office, with an exam table, scale, wall-mounted blood pressure cuff, doctor things; a bank of lockers occupies an entire wall of the third room, along with several dry and empty shower stalls. The entire building is silent, weird, and morose, though which of these qualities contributes more to the other is a probably the sort of robust trilemma that would delight Henry; everything I've seen so far seems deliberately constructed to confuse and menace anyone on the wrong side of it, like some entrepreneurial reimagining of the Winchester mansion. I halfway expect to find doors opening to brick walls and stairways leading into the ceiling. Henry's house is shaped like my paranoia, I think, hoping to comfort myself by rehearsing my reasons for

186

being here at all. But even after following Isidore up a narrow flight of stairs to the second story, and being asked to take a seat in what I can only assume is Henry's office, I have to check the space around my chair to make sure it isn't positioned above a trapdoor before sitting down.

"We ask all new hires to please fill this out," says Isidore from somewhere across the broad desk dominating the center of the room. Something like a manuscript slides across it and lands in my lap, though I can't see a thing. If not for a large picture window behind the desk overlooking the pond and cabins semi-circling it, the room would have no natural light source. I test the weight of whatever is in my lap, and blink at Isidore silhouetted against the window as I ask what it is.

"Mostly stuff for the background check, and the drug test. Hair and urine on that one. Also, a basic physical, but we do need some blood work, and a TB test, plus reference information, obviously, proof of auto insurance, citizenship, and a permanent address. You know. Pretty standard."

"If you and Henry were running a daycare maybe."

"That's not what we're doing up here."

"I think I know that, which is why this-" I say, tossing the manuscript back on the desk with a thump, "is not something I will do."

"You wanted the job," says Isidore, moving straight from reproach to bargaining. "There's also something in there about the 401K."

"I don't know what the job is enough to want it, or why I need a 401K."

"For to someday retire with. You don't want to work forever."

"I don't want to work at all, frankly."

"That may be a problem, going forward," says Isidore, investigating the dimness of the room as if he expects it to produce a remedy to all this, my Zugzwang. "I won't tell Henry you told me that if you promise to do your best."

"So I'm hired then?"

The question appears to confuse him. Rather than answer, he glances at something to my right, which turns out to be Henry and baby, loitering in the shadows like a dimorphic pair of Vesper bats.

"As I said earlier, Isidore: we can dispense with the pro forma bullshit on this one, please," says Henry, taking hold of the manuscript as he steps out of the darkness, and dropping it in Isidore's lap. "Get rid of it."

"The HR folks in town won't like it, Henry," says Isidore, standing up in a cascade of loose pages. "It's your call, as always, I know that. But they're going to ask me to explain it because I'm supposed to be your office manager, and if the paperwork isn't in order, the office downtown turns into a real snakepit. They're like a gang of bullies from a musical comedy. They speak in private slang and have nicknames for each other. I can't just give those guys nothing and expect them to swallow it if you want to add someone to the payroll."

"How'd the last one do? The guy we hired from out west."

"Oh fine; a disorderly conduct charge for setting a trashcan on fire in Spearfish, South Dakota. I asked him about it during the follow-up, and he said he was cold, which makes sense to me. Also, some traffic tickets. But a model citizen, otherwise."

"So Xerox his materials and resubmit them to the people in town if you need something immediately. Just change the name to Walter Ratliff. And don't look at me like that. If the HR people even notice, which they won't, tell them to talk to me after they clean out their desks, and I'll be glad to explain everything. And don't forget, Isidore: You are my office manager, meaning the downtown people answer to you, not the other way around. If you think it's becoming too tribal over there for your comfort, have them eat lunch in shifts, and rearrange their desks to face the walls. You can also remove the coffee pot, and water cooler. Make them bring their own, or drink from the tap. Also, you can take that off now. Change downstairs, and leave it in locker twelve for now."

Henry points at the khaki uniform, and Isidore plucks the lapel as if he expects it to produce music as he exits the office, the sheaf of invasive paperwork cradled beneath this foreshortened sleeve. Henry and his child turn their attention to me. Their heads move in a peculiar sort of harmony, as though attached to the same swivel.

"I asked him to model it for you," he says flatly, taking Isidore's seat behind the desk. "Just to provide you with some idea of what I expect at its most basic. Of course, I couldn't remember your size, and I had no idea it would fit Isidore that way, but it always pays to make a clown of people every so often because it shows them you can."

"Promising words from a potential employer."

"Current employer," corrects Henry. "Isidore has come a long way. You may or may not know that, but now you do. It turns out organization and basic accounting is something he can do well enough. I spent many years watching him be good at nothing, but knew I would I have to someday find work for him, as per my obligation to his father and the estate. An ugly position to find myself in, Walter. But, as you saw, he knows his duty well enough to allow me to dress him like a fool, or forge paperwork when I ask him to; the phrase for this is latent potential. I like to think I can excise the dormant possibilities of a person who has accidentally given up on himself."

"It sounds like I've been hired without realizing it."

Rather than answer, Henry suggests we take a tour of the camp. On his chest, the baby grins at me, toothless behind the corona of a pacifier.

I remember the summer camp as the first place I discovered my inability to cultivate male friendship. After the Frithians were evicted somewhere around my third or fourth birthday, the property sat vacant in the foothills outside Acheron, and became a kind of den of iniquity for the area high school. Those with a driver's license tightened their hubs and ferried those without one up the mountainside on Friday evenings, national holidays, and the odd Wednesday, as I recall from my penultimate visit, sometime before the turn of the millennium, when things between Lily and me were getting serious, according to her. I remember wondering how serious anything between fifteen-year-olds could be, and after reaching the sort of conclusion I couldn't share with her or act upon, I decided to wait it out.

She was the only reason I was invited along, and the driver, Wayne, a lank woodchuck who was a friend of Lily's family through a maple syrup concern, initially balked at bringing me. He was clearly worried I might upset the male to female ratio he'd been counting on for the evening, but said something about not having enough beer for me, even though five out of ten people he drove up the mountain later that night sat squarely on the cases of Loup Garou sliding around the back of his pickup like milk crates on a frozen duck pond. Swine, I thought, as Lily watched me bounce around the rear of Wayne's truck and smiled witlessly through the back window; even after she told him we were dating and he agreed to let me come, I was still made to sit in the back with the three other guys, and two girls who didn't interest Wayne. He framed this seating condition as if it was chivalrous on his part, through it was clear he just enjoyed portaging a cabful of girls up Mt. Abandon like some provincial sultan towing his seraglio around in a forage wagon. For once, I was glad Lily wanted me, and not someone else, someone like Wayne, who would likely be on the outside of all this if he wasn't a licensed driver who was also willing to steal alcohol from the bottle redemption center where he worked weekends.

I'm certain every American town has a bit of forgotten geography where young adults go to practice being bad older adults. In Julian Falls, this was a particular Indian burial mound excavated deep in the woods abutting the St. Margaret's campus. In other towns it might be a disused sawmill or the exit ramp of an abandoned highway, places where roads terminate, and sound doesn't carry. I don't know why these areas attract teenagers; probably for the same reason children build forts out of couch cushions. In any case, as we debarked from Wayne's truck and began milling around the crescent of cabins banding the pond at Camp Frith, I wondered why we never went anywhere without an abundance of decay. I suppose she means for us to sleep in there, I thought, watching Lily carry two sleeping bags into cabin five, which listed so much it appeared polygonal in the composite light of a fading autumn evening, and the hungry glow of a fire kindled by the shore. My fussiness over Lily making our bed in what looked like a goat shed was probably derived from the earlier kerfuffle with Wayne; the truth was I would sleep in a haunted house for sex. No problem. Lust blinded by inexperience will always triumph over fear.

I decided I was going to enjoy myself, and only discovered this was impossible after opening a king can of Loup Garou, and waving to Lily on the other side of the pond where she stood with the other four girls. At some point between leaving the truck and opening a beer, the outing became gendered. I stood with the men, Wayne, and three others who may have all been named Kyle, dowsing for a common topic. The Kyles all played soccer together, a sport I respected for its simplicity and knew nothing about, and Wayne's cousin refereed some of their games down at the Castle Memorial rec field, where Wayne also played softball on the weekends. So there they were, discussing calls, the condition of the facilities, and the greater, wider world of sports, while I became accidentally drunk enough to suggest we all shotgun a beer. One of the Kyles thought this was a great idea, which won over the other two, forcing Wayne to agree, since he wasn't the sort of person to let a moving train pass him by without leaping aboard. He was also the only one of us with a set of keys to puncture the bottom of the cans, since no one in Acheron locks their doors, and Wayne was the only licensed driver. I have accidentally created a hero, I remember thinking, as the Kyles exchanged high-fives with our chauffeur after he produced his car keys like a casino magician ejecting a dove from his sleeve, and set about using them to stab our cans.

Shotgunning was something I had only heard of, but it seemed like the sort of useless activity that would make me less conspicuous in a group of young men my own age; I was committed to appearing normal at all costs, not so much for Lily's sake, but my own. I didn't have any male friends except Grover, and hadn't since puberty. I was out of practice, and it was my fault. The truth was I was interested entirely in women, and the mystery they seemed to suggest. I liked intimacy, or what I mistook for it. Most guys my age were as intimate as a cinderblock. Nothing about this bothered me, but I didn't want to seem maladjusted or socially incompetent in case other theoretical women found it unattractive; I knew Lily and I weren't forever. This may be both my earliest and final example of planning for the future. My father spent most of his time with my mother, and they both seemed happy, so I assumed my life would be at least as good as theirs, if I could only avoid revealing how little I valued the friendship of people like Wayne, or the Kyles, for that matter.

I knew I was going to be sick after I'd sucked half the foaming, malted beverage through a fingernail shaped aperture in the base of the can, and tottered vaguely beyond the cast of the firelight so no one would notice me vomit in the pond. But they heard it, of course, which provoked Wayne to begin calling me 'three beer queer' when I returned from being sick. The ladies had joined us around the bonfire, which may have had something to do with it; women love a man who kicks a cripple. The sobriquet generated laughter the first time, less the second, and a polite eddy the third, which didn't stop Wayne from using it over and over again, though it made even the Kyles uncomfortable. Lily seemed uneasy too, but not enough to tell Wayne to be quiet; maybe because he got the beer and gave us a ride, she figured he'd earned the right to pick his jester for the evening. I didn't need her to stand up for me, but I wanted her to, because I had the feeling if I did it myself, it would turn into a fight I would lose. Wayne was older, bigger, and generally more interested in coming out on top of things; anyone could see that. So, I remember thinking: we're all cowards, and this is how we have fun. Three beer queer it is.

I didn't know what else to do aside from sit quietly on a fallen log at an oblique distance from Wayne and wait for Lily to take me to bed in the cabin she'd chosen earlier. I knew what to expect, and was willing to wait it out, even if this meant watching her laugh at Wayne when he pretended to throw a full can of Loup Garou at my face from across the fire. It didn't matter to me; after vomiting in the pond, bleary smugness gradually overtook me as I watched him bloviate past the flames, struggling to make himself relevant to the bevy of young women whinnying at him, relevant beyond the twin dragons of his car and the alcohol he'd provided. It was clear Wayne didn't want to sleep alone, but lacked the courage to ask for what he wanted, and hated me because I didn't have to; he'd seen Lily claim cabin four. Desperation howls the loudest, I thought, allowing myself to pity Wayne, even when he referred to my father as a 'tard farmer.'

He looked at me across the fire to gauge my reaction to this remark, and something in my face must have provided a clue as to what I thought of him, because he asked rhetorically what I was smiling about, though I didn't realize I'd smiled. And before I could answer, a can of Loup Garou clonked off my forehead, opening a small but sanguine cut above my right eyebrow; a filament of bloody beer slithered down the side of my face and dripped off my chin, and Wayne stopped laughing when he realized no one else was.

A sort of dead man's silence ensued while everyone awaited a cue as to how they should feel about this. The Kyles shook their common heads, and the girls Wayne had failed to impress joined them. Lily came to sit beside me, but I was already on my feet, and walking into the night, back toward the access road. She said something, but didn't follow me, and I was glad. After getting sick, some part of me wanted an excuse to leave. I was mostly interested in sleeping in my own bed, in my own house, without having to remain in a single, intimate seeming position for the entire night so Lily didn't feel used in the morning. My working idea of love involved practical discomfort, but it seemed like a fair enough bargain. If Lily was willing to have sex with me, I'd let her fall asleep on my shoulder without moving all through the night, even if I

194

awoke in the morning feeling like a hemiplegic. At this point in my life, everything still seemed like a more or less even trade.

Also, the drama of the moment pleased me; there was something primitive and martyr-like in forsaking the comfort of fire and companionship to stalk off alone into night, though this faded somewhat when I reached Wayne's truck, and saw the lights of Acheron below. I still had five miles to go before reaching town. It was already cold, and the wind blowing down from the mountainside stung the fresh wound clotting above my eyebrow. It would be an uncomfortable walk, but as I mentioned: drama was in the air. I could see Wayne's car keys swaying in the moonlight, forgotten in the driver's side door of the truck when he'd returned for another case of beer, and I knew I was too young for anything I did to have a serious consequence. Still, my experience driving was limited to evenings spent in my mother's Saab, with her reminding me a learner's permit was not a license from the passenger seat, and she was right. I got scared before reaching Acheron's city limits, and parked Wayne's truck at a service station on the town's outskirt, where I called Grover from a payphone. When he asked me if everything was okay, I just said I needed him to pick me up at the gas station, but when he arrived, and found me sitting in Wayne's idling pickup, smelling like beer with my face bleeding, I told him the rest of what happened.

I spent the time between my phone call and his arrival trying to guess what my brother would say or do, and thought I had a pretty good idea. But when he told me we had to bring back Wayne's truck so the others could make it down the mountain tomorrow morning, and asked me if I was okay to drive, I discovered my grasp of my sibling's predictability was not as firm as I thought. Grover followed me back up the access road, his headlights impelling me as they nodded in Wayne's rearview. I fully expected to have my ass kicked by him and members of his retinue for stealing the truck, but I wondered if returning it would mitigate the severity of this.

However, when we reached the gates of Frith, and Wayne, alerted by the sound of our twin engines, came lurching out of the underbrush into the headlights with a hatchet in his hand, looking like a member of the Jackson-Whites, I understood he was the sort of man who didn't need the excuse I'd given him. He ran toward the cab, and began yanking at the door I'd locked while screaming at me through the window. Since it was his truck, I figured he wouldn't break it to get at me, and I was willing to sit in the cab until he sobered up or felt like negotiating. But I realized this would be unnecessary when Wayne entered the cast of the headlights, backing away from my brother. I saw Grover slap the hatchet out of his hand, and give him a two-handed shove into the darkness. There was suddenly more at stake than I'd realized, and watching it happen from the safety of the truck seemed far worse than being part of it, or helping Grover do what needed to be done. I wasn't sure what this was, but I knew I wouldn't forgive myself if I let him do it alone. I unlocked the door with enough time to see my brother clamp a hand around Wayne's throat, and walk him backward into the trees. I didn't know what to think about what I'd just seen, so I sat in the cab with the radio playing 'Hey Jealousy' and the door open, and only receiving a partial answer from Grover after he reached over me and switched off the ignition in Wayne's truck, and said he would take me home now. I had no idea how long he was gone; probably no more than five minutes, but long enough for me to grow comfortable with my inability to decide between loving my brother more for whatever he'd just done, or fearing him because of it.

There's nothing wrong with loving something that scares you,

196

I thought, repulsing myself with how little ground this actually covered in terms of what I felt for Grover in that moment; it would look nice stitched on a pillowcase, or written in puff paint on a daycare provider's holiday sweatshirt. I wasn't scared of my brother, but I was worried and he might have killed Wayne. Thoughts of driving up to Northern State Correctional in order to have a family Christmas, and my parent's hopes devolving on me as their only non-incarcerated progeny plagued me as we drove in tomb-like silence to our parent's house. By the time we reached Loomis Street, I couldn't continue pretending I wasn't worried, so I asked Grover if he'd hurt Wayne, and he said they'd just talked. When I asked what they talked about, my brother said something about how Acheron was too small a place for anyone to think they could hurt me or say anything about our family like Wayne did and walk away from it without something to think about. Grover just said he gave Wayne something to think about.

As we sat across from each other at breakfast the following morning, I tried not to let my brother see how deeply I studied him over my steel-cut oats. He appeared the same as always, predictable as a weather vane down to the way he quartered his newspaper and leaned it against the percolator, reading as he ate. I understood my brother loved me ferociously, and would probably have killed Wayne if he felt it was necessary, because this was the foundation of Grover's steadiness within our family; he always knew what needed to happen, and always did it. And later the same day at school, when Lily said she had decided to date one of the Kyles and hoped I wasn't mad (I wasn't), and Wayne looked through me in the cafeteria, as if I was a window separating him from the ambivalent world beyond, I couldn't directly attribute any of this to what Grover had done the previous evening, and began wondering if I hadn't dreamed or hallucinated it.

And more than a decade later, as Henry, baby, and I stand
on the exact spot where the can of Loup Garou collided with
my supraorbital ridge, I still can't decide whether my memory
of the night is actually a memory, or some apocryphal, impaired
creation of a closed head injury from the impact of the beer can.
A small, dimpled scar remains above my left eye; perhaps it explains all my problems. I'd like that. I'm always on the lookout
for an opportunity to shed some of the responsibility for all this.

I've followed Henry from his office to the water's edge in complete silence, and am wondering if one of us is waiting for the
other to speak, as we cross a pennant of weedy, unkempt beach,
and walk out on a small dock, against which the hull of a drift-
boat makes a clock-like, baritone music. A ferry to nowhere, I
think as we sit in a brace of lawn chairs set at the head of quay.
Henry spins a crank, and an umbrella blooms between us. He
then removes a two-way radio from a scabbard on his belt, and
taps the receiver.

"Gilkey?"

"Sir."

"Bring it now please. Settings for two."

"Of course, sir. Red or white?"

"Beer, I think will do fine."

"Very good, sir."

"Cell service depends on where you stand and how still you
are," says Henry, sheathing his radio. "Not that we allow that up
here. I hope you enjoy thali."

I don't know if I will, so I try and enjoy the view; we're sitting
facing the majority of the original camp buildings deployed in an
alpine meadow, and intermittently shaded by large, old growth
trees which seem to have peeled off from the surrounding forest.

Within six acres of ovular clearing are five large cottages arrayed around the lake, a two-story dining and meeting hall that looks like a frontier saloon, and a low-slung staff dormitory with a medical wing. The buildings are set at some remove from each other, but federated by a network of dirt trails, some of which bifurcate and twine off into the forest, or up the mountainside rising to the north. The entire property is silent and still, which makes the khaki-uniformed man, presumably Gilkey, clattering out of the dining hall, and down the front steps toward the dock seem like an insurgent rather than a staff member.

He appears to be carrying a stainless steel beehive, which reveals itself as tiered tiffin when he reaches the dock, and begins setting out the meal. A table is unfolded, a cloth draped over it, plates clatter and are revealed; it's difficult to tell where he produces all of this from, the mystery only deepening as he sets two bedewed bottles of Champlain Boathouse Ale beside our dishes, and taps off down the dock in his hobnailed boots. I swear to god I will enjoy this, I think, ladling some dal into the tumulus of rice on my plate as Henry dips a bit of chapatti in the raita between us and stuffs it into the mouth of the mandrake hung from his neck.

"Spring fed," he says, gesturing at the water beneath us. "Which is nice, since we can tap the lake for the cabins. I didn't have to do much to them or any of the other buildings; the property already had a buyer who began renovating before he ran out of money. Tore out the outhouses, which were beyond hope, from what I understand, and installed bathrooms and showers in the cabins and staff housing. He updated the kitchen as well, and brought in a stonemason from Barre to fix up the fireplace with slate from the quarry."

"Quarry?" I say aloud, remembering Mr. Gould's invitation to shoot bats.

"Yes, you'll see it later," continues Henry, pride edging into his voice. "The same man added flagstones to the cabins, a nice, unnecessary touch. A bit too spa-like, but removing them would cost more than leaving them in place. They're three-season, the cabins I mean, although that third season would be a bit chilly, especially up here. But it can be done. I'm looking into weatherizing them, since I'd like to have this become a destination for major holidays, as a sort of Anti-Christmas, or No Thanksgiving. The problem is the toilets and showers. Those pipes will freeze unless we replace them, and that requires some digging, which is a cosmetic concern, and would likely require us to close the facility, since we can't have reality intruding. This is a constructed experience, Walter, meaning the seams involved in the construction should be invisible."

"That must be difficult," I say, puzzling over a bit of pickle on my fork; is it a garnish, or for eating? "I saw a lot of plates in the parking lot from Massachusetts and New York. Those places are a mess right now from the hurricane. Neighborhoods in Brooklyn are under water. Boston harbor is an aquarium. People in Connecticut don't have enough gas to get to work. The people here, the clients, I mean, they must be worried."

"This is not a resort, Walter. The people here have no right to information, no newspaper in the morning beside their cup of just-so coffee. They are here to become less of what most people believe is a problem. So there it is."

"You mean they don't know?"

"It's part of the agreement we ask each client to sign after they are accepted. No mail. No phone calls. No reality other than this, what you see here: land, water, and sky. During the screening process, each client is given a safeword particular to them, which they can use at any time to click their ruby slippers together. But they must leave immediately, and cannot reapply for a year. Terminating the agreement early is allowed only once historically, as in the history of that client as it relates to them patronizing our establishment. Clients who try to terminate services early more than once will no longer be allowed to receive them."

"Accepted?" I ask, not sure what I'm asking. "You used that word, didn't you? Meaning you have to apply to do or buy whatever it is you sell here."

"The sine qua non of cultivating an exclusive experience is making absolutely certain it remains exclusive, Walter. If we allowed anybody in it might as well be a county fair. Or the fucking ashram it was during the nineteen-eighties. Do you know how many homeschooled children were born in this lake?" asks Henry, gesturing at the water beneath our table.

I want to ask: That one? and point to the child bridling him, if only to call some belated attention to it, but stuff a wad of creamed spinach into my mouth instead and chew it like a farm animal. I'm out of my element. That much I know, meaning Henry must know it too. He's not the sort of man to leave anything to the will of the gods. Finding out what exactly I'm doing here, nibbling papadum on the dock at Lake Placenta with my triumphant nemesis and his child, seems imperative.

"Henry," I begin, nearly choking on my beer as I try to imbue my voice with something like dignity. "Thank you for lunch, and explaining what you do here. I guess I'm curious what I'm doing here."

"I had an opening for a camp attendant,"

"What does that involve?"

"It's not complicated; keep the men and women separate, and ensure both do their chores. And supervise the quarry. That's the main issue. Anyone we accept will usually be good about obeying the rules, but people still need to be kept on task."

"What happens in the quarry?"

"What normally happens in a quarry: people move rocks."

"But they have to apply to move rocks?"

"Indeed. This isn't for everyone. The most important thing to remember is that you are not a concierge or a housekeeper; you're a superintendent, and overseer. You will not be expected to facilitate the personal needs of our clients; for your purposes, their needs are rudimentary, and their composite personality begins and ends with obedience."

"Obedience is not a personality."

"Exactly, Walter. It sounds like you're getting into the spirit of things. It's important never to miss an opportunity to remind the clients how little we want to know about them. Our only concern is reducing their Weltanschauung to our routine. On a typical day, we have cabin inspections at 4AM; beds made, bathroom cleaned, uniforms laundered. If any of these criteria are unmet, the entire cabin receives a demerit. Three demerits means a ticket home for the entire cabin, so you shouldn't have to do much policing when it comes to the client's quotidian responsibilities. Chores rotate each week, but everyone is required to work in the quarry. Anyway: a typical day. Breakfast at 4:30AM. Quarrying from 5AM to noon. Lunch. Back to the quarry. Dinner at 5:30PM. Evening chores, laundry, custodial, kitchen help, that sort of thing, from 6PM to 7PM. An hour of personal time; this is when keeping the men and women separated is crucial. Cabins one and two are for women, cabins four and five are for men. The third is gender-neutral housing, because it would be a shame to miss out on that market, and it looks good beside the word 'sustainable' on press material. The dining hall is similarly divided. Clients have other things to worry about down in the quarry, so commingling is typically not an issue, and at the end of a good day, most are ideally too tired to do anything other than stare at the ceiling in their cabins. Some may use the library in the meeting hall, or swim in the pond. But if any of them choose to take a walk on the nature trails, you need to be in the staff offices, monitoring the video feed. Generally speaking, the trails to the east are for women, trails up the mountain are for men. I haven't worked out a gender neutral trail system yet; the last transsexual client we had up here was allowed to go wherever it wanted, which I didn't like, but there was nothing to do about it, at the time. The point is: we have had clients try to arrange woodland rendezvous with one another; they always say they didn't realize which trails were which. Anyway, the property is monitored by a comprehensive network of cameras, microphones and motion detectors, both inside and outside the fence. We see everything that happens inside the perimeter, and anything within a quarter mile outside of it, but anyone who goes into the woods must be watched and, if necessary, intercepted and escorted off property with a minimum of fuss and attention. Where was I? Ah, yes: routine. Lights out by 8PM. Be quiet or get thrown the fuck out. Repeat."

"So I'm basically the sex and toilet police," I say; the baby raises an eyebrow. "That sounds like fun, Henry."

"Naphta seems to like it. You'll meet him shortly when we visit the quarry. I'm not categorically against anyone enjoying their work."

"I suppose my biggest question is: why bother? Caring about what anyone else does seems like a monumental burden to voluntarily adopt for the sake of…I don't know what exactly…Privation vacations? 'Come, and be cleansed of everything that makes you interesting and important.' You have a nice property up here, Henry. Why not let people pay you to frolic in it?"

"Because if they think they've gotten away with anything, the entire illusion falls apart. We're engineering an experience, Walter, an experience of submission, and dominance. We're offering clients a vacation from themselves. In our promotional material, we use 'purity' and 'green retreat' as euphemisms, but what we're doing here is about control, and control is less about fear qua fear than in cultivating the belief in those you wish to control that there is something to fear. Our margin of error doesn't allow for loopholes. If clients think they can sneak off to fuck each other in the woods whenever they want, we may as well have left 'Frith' above the gate."

"I see," I say, even though I don't; I'm not an authority figure, and I dislike the fact that Henry believes he can use me as one in this environment. I don't want to wear his stupid uniform, and wander around slapping the bushes to catch wealthy people *in flagrante delicto*. I know I won't take the job, but I see no reason to ruin our lunch over it. As soon as we finish this tour, or lecture series, whatever it is, I'll tell Henry I'm not interested. I might as well have a look at the quarry.

"You can take your beer," he says, already standing, and walking down the dock. I'm done eating apparently. I always assumed he was the sort of man who can't remain seated after finishing his meal. Now I know.

We transect the property at an obtuse angle to the lake until we reach a ribbon of trail leading into the woods behind the dining hall. A sign with both a male and female insignia indicates the path can be used by either. The phrase: no fucking today! ripples duly through my mind as I follow Henry beneath a verdurous canopy. It gives the forest a dim, slightly enchanted aspect. I'm following a monster, I think, watching Henry's back and drinking my beer as we enter a rough, oblong clearing with yet another fence and gate at the far end. Henry leaves the trail which branches off to the right, running parallel with the fence, and taps a combination into a keypad beside the gate. The door swings open, admitting us onto a canopied viewing platform planted on the lip of the quarry.

"Have a look," he beckons without turning toward me, as if he's narrating. I'm not immediately sure what I see when I join him at the railing. Being fundamentally ignorant of landforms, I think I expected the quarry to be more of a canyon, and the reality of Henry's flagship attraction as just a large hole in the ground full of sedimentary and metamorphic cleavage leaves me with a generally passionless impression of his enterprise, and reifies my decision not to work here. What sort of man wants box seats to this? I wonder, as I begin noticing the rumpled forms of the campers below. Their uniforms fluidly blend with the drab interior of the quarry, making them appear like a deliquescent part of it, tepid brown water washing over the baskets of stones they fill in the gut of the excavation, and carry up a winding flight of stone steps hewn from the wall itself. In what look like burlap pajamas, the men are indistinguishable from the women. Probably the point. A camp attendant in khaki sits beneath a beach umbrella at the top of the steps, watching the proceedings through a pair of binoculars. Naphta, presumably. A plangent sonata of hand tools, pickaxes, chisels, sledgehammers, chipping away at the wall of rock below reaches us at the railing, where Henry seems weirdly at peace. I scour the landscape for something less perplexing to focus on, and find only a solitary client mounting the stairs on the floor of the quarry with a basket of rocks in either hand. He takes each step at an even, steady pace until he reaches the top, where he dumps out his baskets in a slag pile to the left of the landing, fills them again, and mulishly proceeds back the way he came, passing other clients on their way to do the same. In terms of being unusual, watching the clients matches if not bests watching Henry who is now watching me. I need to say something.

"They're not building anything."

"They're building everything," he replies. "They've been given eudemonia. This is what money can buy."

"They're painting a bridge to nowhere," I say, feeling clever until I begin wondering whether the same couldn't be said about my life. "How much do people pay to do this?"

"That depends on how long they stay. Minimum stay is a week; maximum three. Special arrangements can be made for an extension if the client and I agree it's in our mutual interest."

"How much does that cost?"

"That depends on how interested I am. I don't like to see the same people around here for too long. They could be returning to whatever it is they do outside of here, and proselytizing on my behalf. We advertise discretely, and maintain an internet presence. But the best promotion among our clients is a sort of stratified, bourgeois incest. They want to be like each other, and establish themselves as normal. If normal means hauling rocks for ten hours a day over spring break, people will line up to hand you a blank check."

"I operate a field dressing clinic in Red Hook. Urban woodsmen from all across New York City pay me to teach them how to properly slaughter and prepare animals they have never seen except on the median of the Staten Island Expressway. The proceeds from this venture mean I own a converted industrial space overlooking New York Bay where I practice beekeeping, a summer home upstate, and drive a vintage Ford Ranger wherever I go. As a hobby, I sell honey at the Prospect Park farmer's market on Saturday mornings, and donate the proceeds to a struggling axe maker on Court Street because he is a true artist, therefore I pity him. I want to stay at Todes/Stiege for a week. How much will you charge me?"

"We wouldn't allow you in; aim higher."

"I don't know how; I'm looking for a figure, Henry."

Henry produces a business card from somewhere, and scribbles something on it before handing it to me. I try not to react to what he's written, and hand it back to him with a nonchalance so transparent I may as well have screamed 'Great and holy shit fuck!' into the vacuity of the quarry.

"Why are some of them wearing white armbands?" I say, trying to draw Henry's attention away from the subject I was so doggedly pursuing. The figure on the business card wedded to the scene before us leaves me feeling reduced, a little person who could fit nicely in the deep, jangling pocket of the robber barons and baronesses swinging from the end of Henry's leash. I suddenly want to declare myself a simple man, though this probably reads loud and clear.

"They've selected our Quietus package," says Henry. "They will not speak or be spoken to during the duration of their stay. Any tasks not directly announced to the clientele during meals or review will be communicated individually in writing. Other clients are warned in advance not to address those who have selected this option, unless they want to earn themselves and their cabin a demerit. There are many rules here. I don't mean to overwhelm you. All of this is in the employee handbook. I'll give you a copy before you leave, and perhaps have a look at it tonight if you have the time. I'd hoped we could get you up here tomorrow around 9AM to begin training; you'll be paid a regular wage for your time, of course "

"What makes you think I've accepted your offer, Henry?"

Saying this out loud may be the bravest thing I've done in my entire life, though watching Henry smile to himself as he turns to face me undoes whatever I'd hoped to gain emotionally from standing up to him. It's like drawing back the curtain of your cowardice only to find a battalion of dangerous lunatics in your front yard.

"Well, I'm sure you'll find something else to occupy your time," he says flatly. "Isn't Cordelia back in town?"

The threat is there, hanging between us like a bad chess move on my part, the sort of thing you watch happen, and begin praying your opponent doesn't notice as soon as you've removed your hand from the piece. And this is checkmate, after more than a decade. I either work for him, or relive high school.

"9AM?" I ask, draining what remains of my beer and looking hopelessly into the cruel but somehow sagacious face of Naphta as he appears in the doorway of the viewing platform; Henry ignores him and continues speaking to me.

"Yes, and in uniform, please."

"Why not?" I say, swigging at my empty beer bottle. Naphta approaches Henry, and leans in close, whispering something in the taller man's ear.

"Get rid of her. Now," replies Henry, his subaltern nodding and moving toward the door. "And one other thing, Naphta: this is Walter. He'll be training with you tomorrow."

"Bring sunblock. Pack a lunch," says Naphta, clasping and releasing my hand and slipping out the door before I can form much of an impression of him beyond what I've already seen. He's several years older and six inches shorter than me, and projects a goblin-like commingling of superior intelligence and mean-spiritedness, which I'm certain Henry appreciates. The door swings shut, and the baby hisses at it, while Henry confirms something on his radio.

"Gilkey will take you back to the village," he says, which

suddenly seems like an extremely ambiguous turn of phrase, and hands me a key from his pocket. "He'll meet you back at the gatehouse. You'll find your uniform, boots, and handbook in locker twelve. He'll give you the combination, and door code, though you won't need it today. You'll receive a new one each week via company email, so it's important to check regularly. Instructions for activation are in the handbook. Any questions?"

"Are Mr. Todes and Mr. Steige aware of what's going on up here?" I ask, hoping to give myself some sort of edge, moving forward. I don't want to threaten Henry. That can only go one way. But showing him I know more than nothing about his business interests or portfolio or whatever he calls it might leave us with the kind of internecine arrangement that means we all lose together.

"It's nothing I need to explain to you, Walter," says Henry, smiling with a kind pathos; that can't last long. "But out of regard for your brother, I can't have you leaving here thinking you know more than you actually do, so allow me to edify you: Mr. Todes and Mr. Stiege are two unemployed cranks who volunteer with the Waitsfield Repertory Theater. I took them to a tailor in Woodstock, provided them with a loose script, and paid them two hundred dollars apiece to say confusing, Eastern European things to Huld so he wouldn't sit on the paperwork for this place until I told him how I'm financing it. Share that with him if you like. He won't believe you because why should he?"

"How are you paying for it?"

"The right question is really: how am I not paying for it? But that's a story for another day. Any other questions?"

"Is it Naphta or Gilkey's identity I'm borrowing in order to work for you?"

"Gilkey," says Henry, turning back to the railing. "See you at nine."

After collecting my costume and perdition manual from the gatehouse, I follow Gilkey, first name Vernon, through an aisle of
denuded luxury automobiles to a small staff parking area hidden
by grove of white pine from the main lot, and try to remain patient as he combs a mountain of crap from the backseat of his
jeep to make room for my baggage. He wasted no time introducing himself, a friendly sort. That makes a change from Naphta,
I suppose. I try not to imagine what our first day together will
be like, a negation made easier as Vernon and I careen down
the mountainside toward town, and he begins filling the space
where silence and speculation would normally live with answers
to questions I haven't asked.

"I'm the cook, as it stands," he says, removing his peaked cap
and tossing it into the back seat; a mane of blonde hair running to
gray flops out from beneath his hat like a parachute opening, and
joins the tawny van dyke around his mouth. If my hair looks like
a hat, I think, then Vernon's is like a medieval helmet. He's a small
man who looks like a retired bandit; a few scars pucker his cheeks
and neck, and as he rolls up the cuffs of his uniform, crude tattoos
dance from his sleeves as though answering a piratic reveille. "Mr.
Hoffmann says chef, that's what he expects me to call myself, but
there's no art to making porridge three times a day. You know
how to make porridge, Walter? Boil grain in water until it looks
like vomit, and scrape it onto the plate with a chisel. Bon appetit,
shitbirds! For breakfast, add some fruit; lunch, add some beans;
dinner, add more beans to what's left from lunch, and some vegetables. I'm hoping one of these days he'll really let me spread my
wings and make some soup or something for a change, but he
insists. Uniformity is essential, that's what he says. As far as I can
tell, I'm mostly up there to make his lunch, which I enjoy doing,

don't get me wrong there, but it's not the same as preparing a meal for a roomful of folks. They've been in that quarry all day with Naphta, and I imagine they're starving. In fact, I know they're starving because they eat the porridge like it's ambrosia. I saw one young lady so pretty she probably farts marshmallows licking her plate like a wolverine. She would have been yelling for seconds I'll bet, but Quietus, and all that. So, that's my job, in case you think you came on thali Tuesday or something like that."

"Lunch was excellent," I say, more than glad to be relieved of the burden of conversation with my new coworker, and further relieved that Vernon seems to recognize the weirdness of our workplace rather than complement it. Perhaps I'm not alone in all this, even if Vernon can't see past the lip of his own particular foxhole. "Thank you, Gilkey…Vernon. Chef Vernon."

"Just Vernon is fine there, Walter, and let me tell you: my plates should be good. I went to school for this shit, Johnson and Wales, worked in kitchens everywhere, Whitesuntide in Boston, Homoousian and Shabnam's in New York, The Tight Suit in D.C., and Rommel's in Chicago; I designed their Kopeck Menu myself, though did I get credit for it? Shit no! Same with Mrs. Brisby's in Provincetown; created the Moving Day salad, and what do they have me do? Train my replacement, a little wop with a degree from some lapsed black shirt cooking school in Milan. So I said fuck it, and spent some time way out west not cooking anything except what I could make with my Sterno, because sometimes a man needs to take what he knows and put it on the highest shelf he can find for a while. I guess considering my, excuse me, our current gig, I'm still doing that, but it won't be for much longer. This here's a stopgap if there ever was one, and I got something real good on the line. Nothing to do with food service, but you don't need skills when you have a great idea."

"Oh?" I ask, not really interested, but it feels morally asymmetric to let Vernon talk to himself.

"Oh, indeed. Me and Isidore put this little thing together, wrote the business plan, got the investors we needed, and we're both putting in another week or so up at Henry's sleep-away gulag before we put in our notice. Because what we got going on is the future, and you don't mess around with the future, am I right?"

"Absolutely," I wonder aloud.

"So picture this: Grandma is dead. How sad. Arrangements must be made, but not everyone is going to feel right shoving her in a matchbox while some half-pickled funeral director in a cheap suit pats their hand. It's sad on top of sad; the template for cultural ritual fails most people. It's not just about picking the flowers or reading the right psalm. It's about knowing you made a good decision for grandpa."

"Grandpa?" I ask, not sure if I've lost the thread of the extemporization or business pitch or whatever's going on here.

"...and a decision you can both be proud of. And that's why Green Graves is such an interesting company. We cater to clients with an interest in celebrating the life of the people they've lost by choosing a service that will preserve and enhance the lives of the people who are still here. Our clients are the same people who buy their friends a chicken in Bolivia every Christmas, and it's exactly that kind of extremist earth hound who will make us a fortune. Why cremate, when you can opt for an unmarked? No coffin, no marker, nothing that interrupts decomp, and no nasty emissions. How about a nitrogen and ultrasound treatment? Freeze Grandma, turn up her favorite record to ten, and feed whatever remains to a houseplant. We even have our lawyers developing a clause that allows the grave to be reused after a certain amount of time, if the bereaved wishes it so. We have caskets made from recycled materials on order right now with a plant in Stratton. It's an exciting time in the dying business."

"So, let me see if I have this right, Vernon. You and Isidore are offering people sustainable death?"

"Well, that's just it, Walter: Dying is probably the most sustainable thing the human species is capable of, but we overcomplicate it. Most of our business is subtraction, rather than addition. Our plots are dug by hand. The gravestones are quarried and carved by local artisans. We can even provide one made of the same material as the caskets, if the family wishes. Izzy and I are basically eliminating the industrial aspect, and humanizing the business. People are comforted by the idea that the materials and processes behind settling their loved ones in the ground or wherever are both sustainable and handled by actual people rather than machines. Basically, Green Graves is eschewing the ugliness of death, and, who knows? Perhaps a measure of the fear there, as well. And check this out: we just leased a house off Town Hill Road up by the college as a sight for our sustainable mortuary."

"Is that a thing that can happen?"

"It's an experiment, Walter. I like to think of it as a mummification clinic. Isidore found some guys from out of state who are willing to give it a shot, and that's about all we need, because even if we say that particular service is 'coming soon' or something, people will read, notice, and remember it. A great idea doesn't have to work for it to be great, and make money. Just look at Henry back there. Every time something at that haunted house he calls a retreat breaks, he pawns it off on the clients as part of the experience. Has them thinking cold showers, and ticks with corncob stuffing are part of a philosophic manifesto rather than him being a skinflint and a sociopath. I've been up there since the spring, and I've about had it with everything to do with the place, especially that fucking little wackjob Naphta. I can't imagine where Henry dug him up. The man has something wrong with him that thrives in a position of authority. You know I caught him planting poison ivy in the quarry? Had a little tray of plants he'd uprooted from god knows where, and a big thick set of garden gloves, and was whistling to himself like some old lady trimming her rosebushes. And another time, I had to throw him out of the kitchen for trying to dump sawdust in the porridge. One of these days, he'll kill someone if Henry doesn't keep a closer eye on him. My point is: You seem like too good a kid to be spending your days apprenticed to a maniac on a mountaintop, and I'd love to get you in on the ground floor with Green Graves. We could use a guy like you, no question. No need to interview. You're hired, as far as I'm concerned."

"Hired to do what?" I ask, stunned to have been offered two jobs in one day without really deserving either of them. I have no way to compare this to anything else, and am therefore unsure whether I should feel lucky, or the opposite.

"Dig graves," says Vernon cheerfully, as if nothing could be more natural for me. "Remember what I said about how all our plots are dug by hand? That's integral to our entire charter of sustainability and ethical choices for Grandma. But we need some strong backs. Think about it: Just you, a shovel, and the soft, soft earth. Can you imagine anything better? We'll probably start you out at $8.25 per hour, bump that up to $8.75 after your ninety day probation is up, and go from there. Believe me, Walter, this is a great opportunity for a guy who maybe doesn't need too many chats at the water cooler and company picnics, but performs a valuable service nonetheless."

214

"That's generous, Vernon, but frankly, it's been a while since I've had to make any real life choices, and I'm a bit overwhelmed. Can I have some time to think it over?" I ask, feeling definitively unlucky as we pull up outside my house. Would Cordelia be more impressed by me working as Henry's commandant, or a hippie gravedigger? Apparently, these are my only viable employment options here in Acheron, Vermont. All this has the overfamiliar feeling of a nadir gathering like a knot of thunderclouds on the horizon, but who knows? That could just be opportunity battering at the gate. If Henry's costume fails to impress Cordelia, I'll give grave-digging a whirl.

"Well, sure, Walter! Take all the time you need," says Vernon as he hands me my boots through the passenger window. "So long as it isn't more than a week. We only have so many spots open, and they're filling up fast. A lot of people and businesses want in on this thing. Champlain Boathouse brewery just stepped in with a sponsorship opportunity the other day, and after the job fair up at the college, we got a stack of resumes you could stand on to hang yourself. Point is: things are moving. I'd hate to see you left behind up there with Henry and Naphta. You're too young to be up to no good all the time, and it's unavoidable with those two. I don't want to scare you, Walter. But you stay up there long enough, sleepwalking through that place, and one day you'll wake up and realize you can't count all the bodies you've buried for them. You're too gentle and obviously unaware not to consider my offer."

He speeds off into the gathering evening, leaving me puzzled by his penultimate statement, and feeling somewhat twerp-like. Vernon thinks you're too harmless to work with the living, I think as I plod toward the house. Grover meets me at the door, taking in the uniform carelessly folded beneath my arm, the four-hundred-page handbook, and whatever my facial expression might communicate about these items, and asks me if I'd like to have dinner in the backyard. Ruby appears between his knees, and tries to scurry up my ankle. I hoist her onto the saddle of my forearm, and follow my brother through the house, into the backyard, where a serving bowl of whole-wheat linguine and ethically-shucked clams, presumably, sits on a table set for two beneath a tormented-looking willow. A fire smolders in a pit at a comfortable distance from our chairs.

"It's from the store," says Grover, tugging the cork from a bottle of red wine and seating himself at the table. "I was planning on cooking, but one of my deli chefs made this. Plans change."

"Don't they," I say, seating Ruby on my lap and feeding her something from my plate. "Are clams bad for dogs?"

"Well see," says my brother, tentatively raising his glass. "Congratulations, I think."

"You don't think it's a good idea either?"

"Either?"

"It doesn't matter. Or I hope it doesn't. It must be possible to work for Henry without becoming like him. You've been doing it for years."

"Is that really what you're worried about, Walter?"

"No," I say, after a pause in which only the susurrus of the brook interferes. "No matter what happens, he and I will never care about the same things. He must know that, so I can't understand why he hired me."

"I'm also waiting to see," says Grover, shuffling the pages of my employee handbook open on his lap. " 'At no time is a camp attendant allowed to touch a client; however, if a client chooses a partial to full contact package (p. 243, s. 1C), and completes the necessary medical and liability paperwork (p. 242, s. 2B – 3C),

216

physical punishment is permissible at staff discretion. Please see p. 189 – 193, s. 4A – 4C for examples of acceptable physical intervention, and proper use of discipline tools.' "

"Very thorough," I say absently, making eye contact with Grover when he raises his head from the page. "I'm offended by the job, and ashamed of myself."

"Please don't be; I wrote it."

"So then what are you worried about, Grover?"

"He wants the store. But meanwhile, he'll settle for you."

"You told him no this morning," I say, trying to remember what bravery sounds like. "Or you told Huld. Either way, I can do the same."

"Walter, I know the job up there at the camp; I can imagine how you felt when he took you out on that awful little deck he has over the quarry. So, I'm assuming the only reason you came back here with this," he says, gesturing at the employee handbook, "is because he didn't give you that choice. I'm not going to ask what he said. That's your business. But trust me when I say the only way to deal with him now is to allow him to make progress, and stay out of the way. He'll become involved in something else sooner or later, and the coils will relax."

"So: play dead."

"Or obedient, if you prefer."

"It was Cordelia," I say, sluicing the rest of my wine onto my shirtfront in a failed sortie toward indemnity. "Henry knows so much more than I ever realized about it, or her, or us, or whatever's left of it. I know he'll find a way to make me suffer because of her, even if he has his own family now, and that little gorgon to take care of."

"The baby's a nasty piece of work," says Grover. "But it's supposedly Mr. Castle's child, not his. Born after he died to his widow,

Jo. Since he lives up at the house with her, and is Mr. Castle's heir apparent, Henry has taken over parenting the thing. Part of me hopes I don't live long enough to see how that turns out."

"It's already grown into one of those gothic portraits with the eyes that follow you everywhere."

"I think he brings it around to deliberately unsettle people. Speaking of things in frames, Walter: whenever you mention Cordelia, I think of one of those histrionic paintings of eternal wall-to-wall torment by Bosch or Brueghel. Have I ever told you that?" asks Grover, not really interested in an answer. "Which reminds me further: I nearly recycled some writing of yours this afternoon. I think you'd left it in the basket of that awful bicycle of yours…"

"My bakfiets?"

"…And the pages were blowing around the yard. I thought they were just old mail and receipts, but I saw you'd written between the lines."

"Did your read it?"

"Enough to realize it probably was something you meant to preserve. I left the pages on the desk in your room."

"I'm sorry if I've disappointed you," I say, stuffing a clam in Ruby's mouth. I'm unable to look at my brother. "I'm not thrilled with myself either. I can't explain why she means more to me than almost anyone except you."

"It's none of my business," repeats Grover, leaning over the table to refill my glass. "We don't choose each other, as family or lovers. I'm glad you followed her here, because I get to see you now. That's enough for me, though I'd like to see you happy, at some point."

"At some point," I repeat, prevented from swallowing my food by a cravat of emotion swelling my throat. It feels like the final dinner before I go off to war, not an absurd thought considering my appointment tomorrow at 9AM, and what it means, or might mean, for not just me, but my brother as well. I watch him now across the table, calmly chewing his linguine and sipping his wine as he reviews the pages of his handiwork before tossing them into the fire pit beside our table. If I ever did anything to hurt him , I'd kill myself, I think, wanting to share this with him, but worried it might only complement his concern for me. I try to regroup mentally, and get through dinner without thinking about Henry, and only realize Grover has been watching me stare off into the branches of the willow shading our table when he asks if I'm through eating. I notice his empty plate, and realize he's been waiting for me to finish my meal before leaving the table.

*   *   *

At 7AM the next morning, I'm standing on the porch of Cordelia's house in full uniform, gripping the jaw of her doorknocker, with the letter I began while sheltering from Hurricane Eula with Officer Laurel, and completed last night at 4AM, tucked beneath my khaki sleeve, ready for delivery. I haven't slept more than the ten minutes it took to print the thing, and a nugatory hour in the front seat of Grover's Honda. He lent it to me for my commute up the mountainside, pressing the keys into my hand before he went to bed. And with the letter in rough manuscript format on the desktop, and the uniform swaying in the closet like a Halloween decoration, I decided I might as well dress for work and stake out Cordelia's house for a few hours.

Before leaving, I mixed the last of my brother's vodka in a thermos with the last of his cranberry juice and packed it with the remaining linguine and clams as either an early breakfast or late dinner, and parked at the curb across the street from her house where I picnicked in the front seat, sipping my libation from the thermos lid like I'd earned it, and eating the pasta with my hands because I'd forgotten a fork. I somehow awoke on time at 6:30AM with my forehead resting against the horn, still numbed enough by the vodka to feel prepared for whatever came next.

It had to happen sooner or later, and as I mulled over the pages Grover left on my desk the night before, I decided sooner was best. My success hinged on the element of surprise; I hoped to shock Cordelia into loving me as she once did, or seemed to, by presenting myself in the both the first and last place she would expect to see me. It had been over a week since we last saw each other. New York and the rest of the Eastern Seaboard was drying out from the storm; the window for catching her off guard was closing, and without surprise, I'd be left with only begging and horse-trading as options, both too familiar to gain me any real ground. Ideally, I wanted her to see me as a familiar stranger, if possible, and project a sense of stability and well-being mostly absent from our last five years together. I assumed the uniform could only help me there, and tried to wear it proudly as I crossed the street to her yard, and ascended to the steps to the door, adjusting my cap in the sidelight so it sat rakishly on my head with something of the outlaw lover about it. You can do this, and even if you can't it's too late now, I say to myself as I allow the knocker to fall and clack against the door.

I assume I'm ready for anything, even Butch, Cordelia's father, to answer the door; we always got along, but I'd have to turn too many corners in explaining how and why I'm standing on his doorstep in a costume at 7AM with a novella for his daughter. I'd settle for him, if only to plant the manuscript in reliable hands, but I'm hoping for Cordelia; I'd like to leave the property with

220

an idea of how much rubble I have to clear away before we can get things rolling again, at the very least. However, when Nathan Moore answers the door in a pair of tasseled loafers, gym shorts, and the blazer I saw her ordering in Fatale earlier in the week, I don't immediately conclude all is lost. Instead, I'm briefly embarrassed, and stupidly check the number above the door to make sure I have the right house.

"We didn't order a singing telegram," says Nathan, looking me up and down as if he doesn't recognize me, though I can tell he knows exactly who I am by the smile recreating at the corners of his mouth like a coyote frolicking along the margin of a campfire. "Yes, go ahead. Check the house number. Do what you need to do, Walter."

"Where did you get that?" I ask, gesturing at the garment caparisoning his narrow shoulders and bare torso; the lapels of the blazer part like labia birthing a depilated beer paunch, which seems to stretch the outer limits of the suddenly small and common world between us.

"I'm afraid I had to leave New York in a bit of a hurry; I was invited to be an artist in residency at the college, as you may have heard, and I had to set up a show in Chelsea, and leave to come here the same day as the hurricane, and I just didn't have time to pack a bag. Cordelia was nice enough to offer me a ride with her, and accommodate me otherwise, as you can see, and even threw a few clothes into the bargain, for some reason. Women and their gifts...What a mystery...I was surprised not see you with her, Walter."

"...Accommodate?"

"Me, yes. It's nice to see you again, though there is a smell of...vodka, isn't it? Yes, and...shellfish? Where is that coming from?"

"I'm on my way to work," I say, unsure of what I'm even responding to.

"Are you some sort of gamekeeper? Cordelia mentioned you potentially managing wildlife at some point long ago."

"Whatever conclusion you might draw from all this is probably inaccurate," I say, gesturing at myself. This was your competition, I think: A man who treats his Klonopin prescription like a salt lick, and reads Gertrude Stein on the toilet. He is now living in her house, and she is buying his clothes.

"If you say so," says Nathan, his eyes finding the manuscript beneath my arm. "A delivery?"

"Not for you. Is she in?"

"She's at the library. You can leave it with me."

"I don't think so, Nathan."

"I won't read it. I'll put it in a safe place."

"You're a liar; even she knows that."

"Perhaps, if you weren't so unkind, you'd be standing where I am," he says, making a kind of half-hearted grab for the manuscript. "Read me a passage; I'm interested to hear how you express yourself in writing."

"Fuck you, Nathan, you lactating swine," I say, swatting his hand away, and trying to smother an anxious yip rising in my throat. Please god, I think. Not here. "No matter what she said to you about me, I will always know about your breasts and the milk they produce; glass houses, shitbird."

"Oh, how nice, very classy," he says, sounding almost weary. "As if I put myself on Risperdal in order to treat a very serious medical condition, which is frankly none of your business, with a complete understanding of what it would do to me. I'm sick, Walter. I hear voices. Try to have some compassion. Do you even know what it's like to think of someone other than yourself?"

"Don't try to shame me, Nathan," I say, turning on the heel of my boot so he won't see the tears gathering in the corners of my eyes. "Grow a beard. Join the sideshow."

My breathing is short, and my legs unsteady, but I can see Grover's compact, sensible little foreign car on the other side of the street. If I can reach it before I collapse, I'll have almost two full hours to cry and gasp and growl in the driver's seat until I need to go to work. It's not even 7:30AM. But as I take my first step away from the door, I feel a sort of hesitancy beneath my arm, and then a vacuity where the manuscript should be; a door slams, a bolt is thrown. I almost don't bother turning around. The situation is clear, even before a window in the second story above the porch rises, and Nathan begins reading.

"I suppose this is meant to be a work of literature, but I should warn you: I have no formal training in this area. As you know, during the three terms I spent with you at St. Margaret's, I took mostly art and philosophy classes, and one term of elementary Latin. That was a mistake. To be: Sum…Some Latin. *To love.* Some more Latin. *To corrupt.* Ever more Latin…I might trim that a bit, Walter. No need to burden your readers with a mess of dead language so early on…*I'm ashamed that's all I remember.* Otherwise, it's very good you know. A promising start."

I descend the steps pursued by the suddenly unfamiliar sound of my own words, the words I'd hoped would do everything they are not doing. I'm swaying like a drunk, and nearly snap my own leg at the knee trying to take an extra step as I scramble down the front stairs, setting off an anxious sonata of humming and yipping in my throat and chest, and causing Nathan to actually pause in his reading. This is the last thing in the world I want him to see and hear, but I can't help it; my equipoise is shattered and unrecoverable, a total loss. By the time I reach the yard, I'm no longer gibbering or growling to myself, but baying like a blood-hound at the rainclouds knotting the sky above as they open, unable and almost unwilling to catch my breath, because what difference would breathing really make? Pity is my only remaining card, and how better to play it than for Cordelia to find me suffocated on my own abasement in her front yard as the man she exchanged me for airs our common business from her bedroom window like a town crier? Whoever said the worst thing that can happen is never the thing you imagine was wrong; it's always as you imagine it, only worse.

"The Monday after you left began well. I was arraigned at 6AM and out of jail by 8AM, but the subway was shut down for the storm, and the bridges were closed to traffic. I already knew you were gone, because I called you from a holding cell in Chinatown to say I was in a holding cell in Chinatown. But when you asked where I was, I said "someplace bad," instead of something more accurate, because I was embarrassed. So that's why you never showed up…Can I ask what you did? Cordelia wondered where you were, but after you wouldn't stop trying to call her, she stopped worrying about it. What is that noise you're making, Walter? Are you growling?"

I barely hear Nathan as the rain begins to churn the lawn and spatter the street, but I hear enough to know I can't die in the yard, listening to him read my letter as he listens to me lose control of myself. Every man has a limit, supposedly. I guess I've reached mine. I lurch out of the gate, braying like an ass and knocking against parked cars as my vision begins to pulse and blur around the edges. I manage to reach the street before my legs give out, though I'm still not out of aural range of Nathan.

"I watched you become limitlessly beautiful in the shade of a belfry. Poetical, that. Though it's only page four or something and

I'm already growing weary of the digressions, Walter. Is the entire thing like this? I know I'm only a humble painter, but shouldn't a gentleman get to his point? Where are you going? Do you need me to call someone?"

Cocksucker, I think, collapsing in the middle of the street as a car turns the corner in the downpour. The storm enshrouds the valley in a malefic sort of twilight, and drivers have engaged their headlights, but it's unlikely they'll see me lying in the road until it's too late. Perfect! I think, happy to be relieved of the responsibility for taking my own life. My father always said killing yourself is one of the most selfish and brutal things you can do to the people who care about you. He was probably right. At least this way, it will look like an accident. I think back on what I almost said to Grover the night before, about killing myself if I ever did anything to hurt him. It makes this feel like a sort of inverted and preemptive apology. I killed myself to show you how sorry I was for hurting your feelings when I killed myself. In the end, I'm hoping it will amount to no harm done, the same as everything else I do. I want to leave the opposite of an impact, if possible. I close my eyes, hoping to be efficiently crushed beneath a vehicle hissing toward me across the flooded pavement, yet still trying to capture a full inhalation once more before passing out. Breathe deep before the end, you fool, I think to myself, wondering why my will to live remains intact even when all is lost. Because, stupid, you don't want to die, I answer myself. You wanted her attention, and didn't create any other options if she wasn't at home.

That seems about right; plan A failed, and without a plan B, I apparently self-destruct like something you'd expect to find in a comic book. If I'd really thought this through, I might have kicked Nathan in the balls, reclaimed my manuscript, and sat in Grover's car drinking cranberry juice and vodka from my thermos until it was time to go to work, editing the damn thing. Though the idea of physically harming Nathan leaves me feeling the way I did when I saw one of my coworkers at the Brooklyn Association stomp on a mouse scurrying out from beneath her desk, anything beats a slow march toward hysteria. But it's too late now. As the layers of my consciousness drop away, I try to relax like David Livingstone with his lion, and enjoy the rain pattering my face, and the feel of the still warm pavement humming against my cheek as a car approaches. I'm calm, too calm, suddenly breathing evenly, my lungs opening like drapes onto a transparent summer morning, the growl in my throat fading to sonorous and narcotic purr, as if I'm singing myself to sleep.

I try to recall some pertinent comfortable memory to accompany me to my doom, something from a time when I wasn't struggling to stay afloat in Cordelia's wake, and it felt like we were both making the same sort of progress, but can only recall the cake party I was assigned to cover for the college newspaper my first term on campus. This is what the editor at the St. Margaret Record called it: a cake party. He didn't tell me what it was, but said I should go to a particular building at a particular time, and write about what I saw. This turned out to be a group of new students, like me, all white, presided over by an ambiguous third year named Greer, the then president of the White Allies, a group of paleface students there to support the people of color (or POCs) on campus, who mostly didn't want their support, unless one of them had to move or something. Then they called Greer, who would mobilize the Allies to help move boxes across campus. The POCs called this service dial-a-cracker. I only know this because I lived next to one of them, and overheard.

Greer began the meeting by saying, "Fuck the fucking racists." This is how they began every meeting, I found out later, and then said something about how the first and most important part of becoming a White Ally is acknowledging your privilege, and checking yourself on it. A few students nodded, and then she put a box on a table in front of her, and said, "The second part, once you have acknowledged your privilege, is divesting yourself of it. This is not easy, but it can be fun." She opened the box, and inside was a cake cut into slices.

"Lets say this cake represents your privilege as a white person, in this room, right here and now," she continued. Everyone seemed marginally fine with that idea, so she encouraged her audience to line up and get a slice of cake. One of the new students in the queue asked why the cake had white frosting.

"It was all they had at Kroger," said Greer, adding as an afterthought: "And because white is the color of your privilege."

As people returned to their seats, someone asked me why I didn't have a slice of privilege cake, and I said something about how I was on assignment just as Greer shouted that the cake wasn't for eating at another student who was about to take a bite.

"Now that we all have our cake," she said, "which is privilege, in our hands it is time to divest of it. Now, I know you all badly want a bite of the cake. It's yours. You were given it without anything being asked of you in return. In a way, you were born, born into this room and this situation, with that cake. This is where we separate those who will make good allies from those who will not. If you wish to indulge your privilege, take a bite. Go ahead. It's right in front of you. It's moist and tasty. Make a pig of yourself. Go ahead. Do it."

One dim bulb of a first year student actually began eating his cake, and Greer yelled at him until he left. He said something about how he was confused, and thought she was telling us to try a bite of privilege, but it didn't work. He failed.

"Now, we must divest," said Greer to her audience, minus one. "Look at your privilege. Realize everything you love and will miss about it."

People did it; a roomful of students staring at thinly sliced supermarket cake.

"Good. Now, throw it away," she commanded, and no one did. The room seemed reluctant to make a mess, so Greer encouraged them. "Go ahead, it's fine. Here, I'll start."

I didn't realize she'd actually thrown the cake until it landed in my lap, and suddenly, the room was full of flying pastry. And once the last slice of cake had flown, she congratulated everyone on a job well done, and told them to consider themselves ready. On my way out of the room, I heard a student ask Greer if he should have thrown two pieces of cake since his parents were rich. She told him it would be fine, for now. I walked back to my dormitory as if I'd lost true north on my internal compass, wondering what kind of facts about life my kind leftist parents had neglected to impress upon me that would in some way explain what I had just seen. I wasn't comfortable with the possibility that my existence constituted something to make up for, or check, as Greer said. I wondered if life in rural Ohio, with nothing except churches, cornfields, and the single street composing Julian Falls' business district to circle the campus wagon of sociopolitical indignation, hadn't left the St. Margaret's student body so bored we'd begun searching for something to feel guilty about.

I bounced this thought off Cordelia when I arrived in my room, and found her lying naked on my twin mattress, reading a copy of *Gorky Park*, with a plastic cup of Evan Williams mellowing in the vernal air on the windowsill. It formed a perfect cutout of what I considered a domestic scene, at the time. Rather than responding to anything I'd said, she dragged a finger through the

228

frosting jacketing my crotch, tasted it, and said it figured Greer was too cheap to get anything better than Kroger.

"Fuck the fucking racists," she murmured, drawing me beneath the sheet, and synopsizing the adventures of Arkady Renko for my benefit, catching me up, as it were, on everything that mattered to her, or us. At the time, moments like these reminded me why I'd bothered going to college: because Cordelia was special. After watching the students waste pastry, I needed to know I wasn't the only person who was incapable of caring about the point they were trying to make. I figured no one would notice, even after I allowed her to provide the sort of context I needed in order to write my article, or, more accurately: allowed her to write the bulk of it, though she declined credit in the byline when it was published in the St. Margaret Record, and I received a full ration of shit from the student body for what they considered an unfair, sarcastic, and privileged (naturally) summation of their cake party.

"Fuck the fucking racists," she repeated like a kind of benediction when the uproar over the article was at its pinnacle, the phrase turning in her mouth with a rich sort of irony. I felt good, despite everything. I didn't care because Cordelia didn't, and it seemed like we would always agree on the important things, or not spend too much time caring about the unimportant things. There's safety in mutual ambivalence. However, years later, with Nathan warbling my letter from a window above the street in which I've collapsed, and a car hurtling toward me through a translucent curtain of rain, I still feel like I have cake in my lap.

Paranoia is briefly defrayed by relief when I awake alive on a mattress in what looks like a disused medical storage closet; oxygen tanks line the wall beside my head, packages of adult diapers list from a closet left open across the room, and a wheelchair missing a wheel sits cravenly in a corner beside an open window. Past the tattered curtain obscuring it, I hear the crisp report of rain on a tin roof. So: It seems I'm alive. Or can this be hell? I wonder, sniffing the edge of the afghan covering me; it smells of cigarettes, and vaguely rotten, though I notice the odor is not confined to the blanket as I stand, and cross the room to the door. Perhaps something died in the wall, I think hopefully, as I test the handle.

I'm vaguely disappointed when it turns, admitting me into what looks like a kind of destitute boardroom. Beneath a grid of browning asbestos tile, a long table belted by an assortment of mismatched chairs occupies the center of the nearly windowless room; a brace of high, narrow portals, the sort of thing Henry would like, sit in the far corner, showing only a slim polygon of gray sky. Could he have something to do with where I am now? I've clearly missed our appointment, and jilting him has to have a consequence, but what will it be? I try not to think about whatever punishment is probably brewing up at his compound right now as I take in the rest of the room. Folding tables you would expect to find at a Lutheran bake sale, a cabinet leaking a selection of board games and cheap novels through a missing door, and a coffee urn armored in wood-grain Formica comprise the remaining furniture. And as if to admonish, or prove something to me, the twelve steps and traditions are painted on the opposing wall in huge, emollient calligraphy.

So, this is hell, or some department of it, I think, stepping into the dimly lit room onto to what feels like a plush toy, but turns out to be a human hand. The owner thrashes to partial life beneath the folding table where he is encamped, withdrawing his hand, and offering the sort of advice I hope I never have to take.

"Watch where you step, you shit curl bisexual! You're lucky I startle good, otherwise you might see me coming and it would be too fucking late for you! Last time it happened, they only found the guy's hat by the river, and it wasn't me that saw it, so you keep your mouth shut about all that; I don't need another fucking jacket and you don't need the kind of help I'll give you when they find out I had nothing to do with it and I come looking for answers! And I got your picture! I'll know where to look!"

"I'm sorry, sir," I say, feeling suddenly scared of the voice under the table, like a child afraid of a beast lurking beneath his bed, but still compelled to have a look anyway. I slowly dip my head below the surface; a pair of glittering, angry eyes stair back from within the firmament of a tobacco-stained beard. I feel as if I've startled a gnome; the man cowers against the wall, watching me like a raccoon cornered in its burrow. My fear is now yours, I think, as he draws his blanket to his chin with a sort of vicious helplessness. "Can you tell me where I am?"

"Now, you fuck off, buddy. This is my spot, I found it fair and square, and if you don't like that, go talk to the pretty lady in the front office and she'll fix you up maybe, but this here is mine, and I ain't moving."

That's enough for one day, I think, feeling an odd sense of completion as I leave my new friend beneath the table and begin searching for an escape from wherever I am. Two out of the three doors in the room are locked, and the third lets out onto a stairwell. The smell of rot and cigarettes hangs with a kind of certitude in the air as I descend the stairs and pass into a bleak dining room. Tables and chairs are leaned and stacked respectively against one wall, while a battered stainless steel buffet and steam table occupy the other; the two arrangements face each other across an austere half-acre of scuffed maroon tile like opposing infantry. Between them, a man mopping the floor and speaking to either himself or the mop gives me an enigmatic look before returning to his work. Something about all this is familiar, but I only realize exactly where I am when I pass the entrance to the kitchen on my way out of the dining room, and recall the Thanksgiving afternoon many years ago I spent washing dishes with Sticks, the sex offender.

"You need something, pilgrim?" asks one of the two men I've apparently been watching for quite some time from the kitchen entrance; he operates the dishwasher, while another guy fishes pots and pans from an industrial sink in the corner. The man speaking to me wears denim jeans and a denim jacket, not so unusual, but also a pair of spurs, which I've never seen on a person in real life.

"I'm looking for the…office?" I ask, two questions actually, since I'm not sure where it is, or entirely certain it exists. The man camping beneath the table upstairs didn't seem like the most reliable person. I remember standing in a staff office during the bleak holiday morning when my father made Grover and me volunteer here, but have no idea where it was in relation to anything else in the building.

"Down the hallway, first left before you hit the porch door," says the kitchen cowboy.

"And tell her we're about out of dish soap," says the other guy, with a kind of venom. "I don't know how the fuck she and everyone expect me to scrape the shit off this shit without any goddamn soap and you can tell her I said so."

"I'll do that," I say, fleeing from the kitchen in what I hope is the generally right direction. Men and women sit and stand at various points in the hallway like a kind of gauntlet, talking, coughing, and laughing in variable states of decrepitude. Some of them definitely appear homeless, while others pass for what I've always been told is normal. An obese woman with a racing stripe of vomit pasted to the front of her sweatshirt sits slumped over in a folding chair, while a man in nursing scrubs stands nearby, reading a library copy of *The Magic Mountain* and waiting to use the bathroom. The air remains fetid, which I suppose is unavoidable; all humans begin to smell bad if you pack them close enough together. I'm trying not to look at anyone around me, and walking so fast I nearly miss Martha framed, once again, by the doorway of the St. Simeon's staff office, like a figment caught in the window of a passing train. I loop back, but stop halfway into the room, waiting to be noticed or beckoned; I'm unsure whether the conversation she's having is private or not.

"She told him to stay away and now he's here," says a blousy, middle-aged woman with a meddlesome aspect. "Showing himself like he got the right to do it or like she don't see him every night when she falls asleep, and I should know since she's in the bed above me, and when she wakes up crying and shaking and needing someone to hold onto it ain't you people who come upstairs and sit with her until she can go back to bed; nope, it sure as fuck isn't! It's me up there, because I can't stand to see someone I care about suffering like that, because I do care, and you people don't. What he done to her you don't just get over or walk away from like nothing, so how come you people don't understand that?"

"First of all, Marianne," replies Martha, speaking to the woman, though her eyes travel to me in a sort of silent and gentle greeting. I'm glad I have a minute to get my opening remarks together, because I'd forgotten how beautiful Martha actually is, and can easily imagine how stupid this would make me if I had to speak about anything off the cuff. "I'm not a police officer. I don't have any legal right to enforce a restraining order, here or anywhere else. We try to do our best to make sure people feel safe here, and for better or worse, that door swings both ways. Just because we know about a problem between clients doesn't mean we get to choose a side, and exclude someone who might need our help."

"Your help…" snorts Marianne. "No one ever gave me any help when my husband died from what they did to him during that Gulf War. And all the planes they were flying over our house where he was stationed, and one them crashed in our backyard, and now I'm disabled, so I deserve benefits, and I don't see anyone here who wants to help me!"

"Right. Our Help," says Martha, ignoring most of what was said to her. "A clean bed, a hot meal, a shower, services, if you want them: housing, employment, medical, or veteran related, like your husband. If that's something you want to pursue, I can help you make an appointment to meet with the veteran's affairs office. That's what our help looks like. If we denied people the services I just mentioned based on things they did before they arrived here, we would have an empty shelter. And furthermore, Kristen needs to address this issue with staff, rather than sending you. I'm glad you're friends, but it's her business, not yours."

"She's too scared to leave the women's dorm what with him all around this place, mopping the floor like he has every right…"

"Until we hear different from the police department or her lawyer, he does have every right. Tell her what I told you: she needs to file a complaint with the sheriff's office if she wants the order of protection enforced. And any problems otherwise, tell her she needs to come down here, and speak with staff if she wants us to do anything about it."

"I'll tell Kristen," says Marianne. "But she won't do it, and you're just making it harder for her to get better, and easier on yourself, be-cause it means you don't have to do anything! You don't care about us! You're just here for a paycheck and that's it! Now, where's the toothpaste? I'm running low. And I need some shampoo."

"In there," says Martha, twisting her lovely mouth into a rune of irritation as she raises a bronzed, willowy arm to gesture at a closet behind Marianne. "Third shelf from the bottom. The milk crate on the right has toothpaste. The one on the left has shampoo. If you need soap, it's in the..."

"I'm taking two of these," says Marianna already elbow deep in the closet. She shoves a handful of toothpaste boxes and shampoo bottles into her purse, and flounces past me into the hallway.

"You're awake. Hi," says Martha, the tension in her face unraveling as she smiles, gesturing at the door. "Close that."

"Gladly," I say, slamming it on several clients waiting behind me in the hall. Martha crosses the room to flip the lock, and hug me. "It's good to see you, Martha. What are you doing here? And what am I doing here?"

"Which question would you like me to answer first?" she asks, drawing away from me to remove a pouch of tobacco from a backpack hanging behind the desk.

"The second, actually, please."

"I found you passed out in the road while I was driving to work this morning. I was worried until I saw how comfortable you seemed. You also smelled like alcohol, so I figured you might just need someplace to sleep it off. I wanted to take you home, but I wasn't sure where you lived, and I couldn't get ahold of your brother to come get you. And I had to be here to relieve the person who was on the night shift. So I brought you upstairs, and put you to bed. I was actually about to check on you before you came down."

"I think I may have disturbed a...one of your...your patrons. He's sleeping beneath a table upstairs, and I accidentally stepped on his hand."

"That's George," says Martha, rolling a cigarette between her fingers while watching my face; she appears happy to see me. How unusual. "Normally he camps this time of year, but I think he decided to stay the night because of the storm. He doesn't spend a lot of time around people, and he scares easy, but he's harmless. Care for a smoke?"

I follow Martha through a side door communicating with a smaller office, and out another into an alley girding a fenced acre or so of vacant lot; past this, the humpbacked foothills of Maybrick Peak are partially visible through the rain rolling against the tin roof above our heads. It's not a bad view, even through a screen of chain-link. Martha twists a cigarette into being for me, and lights her own from a box of kitchen matches left on the windowsill. I do the same, wishing I remembered whether she and I had sex, and feeling embarrassed at having once again been rescued from myself by a beautiful woman who found me collapsed in a public road during inclement weather. A troubling pattern seems to be emerging, I think. Or can I take pride in this sort of symmetry?

"To answer your first question," says Martha, exhaling parallel barrels of smoke through her nostrils. "I make more here than I ever did adjuncting at the college. I have student loans to pay, and those bloodsuckers don't fuck around. Vermont Student Assistance Corporation are a bunch of jerkwater lowlife motherfuckers. So as much as I'd like to use my education to make a living, it's not allowed. Unless I want to live here."

"So it's about money," I say, puzzled by the idea of St. Simeon's as a nest of profit, and wondering if Martha has discovered buried treasure somewhere on the property. "You work in a homeless shelter for the money. That makes sense, I think."

"No, not entirely. I can live like a human being on what I make, but I'm still renting. It's the difference between a sharing a yurt with a bunch of dope-smoking morons, or having a one-bedroom apartment to myself. And I like the work, Walter. I like making sure people get something to eat, and have a safe place to sleep. No one shouldn't have that. I'd rather have someone like Marianne shout at me all day about nonsense than watch hungover undergrads nod off in my intro to Wildlife Biology. Like you did."

"I was never hungover," I say, justifying myself even though this is obviously meant as a joke. "I was tired from hauling boxes of crap around for my brother."

"I remember."

"And I was only taking classes to impress a girl. No, wait, that's wrong. I didn't want to impress her. I wanted to appear independent."

"Did that work?"

"I thought it did, up until this morning."

"What happened this morning?"

"I think I got my heart broken," I say, humbled by how flat and speculative this sounds coming out of my mouth. "But that's all in the past now."

"If you don't want to talk about it, you don't have to."

"Well, I had a very important document stolen this morning, and it would be easier to contextualize everything for you if I still had it. I don't want to waste your time, Martha, and I'm so glad you found me."

"Speaking of that," says Martha. "Does any of what you're not explaining have something to do with that costume you were wearing when I found you?"

"Costume?" I ask, expecting to see Henry's uniform when I glance down at myself, but finding only a huge pair of denim JNCO's with a massive flaming skull embroidered on the ass and a oversized long sleeve t-shirt with 'NO FEAR' printed across the chest. "Why am I wearing this? Is J.C. Penny having a back to school sale?"

"I'm sorry. It was the only stuff in the clothing box that was even close to your size, and you were so wet when I brought you in here that I thought you might be hypothermic."

"You undressed me?"

"Well, yes. I mean, come on, Walter," she says, grinning through a mantilla of smoke. "It's nothing I haven't seen."

"But…" I begin, wondering if this constitutes an answer of some kind to my earlier question about whether or not we sealed the deal. Hard to say. Seems to still be up in the air. She's staring at you. Say something, anything. Ask a question. Open up the conversation. "So…I was naked in the homeless shelter?"

"You're clothes are drying downstairs," says Martha, ignoring my question. "Your boots are by the radiator in commodities so they won't get snatched. Things tend to disappear around here. If you're too embarrassed to leave here like that, you can hang around the office until everything's dry, or I can drop the stuff off at your brother's house when I get off. I assume that's where you're staying?"

"It doesn't matter now. I needed that stuff for work this morning. It's probably too late now. You can just donate it, I suppose."

"You mean you don't normally dress like you're on parade?"

"No, Martha. I was starting a new job today. The uniform was part of it."

"A job doing what?"

"I wouldn't even know how to begin answering that question."

"Well, you don't seem too sad about it not working out."

"I think I have other things to be sad about right now. And I didn't really want the job."

"Then why did you take it?"

238

"For the same reason I took Wilderness Biology with you," I say, aware that I'm feeling sorry for myself, but not sure how to feel differently. Speaking about the uniform reminds me of Henry's promise to call on Cordelia if I didn't take the job at Todes/Stiege, and I'm wondering if he's already tried to follow through on his threat. Perhaps he did what I did; knocked on the door and met Nathan. I can't imagine a more perfect misalignment of personalities. Though vanquishing Henry's hold over me is clearly a Pyrrhic victory, the possibility of him arriving on Cordelia's doorstep intending to woo her like the old days, only to be waylaid by a ponderous, half naked visual artist tugs at the sagging hem of my spirits. I'll have to start appreciating the little joys in life, moving forward. They may be all I have left.

"Why are you smiling, Walter?" asks Martha, dropping her cigarette in a bucket by the steps we're sitting on.

"I'm imagining someone I don't like wasting his time."

"I have to get back inside. We're going to start check-in. But listen: How do you feel about working nights?"

"I think that might be better for me, actually," I say. It would probably keep me out of the tree beside Cordelia's window. Proof seems redundant at this point, but catching her and Nathan having sex might provide a nice capstone to my experiments in hope. I could bring food. And alcohol. Make an evening of it. "Why are you asking me that?"

"You seem unemployed to me," says Martha over her shoulder as I follow her inside. "And I'm at the point here where I'm going to have to begin working eighteen hour days unless I can get someone steady in here overnight. 7AM to 7PM, Friday night through Monday morning."

"You want me to spend my weekends staying up all night alone at the homeless shelter?"

"You don't seem weekend oriented."

"What are my duties?"

"I can go into it more during training, but basically, we need someone here to maintain a safe and sober overnight environment. You assign beds and chores; everyone who stays here does a chore the next day. No chore is a two-day out. You help the clients with meds and bedding, maybe hand out a few sack lunches, and give anyone who acts screwy a BA."

"BA?"

"Breathalyzer, Walter. Blow till it clicks. Bed checks at 10PM, and walk around the building with a flashlight near midnight to make sure no one is sleeping in the dryer vent. Then you hang out in the office and read a book or watch a movie until 4AM when you start setting up for breakfast. If you have to call the police or an ambulance, you log it and write up a report. Then you go home, sleep for eight hours, come back, and repeat. It's simple, deliberate work, Walter. I need someone, and I know you could do it."

"I don't know if this is my ideal work environment, Martha."

"What is your ideal work environment, Walter?"

"Someplace where I blend in with the furniture, I think."

"Well this is not that," she says, unlocking the office door, and admitting the first in what appears to be a queue of residents stretching all the way down the hall into the dining room. She opens a drawer in the desk, removes my wallet and Grover's car keys, and hands these to me. "But if you're interested in doing something other than the nothing you appear to be doing, come by tomorrow at 7PM, and I can start training you. You'll be paid, of course."

"How much?" I ask, as reflexive as a twitch or knee-jerk. I'm ashamed of myself, but Martha smiles.

"That's the spirit," she says, turning her attention to George, who has shambled in behind me, still spooked from our earlier encounter. He's obviously waiting for me to go before he explains to Martha what he wants, and I'm happy to oblige him. The composite smell of cigarettes, whatever meat is being burned for dinner, and the people stacked up in the hallway awaiting their turn is the sort of sensory input that would normally have me whinnying at the ceiling and gasping for air until my ribs ached if I wasn't still exhausted from earlier today. I need a break from myself, definitely. But in the meanwhile, a break from St. Simeon's will do; Martha must be joking if she thinks I'd spend my nights here. But as I'm cruising toward the door, holding my breath and avoiding eye contact, I realize I haven't asked Martha the most important question of all. How could I have forgotten?

"Do you remember seeing me?" I say, reappearing in the door as she hands off a pharmacy bag the size of a pillowcase to a woman who looks reanimated. "Because I remember seeing you."

"What do you mean?" she asks, amused, not impatient, even with the rough and tumble retinue clawing at my back to get in the door. I suddenly feel wanted, and immediately tell myself the wrong thing: Take the job; she is in love with you. I'm thinking wishfully, I suppose, but maybe there's a granule of truth to it. Perhaps Martha's offer of employment is a kind of lovelorn Potemkin village, erected to conceal her true feelings from me. I have an active internal world, I think, watching the shape of her body as she bends to return the pharmacy bag to a metal cabinet behind the desk, the way she put away the groceries I delivered to her house many years ago. But maybe there are possibilities here I'm not exploring. I've essentially forgotten what I came for, and am entirely lost in imagining Martha and I copulating for either the first or second time on the desk dividing us from each other, when I realize I've also lost track of how long I've been standing in the doorway, watching her in a kind of predatory silence. It's clear she's been waiting a while for me to speak when I finally do.

"It was last week, in the evening," I say, regaining control of myself, and chasing my internal wolf back to its den. It's not your fault, I think. Your love boat was torpedoed just this morning. Please pardon me, Martha. "I was walking by, and you came outside and asked people to come inside. We made eye contact, and you offered me a…a sack lunch? Is that what they're called?"

"Very funny, Walter," she replies, turning away, just in time to see a man lunge at another man in the courtyard through the office window. "Now I have to call the police, and you need to go. Remember: 7PM tomorrow. Don't be afraid."

Did she have to put it like that? I wonder to myself, as I toddle through a cordon of smokers gathered on the front steps to watch two men taunt and spit at each other beneath a sugar maple shading the forecourt. Martha stands beside them as if she's directing traffic, her cell phone cradled between her ear and shoulder as she converses with an emergency dispatcher and struggles into a raincoat, though the drizzle has eased to a light mist. I feel needy, and I'm hoping to conceal this by offering to help her wrangle the two men, if only to spend some more time around her. I want to appear valiant. But when our eyes meet, it's as if she's still wondering if I need a sack lunch. I'm still blending in.

That's not so great, I think, as I wander off in the direction of Loomis Street, hoping the house will be empty so I can be alone with the remnants of the day, or that my brother will be at home, and willing to take me up to Burlington for a new wardrobe, as promised. I should probably warn Grover about shirking on my obligation to Henry. My brother may be able to give me an idea of what to expect, in terms of retribution now that Cordelia is no longer a fulcrum. Maybe I should trying solving two looming problems at once, and give Henry Officer Laurel's number. They could put their heads together, and come up with a mutually beneficial way to punish me. No reason for anyone to wait in line. Henry is probably tendering something unpleasant for me right now, while Officer Laurel stalks around New Hampshire, looking for someone named Walter. I'm sure she already reported the van stolen. When it turns up in Waterbury with an empty gas tank and a missing bicycle, she'll know I can't be far away. If I can defray Henry's vengeance until she shows up, maybe I can get them to fight over me. A bad plan, but trying to defend the corner I've painted myself into after pissing both of them off is more than I'll ever be prepared to deal with, and escaping from it feels redundant. I'm already back in Acheron. There's nowhere left to flee.

I don't notice Cordelia sitting on my front steps until I've already rounded the front gate, and it's too late to turn around. An old scar, the place where Lily's trap closed on my leg years ago, begins to itch. My immediate impulse is divided between scampering up the walk and embracing her, or abandoning the property and reclaiming my room at the homeless shelter for the night. But perhaps she's come to apologize and kiss you, I speculate. There's always that possibility. In any case: this is your home, and all is not lost. What sort of admiral dives overboard during a parlay?

The house stands cool and calm behind her in the early evening with a redoubt of green hillside and black mountain enclosing it, and peepers bleating like a choir of fairies from the creek out back as she rises from the porch to meet me. Try to look at her objectively, I advise myself. Or do I mean subjectively? I always confuse those terms when I have to apply them concretely. Let's give it a shot: I see a meaty little blond with eyes like twin saucers

of Delftware on which my heart sits evenly divided between theoretical love and practical betrayal, a sort of still life with Nathan
lactating somewhere in the middle ground.

This has a subjective feel, though it's too late to revise; we're
embracing like old acquaintances, students, rather than friends,
of formal affection with our pelvises arrayed at a polite furlong
from each other as if we expect a nun to appear from behind
the lilac bush with a ruler. The scent of tanning lotion and sweat
rings in my nostrils like a Pavlovian dinner bell; I have to will
myself not to drool all over her dress as I try to escape the sun-
warmed yoke of her arms and press my mouth to some part of
her face, a face I've always found limitlessly interesting. Cordelia
is more handsome than beautiful, yes. And she doesn't have Martha's ability to make me feel hideous when I look at her, a swamp
troll lumbering into things beside an odalisque. Thank goodness
for that, I think, as my lips finally connect with her philtrum, a
stupid place for a kiss, but a kiss just the same, and an emotional
foul ball maybe, but I'll settle for it. How many little victories
add up to triumph? They never teach you that in school.

"Hi," she says almost without affect, and completely unlike
Martha did earlier, while running two fingers between her lips
and nose. She isn't setting any limits yet, chalking the boundary
of our shared field of war, as it were. That must be good. "I didn't
expect to see you, Walter. How did you even get here? And what
are you wearing?"

"It's a long story," I say, trying to avoid explaining the clothes
Martha harvested from the homeless shelter by skipping the
question entirely. "Actually, I wrote most of it down. Did you get
my letter? I left it with Nathan. And while we're on the topic of
people we didn't expect to see, I should..."

"Parts of it. Enough to get an idea of what you wanted to say to me, I think," she replies, doing the same, apropos of Nathan. That's only fair, I suppose, but it's bound to come up again. I'll try later. "You write like a nihilist."

"I don't know what that means."

"It means you only have one point, and you make it over and over again. But I felt like you were trying to trick me into reading more by making it seem like there was something else coming. I don't have the time for that shit anymore, Walter. I got bored."

"The point is that I love you," I say, pushing past her into the house, and turning a sharp left toward the wine rack in the kitchen. I might as well begin drinking, but need a suitable time-out while I think of a way to steer the subject back to Nathan. He has to be the weak link here. I can easily see why Cordelia wanted to pounce on Henry; he's taller, darker, and handsomer than me, and even at a young age, was talented in a way that would obviously make him rich when he grew up. I don't compare because I can't compare. Fair enough. But Nathan is a slob and a crank, the sort of man who looks more and more like a tortoise without a shell as he approaches middle age. People buy his pots and paintings, sure, and maybe he does hear voices. Maybe that's part of being a tormented genius. Maybe they told him to drop out of MICA and busy himself having "unsuccessful" sex with Cordelia in the garden apartment with Heidegger or whatever it was by the toilet while I was blundering around the campus in Ohio, alone and lonely, waiting for her to return. It now seems like a rehearsal for the current state of things. I'd find it easier to take the voices seriously if I didn't feel like Nathan wanted me to take them seriously, and congratulate him on making it through to the other side of whatever shabby cerebral torment he's engineered for himself and now seems to be profiting from. Mind if I steal your girlfriend on my way to self-actualization? Weirdly enough,

Cordelia always used to say that there haven't been any legitimately tortured artists since WWII, and, fool that I am, I took her at her word, right up until she left me to sink or swim in New York while she escaped to New England with young Werther and his paint box. If I claimed to see it coming, the punch line would be ruined.

Maybe they're both fucking nuts, I think hopefully, recalling my mother's informal diagnosis as I return to the porch with a bottle of red wine and two glasses, out of habit. At some point while I was gone, Ruby waddled through the screen door, and began snoozing like an old drunk in Cordelia's lap. Perhaps now she'll stay until I can think of something to say that she hasn't heard before, I hope as my hands tremble too much for me to pour a glass of wine.

"I'm glad you finally slept with Danielle," she says, taking the bottle and glass from me, and helping herself. "She needed it, I'm sure, and now you know what it's like to finally do something you've wanted to do for a long time."

"I didn't want to do it that much, but I missed you."

"Don't say that to me. Own what you did. Do you think I didn't know why you were going over there every time we had disagreement?"

"It wasn't exactly like that."

"Sure it was, Walter. And that's okay. One rock sinks or becomes unsteady, you jump to another."

"If that's true, why are you here? And why am I here?"

"I came to return your letter," she says, handing me a thick manila envelope; the weight of it in my hand is like a promise of austerity from here on out. "And to let you know that I will be returning to New York with Nathan when they reopen the tunnels and bridges. We're going to live together. I was going to tell you when I got there, but since you're here now…"

"But...you just moved out. All your things, our things, are here," I say limply, as if reversing this is impossible.

"It occurred to me when you didn't meet me that I was only leaving because I wanted to have children, lots of children, and because you wouldn't get me pregnant while we were living in a place you hated. I had to go if I would ever have the full range of human experience. You held my womb for ransom, and I let you."

"No I didn't," I say, though this is basically true. "And even if I did, what's wrong with that? You want to raise your children, our children, in a place with the worst public schools and hospitals in the country, no space, no yard, people crawling all over each other waiting in line for every stupid thing, where the most personality I can ever expect to find in the combination of your genes and mine is a kind of educated consumerism, a small-minded New York City chauvinist in miniature. My son or daughter won't know what it's like to see the stars every night or experience profound silence around them, but she or he will happily direct you to the best place in Brooklyn to get buttermilk fried chicken and a nice habanero sorbet to finish. My god, Cordelia, don't you see what's wrong with that? I wanted to provide my children with things that matter. That's all."

"Well, fortunately for everyone involved, that's no longer an option," she says, already weary of listening to me; she's heard it before. "At least with me. I have a great job; I get to wear tweed jackets, eat the best pizza in Brooklyn on my lunch break, and ride my bicycle to work in a library at an art school. I do this every day because I like being at the center of the human world; you hate being anywhere near it. But more importantly, I need to live in a place where things happen. What am I going to do here, Walter? Wear a tweed jacket to the secular sing-a-long at the Unitarian church on Christmas Eve? Treat myself to eating at the same five restaurants after stacking six cords of wood so I don't freeze to death when winter comes? Hope I make twenty thousands dollars a year so I can buy a car and shop at the J. Crew in Burlington? No, Walter, I don't want any of that, and I won't be your backwoods wife, sorry."

"I never proposed to you."

"It was the most considerate thing you never did."

"So what now?" I say, after we sit in malignant silence for a few minutes, listening to the dog snore. "You marry Nathan and hope his hormones even out long enough to get you pregnant, then raise your offspring in an open sewer?"

"I spent so long wanting to make you happy, but not knowing how to do it," she says, ignoring me. "I think I knew how to at some point, but it just went away after we moved to New York. I'm sorry I couldn't do that for you, Walter. I really am. Ultimately, however, it's not my job, and you couldn't expect me to carry you forever, waiting for you to figure it out. I think my being there is why you never did. I held you back. I'm sorry."

"I dislike whatever you're trying to do right now," I say, accidentally tipping my glass into the flowerbed as I try to pour wine into it, and sipping directly from the bottle with a kind of flourish instead. "You and that swine are perfect for each other. You both don't realize how bad you are at manipulating idiots like me; we notice. Just because you get what you want doesn't mean we don't."

"I think after your parents died I forgot how to say no to you."

"See, that's exactly what I'm talking about! I don't understand how you can say things like that, completely untrue things, and continue to live happily with yourself, as if you didn't want me with you here, or in Ohio, or New York, as if all of it was staged for my benefit, as if you were helping me grieve or something, and all of this is the natural consequence of my taking advantage of your boundless goodwill. No fucking way, I don't believe it, and I don't want to hear it. I'm ashamed for you. And Nathan. Together."

"We're moving to Cobble Hill," says Cordelia; I can practically hear the tracks changing. "I have possibilities."

"That seems to imply that I don't."

"I tried so hard to help you find out if that was true or not. Volunteering for the Parks Department, something to get you out in the woods where you always said you wanted to be…"

"Cleaning a beachside toilet in Far Rockaway is not 'the woods.' "

"…I believe I suggested that. Or maybe blogging about how poorly the city was planned. Do you remember that? You were going to call it 'Urban Warfare,' and take pictures of all the great examples of bad urban planning you found everywhere and write about them. I liked that. Or remember me offering to stay with Ruby, and pay the rent for the summer so you could come back here and clear trails for the Forest Service? What happened to that? All of these were good ideas, and some of them were yours. I wanted to see you do something with your time aside from working at that awful leftist tax shelter and reading mystery novels. I mean, you never even finished college."

"Because I love you," I say, limply.

"Even if that were true it doesn't explain why you continued not to finish when we lived in a place with the best public universities in the country. I offered to help you pay; I filled out applications; I even asked professors from St. Margaret's to write you letters. Do you not remember any of this?"

"I remember. But Nathan…"

"You realize I'm doing you a favor by listening to this?" she says, passing me the unconscious shape of our dog, and standing up as if to leave; what's left of my heart dribbles into my shoes.

"He makes it easy for people like you to deride him, people who are happy to tear down everything around them rather than make something of their own. Go ahead then; say whatever else you need to say about it, but realize when you're done, and I leave here, I'm going back to him, Walter. Not you. I'm sorry. This is over."

"He's a fraud; you'll see."

"You only know what I've told you about him, which isn't very much. And what you know doesn't matter anyway because, fraud or not, he's establishing himself. People want to see his work; they want to show it in galleries, and they want to buy it. And even after he moved to Brooklyn, and I had to pretend I didn't want to see him for the sake of your mental health, I never stopped believing in his talent. I knew it would happen for him. I'm just glad I get to be there for it instead of watching my fertility clock tick away while waiting for us to want the same things."

"Come inside," I say. "I'll give you a baby right now. Or out back. Your choice."

"I have to go," she says, checking the time on her phone and smiling a bit as I scour her features for any sign of interest or hesitation. Nothing, aside from the smile; a face like a set of outdoor furniture. "Nathan's show up at the college opens in forty minutes, and I said I would help him set up. He told me to tell you you're welcome to attend."

"I'm afraid I'd have too much wine and end up snapping his bra, Cordelia. No one needs to see that."

"I guess I should thank you for making this easier than it needs to be," she says, leaning down to kiss my forehead. At even this slight suggestion of affection on her part, my hand inadvertently snaps up from my lap like a rake left out and stepped on to grip her ass beneath the dress, and finds no underwear beneath it. So this is how she goes visiting now. Bitterness is watching newness form and being excluded from it, I think as she removes my hand, and steps back. "I'm sure I love you, Walter, but I like being in love much more. You're going to make some girl so happy. I know it."

"I want to make you happy; I love you," I say to her back, as it recedes down the walk, past the mailbox and out onto Loomis Street. Her bicycle clatters to life, and she's gone, up the hill, toward the college, but effectively banished from my life. Ruby watches through the fence, her tail swishing the dormant air of the evening until the sound of the Schwinn fades to nothing, before returning to me, second prize, swilling what remains of the wine on the steps, for all to see.

"We'll get through this," I say, taking the dog into my lap, and allowing her weight to sooth me, like one of the sandbags Cordelia and I used in our yoga classes, long ago. I hope to reach a point where everything within my orbit no longer reminds me of something we did together. At the moment, burning Acheron to the ground and salting the ashes afterwards seems like the only solution. Either that, or paying someone to poison Nathan. I don't have the stomach for anything more dramatic or gruesome, but I doubt Grover would lend me however much it costs to get the thing done. And who would I even ask? After living in New York City, the roughest corners of Acheron seem like Whoville. And in all likelihood, removing Nathan from the picture would only make room for someone else, someone worse, or more similar to the maverick logician, plumber, and chef I always imagined replacing me. Cordelia made herself clear. She's finished. Hopefully, when Grover comes home, he'll help me blame some of this on her. Right now, it mostly feels like my fault; one too many plates of pierogi, long summer weekends watching me read beneath a blanket in bed when she wanted to ride bikes to the beach, or disappointments, generally. That's basically what I'm describing. Like her twenty-sixth or twenty-seventh birthday, I can't remember which, when I bought her a tea kettle from the Sears down the street rather than something more interesting or exemplary of what I actually felt, anything else, because I was too afraid to leave the neighborhood and she knew it, saw me struggle to pretend I hadn't embarrassed myself as I presented her with the box and a premixed yellow cake, not unlike Greer's privilege cake, but with less personality and a stochastic arrangement of candles, and sang happy birthday to her in a warbling little voice as I struggled to breath evenly and not seem unusual. And this was a special day. Imagine what she had to look forward to normally. Head shit, and lots of it. How easy must that have been? Watching me prowl through life like an escapee of an asylum for the harmless but intractably defective. She opened her gift, frowned at it, blew out the candles, and began a conversation with me about how unhealthy she thought is was that I'd never lived alone. This sounded like trouble on the horizon. But it's your birthday, I thought then, looking at her. Some people like to celebrate with dinner and drinks; others prefer to summarize the failures of the people around them to mark another year come and gone. I have no choice but to let all this unspool.

So we sat together on the couch with the red Sears kettle between us like a mediating hydrant as she casually discussed how nice it would be for her if I found my own place when the lease was up, because it had been years, good or bad didn't seem to matter, just: years, and she needed some space. It felt like she was trying to grant herself a birthday wish by asking me to go away for an unspecific time period, so I agreed, watching my reflection in the polished surface of the lesser gift, my gift, wondering if I looked like someone accepting what they couldn't seem to change. So, this is what those alcoholics in the church subrooms feel like, I thought to myself.

Of course, she changed her mind the next morning, apologizing, and saying how much she needed me in her life and liked having me in her space, all the right things. She even made a show of using the kettle to boil water for tea. Apparently, Cordelia was just as afraid of being alone in New York, or alone in general, as I was, so: good, I thought then, settling in to what seemed like a dead heat. Or so I assumed. Until today.

"Let's drink some water and go to bed," I say to Ruby. It's probably no later than 7PM, and I already slept most of the day away on a mattress at the homeless shelter, but what else is there to do? I can't imagine watching, reading, or eating anything, and I'd be amazed if Grover can get a single straight sentence out of me when he comes home; explaining my day feels like it would take an entire geologic age. Sex with someone new would theoretically be nice, possibly even salubrious, but eligible parties are not exactly queuing up at the garden gate. Could I call Martha, and explain the situation? Certainly, but would it yield the result I think I want? Likely not; I envision myself weeping on her shoulder mid-coitus, an ugly possibility. And she isn't expecting to see me until tomorrow. Probably best to keep it that way, rather than trespass any further on her generosity. I'll pretend it's a date if I need to.

I gather the glasses and now empty bottle, and tuck the manila envelope containing my letter beneath my arm upside down, sending a cascade of pages onto the lawn. My life is a silent film, I think. I consider leaving them there, but remember Grover already had to rescue my epistle from the yard once, and it's probably the last thing he wants to see out here when he gets home from work. It's not as if I don't have the time to clean up after myself. As I

squat to reclaim the pages, and begin combing them into a stack
without regard for neatness or pagination, my eye catches something written on one of them: A letter grade. C minus, in red. What
have we here?

The Beautiful Lyre
A Behavioral Analysis of Alcibiades
and his Refusal to Play the Flute.

*Though never suffering the fate of Marsysas, Alcibiades spent
the entirety of his life chameleon-like, that is, changing skins.
His refusal to play the flute in favor of the lyre prefigures his role
as a statesman in many ways. For a flute involves the use of both
hands and mouth, whereas the lyre may be strummed while the
minstrel is participating in conversation. It is in the inability of
the audience to observe both the actions of mouth and hands
that Alcibiades will eventually find his niche. As in the case of the
Egestaeans of Sicily, his eloquent deception of the Athenians allowed him a possibility of conquest, a whim which launched the
disastrous expedition into Sicily. Wooed by his words, the Athenians never watched Alcibiades' hands, which were already slic-
ing their master a more than fair portion of Libya and Carthage.*

It's one of Butch's term papers. Well, not his exactly, but something written by one of his students. Cordelia's father has taught
classics or Latin or Hellenism or something at the college since
before I was born, and I remember helping him read papers like
this several times over Thanksgiving break after Cordelia left for
St. Margaret's. He didn't need the help, but he wanted the company. I hadn't read the things his students had, and didn't understand most of what they wrote, but we both missed his daughter,

and liked to drink beer and read things. It made sense. What doesn't make sense is how it got mixed in with my letter. I set it aside, wondering what the least awkward way of returning it might be, and begin rifling the stack of paper it came from in case something else got shuffled in. My fingers find one, two, three, four, five more before it becomes apparent that the envelope Cordelia gave me contains only a bushel of carelessly written midterms from Butch's graduate seminar on Thucydides' *History of the Peloponnesian War.*

"There's obviously been some kind of mistake," I say aloud, not really believing it, but hoping the statement will become veritable if I declare it to the dusk beyond the porch like a kind of Hudson Valley Hamlet, chasing my father's ghost beneath the apple trees or something. No, the only mistake was not kicking down Cordelia's door after Nathan snatched the letter from me in the first place. Then I could have avoided all of this. I see where I went wrong. And even though she could care less about anything I have to say, he would be reluctant to surrender my manuscript, even when ordered to do so by her. Why? Because he's a fucking weasel, that's why, and having something personal of mine probably pleases him the way a lock of hair thrills a witch doctor. So he did what any weasel would do: stuffed some papers from Butch's desk in the same envelope, and had Cordelia deliver it to me, assuming I wouldn't notice until it was too late, but not really caring either way, I imagine. Cordelia probably thinks he's too brilliant to punish, and why should he have anything to fear from me? I crawled away from the doorstep as he read aloud from my manuscript, the sound of his voice interrupted only by an anxious bleat from me as I settled down in the road to die. All of this spells victory for Nathan, but then: I remember my brother, mild and circumspect Grover, slapping the hatchet out of

Wayne's hand and walking him into the nightshade of the evergreens outside the abandoned summer camp and feel much better about what I'm about to do, what I must do. Nathan needs to be given something to think about.

I sweep the term papers and dog inside the front door, snatch my bicycle from the driveway, and begin pedaling up the hill to the college.

Twenty minutes later, I'm purring lividly behind a curtain in the Castle Gallery, second floor, Gein Hall, listening to Nathan address a group of art students, professors, and curious townsfolk, as Cordelia beams beside him.

"...attaching life preservers to the canvases in the 23rd street show was a creative choice, yes, but also a practical one. If the gallery flooded, I wanted to ensure that my work survived the storm, and perhaps reached someone who was suffering from it and trapped by it; I wanted to expand my audience by assuming their captivity in the conceit of the work, and provide them with a fleeting moment of meditation amidst cataclysm, so to speak. Because, as artists, we extract harm from the world by making art, and create the opposite of an impact. Leave changing the world to the politicians, empty suits with neither the ambiguity of philosophy, or long, endless view of art; so the artist's job is compensatory: to brighten the corners shaded by the clumsy and cruel hand of humankind. Let all work be a prayer to the universe that we are not alone in it, and if we are not alone, and someone is watching, then we are terribly sorry for what we've done as a species, and our art is our burnt offering, our hecatomb, our poured libation. So imagine being stuck on your rooftop, waiting for rescue, and seeing a bit of art of float past. I, for one, would take great comfort in that. Of course, this actually happened.

The show was inundated, and the canvases washed down Sixth Avenue, floating one by one on the life preservers I'd affixed to them, and out into the East River, or who knows where, possibly New Jersey by now. I was lucky enough to have several friends, who selflessly chose to remain in case of this eventuality, capture the event from the windows of their apartments. One of my documentarians even chased the floating artwork in a kayak all the way to Battery Park, before he had to abandon ship, so to speak. How he managed to paddle and use a camera I do not know, but his photographs are being compiled and released as a book, *UnMoored: Love Underwater,* the proceeds of which are being somehow channeled into art therapy for victims of Hurricane Eula. Some of the text for the book is also on display this evening, and generally, what you see here tonight is thematically federated to this same project, a project in which love and loss are celebrated as a single modality. Please enjoy yourselves, and to those of you who are artists, seek to not matter, or work on mattering less."

Asshole! I howl internally, watching him wheel around the packed gallery with Cordelia's armed looped through the paint-stained sleeve of the same blazer he wore this morning. He's managed to put a shirt on beneath it, and a pair of pants and shoes, which I'm embarrassed to admit leaves him looking more civilized than me. I was angry enough not to care whether I blended with the student milieu when I left the house, but after climbing the hill to the college, and crossing the quad beneath the dome of Holmes Hall, past groups of fashionable, educated young people arrayed on a benches along the avenues of trees shading the campus, I realized I was still wearing the clothes Martha gave me at the homeless shelter.

So it's back to school 1997 for me then, I thought, feeling every inch of my outfit as I slunk like a caterer through the gallery's side door, my formerly magmic ire over the stolen letter cooled to an algid shame as I surveyed the exhibit from the tenuous cover of a fire exit. Paintings on the walls, teapots on pedestals, and a few recent-seeming nudes of a woman who is likely Cordelia, or her epigone. I probably should have expected that. Every trail of salt leads to a wound.

Fuck the world, I thought, recalling Huld as I left my hiding place, not sure where I intended to go, but not wanting to spend the evening growling to myself in the stairwell as I did in the clothing rack at Fatale. There's probably no way out of this without making a scene, I told myself, so I might as well figure out what kind I want to make. But I only got as far as the refreshment table before Cordelia appeared as if dropped from the ceiling, standing with her back to me, but not much farther away than the cheese plate I'd been raiding before I noticed her. I froze like a floodlit raccoon, my mouth stuffed with Wheat Thins and Boursin, the stem of an overfull glass of wine pinched between my thumb and index finger as the familiar amplitude of panic settled in my chest. I inadvertently purred, spraying crumbs across the back of her dress, and withdrew behind a curtain with a bottle of terrifically bad Australian chardonnay to help me regroup just as she turned to see where the noise came from.

I'm still regrouping in the drapes when Nathan launches into the same lecture he gave five minutes earlier, the third or fourth rendition, by my count. How he manages to never assail the same group of people is a mystery I'm unlikely to solve, and not the reason I'm here. Though somewhere between the rack where I left my bike and the long walk past people fulfilling their potential, I began wondering if should shelve my revanchism for the evening, skip the opening, and maybe see if there was a counselor

258

still in the admissions office to generate an upbeat list of options for me. Here, Walter, are five things you can do to feel like less of a social parasite. Would I rather leave campus tonight with my letter, or an application for admission to Acheron College? Both seem like a long shot.

There's still time to make someone proud of me, even if it's only Grover, I thought, and still think, already compiling a syllabus from the interior of my hiding place like a fugitive academic. Revenge suddenly seems like a lot of work, and I'm at the point of simply finishing what remains of the wine and escaping through the already open window behind me, though it's a full story to the ground with only a menacing arrangement of hedges to break my fall. If something happened, I'd be too embarrassed to cry for help with Cordelia and Nathan around, and would have to wait for the groundskeeper to find me in the morning. No more unnecessary risks, I think. This is part of your new life. Leave the same way you came in, and hold your stupid head up when you walk back across campus for the bicycle, no dodging between trees and lampposts like a cartoon villain. Behold me, students, and laugh not: soon I shall walk among you! I'm weirdly invigorated by the chance to become an adult learner as I peek around the curtain to check if the coast is clear, and notice Nathan holding court.

"...released as a book, 'UnMoored: Love Underwater,' the proceeds of which are being somehow channeled into art therapy for victims of Hurricane Eula. Some of the text for the book is also on display this evening..."

He points above his head at a part of the show I hadn't noticed: A kind of laundry line strung between the gallery's walls with loose, typewritten pages clothes-pinned to it as if hung to dry. What have we here? I think, reaching out from the curtain to tug at a cord fed through a pulley affixed to the wall beside the window. Let's have a look. I draw in the pages slowly, not wanting to attract any attention to myself as they pass like a forlorn rack of dry-cleaning above the oblivious heads of the attendees, and disappear into the drapes. After unpinning the first, and re-reading a maundering description of coition with Danielle from my letter to Cordelia, the ink muddied and the paper distressed in some way to give it an aqueous, waterlogged look, but my letter, just the same, I have to restrain myself from yanking the entire contrivance out of the wall and using the cord to rappel out the window after strangling Nathan with it. Be calm, I think. You have everything you need to make this right. Think of it as fishing. You have landed the catch of the day. Good job, Walter! Now keep that tip up, and reel it in.

I weight the first page with the now empty wine bottle, and begin reclaiming the rest of them, one by one, detaching each from the clothesline and adding it to the stack on the window sill, swaying stiffly now in the balmy summer wind rolling down from Mt. Abandon. Beyond the window, the campus murmurs in the late evening sunlight with an expectant gravity, as students pass screens of red brick and viridian ivy on their way downtown. It occurs to me that it's Friday, and a beautiful night outside, and here I am, helping Nathan understand consequences. This, and not assaulting him, will be my good deed for the foreseeable future, I think, as the pulley creaks in my hands. I'd prefer not to believe in evil, but he's made it so easy. What kind of morally insolvent narcissist tries to pass off a stolen, extremely private letter as his own in order to publish it in his golden treasury of disaster profiteering? A veteran one probably; plenty of practice under his belt, and the kind of untrammeled sinister agenda that presages wrongdoing the way a constellation of enemy campfires along a twilit horizon promises battle at dawn. If I had to define evil, I would use the world inevitable.

Either that, or Nathan is sitting on enough benzodiazepine to make life one wall-to-wall magic carpet on which everything is either groovy or approaching it. UnMoored, indeed. If only all of us were so lost. I don't see a third option. Maybe the voices told him to do it.

As I collect the final page from the clothesline, and add it to the stack, a lucidly furious Cordelia yanks the curtain aside, exposing me to a room full of people who appear to be confused about whether or not I'm part of the exhibit.

"You followed me!" she yells, yanking me out of my hiding place in order to display me for Nathan, like a bird dog flushing a grouse.

"You invited me!" I counter, gesturing at myself with the wine bottle. The atonal polka that's been playing in my head for the past week ratchets up several notches as Nathan pauses mid-colloquy before a passel of undergraduates to regard me with a kind of ownership, the creep.

"Ah, Walter. So glad you could come. However," he says, gesturing so theatrically at the stack of papers clutched to my chest that I expect a pastel handkerchief to shoot out of his sleeve. "I'm nonplussed to see you've dismantled part of the show."

"I didn't follow you," I say to Cordelia, ignoring him, and slithering out of her grip as I try to claim some neutral ground in the gallery. This turns out to be a kind of no-man's land between the fire exit and a drab pillar crowned with a conceptual teapot. "I mean, I did, but not because I wanted to follow you. The letter, what you gave me today. It wasn't my letter at all. It was a bunch of your dad's term papers. Nathan switched everything so he could display them here, and publish it in his book because he's a complete bastard, and he doesn't care about me, because why should he? But he doesn't care about you either, Cordelia. If he did, he wouldn't have used you to lie to me so he could put your business, our business, up here on display for all these people to see. Think about it, please! This is the man who you want to have children with instead of me, and he's using you like a broodmare for his nauseating creative impulses! Have you listened to him speak? Do you see any room for yourself or god forbid a family in any of that, anything he says at all? Please! I love you too much to see you waste yourself on anyone except me!"

"That's absurd," says Nathan, slurring a bit, possibly even a little angry, definitely very drunk. So drunk he appears reluctant to get any closer to me because he might have to walk, so we end up arguing like men on opposing sides of a gully. "Why, Walter, would I need to create such a jejune diversion?"

"You tell me, fuckface! This isn't my medicine show," I yell, my voice cracking a bit. The crowd titters, though it's unclear whose side they're taking. Cordelia takes my forearm in her hand, and rotates me away from Nathan.

"He didn't lie to me," she says, her anger fading to a kind of pity "It was my idea to use the letter, and put my dad's papers in the envelope. I didn't think you would notice until after the show, and by then it would be too late."

"Why...would you do that to me? Or to us?"

"Because this is art, Walter. It's serious."

"Goddamnit, what?"

"And because I believe in Nathan's work, like I told you earlier. Also, it's my letter. You addressed it to me, meaning I can do whatever I want with it."

"No," I say, even as I allow her to tug the document out of my hands, and pass it to Nathan. "No. Please, don't do this."

"I should add," he says, accepting and flourishing the pages in my direction, but continuing to address himself to the audience standing by, like he's trying to turn all this into some kind of performance piece. No matter where I stand I seem to be in the way of his art. "These have been altered with a solution to make them appear as if they were recovered from the floodwaters, which makes them no longer a letter, your letter, but a work of art, and therefore mine, as well. It seems you have no claim here, Walter, on anything at all. Ah, greetings, *gendarmes*!"

Two uniformed campus safety officers enter the gallery, sweeping the room for less time than it would take me to leave it on my own before their compound gaze settles on me as the reason they were called. They don't even have to ask any questions.

"You a student here?" asks one of them, halting within grabbing range of me.

"Not yet, but I was thinking of apply. . . "

"You like this art?" interrupts the other, gesturing toward some of it.

"No. I feel a little raped by it, actually."

"Then it sounds like you don't have any reason to be here," says the one who spoke first as both of them move in a kind of lumpy choreography to either side of me. "Now we're going to escort you off campus. As long as you don't have a problem with that, we won't have to call the real police."

"No, I think I'm done here," I say, allowing them to bracket me. This all feels more familiar than it should. Meanwhile, Cordelia seems to be going out of her way to avoid eye contact with me as I pass her, sandwiched between the security guards. But she can't pretend she isn't curious how all of this looks, though when her eyes find mine, it's meant as a sort of envoi, and I can't think of anything to say other than something she has already heard: "Cordelia: I love you so much."

"I don't want to see you again," she replies.

"And I forgive you," I add, watching her cross the room to join Nathan, who has no problem at all meeting my gaze.

"Don't forget to write," he says, waving goodbye with the sheaf of my papers clutched in his hand.

"You shut the fuck up, you terrorist windbag," I shout, loud enough to make my escort nervous. They each take an arm in unison, quickening their pace as I bob between them like a cork in a bathtub, only releasing me after we pass through the hallway, down the stairs and out a set of double doors into the night.

"Thought we were going to have an incident there, for a minute," says one of them to the other as we're crossing the quad. He sounds oddly jovial. These men think their job is funny and want me to laugh with them, I think. This would be the point in a musical where we all break into song. "But it looks like we won't need to call for backup after all."

"I don't think our friend here wants much trouble, do you?" says the other, to me.

"No, not all," I say, as they continue to talk over me.

"Lost his girl it looked like."

"Did her new guy appear to have well, boobs, to you?"

"Little ones, but yeah, there was definitely something there."

"Do you reckon they produce much milk?"

"They do," I say, but neither of them hears me.

"I read a story somewhere about a guy who cured himself of erectile dysfunction by drinking his wife's breast milk."

"Sounds like the young lady back there has a lot to look forward to."

"I imagine it's the sort of thing that never quite seems normal."

"I imagine you're right, but who knows what makes people happy."

Not me, certainly, I think, feeling sort of like a third wheel in the discussion, which lapses into an oracular silence as we wade through a shadow thrown by the neoclassical façade of Holmes Hall. Sunlight fades behind it, casting a cool beryline finish over the campus, and making me wish I had something to do other than returning to the empty house on Loomis Street to pet my dog and watch Grover pity me. If I had any money at all, I might go to a bar and try to pick up one of the pert, smart-looking coeds descending the hill toward town. But I've never been much good at that kind of thing, and inflicting myself on someone entirely new has a vocational feeling to it, the sort of thing I have to do in order to keep pace with Cordelia, who has already replaced me. This isn't a race, I say to myself, not entirely sure it's true. Well, even if it is a race, she already won. Meanwhile, no one deserves to be on the disposable end of your longing. Go home. Pet dog. Drink wine with brother. Wait until you're not sad to see if you're actually lonely.

"The suspect seems to be cooperating," says one of the safety officers, biting down hard on the irony of this assessment and seeming to savor it as we reach the rack where I left my bicycle. "And I have to take a dump. Do you mind seeing our friend here to the gate on your own?"

"Uhyut," answers my remaining warder as his friend peels away from us. He watches his coworker march off in the direction of the library, before turning back to me. "Listen: you want me to call your brother to come get you? I'm pretty sure I still have his number, and I don't feel right letting you ride down Town Hill Road like you are. You smell like you've been pressing grapes all day, Walter."

"What? No, thank you. I'm fine," I say, seeming anything but fine as I stare mutely into the safety officer's face, hoping I'll eventually remember who he is or how we know each other if I look at him for long enough. He's probably six inches taller than me, with a bushy auburn beard, and a kind of general alacrity about him; here is a useful sort of person, I think. He can probably fix all the things people like me break.

"It's Wayne," he says, seeming a little spooked by me. I'm not sure how many minutes have passed while I examined his face for something familiar. I notice myself in the window of the bursar's office over his shoulder: my head is cocked so far to the side it nearly rests on my shoulder as I stare at him, unblinking. That would make anyone nervous. I should get a watch. Time these things. Give myself an appropriate window in which to appear unusual. "I don't expect you to recognize me. We went to high school together. I didn't have a beard then."

"No, you didn't!" I say stupidly, unsure whether I should offer my hand for a shake, or a high-five or what, so it ends up hanging in the void between us as if I expect him to kiss it. "So, you're a security guard now?"

"Well, yes and no," he says, appearing relieved to return to a topic with defined boundaries. "I'm a campus safety officer. We don't have security guards anymore. When the contract with Hoffmann Personnel came up a few years ago, someone wrote a grant proposal, and ended up getting a bunch of money to train students in non-violent crisis intervention and first aid, and put them in these dopey uniforms as part of their work-study package. I can't afford the M.S. I'm getting at the forestry school, even with my fellowship, but his way, I can work fifteen hours a week and pretend I have an income. And I don't really do much. Write tickets, and make sure drunk freshman don't fall out of windows."

"But what happens if something actually goes wrong?" I wonder aloud, intrigued by the idea of students policing their own

266

campus; maybe I could do that if they let me in. Officer Walter, re-porting for duty. "Like, suppose I'd brought a...a...a scimitar with me tonight, and waved it around the gallery? What then?"

"Well, then we call the actual police, which is what a security guard would do anyway. This ends up being cheaper for the col-lege, and keeps the drum circle and ultimate Frisbee folks from bitching about the campus looking like occupied territory."

"That makes sense," I venture.

"To some people," he replies, his eyes combing over me as if he suspects I might be one of them. "I'm sort of surprised to see you here, Walter. I heard you moved to New York. And then, nothing."

"It's still nothing," I say, trying to sound cheerful about it. This is how men talk, I think. "Only I'm doing it here now."

"Whatever happened back at the art show seems like something."

"I was operating with bad information. That's what it looks like."

"I don't really know what you mean, but I'm sorry for you, all the same. It seemed hurtful to me."

"I...appreciate that," I say, trying not to make it sound like a question. I was under the impression Wayne and I were enemies, and yet, here he is, offering to call my brother to come get me and expressing sympathy after watching me humiliate myself in front of Acheron's fine arts community. Maybe he and Grover buried the hatchet without informing me. That, or my brother managed to choke a friendship out of him. What am I supposed to learn from this? Steal a man's truck and you've got a pal for life, I think, as I roll my bicycle to the gate beside Wayne, hoping he won't notice I'm using it as a walker and make the call anyway. The cargo bike won't fit in the back of Grover's Honda unless I walk home after loading it in, which would probably piss him off, and I don't have any way to lock it up on campus. I'd hate to see my poor bakfiets end up in a tangle of community bikes behind the college's metallurgy studio. We've come so far together, and it seems to be one of the only things I own outright anymore, stolen fair and square, as I see it. Cordelia will likely keep most of what we had in common to outfit her love nest in Cobble Hill, all the things we stuffed into a U-Haul on the eve of the storm. Did I detect trouble brewing then? Things hadn't been bad, but they hadn't been good either; so nothing new there. A condition I'd come to consider a kind of stasis in the tiny world we shared together, too small for both of us, looking at it now. Nathan doesn't seem like the sort of guy who travels with a trousseau, so she'll probably need all of it, chairs, dishes, lamps, whatever there was. I can't even remember now, so I'll assume I won't miss anything. Did I even have a favorite coffee mug? I don't think so, but I remember taking my morning coffee sitting in the epicenter of a large Persian carpet Butch gave us last Thanksgiving, stroking Ruby and reading a book before I had to leave for work at the Brooklyn Association. I recall this being a happy daily moment. Going forward, I should start establishing these again, the minute joys that made my life in New York slightly greater than the sum of its parts, more than just dragging one foot after the other each day, hoping I wouldn't have to make any important choices or live through anything painful and horrifying. Maybe that's all there really is to enjoying this, and I was always mostly happy, I think, as I pause with Wayne on the edge of campus, the nascent lights of our town, our home, suspended below us in the eventide, while the remaining sunlight unspools along the undulate horizon in a single fibril of perfect fire. Is it possible to be happy without you or anyone else knowing it? I wonder, thinking of Grover's wish for me; perhaps joy is just knowing joy exists. Can I live this way, underwhelmed and apparently satisfied? Maybe it

268

isn't a choice. I don't have to always enjoy my life to be interested in it. What was it Thoreau said about the supreme condition of life? Wayne might know. Ask him.

"Have you ever read *A Natural History of Massachusetts*. . . " I begin, realizing I've interrupted him in midsentence. He tries to continue speaking and I interrupt him again to apologize: "I'm sorry; what were you saying?"

"I said if you're still awake around 10PM, I'll buy you a beer in town. Grover has my number."

"Why?"

"Why what?"

"Why does he have your number?"

"I get my fiancée's parents gift baskets from the market."

"You place an order, he calls you when it's ready."

"That's right, Walter. It's not mysterious."

"Congratulations on getting married."

"We're not married yet."

"I know that," I say. "I mean: I understand the difference. I think I'm just in a hurry to say it's nice to see you're doing well and have a normal life, because I'm probably jealous of it. Take that into consideration."

"Aside from your friend with the bosoms, nothing I noticed about your life tonight seemed abnormal. People separate. It's something that happens when they care about each other for the wrong reasons. Last time it happened to me, my friend Kyle took me out for a beer, and we didn't talk about it. That was best."

"What did you talk about instead?"

"Softball."

"Do I seem like I need to talk, Wayne?"

"I don't know. You seem like you need to be distracted maybe. Either way, I'll be down there when I get done up here."

"I think it would behoove me to drink some water and go to bed," I say. It's technically true, but feels reflexive, a residuum of the contented ambivalence that probably drove Wayne to swat me in the face with a beer can so many years ago. Do I still not want his friendship, even a decade or so later, or am I too afraid of men to be one? Possibly both. At least we're not hitting each other. Maybe I'm growing into it.

I don't have much practice making friends anyway, but I sense I may want them sometime soon, unless I can quickly clog the hole left by Cordelia with someone new. It's short notice, but someone has to be the Band-Aid in all this, right? But who? No candidate paddles to the immediate surface of my selfishness, and imagining myself entirely alone as a result of my bad decisions has an irritating, parabolic aspect. I'd prefer to avoid confronting anything major for the time being; I have my whole life to come to terms with myself. Meanwhile, I'll do anything I can to delay the feeling of having been buried alive, so to speak, at a Viking funeral; set adrift and burning on the waves as my funeral party watches, deaf to my screams over the roar of the flames, my loneliness irrevocable as the pulse of the ocean beneath my diminishing bier. Cordelia told me once this isn't actually how Norsemen dispatched their dead; they got drunk, raped a slave, and arranged stones in the shape of a boat or dragon or something. But it isn't them I see on shore; it's her, and Grover, my parents, a few others perhaps, all watching and receding.

Yes, my nightmare of isolation is historically tenuous, but I'm past the point of trying to prevent what I imagine. Thus, I try to justify and absolve myself before Wayne instead, whose opinion of me has suddenly become important; a peculiar development, considering our history.

"I don't know anything about softball," I say, "but I think talking about softball at the bar sounds good, though if I'm awake, I'll assume she and he are too, and start wondering what they're doing. So I guess if that happens, if I'm awake after I drink some water and go to bed, I'll probably call you anyway."

"It's going to hurt either way for a while," says Wayne, nodding to another peace attendant or whatever they're called in a booth beside the gate as we pass beneath it. "Twisting the knife is one thing. Some people hang a trapeze from it."

"I know," I say, not sure I do.

"Maybe you do. Just make sure you're not the one swinging from it," he says, touching my shoulder in a kind of salute on his way back inside the gate. "Good to see you, Walter."

"Uhyut," I say, still not sure what he means, but glad to have something to puzzle over as I walk my bicycle home in the bat-flung dusk. So, I think. Time doesn't heal old wounds. It salts them. I'm determined to find joy in that.

III.

"If you do not become a hypocrite…perhaps you will be a man."
—Stendahl, *The Charterhouse of Parma*

Dear Cordelia,

I'm writing this in the spirit of good faith, I promise. Bona fide; from my Latin, recall, part of the degree I never finished. And also as a coda, of sorts. I promise I will not apologize, because I don't think you're expecting an apology, and I believe dropping one in your lap, too late it seems now, will annoy you. So: I'm not sorry, at least not until the end. But seeing as you're planning to publish the letter I gave you, I'm hoping you might include this, if not in the body text of "Love After the Flood" or whatever Nathan calls it, then perhaps as an appendix or something. I wish I didn't have to write anything; I'm a little bored with myself at the moment, so I can't imagine how you must feel reading this, assuming you're reading it at all. But, listen: I promise not to bore or depress you. Or not much. A tall order, considering me, but it's important for you to know that even after all these years, there are still things you don't know about me, and if you never want to see me again, it's important for me to share them. It won't take long. There aren't many. Just one really. But I'd like to see them in print along with everything else to give you and your readers a full understanding of what you're leaving behind. You've allowed Nathan to make us into characters; I hope you both will allow me to develop mine.

Also, after I ambushed you at the gallery, I walked home thinking about how sexy you looked when you were unpredictable, and how long it had been since either of us surprised each other. It made me sad for a variety of reasons, none of which I'll share with you, as promised. But I was also comforted by it, the thought that I might have been as bored with you as you were with me, and maybe you'd just realized it first. I can live with that; second prize still implies an achievement. I'm sure I would have continued to love you for years, bored out of my mind by it, but with love just the same. However: I'm glad you had the foresight to help us escape each other; I will always love you for it. Please don't feel guilty, or feel like I'm trying to make you feel guilty. It's no longer important for you to love me back. I mean that. And I know I said I wouldn't apologize, but I'm sorry for blaming New York City for everything, a place that meant so much to you, when it was us, our fault, all along.

Speaking of New York, I wanted to share the most embarrassing moment I ever experienced while living there with you. I'm sure you think you know what it will be; the time I had an anxiety attack on the security line in the Jet Blue terminal at JFK and had to lie down in the middle of everything and hum to myself on the floor, while you shooed people away and told them I was just 'wigging out a little.' Or the Christmas party one of your coworker's hosted at her apartment, where I sat in the corner the entire evening, reading a copy of Legends of the Fall *I'd found in her living room, entirely absorbed and content, occasionally crying to myself in front of the people you worked with at the library, until it was time to go. What about the winter Butch attended a symposium at Columbia, and tried to take us to see a ballet by Tchaikovsky at the Metropolitan Opera, and I was so worried about 'wigging out' during the performance that I broke three glasses during dinner with him at a somewhat up-scale restaurant on Amsterdam Avenue, finally opting out of the evening altogether and citing a vague objection about good old Pyotr Ilyich being a pederast, how wrong it was to celebrate his work and so forth with his passion for young boys; your father, being a classicist, had no idea what to say to this, but was kind enough to reserve judgment, even after a copy of* Death in Venice *came flapping out of my backpack while I was threading myself out of the front door of the restaurant. I didn't even bothering picking it up; you brought it home with you after the ballet. I still haven't read it.*

But no, none of these, and I'm confidant you don't know what I'm talking about, because I never told you. And it is my own memory; you had no part in making it. A strange concept, I know, considering how much information we stored with each other over the years, and you being a librarian; everything new must be checked in, given a call number, and stored to ease rec-ollection or recapture. But I'm afraid the foremost humiliating incident of our tenure in New York occurred recently, while you were at work, and I was alone one warm afternoon in August, running through Prospect Park. You'll remember this phase: I wanted to run, and didn't know how, but thought I should try it, and see what happened. Yoga was something I did for you, my love, I'm sorry to say. I wanted you to believe you had a modern, sophisticated gentleman at your side, not a jittery lunatic whose fight or flight mechanism was so impaired that he couldn't sit in a

274

restaurant for more than five minutes, or meet new people without immediately being suspicious of them. I always assumed I had no business running anywhere, but wondered if forcing myself to flee each day after I got home from work might make me easier to live with, so it was really a decision I made for us. You'll recall: I bought hysterically ugly shoes anyway, mannish tights, and a nylon jacket to break the wind, and wore them each day, bouncing like a disunited piston along the asphalt hamster wheel encircling the park, beside the performance cyclists and other runners in better shape with nicer gear, wheezing and gasping like the Canadian geese gassed by the city department of parks and recreation, but loving you deeply enough to torture myself this way as a hobby. Once again, I'm not trying to curry guilt; some people want to stay in shape for their partners; I wanted to stay sane for you.

What happened this particular afternoon in August was a basic New York problem. As I rounded a bend in the trail near the boathouse, I was seized with the sudden urge to evacuate. I glanced around for a solution, even a clump of bushes to conceal myself, and found nowhere this could happen. I felt very alone with myself and my urge, rapidly growing into a need, to void my bowels in a huge, alienating city without public restrooms. New York doesn't care if I shit in my running shorts, I thought with a kind of petulance as I glanced frantically in the direction of the Brooklyn Public Library, too far up the hill with Grand Army Plaza encircling it like a moat to do me much good, and closed at his hour anyway, and back at the dormant barrack of the boathouse, and at the coverless ground extending from where I'd stopped in every direction. There might be a chemical toilet somewhere in the park, but the city seemed to reshuffle them every week or so, like a kind of septic musical chairs, meaning if one existed, it could be anywhere. This is happening whether

I or anyone else likes it or not, I thought. The only question is: where?

Cordelia, I don't want to gross you out, but there is no other way to explain this. I had to go, I couldn't hold it, and there was nothing to make these two facts of life agree with one another. I was too far from the apartment to make it back, and wasn't in good enough shape to get there with any real speed. I mutely envied the divisions of runners passing me like gazelles, and considering toppling a cyclist off his bike and pedaling myself home. I had nowhere to run, and nowhere to hide, so I improvised: I ran across the great lawn until I found a good size tree, a Maple I think it was, with a fresh coat of opaque green leaves shielding its crown, and hauled myself up into the foliage, climbing until I managed to find a bifurcated branch which bifurcated then again, forming a pair of organic stirrups to hold my feet and legs in a position of easement as I relaxed into what I was doing. My tights dangled raggedly from one ankle like a pelt hung out to dry, and I'd lost one of my shoes during the struggle to remove them. Down it went, hitting every branch on the way before landing in a bed of mulch. I hoped my droppings wouldn't hit it, but if they did, I could live with that; Shit on My Shoe: A New York Travelogue, by Walter Ratliff.

I was strangely at ease with myself, my body at a relaxed right angle as I rested my back against the trunk, and used the crotch of a branch holding my feet as a sort of toilet seat. I was too relieved to care about the shoe, and strangely proud of my ersatz latrine, and myself for finding it. I'd managed the impossible, hadn't I? I'd finally triumphed over the inhuman city of New York, and its endless raft of humiliations! I was so unused to the feeling of success that I luxuriated in it, embowered in the verdant branches with my pants down, dropping my dung on the impatient world below like a feral pigeon. Life was suddenly good, so exquisite in fact that as the last tuft of waste left me and plummeted to the earth, landing squarely between the boots of an NYPD officer peering up at me from the mulch bed, I remained oblivious until he actually spoke, wondering if I could pat myself on the back without falling out of the tree.

"Okay, my man," he said, sounding almost sorry to bother me. "I'm going to need you to come down from there. I'd prefer with your pants up."

I considered climbing higher, but did as I was asked instead, pulling up my shorts, and fiddling with the belt I wore with them, and gingerly descending the tree. The day's emotional amplitude was clearly beginning to devour its own tail; no running from that. I narrowly avoided my own waste as I reached the ground, but was momentarily relieved to find my lost shoe untouched. The cop allowed me to put it on before leaning me against the trunk of the tree where I'd enjoyed such happiness only a moment earlier, and handcuffing me.

I never found out who called, or how I got caught, but as I was led toward a cruiser idling nearby I noticed another officer speaking with a wedding party gathered on the lawn. The bride and her dovecote of maids seemed to be awaiting a behavioral cue from a chorus line of strapping, Italianate groomsmen men in rented tuxedos who looked like the sort of people you would expect to find either waiting tables on a Mediterranean cruise line or burying someone like me in a fifty-gallon drum outside the Meadowlands. Their compound poise suggested either the beginning of a fight or a tap dance routine. In the foreground, a photographer raked his shoe through the grass, muttering to himself, but looking at me. This was not how I imagined our wedding, the one I'd half-suggested the night of the fireworks in Julian

Falls, though I noticed things about it that would have appealed to you. The groom had strong hands, a feature I didn't possess, but something you always admired in men, and the bride was pregnant, second trimester by the look of things, and everyone appeared happy to see them together. With a few adjustments, I could see you in her place, but didn't find room for myself anywhere in the wedding party except the treetop. I wondered what the odds were of finding everything I had always feared about you and hated about myself in one place as the cop ducked my head inside the rear of his patrol car, seating me beside a tall, handsome West Indian wearing cleats clotted with dirt and a soccer jersey.

"Man, officer, this guy smells like poo, for real," he said to the cop, now leveraging himself into the front seat. "You going to sit me next to a guy who shit his self?"

"You want to ride in the truck?" asked the officer, while his partner examined my driver's license under the console light. "Walter here likes to climb trees and shit on folks. Give him a break."

"That's gross," said the West Indian. "And fucking crazy."

"I didn't shit on anyone and I'm not crazy," I said, not really thinking my response through. "But I had to go and there wasn't anywhere else."

"Is that some kind of Vermont thing?" asked one of the officers, sounding genuinely curious, as he typed information from my license into a computer in his lap. "Where is that anyway?"

"It's like six hours north," I said, unsure whether or not I was being made fun of. "Next to New Hampshire."

"Is it a country place?" asked the West Indian.

"Yes," I answered. "Not so many people live there, so there's more room for trees and things."

278

"They got bed and breakfasts?" asked one of the cops.

"Well, sure, I mean, it's New England; every third house is a bed and breakfast."

"Sounds nice," said someone.

"It is," I agreed. "In fact, I'm supposed to be on my way there in a few hours. Is there any chance I can pay my bail or whatever I need to do and get going with enough time to avoid the storm?"

"You don't just pay bail," said one of the cops. "You have to be arraigned first. And the court's closed right now with the weather. Should open up tomorrow morning so they can clear out some of people before the storm hits."

"So I'll be spending the night in the city jail?"

"Bring a toothbrush," said the other cop. "And hang onto your soap."

So that settles it; all is lost, I thought, as we drove toward the Brooklyn Bridge. I watched the passage of overfamiliar personal landmarks from the window of the police car. The corner of Flatbush Avenue and Bergen Street where a motorist threatened to shoot me for yelling at him from my bicycle after he nearly killed me in afternoon traffic. The upscale market where we bought the same gentrified groceries each week. The single tree outside Long Island University under which I spent the most interesting hours of my workday. There was clearly nothing to miss, but I'd imagined seeing all these places for the last time from the window of the moving van parked outside our apartment on Caton Avenue so many times, had buttressed the interminable days at the Brooklyn Association with fantasies, it seemed now, of escaping the city with you. And on the day of our departure, here I was, headed to central booking. Because of the approaching storm, all criminal idiots like myself were being stored in the main branch of the city jail in case we needed to be moved to Riker's Island or something. At the time, I imagined you arriving at 100 Center Street, and rescuing me. Now I understand why you left. It may have been your only chance. But I want you to know I was waiting for you.

By now, you may have guessed this is the reason I never showed up to leave with you for Acheron the night before Hurricane Eula hit the city. This was something my original letter never mentioned, and I was too embarrassed to share when you showed up on my porch with that spurious batch of your father's term papers. What could I say then? That I had nearly shit on a blushing bride from the upper reaches of a mature Maple tree in Prospect Park, and was being charged with public excrescence and criminal mischief? Even though we told each other almost everything, I couldn't tell you that. But I thought I might owe you and any potential readers of 'Drowning Love' or whatever Nathan calls it an explanation, so I hope you'll consider appending this to my original letter as an epilogue.

In closing, I want to mention that I've been thinking about what you said; how I will make some girl so happy, and I've decided it's probably true, though perhaps not in the way you meant. I realize I'm nobody's prime cut. I'm handsome in a way that attracts people, usually women, who want to improve me, or need someone to fill space while they grow up. You never wanted to improve me, and for that, I'll always be grateful. But I've decided this may be my romantic niche, and it's really not such a bad one. As a fixer-upper, I can always count on never having to entirely pull my own weight, and as placeholder, it's not like I need the husband practice. I'm actually sort of thrilled to be at the center of a perfectly closed system. This wasn't enough for you. I understand that now. But for someone else, it might be, and if I can make them happy without having to change, then it's possible I won't be alone forever, hopping from rock to rock, as you said. I'm sure neither of us sees much self-work in my future. Someone on planet earth has to be okay with that. Maybe even attracted to it, if I'm lucky. The other possibility is too horrible to consider. Not to be dramatic, but losing you scared me more than losing my parents, because when they died, I still had you. This was unhealthy. But when you said you didn't want to see me again after the art show, I remembered something Paul told me on the roof of the Brooklyn Association shortly before he died. We were talking about having children. I said I didn't want any, and he expressed a kind of resignation over his own childlessness. I've had three families, he said, and none of them want to see me, so I don't think I'm meant to be part of something like that.

He was talking about being adopted by people who didn't like him as a child, getting married to a woman who didn't love him and who he didn't love, divorcing her, reconnecting with his birth family, and eventually falling out of touch with them one Thanksgiving when he took the train from New York to Boston to visit his sister and her kids. He came alone, and she met him at the station and explained her idea of family, which, she said, was people getting married and having children, and getting together at holidays to watch these children play. She told him he didn't fit into that, so he got on the train and came back to New York.

The reason I'm sharing this is because I realized then, as Paul and I stood beside the cell phone towers on the roof of the building on Nevins Street, watching Flatbush Avenue fart and whistle below and Brooklyn ripple in the near distance, that I wanted a family of my own, just not with you. We had done so much during our time together, but this was something I couldn't imagine us doing. I'd been working on bribing you with insemination in order to get you to leave the city with me, and assumed I would find a way out of fatherhood once we'd landed back in Acheron. Something would get in the way; I was counting on it. But the concrete part of what it meant to actually have my own children got a bit lost until Paul inadvertently helped me excavate it. Seeing him basically alone, except for the occasional liaison with Linda the bodybuilder out in Bergen County, and knowing he died alone shortly afterward, I saw myself beginning to lope along in his footsteps, and it scared me. The unbearable lightness of having no one who gives a shit about you, how easy it was to achieve, but don't misunderstand me. At this point in my life, I know I would make a very kind, bad father, but I'm hoping when I meet someone who isn't waiting for me to get it together, and is just fine with a fixer-upper, I might be able to relax long enough to seriously examine the parts of my life I need to work on in order to be a parent. I was always waiting for you to leave, but hoping you wouldn't, so there was never time for that, though I want to thank you for helping me eventually understand what I want and what I need are not mutually exclusive. I'll always remember you as the person who taught me this. I'm sorry there was nothing I could teach you, but I never finished college, as you know, and am kind of a land-going dummy as it is. I'm sure our expectations had never been lower than they were the last time we saw each other, but you were still able to surprise and edify me even during this, our nadir. Thank you, yet again.

I hope and assume you'll be doing everything you want by the time this reaches you, and I miss whoever I thought you were very much, and continue to love her, mightily, I think. Not to sound petulant or sanctimonious. I don't consider this a cross I must bear to a little Golgotha all my own. On the contrary: when I look around, I'm relieved to find my life a mess, with or without you in it. Perhaps someday our children will play together on the village green outside Acheron town hall while you're visiting your father for some holiday, and I'm still here, fiddling around. Until then, I remain,

Affectionately yours,

Walter

P.S. Thank you for allowing me to keep Ruby. I realize you paid the adoption fee, and footed most of the vet bills, but these past few weeks would have been very difficult without her unwavering support, and I am eternally grateful to you for allowing that to happen.

Martha looks up as she finishes reading, and begins spinning a cigarette between her fingers rather than commenting on the letter. It's 3AM, and we're approaching the homestretch of my cotillion with Acheron's homeless community. I've spent most of the evening watching Martha do my job, not sure how she expects me to do it. Shortly after arriving, I stood with her in the hallway outside the kitchen, as clients lined up. She assigned them chores while I juggled beds, scribbling names on a clipboard with the berths listed on it with a kind of abandon as I rerouted residents through the laundry room to get bedding. Between lulls in the check-in line, I studied my bed sheet like a catechism, trying to get some idea of which names went with which faces. Martha told me this would make my job easier, shortly before introducing me to hundred or so people waiting in the dining room.

"And finally, this is Walter," she said, gesturing at me at the tail end of the evening's announcements: Thank you for doing your chores, please do not prop the doors; if we catch you propping the doors, you will be asked to leave, this is a safe and sober nighttime community, so we will be doing random BAs. Several voices fresh from the NA meeting upstairs said: Hi Walter. "He'll be here at night on the weekends. Be nice to him. Now, let's get rolling. You're checking-in with me for a chore, Walter for a bed, and if you're new, get to the back of the line."

How on earth am I supposed to remember all these people? I wondered, as chairs scraped against the tiles of the dining room, and people stood as if their flight was boarding. Years in New York City had left me quietly repulsed by homeless people, even the family-friendly ones who occasionally become local personalities in certain neighborhoods. I remembered the guy outside the Brooklyn Association, doing chin-ups on the walk-sign between four lanes of traffic on Flatbush Avenue, and tried in some way to square his imprint with the denim clad kitchen cowboy who helped me locate the office earlier in the week.

"Avery Von Spitzmäuse, bed fifteen," he said, tapping the clipboard, and extending his hand. "Welcome aboard, pilgrim."

We shook hands, and he clinked away on spurs toward the laundry room. Name like a hillbilly count, I thought, that should be easy to remember. Up next, Linda Blossom, bed twenty-two, name obviously fake, early forties, no teeth, glasses, long gray hair, probably weighs ninety pounds, looks content and crazy. Moving on: Lurk, bed seven. Just Lurk apparently. Early twenties, built like a short-faced bear, face tattooed with what look like peacock feathers. I'm sure I'll remember you, I thought, checking him off, as Martha shouted a last call to anyone we might have missed. The night unspooled this way, with me hugging close to her and trying to remember everything she did as she went about her duties, handing out sandwiches and juice to people too intoxicated to stay, performing bed checks after lights out, and patrolling the alley between the shelter and the building next door every few hours after sunset. As we walked together around the dumpsters behind the kitchen, shining flashlights in any likely ensconcement along the way, I said something about how watching her work made me feel utterly incapable as she paused to light a cigarette.

"It's the easiest job in the world if you can do it," she said, offering me a puff; I accepted. "And I wouldn't have you here if I didn't think you could do it."

"I'm afraid I'll embarrass you," I said, meaning it. Martha hooted.

"Have you forgotten where you are, Walter? It's not like I gave you an internship at my dad's law firm; you got grandfathered in to the graveyard shift at a homeless shelter. Embarrassment isn't an option."

"I just want to be baseline competent for you, Martha."

"You'll understand it all in a week or two," she said, nudging a bundle of blankets on the side porch with the toe of her shoe before speaking to it. "Whoever is underneath all this, you need to move off property. We're closed to the public after 7PM, and it's now 2AM. If you leave now, I'll let you keep your beer, but if you don't move, my friend is going to dump it out."

She handed me an open tall boy of something truly vile, and tugged the blankets away to reveal a middle-aged guy with an eye-patch glaring monocularly at us. Just like Ruby, I thought, wrongly.

"Give me my shit, cutie pie," he growled at me, a pair of dog tags chiming against his chest as he raised himself to a sitting position. "Or I'll skullfuck you silly and take it anyway."

"I don't want to hear that," I said, surprising myself as I emptied the can onto the pavement. Did I just stand up for myself? That never happens!

"Fuck this donkey dick!" said the guy, speaking to Martha

and pointing at me. "What do I got, PTSD, fucking depression, and all kind of other shit from serving this goddamn shithole of a country so you come-to-do-good, stay-to-do-well types can dump my fucking beer out and tell me where I can sleep!"

"We're telling you where you can't sleep," said Martha, beginning to walk toward the front of the building. "You have five minutes to get your stuff together and move along; then we're coming back out here. If you're not off property by then, we'll call the police."

"I'd knock a little faggot like you through the wall," said the guy to my back as I hurried to join Martha. "Not that I'd need to do all that. Constipated little blouse boy like you. You've never been afraid of anything that matters in your whole shitty life. I can see that even with one eye in the dark."

That's probably true, I thought, scurrying after Martha. I was afraid I'd embarrassed her, or made something worse by dumping out the beer, and apologized for this when we got back to the office.

"Probably you did make it worse," she said. "But you also did the right thing. Our policy is to dispose of any alcohol we find on property, and there are more than enough other places to drink yourself stupid in this town. Coming here to do it makes no sense. I only offered to let him mosey with it because I know the guy, and I figured it would move him along."

"But he didn't move along."

"Right. So he lost his libation. We couldn't take away his extension because he already lost it."

"What do you mean?"

"Every client gets forty-five days here at the outset, so roughly a month and a half. Anything beyond that, and they need to file an extension request for another two weeks. Supposedly we grant extensions on a case-by-case basis. The committee doesn't hassle people too much about it, but we need to have something in place to check the malingering, and motivate clients to find jobs and apartments. The point here is if you're caught drinking or drunk on property you automatically lose your extension and can't come back for a month, which doesn't deter most people, as you saw with our friend just now."

"Does he react to everyone that way?"

"Mostly. You did fine, Walter. Please don't make me give you a performance review every ten minutes. Haven't you ever had a job before?"

"My last job no one cared what I did because what I did didn't matter."

"Well, assume your instincts are good, or you wouldn't still be here, at 2AM, discussing them with me," she said. Don't be so sure, I thought, admiring her in the jaundiced light of the office. Long tan swimmer's legs extending from a pair of men's Carhartt cutoffs. The outline of a sports bra beneath a leaf print t-shirt. Hair kept in a sort of stylized bowl-cut, *sine cura*, beautifully ugly in its own way. These are the things I like apparently. So, yes, still carelessly stunning, I thought further, content to admire her in silence for the remainder of the evening, and I'm still admiring her now, at 3AM, as we walk outside to share one of her cigarettes and discuss what she's just read.

"Gospel according to fucking asshole," she says, jutting out her chin to emit a plume of smoke. Like a dragon, I think whilst speculating: My dragon? "Maybe that's a bit harsh. You really want all that to be somewhere people who don't know you can read it?"

"Why do they have to know me?"

"Maybe it would be better if they don't," she says. "But you said something in it about that guy..."

"Nathan. Not a guy as you and I might understand one."

"Okay. Whatever. You said something about him casting you as a character, right?"

"Yes. Being around him makes me feel like a marionette. I wish I knew why."

"None of that really means anything to me, Walter. But when I read what you wrote, I get the overwhelming sense that you've cast yourself as a bumbling fucking idiot who things just happen to; maybe you enjoy this, but pretending it's up to him and not you just seems like a typical cart/horse problem."

"I'm finding wherever I put the horse doesn't matter, Martha; the cart never has any wheels."

"Is that some kind of riddle? You're avoiding responding to what I just said rather than denying anything, so I'm going to assume you see some unfortunate truth in it.

"Maybe I just don't want to argue with you."

"Maybe you just don't have an argument. Pity has a terminal velocity. You can only hang out in the foreskin of victimhood for so long before everyone starts wondering why you don't just go somewhere else. Many of the people here are great examples of that. Do you really want to tell the women you supposedly love that you got arrested for shitting from tree branch in a public park? Is that the last thing you want her to know about you?"

"Considering the context, do I have choice?"

"Of course you have a choice, fucking dummy!" shouts Martha, tossing away her cigarette and jerking open the door to the office. "It's like when you have nothing to say you just debase yourself for her, and hope someone will notice and redeem you. Like, good job, Walt; here's the prize for hanging in there when it made no sense. Does it ever occur to you that you don't have to say anything? She fucking dropped you. Fuck her. Don't send the letter; burn it."

"Well, thanks for reading it and giving me your opinion. How long have you been single?" I ask, thinking: I love you a bit, yes; let's talk about you now.

"Oh, fuck you, Walter," says Martha, not unkindly, as I enter the office behind her, and close the door to the alley. "Long enough to recognize how afraid you are of being alone."

"I want to pretend I'm not, but I'm curious how obvious it is."

"It's almost 4AM," she says, rather than answering. "We have to go put out breakfast."

In the kitchen, she makes coffee in a huge, doubled-barreled urn, while I dig through milk crates of donated baked goods, wilted Danishes, desiccated strudel, muffins like hardtack, searching for something I wouldn't be ashamed of feeding to the clients.

"Just bring out whatever's here," says Martha, grabbing one of the crates as the urn burbles malignantly somewhere in the background. "Donations run a bit thin toward the end of the week, and people mostly just come for the coffee anyway."

I follow her to the main area of the kitchen, and begin helping unload the comestibles, following her lead as she stacks boxes of donuts and plastic trays of croissants on the buffet like she's building a retaining wall between us and the dining room. At some point, our hands touch as we're arranging bags of week-old bread, and I get an erection. Fine time for you to show up, I think, heading toward the walk-in freezer to cool off before Martha notices anything. I select a packet of frostbitten chicken breast, and press it against my groin, not realizing the labels says Grover's Market, until I've subdued myself and returned the frozen meat to the shelf. Nice of my brother to donate, I suppose. Maybe there's a way to apologize to him for this without admitting what I've done. I suddenly want a shot and a beer more than anything I've ever wanted before, but settle instead for three bottles of orange juice substitute, victory juice, and two jugs of one percent milk, which I drag out of the cooler like a man escaping a house fire, intending to set them on the buffet beside everything else. I'm hoping I look like a man doing his job in front of Martha.

But she is already out in the dining room, setting up tables and chairs with several clients risen early; Milt Cohen, bed 23, older, schizotypal, friendly enough to me during check-in, and a gentle, self-destructive soul, according to Martha. Teresa Rush, bed 7, young but older than me, dishy, weird, works at a Taco Bell somewhere in Shelburne, offered to help me look for blankets down in the basement earlier in my shift, and, god help me, I nearly went, just to see what would happen. I suppose I just answered my own question about how scared of being alone I must look. She catches me watching her straighten chairs in the dining room, and I nearly kill myself stumbling over Thomas Winter, bed 17, as I try to scurry out of eyeshot; Thomas carries a carafe of coffee out to the dining room, meaning Martha is about to open up. He's ex-military, built like a steamroller, probably just old enough to drink, with 'WARRIOR' tattooed across his throat. During our limited encounters, he always seems to be on the verge of losing control of himself, and even as he swerves around me with the coffee, being helpful, I'm poised for a backdraft of some kind, waiting patiently to be knocked through a wall. But Thomas continues on, not even turning around as I follow him into the dining room, where he sets the carafe on a folding table, nods good morning to Martha, and pinches Teresa's ass before going out on the porch to smoke.

I guess they're morning people, I think, watching her gaze ardently at the door through which he exited the dining room, ashamed to find myself jealous of them, and wondering what the hell she meant earlier by asking me if I wanted her help getting

290

blankets from the basement. Maybe she just wants to be helpful, stupid, I think further, watching a line of people enter the dining room through the porch door, and shuffle past the ziggurat of baked goods on the counter behind me as they sip thin coffee from chipped mugs, and exchange cheerful information with each other. Gary Gibson, bed 16, fortyish sex offender in a fringed leather jacket and a service animal, a puppy named Mr. Mason, brings in a bundle of newspapers, Acheron Monitor fresh off the press, and begins distributing them around the tables. I don't notice Avery Von Spitzmäuse until he leaves a table by one of the windows, taps up to me on his spurs, and asks if he can switch on the kitchen radio. I'm so pleased to be reminded of my authority that I assent, and soon, a soft, mawkish country song, something by Carl Smith, accompanies the general calm and leisure of the dining room at 5AM, as residents hum or whistle along to the music, sipping their foul coffee over the local news like inmates of a patisserie in the 16th arrondissement. I'm irritated by the possibility that everyone here is having a better morning than I am, including Martha, who finishes speaking to several clients at Avery's table, and gestures toward the office when she notices me gawking at her. Follow you? I think, watching the tired shape of her body sway as she sways down the hall. Why, of course. Any-where. Into a volcano, if that's what it takes.

"Good morning," she says, closing the door behind me as we enter the office. "I need to know now if you can do this job. I'd like to give you more time to think about it, but the fact that I don't have anyone else to ask if you say no means I have to do this now. Not to put pressure on you, Walter, but this is how it is. I'd like to have some of my nights back."

"So, I'm hired?"

"Yes," replies Martha; neither of us seems to know if I'm joking.

"Do you feel prepared? I mean, I'll be working the swing shift with you, but can you handle breakfast and whatever else comes up?"

"If I can't, I'll figure it out," I say, not entirely sure this is what I will do, but it feels like something I need to say to put her mind at rest. She doesn't know how long it's been since I've had to demonstrate anything I've learned. Maybe if we're both lucky, the decision to hire me won't come back to haunt her. But the false confidence seems to have done its work. Martha appears grateful as she comes around the desk, and I'm hoping for a kiss on the cheek at the very least, or some sort of lady's favor to hang from my lance as I go forth on my own to act as zookeeper for the residential population of St. Simeon's. I seek only virtue, but will accept love in aid of it, I think, cocking my head to the side and presenting my cheek. Bedizen me, fair maiden.

Instead, she surprises the shit out of me by posting up for a high-five, and I rear back like a startled show pony, afraid I'm about to be slapped. You never ask yourself 'why?' in these situations, I think, barely recovering myself enough to conceal how disappointed I am as she thanks me for saying yes, and we shake hands like aldermen at a groundbreaking. Well, if we're going to work together, I suppose we should both get used to this kind of thing until I learn how to not beg for what I want. It's odd; I don't miss Cordelia. But I miss loving her enough to make every pitfall along the way to loving someone else seem irrecoverable; please pardon me, Martha, while I trip on my dick and fall down a well.

No, this won't do at all, I think as she settles down behind the desk, tired, pleased, ruggedly erotic, and I park myself on a folding chair in an alcove by the client telephone to watch her do my job. She passes Linda Blossom a bindle of prescription medications from a metal cabinet behind the desk, gives Lurk the address and phone number for a vocational rehabilitation center in Burlington, and goes upstairs with Parson Whitaker, bed 14, an ancient Texan, former military sharpshooter, ex-shrimp boat captain, recovering from a post-op E. coli infection contracted at the VA medical center in White River Junction. Even watching Martha leave with Parson to help him retrieve his belongings from a closet outside the second floor men's dorm makes me jealous. Good god, I need to get a handle on this if I want people to treat me like a grownup.

Linda returns with her sack of medicines, and hands them to me, a white plastic garbage bag with her name taped to it, signs the medication log I slide toward her across the desk, and asks if I have any toothpaste. I take a cue from watching Martha the day before, and point to the closet behind her.

"Oh good," she says, tugging at the door with an arm like a broomstick while I try to guess whether I need one or both hands to completely encircle her waist. "I don't have any teeth, but I like to brush my tongue."

I didn't need to know that at all, I think, as Martha returns with Parson, who gives me the kind of steady, appraising look my father used to use when I lied to him about unimportant things before thanking Martha, shouldering his backpack, and leaving the office. Linda, gumming a tube of toothpaste, follows him out the door. Thank you, Linda for teaching me something new about what I find disgusting, and thank you, Parson, for reminding me I'm no good at man-to-man stuff.

We're suddenly alone, Martha and I, like the young man and woman occupying this same office on Thanksgiving morning many years ago, I fancy. I always thought they might have been in love, but now I think they were just too tired to know whether they were unhappy. Both are a kind of contentment.

So am I content? I wonder, and continue wondering when I leave two hours later, replaced by a Jesuit volunteer from St. Michael's up in Winooski, feeling suspiciously at peace with myself as I walk home at dawn through the fogbound, verdurous streets of Acheron. The constellated lights of homes, and an occasional, solitary driver hang and pass respectively in the brume, and I'm nearly home when I notice the footsteps behind me.

Am I being followed? I wonder, too tired to be afraid, but curious enough to pause outside the gate to my house, waiting for whoever is behind me to emerge from the palisade of mist at the end of Loomis Street. When nothing happens, I'm almost disappointed. The footsteps pause before receding, their hesitation a kind of silent prayer to the paranoia I normally court at all hours of the day and night. Despite this, I take several steps away from the gate, and call her name into the mist.

"Cordelia?"

I try several more times before giving up, and going inside. I'm not sure what I expected. Grover is awake and fussing around the kitchen, preparing for work. The look he gives me when I walk through the front door makes me feel like I'm returning home after a year at sea.

"Was that you yelling outside?" he asks, sliding a Platonic omelet from a pan onto a plate beside two wedges of perfect toast, bronzed with butter.

"Yes. I thought someone was following me."

"Why would they do that? Was someone there?"

"I don't know, and yes there was," I say, only realizing I've taken a piece of toast from his plate and begun eating it after I nearly choke, and have to scurry to the fridge for a beer to wash it down. "I've decided not to worry about it. Eventually they'll figure out I'm not meant to lead."

"If you're hungry, I can make you something," he says, watching me shake my head as I eat his breakfast. "And, also: where have you been? When you didn't come home last night, I tried not to worry, but you've made that kind of impossible with everything that's been going on, so I drove around looking for you. Stopped at the town jail. Dropped in at the bars on Clamence Street. Called the hospital. Felt stupid and came home. Now that you're here, seemingly intact, I'm glad I didn't round out the night by showing your picture to the habitués at the pool hall."

"Sorry, Grover. I was with Martha."

"Oh. Good, I hoped it was something like that, but I didn't want to go peeping in keyholes to find out. Anyway, good for you, I think. How's she doing?"

"Fine, maybe, but she doesn't seem to want me like that. We were at the homeless shelter."

"I see," says Grover, nodding as he chews, like this is what he expected me to say. "So...you're hanging around the homeless shelter now?"

"I'm not hanging around. I'm paid to be there. So is she."

"Oh. So it's a job," says Grover, relieved. "You have a job. Well, Good. Very good...But is that really what you want to be doing right now?"

"I don't know. It was nice to spend the evening worrying about other people for a change."

"I feel like that's all I do anymore," says Grover, standing and sliding his plate over to me; a perfectly bisected omelet leaking a tendril of Gouda and wisps of chive remains.

"Please don't worry about me," I say, tucking in. "I'm not going to do anything stupid. Or more stupid, I suppose. What I mean is: I won't embarrass you. Again."

"That's not what I'm worried about. Wayne told me what

happened at the campus," says Grover. "I saw him at the bar last night while I was looking for you."

"I'm glad you two made up."

"I'm sorry, Walter. You could have called or something. You can always call. I just wish you told me."

"Sorry. Explaining everything felt like living through it again. Still does. It's okay. I don't have anything I need to unpack, and no one needs to know."

"I think I understand that. But you're living here now," he says, gathering his keys from the table, and removing his jacket from the back of a chair. "And when I hear things like what Wayne told me, I imagine you suffering and I'm not okay with it, even if you are. I don't want it in my house."

"Remember when dad first got the us internet?" I ask as I tuck my plate in the sink, trying to worm my way out of a serious discussion of how I'm feeling. "It must have been in like 1995-96."

"Sort of. What does that have to do with what we're talking about?"

"We're talking about suffering. In this house, as you said."

"I still don't see what this has to do with that."

"Well, dad asked you to make me an email for school? Remember?"

"No. I don't."

"Well, I ended up with beep_beep_shitheap@aol.com as my first email address. And you said if I told dad or mom about it, you would show them the collection of adult magazines my friends and I stole from the beverage redemption center hidden in the treehouse. So, until I figured out how to change it, I got to be beep_beep_shitheap whenever anyone at school asked for my email. I used to tell people it was pronounced 'shy-theep.' Where did you even come up with that, anyway?"

"I'm sorry. I was a rude child."

"You were almost fifteen," I say, watching my brother smile for what may be the first time since I've been home. "And I suffered in this house because I trusted you."

"Part of trust is knowing when to abuse it," says Grover, stepping over Ruby on his way out of the kitchen. "You're on the night shift?"

"Indeed. Seven to seven."

"Well, there's food in the fridge, but if you want me to have someone from the store drop something off at the shelter for you and Martha later on, let me know."

He leaves before I can thank him, swallowed by the fog. I wash my plate, and set it in the rack beside the sink, beckoning Ruby as I head upstairs to bed. I'm strangely fine with the last twenty-four hours, an unusual feeling, considering where I spent the past twelve. I feel like I should be a little depressed after seeing people struggle with themselves, or the indifferent world, whichever it is, but I'm mostly just glad to come home at the end of my shift to someone worrying about me and asking if I want my dinner delivered. Sometime late last night, or early this morning, after the clients were in bed, Martha was walking me through the paperwork, and said something about how aside from all the obvious reasons people came to St. Simeon's, drugs, mental illness, medical bills, injuries, abuse, trauma, debt, unemployment, the one thing they all had in common was no one caring about them. I sat with that for what seemed like an appropriate amount of time, and then asked Martha to read my letter.

*　　*　　*

I no longer wish to be taken by surprise, I think to myself, as I pass Cordelia's house the following evening on my bicycle, and notice the moving truck in her driveway. Not the same one, of course, but an identical model, freshly rented. At least this means she'll leave soon, and I can start developing theories about how successful and content she is without me, instead of seeing evidence of it each day on my way to work. A bright thought, though I spoil it by imagining Nathan's paints and clay sliding around the back of the moving truck in place of my books, hundreds of promiscuous volumes without focus or order, suggesting a kind of birdbrained autodidact rather than an eclectic knowledge of anything in particular. The nearest thing I had to a legacy on this earth, my gentlemen's library. Reading was most of what made the days in New York pass without feeling wasted, so I suppose in the end, owning enough books to entomb myself made sense. And they were the one physicality I assumed would always anchor me to Cordelia; if getting rid of Walter also involved removing the archive he'd made of the spare room, it would be easier for her to keep me, and take it from there. The idea of erecting a fort to keep things in rather than out seems profound until I remember it's called a cage, not a fort, in English.

But whatever it was, prison or palisade, it took less effort to collapse than I thought, because here we are, or here I am, witnessing the closing movement of it all as I creak past on my bicycle, trying not to scowl in the direction of the house in case she or Nathan are home. Nothing adds ardor to new love like watching someone else fail at it. I would hate to be a reminder of what happens when you no longer know how to make yourself interesting to the person you care about most.

I soften my scowl, and direct it ahead of the bicycle, toward Martha, I imagine, waiting for me at the gate of St. Simeon's like a pioneer wife standing in the door of her cabin as her husband crests the last hill before home, bearing gifts and stability. I don't know what I want or expect out of all this, but it's nice to spend the evenings with her, and a group of people worse off then myself.

How strange to anticipate going to work with a measure of joy; this may be the first time it's happened. Is that what real life feels like? Perhaps; the first thing I did after waking up at 5PM and having a cup of coffee in the backyard was call Grover to take him up on his offer. Dinner for Martha and I, will be delivered around 11PM by one of his deli adjutants. I'm hoping a nice meal at the homeless shelter will seem like a date before she realizes it. Since the circumstances surrounding our reunion prefigure me as a kind of romantic event horizon, it's important to fly below the radar on this one. I attempt to put myself in her place: Would I invite someone into my bed after finding them waiting to die on a public street in the pouring rain? At this point I just might, but Martha's expectations are probably dialed a bit higher. Still, stranger things have happened recently. How can I forget Officer Laurel? I'm sure she hasn't forgotten me. At some point, the police van malingering at the rest stop in Waterbury will be discovered, and it's only a matter of time before the stunt in Springfield comes back to haunt me. But when? I ask myself, saved from answering when someone calls my name from Cordelia's yard. I swing around in the saddle, and notice Butch waving beside the mailbox, and I wave back automatically, catching myself too late. No hope of ignoring him now.

"You don't need to be scared, Walter. She isn't here," he says, drawing me into a man hug as I dismount my bicycle and lean it against his fence; I hadn't realized we were so close, but then, Arvin's hug also surprised me. Perhaps people are kind. "She and that nitwit are up in Burlington for an opening. I guess he got some of his naked pictures of my daughter in a show at the ferry terminal by the lake. How are you then?"

"I expected to be doing a whole lot worse," I say, trying to avoid his eyes, a deep, almost royal blue Cordelia inherited from him. They're frankly spooky mooning out from behind the kind of spectacles a college health plan pays half of, and beneath his blonde stockbroker haircut, fading to gray now. What else? Not so very much. A slight, lusterless frame beneath the sort of polo shirt and checked shorts getup that only looks right if you're watering your lawn with a beer in your hand. Butch fulfills only the latter criterion, since no one in Acheron waters their lawn; it's a town of bad Americans like that; career subversives, and lifestyle terrorists. Butch offers me one, which I refuse by explaining I'm on my way to work, and he asks where.

"Oh, man. You've got to have a big heart to do that shit," he says, when I tell him. "A music teacher friend of mine up at the college, he used to play his cello for those folks during lunch. No one knew what to make of it. He stopped after someone started following him home from the shelter. He never figured out who it was."

"That happened to me the other night."

"Someone from the there, you think?"

"I don't know, too foggy to see. I just heard footsteps."

"Be careful; small towns are where things happen sometimes."

"I thought it might have been your daughter. Maybe she forgot to tell me something."

"You miss her, Walt. That's okay."

"I'm not really sure what I miss, but I think it has something to do with her, yes."

"I miss her mom everyday," says Butch, in a way that doesn't promise expansion.

300

"I miss my parents," I reply, hoping to provide parity.

"Well, you know life was good when you miss people who were part of it," he says, knitting the looming awkwardness we share into a kind of joint aphorism. I'm grateful, but can't thank him without ruining it. "Listen, she wanted me to call you about your stuff after they'd left, but since I saw you, what's the point of waiting? You know what she's doing."

"I think the point is that she doesn't want to see me, Butch."

"Well, they're up in Burlington tonight, as I said, and she mentioned something about fucking Nathan being invited to an after party at a lake house in North Hero or some such horseshit. I realize none of this is making you feel any better, but the point is if you wanted to drop by and claim anything after work, I'll be here, and we can have that beer."

"Unless you want to drink beer with me at 7AM, it may have to wait until after she leaves, Butch. Though I'm glad to find you don't like him much more than I do."

"Nothing to like there, Walter. Boy with paintbrush seeks SWF to hold easel and stoke self-love. But her body, her choice, as you know. If it's any consolation, she never asks what I think of anything. That might be why you're getting to hear this. And a guy from my department was at the gallery, and he told me about it. I didn't even know you were back in town, but I figured it was you. Sorry she was part of that."

"*Vae victis,* I suppose."

"*Vae victo,* Walter. It was only you."

"Well, Nathan obviously has a good idea of what she needs; I never did."

"It's hard to tell what you need until you dump it overboard."

"I didn't realize you thought we were such a great match, Butch."

"Oh, I don't. Never did, actually, and I always figured something like this would happen, but I didn't want to make myself into some kind of Henny Penny by warning you. And after you guys started going to school together in Ohio, I thought maybe I was wrong."

"I think she only asked me to come out there because Nathan dumped her, and dropped out of St. Margaret's. He moved to Baltimore; she needed a friend."

"Well, you and her got a few good years together. That's all anyone gets from the people they see every day."

"I'll keep that dreary thought in mind, Butch," I say, extending my hand. "I have to go to work."

"Come get your books out of my basement," he says, taking my hand, and drawing me into another hug. "We'll have a beer, and grade my student's shitty papers. I need a friend too, occasionally."

So do I, I think, waving to him as I mount the cargo bicycle, and continue on toward the shelter, and Martha, trying to resume my scheming where it left off, but find myself snagged by a memory of Cordelia removing her shoes, and running away from me along the deserted horseshoe of Bondi beach beneath a slate winter sky while my insides churned like the apparent ocean itself from a seemingly benign breakfast I'd had an hour earlier; poached egg, smoked salmon, toast with jam. I couldn't digest Australian cooking; this was a problem I'd developed the first day in Sydney, where we'd come to stay for two weeks with a friend from St. Margaret's, who'd emigrated to escape his credit card debt. He took us to a fish market beside the harbor to eat oysters, and during the walk, I had no choice but to announce to both him and Cordelia that I had diarrhea, and needed to find a bathroom immediately. We were embarrassed in canon, but there was no way to escape it; our friend and his partner allowed us to stay in their spare room, where we listened to them drink and fight like longshoreman late into the night, fancying ourselves above the kind of conflict resolution that ends up moving furniture around a room.

And yet, when I watched her run from me, down the beach with waves unwrapping against the shore like doors closing, one after another, I knew she knew I couldn't follow, because I needed to find a bathroom. I'd told her this, and I realized she didn't care. This was no longer an experience we were having together, and not the sort of thing I could solve by slapping a reading lamp off an end table. I was sick, and she was well; that settled it. I'd always thought of this vacation down under as part of one of our good years, as Butch said, long before I stopped being able to breath, but in point of fact, it presaged the shape our relationship to come. She, at home in the world, and I, needing to find a low traffic area to shit in it. All the warnings were there, and I'm sure many others will pop up in the rearview as time passes, and I remember more. Plenty to look forward to, no matter what, even if the obvious is only obvious after it happens. Still, I wish Butch had said something, but I suppose we became friends too late.

Paranoia is wondering whether Martha dressed up for me or someone else as she delivers the night's announcements in the dining room before starting check in.

"...as you know, it's now 7:30PM, and we are closed to the public. Doors are locked, friends; please do not prop them. If you need to smoke, use the back door off the TV room, or utilize door times; these are 8:15PM, 8:45PM, 9:15PM, and 9:45PM. We will not answer the door between these times, so plan accordingly if you want to leave after check-in to go to town or out for a walk, a movie, anything like that. Yes, these policies are annoying, but they're designed to keep us all safe. If you think you'll miss the last door call before 10PM lights out, please use the late sign out sheet in the office, and expect a BA when you get back, so make sure you can blow zeroes. We need to know who's here, and make sure everyone contributes to making this a safe and sober place to live…"

She's exchanged the Carhartt cutoffs for a skirt, of all things, a garment I never expected to see on her, which she wears like a kilt above a pair of soft leather boots breaking at the knee. Absent also is the mossy oak t-shirt, replaced with a sort of night-going tank top worn beneath a secretarial-looking sweater, the sleeves quartered at the elbow as she reads through notes clamped to her clipboard.

"…And thank you once again for doing your chores; this place doesn't work without your help, and we are all grateful. But please remember to ask staff for permission before entering the kitchen, even if you have a chore in there, cleaning the hoods, emptying the grease trap, rotating the bread, anything like that. A lot of stuff is going missing, so if someone is in there who shouldn't be, that's an automatic thirty-day out. Theft, of course, is a pending permanent out. So please ask folks. Walter and I are here to help you, and we're not going to let anyone go hungry…"

At the sound of my name, I raise my eyes from examining the shape of Martha's butt beneath the nearly diaphanous skirt, finding myself pilloried with desire by the lack of a visible panty line, to nod affirmatively at the crowd waiting for her to finish speaking. Yes, I too will feed you, hoping none of them caught me, but too interested in the outfit to care who notices. The colors and cut of what she wears don't really matter to me. All of them combined announce big plans after work. I hope it isn't true, but perhaps this is why she was so eager to have a night off. I could blame myself for making this possible by taking the job, but that feels almost hubristic. I'm still adjusting to the idea of love finding a way to triumph over interference from people like me, I tell myself, as I watch Martha speak, poised, lush, quite near, quite far.

"...and last, I know it's summer, and I know it's hot in here; thank you, as always for staying civil, and maintaining a respectful, community atmosphere when it's not always easy. It's hard to live this way, and what staff don't know about it, we try to acknowledge, so please, always communicate with us if there's a problem, or if you need to talk something out. That's what we're here for. Thank you all for being here for this; you're checking-in with me for a chore, Walter for a bed, and if you're new, please get to the back of the line."

She smiles at me over her shoulder when she says my name, and our eyes meet, hers betraying nothing, my own probably wailing an oratorio of neediness. I notice in addition to the change of clothes, she may have also trimmed the bowl cut into something a bit less squirish, which provides some food for thought as I barricade myself with the bed sheet and breathalyzer behind a Dutch door past the kitchen entrance, and begin taking names and redirecting foot traffic in need of bedding toward the laundry room.

Earlier in the evening, several clients smoking in the courtyard, Avery, Thomas, and Linda Blossom, greeted me as I wheeled my bicycle through the side gate, and I managed to return their greeting without have to dig too deep for their names, startling myself. I lived next door to the same nice, tea-drinking, cat-oriented couple on Caton Avenue for three years, and couldn't remember what either was called, even though our indolent postwoman regularly gave me their mail. And yet, as I shuffle the St. Simeon's residents between beds, I find my recollection of each of them, their name, their face, the small details of why they're here, nearly perfect, or perfect enough to keep the line from backing up into the dining room and irritating Martha. Warren Green, bed 32, late twenties, career transient, serial arsonist, and painter of bizarre but not very good miniatures, several of which are displayed in the staff office. Leslie Vollmer, bed 4, early thirties, drools, clearly deranged, sleeps with a CPAP machine so: needs a bed near an outlet, diagnosed with scabies and proscribed cream which she asked me to apply to her back at 2AM because she couldn't sleep; both of us were rescued by Martha. Andy 'Red' Martin, bed 22, solidly in his fifties, no idea how he got the nickname, though he reads Tolstoy in the alley when the weather is nice, so may have given it to himself, traumatic brain injury from a logging accident two years ago for which he receives a small disability check, currently waiting to receive a settlement, so he says, enjoys prepping lunch salads in the kitchen, and has a fucking fit, according to Martha, if you move him to anything else.

I wonder if remembering all this crap might be a sign of an even greater, unrealized talent, something I could really use to my advantage, but find myself returning to the corporeality of Martha, standing in the entrance to the dining room with her clipboard as she assigns someone I don't recognize a chore. The important things in life will always escape me, I think, as the man approaches, raising the brim of his baseball cap like the visor of bascinet to reveal the sunburned face of Vernon Gilkey. It's unclear which of us is more surprised to see the other; probably me.

"Gilkey! Sorry, I mean…Vernon. What are you doing here?" I ask.

"I live here," he says, readjusting his hat and lowering his voice as if we're discussing something secret. "I mean, I did for a bit, when the weather was bad. I was sleeping in my jeep for the past few weeks, just came here to eat and shower before going up to the camp in the morning. But my gear got snatched last night by some of the lowlife punks who hang around under the bridge out by Quim Crossing, so now I'm here, where I guess you work? Is that right?"

"Since yesterday," I say, offering my hand. "Sorry, I didn't take you up on your offer."

"Well, it's good you didn't," he says, taking it. "At this point, I'm just waiting for the check to clear, and I'll be on my way. No idea where that would've left you as the low man on the totem pole. Though I'm glad to see you down here instead of up at the camp with that fucking Naphta."

"I don't think I understand. The last time we talked, you were all set to go ahead with…Green Grave? Is that what it was? What happened?"

"Got bought out," says Vernon. "Like I said, a great idea doesn't have to work for it to be successful, and now I'll never know. I guess Isidore was approached by Mr. Todes and Mr. Steige, who got wind of it somehow; knowing that boy, he probably left a prospectus or something in the copier at the downtown office for one of the little ghouls over there to find and run up Henry's flagpole. Or maybe fucking Naphta spilled the beans, lapdog son of a bitch, but it doesn't matter anymore. They made us an offer, with options, for everything, the intellectual property, and the supplies we ordered, even the mummy clinic on Town Hill Road, up by the college. All gone, and their problem now."

"So…You're rich now?"

"I'm signing some papers tomorrow to make all this official, but the short answer is: that's right."

"Sounds like good news, Vernon."

"In a way, Walter."

"I'm wondering why you're not happier about it."

"Since Izzy and I never got this thing off the ground, I don't think it had any integrity to preserve. But it would have been nice to see a thing we built succeed, like the way I used to write a menu at home, and watch it change and grow into something completely different when I brought it to the restaurant. The way they framed their offer left me with the impression that taking it was the only way I'd get to see that happen, at least in this town. And neither of us had the capital ready to just uproot the entire operation and move it somewhere far enough from Henry to keep him from being interested. So we took the deal. I'll know how well Green Graves does by the size of the check I receive in the mail each month. Sort of everything and nothing at once."

"I want to say I'm sorry, but I envy you," I say, watching the line of people building behind Vernon; time to move him along. "You want a bottom or a top bunk for the night?"

"I know everyone around here prefers a bottom, but I'd be much obliged if you'd put me up top, in the corner of the second floor dorm if you can. Lots of leaky folks around here. No one wants to wake up to that. Also, I can read with the light from the exit sign and not bother anyone."

"You got it," I say, writing him in on the bed sheet with one hand, and shaking his with the other. "Nice to see you, Vernon. I'm sorry you're disappointed, but I'm glad you won't be hungry, wherever you end up."

"Well, I appreciate that, Walter, but don't envy me. It's just money, and I expect it'll get me through the next few years. Then I'll be right back here, asking you for a top bunk. Or maybe you'll be gone by then," he says, turning to walk away and collect his bedding, but pausing, as if something just occurred to him. What now? "Speaking of hungry, those folks and I, Henry, Mr. Todes and Mr. Steige, we're all having dinner at the Herrenhof Inn tomorrow night to sign the rest of the papers, all that shit. They told me I could bring a guest if I want, and you might as well come along. They probably meant a lady, but I don't really know any in this town, and women don't usually eat much at a dinner with strangers, and they're paying so we might as well take advantage. Should be right around 6PM."

"Thanks. I'll think about it," I lie as he disappears into the laundry room, having no intention of going anywhere near Henry for both the near and distant future. I'm sure bailing on the job at the camp will catch up with me eventually, but there's no reason to invite punishment when it's already in the pipeline. I return to my work; who's next? Muriel Falwell, bed 9, could be anywhere from fifty-five to seventy, BPD, OCD, PTSD, epilepsy, emphysema, MRSA infection, tattoo on her right breast of either a fierce-looking bird or a dragon, don't want to look long enough to be sure, and the proud of owner of between five and nine plastic grocery bags of complete crap. As she whistles through a litany of woe I can do nothing about, I search the space above her head for some sign of Martha to reanchor myself in reality, or fantasy perhaps, but see only a line of people, waiting to sleep.

Later in the evening, I watch two drunks waltz around the ally beside St. Simeon's, following them with my flashlight like the entire thing is a floorshow, not really sure what else to do, because I'm alone, and shocked to find myself in charge. I would like someone to order me around now, I think, but Martha excused herself early, asking if I minded and whether I felt comfortable on my own after I returned from doing bed checks around 10:30PM. Of course, I said I did, assuring her all would be well, trying to maintain a duckblind of competence and fortitude, keep up appearances, while quietly furious with not so much her, as the meal I'd ordered for the two of us, due to arrive in an hour. I would have to dine alone.

It wasn't Martha's fault. I'd meant it to be a surprise, so she had no idea how excruciating having a nice meal with only myself sounded. Chew, stare at the wall, don't think about it, I told myself, knowing I should have called the entire thing off after seeing her outfit, an obvious sign of trouble brewing, but I wanted to believe she'd dressed up for me; my experiments in hope continue. I watched her from the staff office through a slat in the blinds, slipping into a newish-looking pickup idling at the curb, a hillbilly chariot of some sort, though I couldn't get a look at the driver. It pulled away in a thrum of horsepower, and I withdrew to a desk chair and my paperwork, missing her even though I didn't have a right to, and upset with myself for forgetting how little I had to offer someone realistic, like Martha.

But I could use her help now, if only to manage the two men circling each other in the alley, shouting sanguine, imprecise threats in the moonlight, and entirely ignoring me as I try to insert myself in the conversation from a safe distance.

"Look shitbird: I seen what you done down at Quim Crossing, and everyone knows he didn't deserve it cause that boy's blind in one eye from trying to pull out on his motorbike with the kickstand down, but I got two good eyes, pigfucker, and both of them saw you going through my kit!"

"You won't have two good anythings after I get done with you, and you talk to the right people, you'll see that little fuck had it coming both ways, trying to tell people he seen me with Michelle the night she went to the lake with those boys and got hurt by them. She and I been done, and I don't want nothing to do with her anymore. She's trouble so I don't see how anyone is surprised it caught up with her. You know it too.”

“This ain’t about her at all, it’s about you with your hands in my shit. My things is mine!”

“What do I want with your bag, old man? I got everything I need, and I never stole nothing from anyone. But you should know if you keep accusing me, you better knock me down with your first punch, and I’ll let you have it, cause otherwise I’m going to get up and kill you with mine.”

“You don’t know anything about killing; you couldn’t even kill a dead man already in his coffin.”

“We’re all dead, old man, where you been?”

It’s too dark to tell who is saying what, but it’s getting a little existential for my taste, and would probably go on all night if I let it. I need to do my job, and get these morons to move somewhere else before the neighbors call the police for me. I don’t know them by name, but I know neither can come inside, permanent outs, as Martha says. Even if they weren’t, they’re both too drunk to pass a Breathalyzer, meaning they also can’t be on property after 7:30PM. Though the demarcation is vague, the other side of the alley is generally considered to be the sort of public space where men can drink hard, get stupid, and kick the crap out of each other without constituting a policy breech on my end. I take a deep breath, and another, before taking three large, slow steps, and planting myself athwart the men, both with a combined six inches and one hundred pounds one me. I am about to be torn apart, I think.

“Evening, fellows,” I begin, trying to control the quaver in my voice as I flourish a lanyard with a staff I.D. Martha gave me earlier in the evening. “I work inside, and I’m afraid I can’t have you down here, making a commotion, so if you could move to other side of the…”

"Making a what?" asks the younger.

"A…commotion. A lot of noise."

"Boy: men are talking. Give room," says the other, sounding almost kind about it.

"You're not listening. If you don't move along, ten feet over that way, I will have to call…"

"Nope, you're not listening," says the other one. "We got things to settle here, and this is my town, so you don't get to tell us where to do that. When we're done, I'll go ahead ring your little doorbell over there. You don't need to come out. Just call an ambulance for this fucker."

"I'm afraid that's the end of it for you, friend," says the older guy, stepping past me. I don't actually see the knife, but I hear the blade release, and notice a glint of metal between the men as I flee to the incomplete shelter of the side porch, watching them fence with one another in the moonlight as I call 911, stumbling over myself when the dispatcher asks for a description of my emergency.

"There's knife fight in the alley beside St. Simeon's," I say, which sounds almost romantic compared with what I'm watching: two brutal idiots cutting the air between them to pieces in a kind of ballet of low expectations. The dispatcher asks me if anyone is injured, and when I say not yet, tells me to keep my distance until police arrive. As if I was planning on mediating this bullshit, I think, ending the call, just as a police cruiser pulls off the street, into the alley, revealing the duel in a fan of headlights.

That was quick. Did I just experience a fugue? I wonder, as Officers Roland and Downing exit their vehicle, two people I haven't seen or thought about since we went to high school together, the former a gentle, almost friar-like man who surprised us all when he chose the police academy instead of the seminary, and the latter a maladroit lunatic who everyone in our graduating class knew would become a town cop. Roland hangs back in the shelter of the door, mildly addressing the men over the car's loudspeaker as they continue swiping obliviously at each other.

"Evening, Bugs, Percy," broadcasts Roland, sounding tired, and worried. "We seem to have caught you fellows in the middle of a pretty serious disagreement, but I wanted to remind both of you that whatever it's about isn't worth either of you getting hurt, and us having to come down here like this, and take you in. You guys are friends, remember? Separate, and sleep it off, please, before one of you ends up needing stitches."

This doesn't produce a noticeable effect on the proceedings. Downing allows his partner to negotiate for ten more seconds before wading between the drunks, Bugs and Percy, slapping the knife out of the hand of the older guy, and kicking the younger one squarely between the legs. Full stop. Roland approaches, looking disappointed as Downing cuffs and frisks both men, rolling them onto their sides in case they need to throw up, which may be the most considerate thing I've ever seen him do. He notices me as I step off the porch, and begin crossing the alley.

"Stay back, sir!" he shouts, throwing up a hand. "This is a crime scene!"

"But, I work here," I say, gesturing at the building behind me, and plucking my lanyard off my chest, sort of relieved Downing doesn't remember me. "And I'm the one who called."

"We didn't get a call," he says, murmuring something into a radio attached to his epaulette. "Now, go on inside. This is under control."

"I'll handle this, Downing," says Roland, holding out his hand as he approaches me. "Evening, Walter. I didn't realize you were back in town."

"Uhyut, seems I am, Roland. Nice to see you, and Downing too, I suppose."

"Don't let him bother you; our softball team had a rough weekend. Playoffs against the fire department. You said you called this in?"

"A few minutes ago. I thought that's why you were here."

"No, we were coming by to drop someone off, if it's not too late. We got a call about a woman soliciting at a rest area just past the exit, and found this lady trying to sleep in one of the picnic shelters. She said she just needed a ride up to the Canadian border, but no one would pick her up, so she was walking. I don't think she was soliciting, and Downing actually agrees with me. It looks like someone maybe misunderstood her. Since we just got a call and have no witnesses, we brought her into town, hoping we could drop her off here; we couldn't leave her sleeping out by the highway."

"She ever stayed here before?"

"She says she hasn't."

"Is she drunk?"

"Nope. We gave her a BA. She's fine."

"Anything else I should know, Roland? Sorry. Officer Roland?"

"She seems pretty scared of something, but won't tell us anything about it," he says, leading me over to the cruiser, and unlocking the back door; I notice the dim outline of someone in the back seat. "I have to cancel your call, Walter, so please pardon me. But I assume since you're working here I'll see more of you in the future."

He says something into his radio, and crosses the alley to help Downing with Percy and Bugs, as I tap on the car window, trying not to alarm the woman inside. I don't get much of an impression

314

of the her as she steps out of the car into the alley, but I introduce myself, explain who I am, and what I can provide. She doesn't say anything, but follows me around the building to the front steps, where Oliver Himmel, the produce manager at Grover's store, is waiting with several lukewarm cartons in a plastic bag, glaring at his watch.

"I have been standing here since 11PM, ringing this doorbell," he says, pointing at it as he hands me the bag. "It is now almost midnight. I don't want an explanation; I want an apology."

"Sorry, Oliver. There was a situation," I say, wondering how he could have possibly missed the commotion, that word again, in the alley. "Thanks for waiting."

"I'm not doing this again," he says, wanting to say something else, but worried I might tell my brother.

"No one will ask you to, Oliver. It was an experiment. It failed. Thanks for coming by," I say, though he's already down the steps and off into the night, just as a car, a yellow, new-looking Mustang, clearly some kind of asshole-mobile, sweeps around the corner, and parks across the street.

"Can we go inside please?" asks the woman at my elbow, startling me. I'd nearly forgotten about her.

"Yes, of course. Sorry," I say, unconsciously handing her the bag with my dinner in it as I unlock the door. "Most of this is new to me. All of it, for the most part."

She doesn't reply, but follows me inside, through the vestibule, and into the staff office, seating herself in the chair by the telephone while I root through a file cabinet, assembling the new client paperwork, and wondering if I should worry about anything in particular tonight, or just the normal stuff. No way to be sure until it's too late, I think, trying to seem cheerful as I pass her a clipboard with forms affixed to it and a pen.

"Any problem with a top bunk?" I ask, and she shakes her head. "Bed 8A, then. It's a good spot, right by a window, so right by an air conditioner; I won't joke around, it gets pretty steamy up there, but I think you'll be comfortable. Can I get your name so I can write it in?"

"Millie Shaw," she says, not even looking up from the paperwork as she hands me a driver's license across the desk.

"That isn't necessary," I say, taking it anyway, and reading the thing before I can give it back. "I thought you said your name was Shaw."

"I'm married. Oliver's my maiden name."

"I see. Is Millie short for anything?"

"Millicent."

"Right. Of course," I say, sliding the license back to her across the desk, and trying to square the person sitting before me with the nubile fifteen-year-old ward of the state of Vermont, stockings ripped, hair spiked and styled with gelatin, makeup applied with a dry mop, who never looked forward to anything, not even me coming over after school to listen to Spazz records, and roll around in her twin bed before the foster parents got home from work. She doesn't appear to recognize me, so I don't feel too bad about not recognizing her. Millicent has gained around fifty pounds, probably more, and her hair isn't spiked or styled, but cut in a way that makes her look like a dowager countess lost at the town pumpkin festival. And the makeup is now less daring, more careless, and maintenance oriented; the faded corona of a black eye shows through a patch of concealer, and her lipstick is beginning to cake around a split lip. It doesn't look good, any of it, and I'm too shocked and saddened by what I see to ask anything except what I want to know.

"What happened to you?"

"You saw the car pull up," she says.

"Your husband?" I ask, and she nods. "What did he do?"

"He beat the crap out of me. What it looks like. And now he's here, outside."

"I'm so sorry," I say, feeling tears bud in the corner of my eyes, surprised by them. I'm obviously losing control of myself, but I hope Millicent won't notice. "The police who picked you up. They said you wouldn't talk to them. Can I ask why you're talking to me?"

"I've been in these places before," she says, handing me back the clipboard. "The people who run them always make you reveal your situation as part of their protocol. I might as well get it out of the way now."

"I think they can help. The police I mean. If he's out there, and you feel threatened. I know them. They're good men. Or one of them is."

"They never help," she says, sounding not bitter, but certain. "His brother, my brother in-law, is a Barre town cop. The one time I went there it made it worse, and everyone pretended not to notice."

"This is a different town."

"I grew up here, and I remember everyone pretending not to notice lots of things. Places like this are where people turn away from each other. I wasn't even going to stop by until I got picked up."

"The officer said you were walking to Canada."

"I visited Montreal when I was a kid, living here. It was nice, like Europe, I think. Another country seems safer. He already knows I'm here. Maybe an international border will trip him up."

"Is he some sort of private detective or something?" I ask, worried the question sounds sarcastic, but she doesn't seem to think so.

"No, he owns Shaw Sports, a racecar track. Likes to watch things crash. He has enough money from it to make finding things easy."

"You're not a thing. I wish you would let me help you."

"I don't want solutions or help right now. I just want to go to sleep."

"Are you hungry?" I ask, and she doesn't say anything, but doesn't refuse the food either, as I open the containers, and divide it between us. Grover sent me a bouillabaisse, with jars of seasoned mayonnaise and bits of toasted bread. It looks delicious, but I have to search the internet on the staff computer to figure out how to eat it. Millicent and I slurp our soup, chewing bits of seafood in silence, already knowing everything we seem to want to know about one another, the past existing between us without acknowledgment or recognition. The quiet suits me, as I'm trying to swallow my food past a lump in my throat, only growing more swollen while I watch her eat across the desk.

How could this happen? I wonder, but have no one to ask, except Millicent herself, and I don't think her answer would match my question. I want to help her with more than just this, I think as she follows me into the laundry room for her bedding, and then upstairs to the dorm, where I point my flashlight at her bed, 8A, holding the beam steady as she hoists herself up. I say goodnight, and she echoes me, but I pause in the door of the woman's dorm, wondering if I heard her right. It sounded as if she used my name, but I'm not about to shake her awake to ask. Instead, I sit in the staff office, watching her husband's yellow Mustang through the blinds and weeping silently, wondering if I should do what I'm thinking of doing, even though I know the answer inherently. The last time I felt this bad about something I just let it happen, I think to myself, and then: because it was only you feeling bad about it. I close the blinds, terrified of myself.

*　　*　　*

I arrive late the following evening at the Herrenhof Inn, and nearly come to blows with the headwaiter when he refuses to admit me to the restaurant for wearing shorts and flip-flops, but I'm rescued by Vernon, who appears between the velvet drapes fringing the dining room entrance looking like something between a provincial viscount and a croupier in a freshly cut suit with a pocket square dribbling from his breast, his iron blonde hair sutured in a gentleman's pony-tail, and cufflinks chiming against a drink in his hand, a Herronhoffman; five to six shots of anything in a glass, no ice. A mixed bag, named for Henry's mother, Winifred, who used to run the inn.

"I probably should have reminded you to dress up," says Vernon as he escorts me to our table. "But I figured you were from here, and would probably know the place."

"I buried my parents in the only suit I own."

"So you still own it."

"I'm waiting for someone I care about to die before I wear it again."

"That sounds like a joke but probably isn't."

"You look like you already signed the papers."

"A man should be kind to himself when he can, Walter. Henry's bringing the last of them."

"He isn't here now?"

"On his way. Meanwhile, we have these two clowns to keep us company," says Vernon, pulling out a chair and undoing the bottom button of his suit. He's obviously visited Henry's tailor, the same place where Mr. Todes and Mr. Steige were costumed, because here they are as well, table 9 by the bay window looking out into the garden; when Vernon sits down beside them, they look like the three tenors at rest or something. And even after Vernon introduces the two frauds, I have trouble telling them apart. One is balding, bearded, middle-aged, owlish; the other is tall, skeletal, pale, possibly my age and a little gay. Both speak with the kind of Indo-European accent that isn't from anywhere, ricocheting between cartoon skunk French and Nazi vampire German, but sounds both villainous and credential to North Americans.

"Ah! Ay lookal!" says the younger one when I'm introduced, looking excited. "Vaht vood yoo zay vee shood ahder?"

"I have no idea," I reply, thinking: Here I sit, trapped in an elevator with Vlad the Impaler. "Locals don't eat here because it's expensive."

"Ah, baht shoolee toonaht, prahs ees nough objay!" exclaims the owlish one, gesturing expansively at the empty table as if to say: join me in filling this; what you don't eat, I will.

"Was that a question?" I ask Vernon, who shrugs.

"Let's just ask what the waiter recommends," he says, looking like he might be trying to hide behind the wine list. "Or maybe Henry will have some idea when he gets here."

"Yees, Henri veel knough vaht ees bayst," says the skeleton, shooting his cuffs.

"What country did you say you were from?" I ask either of them, feeling like I'm part of a knock-knock joke. Who's there?

"Zagreb," says the older one.

"That isn't a country."

"Tue sahm, eet ees," says the younger, mysteriously. Vernon looks like he wants to jump out a window.

"How interesting," I begin, wondering if what I'm about to do will impact the conversation I plan to have with Henry whenever he arrives, but hoping I'll get to speak with him before Mr. Todes or Mr. Steige are able to report back. "I spent a little time up your way a few years ago, gentlemen. Lovely country, Croatia. Or Zagreb, whatever you call it. I stayed there for a few days, went to the museum, watched a soccer riot. But I remember an equestrian statue of someone in Ban Jelačić Square' and I can't recall who it is. Surely one of you can remind me?"

The actors look crestfallen as Vernon titters at them into his waterglass, but are saved from answering my question by the arrival of several platters of food none of us ordered, and Henry, who appears at the last place setting as if he was hiding under the tablecloth.

"Good evening, gentlemen," he says, resting his elbows on the table and knitting his hands into a pediment beneath his chin. "I took the liberty of ordering for us. I'm sorry you were given menus. That was a mistake. If you became attached to anything on it that isn't here, feel free to order it."

"Comrade!" shouts the older, owlish charlatan, approaching our host as if he intends to kiss him on both cheeks, but Henry deflects him with a look saying exactly what Percy said to me in the alley last night: Men are talking. Give room. Or man, in this case. This is clearly Henry's table.

"Walter," he says, speaking to me, but nodding to Vernon as he passes him a file and a pen. "I assume Vernon invited you, since I didn't, and you do not know Mr. Todes and Mr. Steige."

"Yes, he did, and no I don't," I say, focusing on a statue of Mercury jailed in the garden, hoping this will make me look expansive. "We were just getting acquainted before you arrived."

"Zat ees akurot," confirms one of them from beyond the purview of the conversation.

"Well, it's good you're here," says Henry, to me, ignoring whoever spoke. Vernon's pen squeaks beside me as he signs away his integrity. "I have a question I need to ask you."

"Then we should talk, Henry," I say, trying to keep the frenzy out of my voice by reminding myself there's no way to win with him. At most, I can expect to lose less. "I have to ask you something. It's important. And I need an answer right now. I have…"

"Not here," he says, the tone of the conversation suddenly shifting as he scents an opportunity. The chum of our power differential clouds the surface of his bathing pool. It's clear I've already lost, a relief. All downhill from here.

Henry knows too, of course. The pediment beneath his chin falls away as he signals a waiter, who appears from absolutely nowhere with two glasses and bottle of wine swaddled in a napkin, and follows us out of the dining room, and through an emergency exit into the garden, where we interrupt two other waitstaff laying a cloth over a wrought iron table on the redbrick patio. We seat ourselves in Mercury's shadow, guarded by Victorian-looking hedges, and fussy beds of summer flowers. My mother would have known each of them by name.

"You go first," I say, trying to collect myself as the waiter pours a measure of wine into our glasses after allowing Henry to taste it.

"You need to learn how to ask for what you want," says Henry, watching me with what a stupid person might mistake for pity; in many ways, it still looks like pity to me, and I want to believe it is. My experiments in hope spring eternal. "For instance: I want to know why I saw a transient beneath the Quim Crossing bridge wearing the uniform I gave you just the other day."

"It would take too long to explain."

"I have mostly time."

"I don't, Henry. I have to be at work in twenty minutes, and need to know if you can help me tonight. I'll pay for the uniform, if that's what you want, but…"

"I've already mailed a bill to your brother's house, and it's not important when you pay it. What I want to know is of why Patches from Shantytown is walking around Acheron dressed like one of my employees. But in the interest of time, I'll assume it had everything to do with your new job."

"How do you know where I work?"

"It's not private information, Walter. But maybe you've forgotten where you are."

"You've always been a phenomenal creep, Henry."

"And yet, here we are," he says, touching his glass against mine, enjoying himself, why not? "Now, what did you want to ask me?"

"I need a favor," I begin, quelling an anxious growl, or warping it into a noise I hope sounds pensive, and controlled. No need to fall off the rails before I've asked for what I want. No, not want. Need. "I need you to make someone go away."

"What makes you think I can do that?" he asks, smiling even after I don't answer by summarizing the fiefdom he's made for himself in Acheron. I refuse to recite your resume, I think, barely able to look at him, waiting as patiently as I dare with the clock ticking. "Walter, she was never yours, because no one is ever that to anyone else. I watched you fail to understand that over the years. Now you know; that's a gift. And they're leaving tomorrow, so dispatching that mope she's taken up with would be a waste of both our time and resources. If it wasn't him, it would be someone else who isn't you. Will that be all?"

"No, Henry, it most certainly will not be fucking all!" I shout, my untouched glass of wine shattering across Mercury's sandals, surprising me, but not Henry. I almost expect a waiter to jump out of a shrub with a broom and dustpan. "You assume you know everything, but maybe you only know what folks around here let you know, and what this place allows you to do. I'd love to see you on the corner of East 21st Street and Regent's Place telling people about themselves while trying to figure out which way North is. You wouldn't make it to the end of this sentence."

"So, edify me then, Walter; add to what I think I know," says Henry. "Tell me who you want to disappear."

"His last name is Shaw. I don't know his first name. He drives a yellow Mustang. It was parked outside the shelter yesterday evening, and it will probably be there tonight."

"How long has he been in town?"

"Since last night."

"Describe him."

"I can't. I've never seen him before."

"First name?"

"No idea. But he owns Shaw Sports in Barre. It's a racetrack."

"Plate number for the Mustang?"

"I don't know. I can probably get it tonight."

"Do that. And when would you like him gone?"

"As soon as you can, Henry. Tonight, if possible."

"Normally, that wouldn't be a problem. But it's graduation night at Todes / Steige, and I need to be up there to conduct exit interviews with the clients before they all leave tomorrow. So, noon, at the latest."

"That's fine, I hope."

"Good. Now, before we go any further," says Henry, nodding to a waiter who has crept up behind me to replace and refill the glass I broke. "We need to discuss terms."

"I'm aware I don't have anything you want."

"No, you don't. And yet I'm providing a service which must be paid for."

"If you want me to come work for you up at the camp, I will."

"That offer is no longer available, I'm afraid."

"I don't have any money."

"I know. Everyone knows. You make it so obvious."

"I'll get your uniform back. Maybe even the boots too," I offer, watching him watch me in silence, not liking a moment of it. He appears to be savoring some part of this, deeply. "So, what then, Henry? Do you want to fuck me or something?"

"You know exactly what I want," he says. "Make the call. I'll wait."

You lose, I say to myself as I leave the table and walk to the edge of the garden, where I sit on a frail bench beneath a weeping willow, watching my reflection in the surface of an ornamental pond as I dial my phone. I can't tell if I'm doing this for the right reasons, but I'm doing something, something for Millicent, who needs the kind of help only evil can buy. I have the rest of my life to feel bad about this, I think, as my reflection raises the phone to its ear. Grover answers almost immediately.

"It's almost 7PM," he says, water running, and pans clanking together in background as he prepares dinner. The idea of my brother eating alone after what I'm about to ask him horrifies me, and I nearly sob into the phone before I can even get it out. "I thought you were working tonight. Is something wrong?"

"No, everything is fine," I lie. "But I need you to sell the store to Henry."

"What happened, Walter?" he asks after a resonant pause.

"Nothing, at least, nothing to me. This is for someone else."

"A girl?"

"Yes."

"Not her?"

"No, someone I used to know. She's in trouble. Henry can help."

"Can anyone else help?"

"I wouldn't ask you to do this if I thought so."

"Then tell him: same terms. And I meet with him, not Huld, at the store tomorrow, my office, 9AM."

"I expected this to be a more difficult conversation. I'm sort of alarmed that it isn't."

"I've enjoyed saying no to Henry for a long time, but I always assumed he would get the store, because he wants it more than I do. I just never had a reason to give it to him. But it seems you do. That's good enough."

"I hate myself and wish you didn't trust me, Grover."

"We all hate ourselves in one way or another. Think of it as a gift."

"I'm so sorry."

"Try not worry about it. You shouldn't hang on to something you don't want just so someone else can't have it. And I love you, Walter. Everything will be fine. Go to work. See you tomorrow."

He hangs up, and I spend a moment watching my reflection weep in the lily pond before leaving the bench, and recrossing the garden to find Henry exactly as I left him, as I've always left him: A man never held in suspense. He knew he would get what he wanted tonight as soon as he saw me in the restaurant, who knows how. He appears to have a better idea of how much Grover trusts me than I do, or perhaps we both knew, and he's just more honest about it. Only a truly stupid man is never surprised, I think, or hope, perhaps because this standard artificially frames recent events as a work of genius, on my part, rather than a kind of emotional paintball. It's never too late to imagine things differently.

326

"Tomorrow at 9AM, his office. You, not Huld," I say, reclaiming my seat, adding: "Fuck you, Henry."

"Text the plate number here," he says, ignoring me, and sliding a Herronhof Inn business card with a phone number written on the back across the table. "And if anything changes, use this number. Leave a message saying you're canceling your reservation. Do not call me about this, or speak to me about it after you leave here. The store is forfeit either way, of course."

"What are you going to do?" I ask. When he doesn't respond, I add: "I would prefer you didn't hurt him. He doesn't need to be hurt. He just needs to be escorted to the county line and told something menacing about what will happen if he comes back."

"It's really up to him, isn't it, Walter? From the little you know of Mr. Shaw, does he seem like the sort of man to go quietly?"

"No, but I'm the customer here, Henry, and I haven't given you the right to do whatever you want."

"Don't be absurd, Walter. Of course you did; that's what this is. You can't do what you want, because you're afraid, and I can, because I'm not. You're buying my courage, and all it entails. Or were we having a different conversation?"

"I want a guarantee that Mr. Shaw will drive his stupid Mustang back to Barre and stay there. That's it."

"We're finished talking about this. Go to work. You're going to be late."

"Fine, Henry," I say, knocking over my chair as I stand up, intending to exit dramatically, but one final question leaves me hanging between the two hedges, unable to leave without an answer: "I have to ask why you deployed those two quacks at dinner. You're not fooling anyone, except Huld maybe, but he'll do whatever you say anyway, because that's his job. Vernon doesn't buy it; he's only here to take your money."

"Some men collect horses, or fine art," says Henry, shrugging. "I collect idiots."

"You're getting your money's worth," I say, thinking: So, what's one more? as I leave the garden, afraid of what I've just done, and hoping it will turn out fine without requiring me to do anything worse.

"That's the idea," says Henry as I turn a hedgecorner, he placid, victorious, drinking his wine alone. I walk around the building and find Vernon waiting beside my bicycle at the foot of the staircase leading inside, a crescent of cigarette ends at his feet.

"So who is the statue?" he asks, smiling and taking my hand, noticing but ignoring how defeated I must look after horsetrading with Henry.

"Josip Jelačić," I say. "The square is named after him."

"And what did he do that deserved a statue?"

"No idea. I just remember the name because the woman at my hotel kept warning me not to go there after a soccer game. She was right. What Eastern Europe lost in fascism, they make up for with soccer."

"I can never remember what statues did," he says, watching an attractive, well-dressed woman descend the stairs and accept her key from a valet. His expression says something like: I've had better, but not recently. "I just came out here to say goodbye, or adieu, maybe. I figured even if you wanted to eat after listening to those two jokers, a preprandial conversation with Henry would probably put you off the meal. You only came because you needed to talk to him, right?"

"Yes. I'm sorry, Vernon. It was important."

"Must be. You looked like you lost a lot."

"I expected to. I'm just surprised by how fast it happened."

"It's nice to know how quickly you can lose everything; makes

328

it easier not to worry about it. We are ashes on the tongue of infinity, and so forth."

"Who said that, Vernon?"

"I just did. Anyway, I'm going up to Montreal tomorrow to begin spending my new money on French Candadian women in low places. Thus, *adieu, mon frere.* I hope what you lost tonight was worth it."

"We'll see," I say, realizing we're friends as he shakes my hand for the second time, and as friends, it wouldn't be unusual for me to ask him for a favor. "Would you mind giving someone a ride tomorrow?"

When I arrive at the shelter, I'm relieved to find Mr. Shaw's yellow Mustang absent from the curb where it was parked the night before. Perhaps, he gave up, and went back to his racetrack. Or maybe Millicent agreed to leave with him, which would be sad, but it would also mean she and her husband are no longer my problem, together or apart, and I could stop worrying about Henry's hatchetmen doing something I could never forgive myself for. How nice it would be to return to a blameless life.

But the consolation lasts only as long as it takes me to greet Martha, apologize for being late, and lie to her about being just fine when she asks how I'm doing, because as we enter the dining area to begin check-in, I notice Millicent Shaw nee Oliver sitting alone by a window, looking terrified as she watches the alley. And as Martha begins announcements, a yellow Mustang cruises shark-like past the window, heading toward the front of the building.

So, we're all doomed; that settles it, I think from behind the shelter of my Dutch door, as clients begin cycling through the hallway. Millicent is somewhere at the back of the line, and I'm rushing those in front of her, chatting minimally, and checking off their names in a flurry as I assign and confirm beds for the evening, trying to move her closer to me. As the queue rapidly shortens, Avery Von Spitzmäuse says something about how I seem to be getting good at this before clinking away on his spurs in search of bedding. He's right, I suppose. Were it not for Boone James, bed 20 (in the medical annex), sixties, malingering, walks unnecessarily with a cane, often tells people he disagrees with that he'll show them what he did 'in the war,' clogging up the line as he deliberates with Martha over cleaning doorknobs, or counting the folks who turn up for lunch, both easy jobs, we'd be finished by now. But what a surprise to have someone notice I'm good at something, even if it's only remembering the sort of faces most people would rather forget. That isn't a marketable skill at all. More of a party trick. But it never happened at the Brooklyn Association, perhaps because no one was paying attention, or I never did anything well there. Maybe both. But next time Avery shows up in the middle of the night in his pajamas, asking me to unlock the door so he can have a cigarette in the courtyard, I might just say yes, even though Martha specifically said this will not happen during tonight's announcements. Power is only a friend to the people if does things for them.

Millicent doesn't acknowledge me when I confirm her bed, normal enough I suppose, nor does she thank me, or do much else, when I tell her where and when to meet Vernon tomorrow morning. Not that I expected her to kiss the hem of my robe or anything, but considering this is only part of what I've done to make sure I remember her the way I want to, I can't expect much more. Still, it would have been nice to know she appreciated the ride.

"Okay, Walter," she says, the last person in line. She slouches off toward the laundry room, trailing fear like a pennant, and

I plod down the hall to the staff office, where I close the blinds to prevent myself from staring at her husband's car, now parked across the street, and try to remember whether or not I introduced myself to her the night before. It's the sort of question that's impossible to ask, and even if she did recognize me, that wouldn't change much; we'd both still be waiting for something good to happen to her. Or something bad to happen to someone else. Much more likely, at this point.

Martha enters the office, which always makes me feel like a creature lurking in some grotto along a bleak and windswept coastline, waiting for something wounded to wash ashore so I can have dinner. I'm relieved to see she's returned to her normal deportment: Carhartt cutoffs, Mossy Oak t-shirt, tactical looking sandals. If you were mine, I think, as she closes the office door, and asks me to join her outside for a cigarette, I'd never ask you to wear anything else. I want to find out how her date went without actually asking any questions about it, but don't get the opportunity until after midnight, with the homeless people tucked into bed, and our paperwork nearly finished. Between handing out bag lunches and medications, breathalyzing and assigning beds to several clients who arrived late from a concert in Burlington, and calling an ambulance for Lurk, who had a small seizure in the TV room, I'd almost forgotten about the car outside, until Martha and I patrolled the alley, and there it was, dormant and sporty beneath the ochre light of a sodium vapor lamp across the street. I froze on the steps as Martha fiddled with the lock on the front door, aware that I appeared suspicious, but not knowing how to appear otherwise, and feeling guilty for consigning someone to a fate I couldn't articulate. I wanted to knock on the Mustang's window, and tell the driver to leave, save himself, but went inside, and began updating the bedsheet. At least you're here till

1AM to keep me from doing anything stupid, I thought, watching Martha then with less apprehension then I do now, shortly after midnight, when she asks if I mind her leaving early.

"A second date?" I ask, figuring it's all out the window anyway; Cordelia's love, my brother's store, Mr. Shaw's life. Might as well toss another log on the *auto-de-fe*.

"Jealous," she says. It isn't a question.

"Extremely."

"No. I just want to go home tonight, Walter. He was nice. I'm not seeing him again."

"Why not?"

"Because he drives the kind of truck I find embarrassing to stand next to, let alone ride in, and loves the shit out of it. He talked exclusively about softball like I was on his team, and when I asked, 'That's baseball for fat drunks, right?' he didn't laugh. And he told me his dream job was 'dogcatcher,' and I laughed. I thought he was being ironic or something, because it made too much sense."

"That's not irony."

"You told me once you wanted to be a philosopher," she says, weary of talking about herself. "How's that coming?"

"You're looking at it, I imagine."

"Please. Don't be jealous; you'll find someone. Maybe we both will."

"What if I've found you, Martha?" I ask; it seemed unavoidable, but probably wasn't.

"You want anything. Before I pulled you out of the road and gave you a job, when was the last time you thought about me?" she asks, not waiting for an answer. "Besides, we tried all that, and it didn't work. Because of her, I think, but now that she's gone, I just see you suffering and alone, and don't want to fill space until you get it together. You taught me a lesson about asking more questions before I agree to a sleepover with the grocery boy."

"I'll admit I'm not entirely sure what happened that night."

"You burst into tears during your big moment. I mean, our big moment. And I was so drunk that I felt bad for you rather than myself, so we talked about Cordelia until you'd had enough of it and passed out. Do you think I want that as some kind of regular thing?"

"So, maybe less alcohol next time?"

"Walter. Look at yourself."

"I know. It's bad. I'll stop," I lie, hoping she doesn't want me to honestly assess myself, right here and now, with Mr. Shaw parked outside, doomed for being a predictable bastard. We could share the same cross. I should call Henry. See if he'll make room. "But you should know you're wrong about the last time I thought about you."

"I don't care right now."

"And I know I don't deserve anything from you, Martha, but I would like a frank assessment of how much I have to grow up before I can see you outside of work."

"I like you fifty percent," she says, suddenly nervous, moving things that don't need to be moved around the desk, watching me with her body rather than her eyes, which is good, because my face probably screams something about liking those odds. "But I don't know how you can think you want something, someone, me, when you don't understand love well enough to let it die without humiliating yourself. How do you expect me to believe you want me after I read your letter? That doesn't make sense."

"I don't know. I think it makes sense because I'm nice, and I want someone to be nice to," I say, feeling like I could have sold myself a little harder. "And you're also wrong, I think, I hope, about understanding love. I mean, maybe you're right in relation to me, but I know what it looks like, so I think I'm allowed to want it."

"I'd like to know what you think it looks like, Walter."

"Well, it's probably different for everyone, but for me, it looks like the only time I saw my parents dance. We were in a small town on the Yucatan; it's a Spring Break shithole now, looks like Daytona, but when we went it was under construction, just on the verge of becoming a shithole. Locals were paid to drag rocks out of the ocean by our hotel so that tourists wouldn't hurt their feet when they swam off the beach. Anyway, we were walking down the main street at night, and there were people like us everywhere, so we felt like we were doing the right thing I guess, as a family. And Grover and I walked into a shop that sold switchblades and fireworks, and when we turned around, our parents were gone. So we walked back outside, and they were there, dancing in the street to a band playing something appropriate in a restaurant across from the shop. They were happy, and Grover and I were happy because they were. I was twelve, so always remember that as what love looks like to the untrained."

"I have to get the chore sheet out of the printer," she says, practically bolting from the room. Paranoia is ambiguity, I think, lifting the blind to check the yellow Mustang across the street against my guilt regarding it, and dropping the shade as Martha returns, organizing her papers, packing her things, armoring herself against anything I might say. So I say nothing, listening to her movements, wondering if there's any way to come back from this kind of mutual honesty. I suppose this is goodnight, I say to myself, trying to look absorbed in updating the bedsheet, not prepared when she crosses the office, and hugs me, like Arvin,

Catalina, and Danielle did when I left New York, like Butch did the night before, like my brother does sometimes. I'm afraid if I get up, I'll ruin the moment, so I grasp her forearm with both hands where it crosses my chest like a safety belt, enjoying the feeling of her jaw resting against the crown my skull as I try to memorize her odor: smoke, sweat, castile soap; I need something to cling to after she leaves, my huntress.

"If you still want this, me, or something when you're not all screwed up, maybe we can talk again," she says, letting me go, and passing Parsons on her way out of the office. He bids her goodnight, parks in a chair by the telephone, and asks what I'm reading. I'm too stunned to answer so I slide the book I brought with me across the desk, a brittle copy of *Andersonville* I found in my mother's potting shed.

"I can't read fiction," he says after examining it. "Last time I read novels was after I sold my boat to some Koreans in Louisi-ana. I wasn't shrimping so I had time on my hands. You like that girl?"

"I suppose I do," I reply, not sure how his boat and Martha relate, but glad to have someone ask me the kind of question I want to answer.

"She reminds of this little sweetie pie I met on Christmas Eve in Chicago. She was just as sweet as she could be. I asked a taxi driver to take me to the finest Italian joint in the city, and she was the only person in there aside from Mafiosi, so I walked right up, sat down at her table, and asked if I could buy her dinner. So we're drinking, eating, and when we're done, it's snowing hard, and ev-erything is silent, and cold. The wind off the lake was throwing us around the street, so she asked if I would walk her home. I do, and she invites me up for a nightcap. We're sitting down on her couch, enjoying ourselves, when suddenly I hear this honest to god roar from the bedroom. I ask what it is, and she says it's just her cat, and asks if I want to see it. So we go into the bedroom, and what do you think she has in there but a full-grown lion in a cage, pacing around and yowling to itself. Scared the living shit out of me, but it quieted down after she fed it a steak through the bars. When I told Martha that story, she asked where its litter box was. Smart cookie. I'm not surprised you like her."

"Is there anything you haven't seen, Parson?"

"They got a three hundred pound belly dancer at the farmer's market on Saturdays," he says, scratching his head beneath his all-season watch cap. "I ain't never seen anything like that."

"Hard to forget, once you've seen it, I imagine."

"But there's plenty out there none of us see or know about," he says, ignoring me, moving along. "For instance: did you know there are human and dinosaur footprints walking together down a riverbed in east Texas? Same thing exists in Turkmenistan, near the Uzbek boarder. Then there's the ten-foot skeleton they found in a cave somewhere in West Virginia, but the government filled it in with concrete before anyone could get a good look. This stuff never makes the news, because they don't want us to know about it. But if you keep your ear to ground, you can figure out what's really going on. If they don't want us to know giants existed, what else are they trying to keep secret?"

"Good question," I say, wondering if we both found the idea of an intellectual ghetto attractive because it seemed to imply four walls and a roof. "But maybe if we knew all the things we don't, the world would be less interesting."

"Well, I'm ready when they come for me," he says; we seem to be having two different conversations. "As soon as I get cleared with the VA, I'm going back up to my cabin in Derby. You know, some little pipsqueak know-it-all from the college came up to me

336

at the farmer's market with a clipboard, telling me he wanted my signature to get something on the ballot about tighter regulations for gun ownership. I told him, 'Son, a well-armed citizen is an informed citizen and patriot,' and asked him if he even knew who he was working for. But I need to get back up to the cabin, pull mine out of the ground and oil them before winter comes. Would have done it all ready if this goddamn whoreson infection didn't leave me stuck in this shit palace all summer."

"How many guns do you own, Parson?"

"One hundred and seventy-seven," he says, after doing some private arithmetic, and switching gears, "I suspect she likes you too. The boat took me all over the world, shrimping and fishing wherever it was good, so I've seen my fair share of women, and you notice things after a while. I'd say don't tell her what you think yet."

"Too late, Parson."

"Well, then you just have to wait for a knock; it'll either come, or it won't. I remember a real sweetie pie I met when I was way down south, off of Balboa, by the canal..."

Parsons tells stories until it's time to set out breakfast, as I listen and do paperwork, grateful, as the hours tick past, that he doesn't expect me to contribute anything. Why should I? He's had a much more interesting life than I have, so there's nothing to add. And it's nice to be an audience for once, part of the background or scenery, the sort of necessary element that's easy to ignore. This may be my natural state; Walter at rest. I used to love listening to Cordelia talk at the end of her day, the way her voice and the small details of her life eclipsed the mundane silence of our common world, my contribution. It wasn't the same as having my own experiences, but it worked well enough for a while; she was my radio. This may be what I miss most about her: she helped me pretend my life wasn't an endless conversation about one thing.

When I excuse myself to go make breakfast, Parson follows me to the kitchen, and asks for something to eat. We're out of sack lunches, and nearly everything else, so I give him an entire box of stale donuts, and cup of leftover coffee that tastes like it was brewed in a tar pit.

"You're a kind man," he says, accepting this garbage. The cup steams as he tucks the box beneath his arm, and walks off to bed with it. Am I? I wonder as I walk back to the office after setting out breakfast, and part the blinds to find Mr. Shaw's car still at the curb. No one has ever said this to me before. Stale donuts and shitty coffee; is that all it takes? Henry said noon, at the latest. It's now 4AM. I go home in three hours. That leaves plenty of time for something bad to happen while I'm here, so I suppose I'll leave the shades closed until the Jesuit volunteer relieves me at 7AM. Go home, have a beer, and try to go to bed. When I wakeup, it will be like Mr. Shaw never arrived. He will disappear, as requested. As long as I don't see it, I'll probably be able to sleep.

I return to the desk, looking around for some circumstantial evidence to prove I've done the right thing, and settle into listening to the sound of clients beginning to stir. Someone coughs. A toilet flushes. The kitchen radio starts playing Faron Young. Linda Blossom passes the office door with Thomas Winter, both of them going outside to smoke. We all say good morning, and leave it at that. Avery taps up a few minutes later to grab a clean towel from a bin by the office door, spurs on at half past four in the morning. He must sleep in them. Milt Cohen taps out a rubric of some kind against a supporting wall beside the closet, and asks if he can sleep in an extra hour; he was up all night with headache. I tell him he can, and feel briefly noble. Here I am, doing my job well, I think, resisting the urge to look through the blinds. I am a reasonable person, and homeless people like me. Surely in this context, I don't have anything to confess.

Your life would be so much simpler if you believed yourself, I think further, tugging the cord, and raising the blinds entirely as the sun rises over Maybrick Peak, unable to square the lingering reality of Mr. Shaw's Mustang beneath the streetlamp with Parson's earlier assertion of my kindness, and manhood. When Teresa Rush appears in the office door to complement the coffee I made, I want to beat my head against the wall, and ask her how good it would taste if she knew it was brewed by a hangman. This is guilt, as I know it. Sun glints off the buffed hood of the Mustang through the office window into my eyes, blinding me as I recall my father, speaking about Sticks, the sex offender from Thanksgiving past: A good, firm belief in intractable evil makes us all great citizens and god fucking awful people. I don't have to think very hard to imagine what he would say to me right now, and that settles it. Time to go meet Mr. Shaw.

I reach beneath the desk, and remove a box of weapons confiscated from residents. Martha and I went through it my first evening for a laugh, so I know it contains a BB pistol, which I disentangle from the knives, hatchets, and one pair of homespun nunchaku, and tuck in my waistband as I cross the office and close the door. I pull out the pistol, modeled stupidly on a German Luger, cock the thing, and fire a shot into the communicating room; something ticks around the furniture before coming to rest. Okay, so I know you work, I think, stuffing the pistol back into my pants, and locking the office behind me as I walk outside. Hopefully, it won't come to that.

Avery, Thomas, and Linda share cigarettes on the steps, and

spill coffee on the flagstones of the patio, making a mess, enjoying themselves. We've already said good morning to each other, so they ignore me, assuming I know what I'm doing as I cross the courtyard to the street. But as I fiddle with the gate, the pistol slips from my waistband, and drops out the leg of my shorts with a clatter, drawing their compound attention. I feel them watching me as I dip to retrieve the thing, but Thomas is the only one who speaks.

"You need help, Walter?"

"No, thank you, Thomas. We'll see. You'll know," I say, jamming the gun in my pocket and holding it there as I walk across the street to the Mustang, open the passenger door, and get inside. The interior smells like mid-shelf bourbon, the sort I used to buy whenever I visited Arvin and Catalina, day-old cologne, and one mentholated cigarette after another. A bowling bag sits on the floor between my feet. A picture of Millicent, smiling for the camera, lighter and outwardly happy, wearing a bikini, on a beach somewhere, hangs in a tacky frame from the rearview mirror. All these details add up to Mr. Shaw, who I had hoped to find asleep. Instead, he's seated across from me, wide awake; larger than me by many pounds and inches, middle thirties, hair raked over a bald patch, rumpled, off the rack suit worn with a gold chain in place of a tie, looks seedy, though not prototypically mean. Beneath the neckbeard and the rest of the hillbilly omertà is a fellow Vermonter who likes to watch things go around a track and catch fire. Not unusual; the sort of person who's harmless until they cause harm.

"You're not who I'm looking for," he says, more curious than alarmed. "Wrong car, maybe?"

"No, I don't think so," I say, focusing on the large, silver pistol in his hand; it isn't exactly pointed at me, so much as cradled in my direction. His other hand holds a newspaper, folded against the steering wheel.

"I saw you from across the street," he says, calm, in no hurry. "Put it on the dashboard."

"It's a BB pistol," I say, withdrawing the Luger from my pocket, and doing what he asks.

"I look like a paper target to you, boy?"

"I wanted you take me seriously."

"We're a long way from that. Consider what a man keeps under his seat."

"I figured if it hit you in the eye, it would sting like fuck and maybe make you blind."

"Nice thought. Do you need money or something? Maybe the breakfast in there doesn't agree with you?"

"What? No! I don't live there," I say, jerking my head in the direction of the shelter across the street. Why is this always happening? "I'm an employee. I left my I.D. inside."

"Sure. I'd go now, if I was you. Your boss should expect a call from me."

"I need you to listen to me, Mr. Shaw."

"How do you know my name?"

"Your wife told me."

"She in there?"

"I can't reveal that. What I can tell you is that if you don't leave town right away, something bad will happen to you. I can't say exactly what it will be, because I don't know. But you're in danger, and you need to get out of here."

"How do you know?"

"Because I paid someone to hurt you."

"Call him off."

"I can't just yet. I need to know you'll leave her alone first."

"She's my wife. How stupid do you think I am?"

"I think you're really stupid," I say. "But that doesn't mean you deserve to get hurt because of it."

"I think you're bluffing."

"Wait and see, I guess."

This appears to get his attention. He scratches his neckbeard thoughtfully, sliding the pistol into his newspaper and laying it on the backseat, his free hand hovering over the ignition, undecided, deciding, I hope.

"I'll remember this," he says finally, not starting the car.

"That's fine, just remember it somewhere else."

"My brother's a cop."

"I know."

"If I call him up, you'll have a problem."

"I'm used to problems. But if you think he'll help you make a smart choice, I'd say call him right now."

"Get out of the car."

I do as I'm told, stuffing the pellet gun back in my pocket, feeling like I've really rounded the bend on my own meddling as I open the door, and step out of the Mustang. A crowd has sprouted in the courtyard across the street, each member watching me from a froth of cigarette smoke; I make eye contact with Thomas, standing by the fence, coiled, vigilant, looking ready to vault over it at the first sign of trouble, and dispatch Mr. Shaw. I shrug, and he salutes, a good soldier, rejoining his retinue on the steps. I'm almost sorry to disappoint him, and wish I had a better understanding of why some men are so eager to fight other people's battles.

"I miss her a lot, you know?" says Mr. Shaw, as I lean down to close the door. Yes, I know, you slob, I think, slamming it without replying, and removing my phone, and the Herrenhof Inn business card with Henry's contact number from my pocket, dialing it as I cross the street toward the shelter. I'm not sure Mr. Shaw will leave after our conversation, but I know I don't want anything bad to happen to anyone else because of me. If justice were your job, you'd be a god, I tell myself, listening to Henry's number ring endlessly. I don't know how juries do it, live with themselves after casting judgment on someone else. The only time I was called to serve, 360 Adams Street in downtown Brooklyn, I spent five hours in the court's waiting area reading a collection of Thoreau's essays before being tossed out during voir dire after telling the triptych of lawyers questioning me how uncomfortable I was with the idea of punishing someone I didn't know for something I probably didn't care about. It was Friday, so I wished them a nice weekend, and they gave me chit asking me not come back for eight years. Stalemate. I left comfortable with the idea of being a bad citizen, if being a good one meant pretending my own casual, low-average existence qualified me to make important choices for other unimportant people.

As I reach the gate, a taxi pulls up, with Lurk inside. The driver helps him out of the backseat, and he wobbles a bit on the sidewalk, heavily doped from his night at the Fletcher Allen ER, so I support him under the arm, this huge, fearsome man with peacock feathers tattooed on his face, and get him into the courtyard, where Avery and Thomas help him up the steps to the front door.

"We'll put him to bed," says Avery over his shoulder as they struggle inside.

"You work here?" asks the driver, holding a white pharmacy bag on the sidewalk, and curiously eyeing the shelter's façade. "He left this."

"I do," I say, glad someone finally noticed, and take the bag. "You've been paid?"

"Uhyut. Hospital took care of it," he says, returning to his vehicle. "Also, your barn door's open, so to speak."

I look down and realize the grip of the BB pistol in my waistband is riding up over my shirt, and has probably been that way since I crossed the street, unambiguously displaying itself for all to see. Fantastic. Half-armed and full-stupid. No one ever tells me anything I need to know, I think, as the taxi pulls away, and I redial Henry's number, continuing the call I canceled in order to assist Lurk.

As I listen to it ring, an engine murmurs behind me, and I wonder if Mr. Shaw has finally decided to flee the county. That would make my morning. But before I can turn around to find out, a car door opens and two strong hands seize my wrists, forcing them behind my back, and cinching them together with what feels like a zip tie. My phone drops to the pavement, and the battery detaches, skittering off the sidewalk into a storm drain. I'm being kidnapped, and Thomas isn't here to rescue me, I think, hoping this looks like a mistake to the clients watching it from the courtyard, though they seem to take my abduction in stride; some gape, a few sip coffee, all smoke. Just another morning in America. None say much of anything, except Linda Blossom.

"You want me to call the cops, Walter?" she asks, sounding eager to help or create mischief, impossible to tell. Before I can answer, a hand holding a badge appears beside my face. Linda looks sorry for me, and disappointed.

"That won't be necessary, ma'am," says Officer Laurel, spinning me away from the crowd, toward an unmarked cruiser parked at the curb. She's dressed casually, in slacks and a windbreaker, something new, for me. Until today, I'd only seen her in

344

uniform or naked, never anything in between. Not that it makes much difference. She looks lovely, as always, and regal in a way I probably wouldn't have noticed if she wasn't arresting me. I want to kiss you now, I think, meaning it. And for whatever idiotic reason, I'm sexually excited by her adamantine grip on my forearm, the front of my shorts tenting in a kind of salute to priorities gone astray as she leads me to the car. Not my fault, and nothing I can do. As with the BB pistol stuck in my waistband, it's out there for all to see, and both the clients and Officer Laurel notice. They laugh, she doesn't.

"Hi, Walter," she says joylessly, ducking my head into the back of her cruiser, and closing the door. Through the window, Mr. Shaw watches across the street, his elbows resting on the roof of his Mustang, his hands joined around a smoldering Newport, and a pint of Evan Williams mellowing beside him in the early morning sunlight. We notice each other, both content in our own way, I suppose; he with his booze and cigarettes, me with my erection. I nod, he shrugs, and Officer Laurel starts the car.

I hoped to be taken somewhere in town for questioning or whatever Officer Laurel plans to do with me, but this hope recedes as she retraces my path from earlier in the week, Walter Ratliff entering Acheron on the back of a stolen cargo bicycle; down Clamence Street, up the hill out of town, and onto the interstate 89, southbound. Fuck, I'm doomed, I think again, as the Waterbury exit passes the window, and signs indicating the distance to Montpelier begin to appear. On the off chance of whatever I say being used against me in a court of law, I remain mute, sitting on my hands, and staring at the back Officer Laurel's head through the steel mesh separating us as my home ebbs away from me. The way she drives, we'll reach the junction of I-91 in an hour, and from there, it's four hours to New York. We'll probably be there just in time for lunch, and I'll have to hangout in the Tombs with the rapists once again, while some justice finishes dribbling marinara sauce on his ceremonial robes. I'm guilty of whatever I've done. I know that. Perhaps if I admit it outright, and don't cause any trouble, I can get myself transferred to Northern State Correctional, and serve my time in a little cell overlooking the lake. Paranoia is realizing you'll wrap your dreams around anything, I think, already imagining myself wheeling a trolley of donated library books between the cells of my fellow inmates, Grover visiting once a week, Martha less often, but sometimes,

"This is Donald's car," says Officer Laurel out of complete nowhere as we pass the Middlesex exit, less than twenty miles from Montpelier. "You remember Donald."

"I think I still have his raincoat, if he wants it back. We could turn around, go find it."

"He let me borrow it, the car, to come get you."

"Nice of him. How did you find me? I don't think I even told you my last name."

"You left an overdue library book on top of my stuff when you dumped it in that parking lot in Springfield. That was enough with the Patriot Act, and all. I returned it for you. I don't understand why you left it behind."

"There was supposed to be a note underneath it. Maybe it blew away."

"What I wanted to say was we're seeing each other again, Donald and I. I'm very happy."

"Glad to hear it," I say. She sounds miserable.

"He's my new boss; he did a good job during the storm, got a promotion. And even after what happened, after what I did for you, he gave me my old job back. I'm very lucky."

346

"Very happy and very lucky," I say, not sure what I can really add to that. "It's good to know these things about yourself."

"You're in so much trouble, Walter."

"I figured."

"Someone else will explain it to you when we get there."

"Fine by me."

"I wanted to talk to you about it. I followed you home one morning after you left work because I thought we could talk. But decided to do this instead."

"I thought that was someone else."

"No. It was me."

"Well, thanks for clearing that up. Can I make a phone call?"

"When we get there and you're processed. You should know how this works."

"It's important, time sensitive; a man's life may be in danger," I say, noticing Lurk's pharmacy bag on the seat beside me. Ah, added leverage! "Also, the medications back here belong to someone at the shelter. He needs them or he might have a seizure and die. So, unless you take me back to Acheron, you'll be endangering two people so you can have revenge. Think about it."

"Nothing is turning this car around, Walter," she says, accelerating. "I don't want revenge. I want to repair the trust of the people I betrayed when I agreed to leave the city with you. I wanted to love you so much, I think. It made me cruel."

"And now you're very happy," I say, feeling sorry for her and myself in equal proportion. "That makes one of us. I'm glad you figured out what you want."

"I thought I wanted to marry you," she says, tenderness or resignation entering her voice, I can't tell which it is without seeing her face. Her eyes, watching the road in the rearview mirror, betray nothing. "I can't want that anymore because it was never real. But Vermont is nice. I see what you meant even though you called it New Hampshire. I could have lived here with you."

"You still can," I say, cautiously, thinking: Why not? Worth a try. "We could be very happy if you want."

"How stupid do you think I am?"

"You're the second person to ask me that this morning."

"You think if you say the right thing, I'll drop everything again, turn the car around, leave my job, my house, Donald, everything that makes me a real person, and not some kind of reptile psychopath like you, someone who just camps out in the lowest common denominator figuring whatever he can't drag down with him he'll use to pull himself up, out of some other mess he's made. No, Walter. I don't want whatever you think I want, and you're not getting out of this. You lied to me and broke my heart; now you're going to jail."

"You know it isn't like that," I say, leaning forward in my seat, trying to get closer to her, put my mouth beside her ear, but only succeed in placing my lips against the mesh and begging through it. "Please. You're doing the right thing for the wrong reasons. That makes it the wrong thing. Please listen to me."

I can smell her hair, and feel the heat from her body through the grating between us, and I know something is up. The most miserable people I knew in New York always went around telling everyone else how happy they were. I don't want Officer Laurel to be sad; I never did. I say 'please' again, no longer entirely sure what I'm asking, there may not be a word for it. But I know she'll understand if I can just communicate with her somehow other than language. I press my lips between one of the wire diamonds framing my prison, comprising our distance, saying 'please' once more, and ejecting my tongue, reaching with it, straining to the very root of my lingua until it touches the back of her ear, probing

the perspiring helix, no longer saying please because I have what
I want: contact. She remembers my mouth, so she remembers my
body, which is the same as remembering the irrational part of us
both, and she moans, her eyes closing dangerously in the rearview mirror, her moan quavering as the car begins to drift. I'm
winning, I think, just before the brakes screech, mashing my face
against the grating, and throwing me backward into my seat. My
head clonks the rear window, stunning me, my vision browning
at the edges like burning paper, but I can see enough to notice Officer Laurel absent from the front seat. My door opens, and she
pulls me out, dumping my body on the shoulder, and crying over
me as I lie there, her tears dripping into my open mouth as I gawk
at the sky, waiting for my head to clear, expecting to be executed.
But no: footsteps scrape the pavement, a car door clunks, tires
spin, and as I hoist myself to my feet, my sight returns, revealing
an empty road; Officer Laurel is gone.

That may have worked too well, I think to myself, trying not
to feel like I missed out on something potentially good for me as I
begin walking toward home with Lurk's pharmacy bag clenched
between my teeth. Though she didn't remove the handcuffs, Officer Laurel was thoughtful enough to include the medication when
she yanked me out of the car, but I couldn't find a way to pick the
thing up without sitting on it first, and crushing the contents. The
medications need to get where they're going, leaving me no choice
but to proceed as I am down the wrong side of the interstate; a fugitive and his Happy Meal. I'd hitchhike if wasn't heading against
traffic, and my hands weren't cuffed behind my back, though if I
saw myself on the side of the road, I probably wouldn't stop.

When I reach Waterbury, the libertarian guy who owns the
town gas station is nice enough to clip off my disposable re-
straints without questioning me, and asks a friend of his tanking

up outside to give me a ride as far as the Acheron exit. The friend waits by his truck while I use the station's phone to call the number Henry gave me, which rings and rings without allowing me to leave a message. I hang up, and try again with the same result. I don't bother dialing a third time, and walk outside feeling like the newest addition to Henry's stable of idiots. I bought his courage and all it entails, as he said. So, this is what it entails. Now I know.

The friend doesn't say too much during the drive, mostly because we share the cab of his pickup with a gigantic mongrel dog sitting between us on the bench seat, its breath fogging the front window so completely that we nearly miss the exit. Still, he allows me to bum a smoke, and I thank him as I step out onto the shoulder, though I may as well be thanking his dog for all he can hear or see of me. But an unspoken 'uhyut' hangs between us as I close the door, and he drives off, a small reminder of what I escaped from a few hours ago, and what I'm returning to now; home, whatever that means in real life.

As I sit on the guardrail finishing my cigarette in the midmorning sunshine, enjoying myself, multiple engines rumble from the other side of the interstate, heralding a caravan of devastated luxury automobiles. They appear at the mouth of the entrance ramp, and merge onto I-89, heading south, retreating in a single column toward the horizon, rattling, choking, dropping parts, followed, at a polite distance, by a moving van chugging along in their composite wake like a kind of caboose. Perhaps it's the same one I saw in Cordelia's driveway, perhaps not. I'm too far away to see who's driving, and knowing wouldn't make a difference at this point, or any other. Still, I watch the van grow less distinct until the contour of the land absorbs it, wondering if I'm forgetting to regret something.

Trying to learn from this will make you think you deserve better things, I tell myself as I descend an embankment toward the road that eventually becomes Clamence Street. You don't; no one does.

When I reach town thirty minutes later, I walk straight to the shelter to return Lurk's medication. Millicent and her husband are gone.

* * * * * * * *

Fomite

A fomite is a medium capable of transmitting infectious organisms from one individual to another.

"The activity of art is based on the capacity of people to be infected by the feelings of others." Tolstoy, What Is Art?

Writing a review on Amazon, Good Reads, Shelfari, Library Thing or other social media sites for readers will help the progress of independent publishing. To submit a review, go to the book page on any of the sites and follow the links for reviews. Books from independent presses rely on reader to reader communications.

For more information or to order any of our books, visit
http://www.fomitepress.com/FOMITE/Our_Books.html

During This, Our Nadir
Joshua Amses

Nothing Beside Remains
Jaysinh Birjépatil

*The Way None
of This Happened*
Mike Breiner

*Summer on the
Cold War Planet*
Paula Closson Buck

*Foreign Tales of
Exemplum and Woe*
J. C. Ellefson

Free Fall/Caída libre
Tina Escaja

Fomite

Speckled Vanities
Marc Estrin

Off to the Next Wherever
John Michael Flynn

Derail This Train Wreck
Daniel Forbes

Semitones
Derek Furr

Where There Are Two or More
Elizabeth Genovise

Snake in the Spine, Wolf in the Heart
Barry Goldensohn

The Three Lives of Jonathan Force
Richard Hawley

Father Figure
Lamar Herrin

The Fall of Athens
Gail Holst-Warhaft

Fomite

In A Family Way
Zeke Jarvis

*A Rising Tide of People
Swept Away*
Scott Archer Jones

A Free, Unsullied Land
Maggie Kast

*Shadowboxing With
Bukowski*
Darrell Kastin

Feminist on Fire
Coleen Kearon

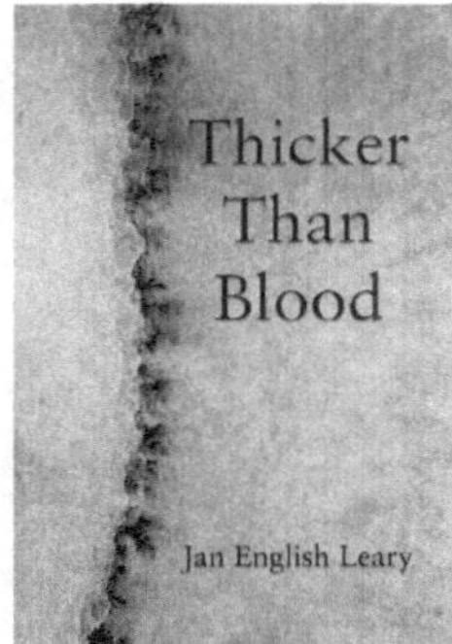

Thicker Than Blood
Jan English Leary

*A Guide
to the Western Slopes*
Roger Lebovitz

Confessions of a Carnivore
Diane Lefer

Born Speaking Lies
Rob Lenihan

Fomite

What She Was Saying
Marjorie Maddox

Unborn Children of America
Michele Markarian

Boom-shacka-lacka
Willliam Marquess

Interrogations
Martin Ott

Connecting the Dots to Shangrila
Joseph D. Reich

Shirtwaist
Delia Bell Robinson

Isles of the Blind
Robert Rosenberg

What We Do For Love
Ron Savage

Bread & Sentences
Peter Schumann

Fomite

Faust 3
Peter Schumann

Principles of Navigation
Lynn Sloan

A Great Fullness
Bob Sommer

To Join the Lost
Seth Steinzor

Among the Lost
Seth Steinzor

Industrial Oz
Scott T. Starbuck

Among Angelic Orders
Susan Thomas

A Day in the Life
Tom Walker

*The Inconveniece
of the Wings*
Silas Dent Zobal

Fomite

More Titles from Fomite...

Joshua Amses — *Raven or Crow*

Joshua Amses — *The Moment Before an Injury*

Jaysinh Birjepatel — *The Good Muslim of Jackson Heights*

Antonello Borra — *Alfabestiario*

Antonello Borra — *AlphaBetaBestiaro*

Jay Boyer — *Flight*

David Brizer — *Victor Rand*

David Cavanagh — *Cycling in Plato's Cave*

Dan Chodorkoff — *Loisada*

Michael Cocchiarale — *Still Time*

James Connolly — *Picking Up the Bodies*

Greg Delanty — *Loosestrife*

Catherine Zobal Dent — *Unfinished Stories of Girls*

Mason Drukman — *Drawing on Life*

Zdravka Evtimova —*Carts and Other Stories*

Zdravka Evtimova — *Sinfonia Bulgarica*

Anna Faktorovich — *Improvisational Arguments*

Derek Furr — *Suite for Three Voices*

Stephen Goldberg — *Screwed and Other Plays*

Barry Goldensohn — *The Hundred Yard Dash Man*

Barry Goldensohn — *The Listener Aspires to the Condition of Music*

R. L. Green When — *You Remember Deir Yassin*

Greg Guma — *Dons of Time*

Andrei Guriuanu — *Body of Work*

Ron Jacobs — *All the Sinners Saints*

Ron Jacobs — *Short Order Frame Up*

Ron Jacobs — *The Co-conspirator's Tale*

Fomite

Kate MaGill — *Roadworthy Creature, Roadworthy Craft*

Tony Magistrale — *Entanglements*

Gary Miller — *Museum of the Americas*

Ilan Mochari — *Zinsky the Obscure*

Jennifer Anne Moses — *Visiting Hours*

Sherry Olson — *Four-Way Stop*

Andy Potok — *My Father's Keeper*

Janice Miller Potter — *Meanwell*

Jack Pulaski — *Love's Labours*

Charles Rafferty — *Saturday Night at Magellan's*

Joseph D. Reich — *The Hole That Runs Through Utopia*

Joseph D. Reich — *The Housing Market*

Joseph D. Reich — *The Derivation of Cowboys and Indians*

Kathryn Roberts — *Companion Plants*

David Schein — *My Murder and Other Local News*

Peter Schumann — *Planet Kasper, Volumes One and Two*

Fred Skolnik — *Rafi's World*

L.E. Smith — *The Consequence of Gesture*

L.E. Smith — *Views Cost Extra*

L.E. Smith — *Travers' Inferno*

Susan Thomas — *The Empty Notebook Interrogates Itself*

Tom Walker — *Signed Confessions*

Sharon Webster — *Everyone Lives Here*

Susan V. Weiss —*My God, What Have We Done?*

Tony Whedon — *The Tres Riches Heures*

Tony Whedon — *The Falkland Quartet*

Peter M. Wheelwright — *As It Is On Earth*

Suzie Wizowaty —*The Return of Jason Green*